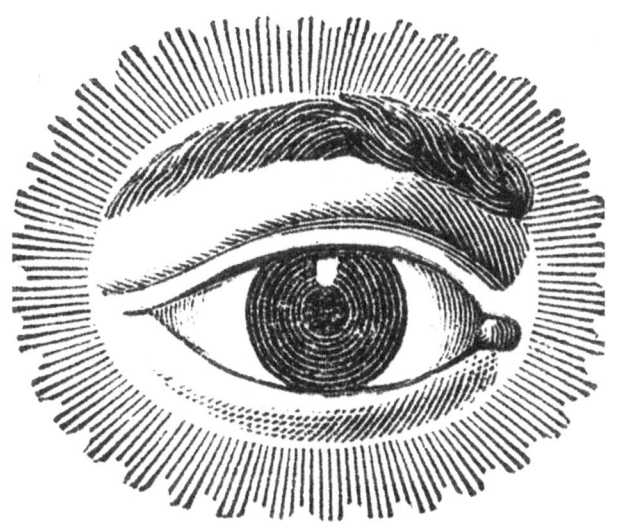

Hypnotism in Victorian and Edwardian Era Fiction

Volume I
Death by Suggestion

Volume II
The Hypno-Ripper

Volume III
The Hypnotic Tales of Rafael Sabatini

Volume IV
The Female Hypnotist

Hypnotism in Victorian and Edwardian Era Fiction
Volume IV

The
Female Hypnotist

Stories from the

Victorian
and
Edwardian
Eras

Edited by

Donald K. Hartman

THEMES & SETTINGS IN FICTION PRESS

Buffalo, New York

THEMES & SETTINGS IN FICTION PRESS

Buffalo, New York

First Edition, 2025

Layout by
David J. Bertuca

Original cover artwork by
Laura Schmitz Lubniewski

Text set in Adobe Jenson Pro

Publisher's Cataloging-in-Publication Data

Names: Hartman, Donald K., editor
Title: The Female Hypnotists: Stories from the Victorian and
   Edwardian Eras / edited by Donald K. Hartman.
   Series: Hypnotism in Victorian and Edwardian era fiction ; 4
Description: First Edition. | Buffalo, N.Y. : Themes & Settings in
   Fiction Press, 2025. | Includes bibliographical references.
   Summary: Fourteen stories on female hypnotists by various
   authors, with extensive bibliography and resource guide.
   Identifiers: Library of Congress Control Number: 2024943986 |
   ISBN 9780960082339 (paperback) 9780960082346 (hardbound)
Subjects: LCSH: Hypnotism and crime—Fiction. | Hypnotism
   in literature. | Mesmerism in literature. | Animal magnetism—
   Fiction. | Murder—Fiction.
Classification: LCC PN6071.H9 H767 2025 | DDC 813.08 H765--
   dc23

Contents

Woman attempting to hypnotize a friend
(Minnesota Historical Society Collection)

Introduction

Literary works about hypnotism were immensely popular in the latter half of the 19th century and on into the early portion of the 20th century as well. One of the most successful novels of the entire 19th century was George du Maurier's novel *Trilby*, whose plot revolves around a menacing male hypnotist controlling a young female subject. Other prominent novelists like Bram Stoker, George Eliot, Wilkie Collins, and Charles Dickens were all interested in the relatively new quasi-science of hypnotism, and Arthur Conan Doyle was especially influenced by the topic, for he would integrate the subject into several of his works of fiction, two of which are included in *The Female Hypnotist*. How popular a theme was hypnotism for 19th and early 20th century authors? *Trance Fiction*, a forthcoming reference book to be published by Themes & Settings in Fiction Press, lists over 1,000 works of fiction (novels, dime novels, and short stories) published between 1840 and 1910, in which hypnotism and mesmerism play an important role in the plot. Less popular, were authors that used female hypnotists as characters—out of the 1,000 or so fictional works published in the period 1840-1910, less than 16 percent had a female hypnotist.

The lack of the female hypnotist as character should not be surprising given the status of women in the Victorian era. Viewed as the weaker sex physically, spiritually, and intellectually, it was assumed that women must be weaker when it came to willpower. A female hypnotist upended societal norms of women having weaker wills, and the thought of a woman subjugating a man's mind was a disturbing concept.

The Female Hypnotist provides a glimpse at the gendered power relations of the Victorian and Edwardian eras through the textual window of a collection of 12 short stories and two novelettes organized around the theme of the female hypnotist. In the book's Foreword, Amy Ellingham, a communications professional, hypnotherapist, and co-founder of the hypnosis blog "Cosmic Pancakes" (https://www.cosmic-pancakes.com), brings her considerable knowledge about the history of hypnosis to bear on the portrayal of women characters' use of hypnotism in the fight to free themselves from the role of the submissive Victorian lady. Avid readers and literary researchers will appreciate the book's inclusion of an extensive annotated bibliography of 19th and early 20th century novels, dime novels, and short stories having female hypnotists/mesmerists as characters.

Donald K. Hartman

Series editor, *Hypnotism in Victorian and Edwardian Era Fiction*

Foreword
by Amy Ellingham

It has been my pleasure and privilege to make a study of hypnotism, past and present, since 2019. Prior to that, hypnosis—and, specifically, the art and science of blending suggestion with 'fascination'—has been a feature of my lifelong passions for writing, communication, and human potential, both wittingly and unwittingly.

I say 'unwittingly' because, as a woman, I could not initially see why I was drawn to hypnosis as a modern field, vocation, or community. Women practitioners dominate the hypnotherapy scene, but from beneath a mostly male clique of trainers, gurus, and—yes—charlatans, who propagate a flawed knowledge base and narrative. The academic science of hypnotism, meanwhile, is my husband's specialty, with male researchers far exceeding names such as Judith Pintar and Amanda Barnier. And, whatever their gender, I prefer to see considered professionals—rather than giddy, misguided amateurs—perform stage, screen, and street entertainment hypnosis.

For me, there instead seemed to be a nascent space between the showmen, myths, and misconceptions of hypnosis as it was and is, and my written fictions and fantasies of what it could be. The *fin de siècle* was a pivotal time for hypnotism (and magnetism/mesmerism) as a social construct and cultural phenomenon, with Franco-British writer George du Maurier's (1834-1896) novel *Trilby* sparking a publishing sensation. The somnambulistic passivity of the tragic titular heroine may be all but forgotten (aside from as a style of hat). Yet Svengali as a sinister hypnotic 'puppet-master' lives on as both a common noun, and as a recurring reference and aesthetic for modern 'hypnotist' entertainers, such as British 'psychological illusionist' Derren Brown.[1]

This clichéd power dynamic between hypnotist and subject prevailed in the parlour and public hypnotic demonstrations that swept Britain,

1 https://derrenbrown.co.uk/shows/svengali/

Europe, and the U.S. during the Victorian and Edwardian eras. Women were amenable subjects and/or loyal fans; a few were vocal pundits or critics; vanishingly fewer were practitioners themselves.[2] Women became, to me, a homogeneous backdrop to the white male prestige of The Hypnotist role. Only tragical female figures from fiction and reality (say, Trilby or the 'professional hysterics' of medical mesmerists John Elliotson or Jean-Martin Charcot) glinted behind the luminary males engrossed with mesmerism in the mid-1800s to early 1900s; figures such as Alexis Didier, Chauncy Hare Townshend, Wilkie Collins, and Charles Dickens, spring to mind.

That's why I was so grateful to discover the work of Donald K. Hartman. His three prior works on hypnotism in the Victorian and Edwardian eras—*Death by Suggestion*, *The Hypno-Ripper*, and *The Hypnotic Tales of Rafael Sabatini*—are treasure troves of contemporary short stories and novellas featuring female characters and plots. But this latest collection, *The Female Hypnotist*, is my favourite yet. The 14 tales of female hypnotists and women wielding hypnotic powers are penned by both male and female authors, some famed, some forgotten. What binds them is the foreboding sense that a woman hypnotist is— to contemporary minds—taboo; that such outliers are a scourge upon 'good,' 'legitimate' male mesmerists to be stamped out; that women who use their eyes, and tongues, to persuade, seduce, and deceive are, essentially, witches.

So, whether you came upon this book as a researcher or simply as a curious reader of works concerning hypnotism, I'm sure you'll relish the women hypnotist characters within. Most are mad, bad, and dangerous to know! Many are clever, ambitious, and innovative… if morally vacant. Some are depicted as evil only by dint of their cool independence, or the crude 'exotic' (i.e. racist/antisemitic) or ableist stereotypes of the times. All, however, are more than a match for the male protagonists and antagonists drawn into their hypnotic, psychotic webs, schemes, and crimes.

In that respect, this book provides ample inspiration beyond the vacuous 'innocence' of *Trilby* and Trilbyana.[3] These 14 tales also feature, for instance, favourable female characters who are able conversationalists—experts, even—on the topic of hypnosis within

2 See *Mesmerized: Powers of Mind in Victorian Britain*, by Alison Winter, 1998
3 https://en.wikipedia.org/wiki/Trilbyana

male company, while a lady-gambler-cheat's knowing 'diss' of Charcot's methods spooks her male confederate. Such devilish details capture, for me, the reality behind the fiction: of the anxiety and allure of women possessing not just 'forbidden' knowledge but *superior* forbidden knowledge.

Perhaps that is the Pandora's box that du Maurier ultimately opened? His friend, Felix Moscheles (1833-1917)—a keen mesmerist upon whom Svengali was based—reflected in 1896 on the young woman who partly inspired Trilby. Moscheles and du Maurier formed a close, flirtatious bond with Carry, the daughter of a respectable Malines widow, during their time in French Bohemia. Moscheles—or 'Mephistopheles', as du Maurier dubbed him—would play mesmeric tricks on customers while Carry worked in her mother's tobacco shop, with Carry taking pleasure in the pain of a young man holding an imagined 'red hot' key. Moscheles implies that mesmerism corrupted her. "[I]t was not without concern that we noticed in her a certain restlessness and a growing tendency to discuss with the serpent questions relating to the acquisition of prohibited apples," he writes in his memoir. "She tasted of the apple her friend the serpent had told her so much about. Then [...] she tried another; such a bad one unfortunately. It was a wonder it didn't poison her, body and soul, but it didn't." Whatever her despair or disgrace, Carry was cut off from Moscheles and du Maurier on their return to Britain, and then married off to a Parisian doctor. Moscheles named his dog in her memory.[4]

That women must be protected, policed, and prohibited from harnessing the powers of hypnosis underscores all the stories that Hartman has collected into this quartet of books. The most malevolent imagined misuse of this dark magic seems, though, to be 'mesmerising mesmerists', and hypnotic women treating men with the same indifference—or predatory playfulness—that Moscheles manifests for Carry. The first tale in this book, written by a woman, is the perfect introduction to this slippery moral slope that preoccupied Victorian and Edwardian minds during this hypnotic heyday. A neglected new wife uses her 'magic eyes' and guiles to win her painter-husband's love for his art for herself...or to destroy him for valuing art over devotion. That readers of such stories could witness conventional wives, lovers, ladies, and visitors in the role of villainous hypnotist must have made for thrilling reading.

---

4 See *In Bohemia with du Maurier*, by Felix Moscheles, 1896

"Never teach a woman the power of hypnotism again," one repentant mesmeric mistress, who you're soon to meet, implores her male hypnotist mentor. "You place a dangerous weapon in the hands of the most irresponsible possessors in the world." A delicious ambiguity in many of these stories is whether women can resist using their hypnotic powers for their inherently 'wicked' purposes, or if the sin is simply in using their 'feminine' words and wiles full stop? A recurring theme is that 'good' men must act as gatekeepers to protect society against 'magic' women; but, thankfully, such outmoded patriarchal sentiments and moral panics no longer stand in a woman's way.

My own study of hypnotism has given me a taste for friendly snakes and bad apples, and I feel great affinity with Carry and the myriad characters she inspired. So here's to hypnotism's original sinners, whatever their gender! Enjoy Hartman's superb book!

Amy Ellingham
Cheltenham, December 2024

Read Amy's writing on hypnotism at
https://www.cosmic-pancakes.com/

Biographical Notes

Louisa May Alcott (November 29, 1832–March 6, 1888) b. Germantown, Pennsylvania.

An American author known for her children's books, especially the classic *Little Women*.

Montefiore Bienenstok

No biographical information could be located on a Montefiore Bienenstok, but it is quite likely that he is the Montefiore Bienenstok (also spelled, Bienenstock) who headed several Jewish philanthropic groups in the city of St. Louis, Missouri; Bienenstock was also a contributor to many Jewish periodicals in the early portion of the 20th century.

Dick Donovan (May 28, 1843–January 23, 1934) b. Southampton, England.

"Dick Donovan" was the pseudonym for James Edward Preston Muddock, a prolific writer of mystery and horror fiction. He also wrote under the name J. E. Muddock.

Arthur Conan Doyle (May 22, 1859–July 7, 1930) b. Edinburgh, Scotland.

Practicing physician in the early part of his life but best known for his detective fiction featuring the character Sherlock Holmes.

Erckmann-Chatrian

Erckmann-Chatrian was the name used by the French authors Émile Erckmann (1822–1899) and Alexandre Chatrian (1826-1890), nearly all of whose works were jointly written.

Benjamin Leopold Farjeon (May 12, 1838–July 23, 1903) b. London, England.

Prolific English novelist, journalist, and playwright.

Emeric Hulme-Beaman (1864–1937) b. Cudapah, India.

A journalist and fiction writer; together with William Senior Ellis, he wrote four mystery novels under the pseudonym "Ben Strong."

Marie Madison (1865–June 8, 1913) b. Cincinnati, Ohio.

May Fleischman was a playwright, actress, and short story writer whose stage name and pseudonym were "Marie Madison." Author of *The Witch* and several other plays, and a regular contributor of short stories to the *New York Clipper* and the *Philadelphia Evening Call*; later wrote under the name "Marie Madison-Brotman."

Richard Marsh (October 12, 1857–August 9, 1915) b. London, England.

"Richard Marsh" was the pseudonym for Richard Bernard Heldmann; a prolific author of the late 19th century and the Edwardian period, Marsh is best known now for his supernatural novel *The Beetle*.

Edward Page Mitchell (March 24, 1852–January 22, 1927) b. Bath, Maine.

An American short story writer and longtime editor-in-chief of the New York City newspaper *The Sun*.

Note on the Texts

The following is a list of the sources of the texts included in this volume, listed in the order of their appearance in this volume.

Louisa May Alcott. "A Pair of Eyes; or, Modern Magic." *Frank Leslie's Illustrated Newspaper* Vol. 17, no. 421 (October 24, 1863): 69-71. [Note: "A Pair of Eyes" was published anonymously in two parts in *Frank Leslie's Illustrated Newspaper*, second part was published in the October 31, 1863 issue on pp. 85-87].

Marie Madison. "A Scientific Revenge." *New York Clipper* (October 12, 1895): 499-500.

Richard Marsh. "The Burglar's Blunder." *Gentleman's Magazine* Vol. 268 (May, 1890): 433-448.

Edward Page Mitchell. "The Facts in the Ratcliff Case." *Evening Star* (November 22, 1879): 6.

Anonymous. "Suggestion." *Romance* Vol. 3 (September, 1891): 186-191.

G.F.G. "One Woman's Will." *Every Week* (August 28, 1891): 189-191.

Erckmann-Chatrian. "Suggested Suicide." *Romance* Vol. 2 (July, 1891): 332-346.

Arthur Conan Doyle. "John Barrington Cowles." In: *The Captain of the Polestar, and Other Tales*. London: Longmans, Green & Co., 1890. pp. 230-266.

Anonymous. "An Apt Pupil." *Ovens and Murray Advertiser* (August 5, 1905): 7.

B.L. Farjeon. "Philip Darrell's Wife." *Weekly Irish Times* (August 8, 1903): 4.

Montefiore Bienenstok. "An Experiment in Conscience." *American Jewess* Vol. 2 (January, 1896): 202-208. [part 2 of this short story published in the February 1896 issue of the *American Jewess* on pp. 261-265].

Emeric Hulme-Beaman. "Madame Valprez: A Monte Carlo Romance." *Harmsworth Magazine* Vol. 6 (February-July, 1901): 449-458.

Arthur Conan Doyle. *The Parasite*. Westminster: A. Constable & Co. 1894

Dick Donovan. "The Woman With the 'Oily Eyes.'" In: *Tales of Terror*. London: Chatto & Windus, 1899. pp. 1-50.

A Pair of Eyes; or, Modern Magic

By Louisa May Alcott

[Note: "A Pair of Eyes" was initially published anonymously in two parts in *Frank Leslie's Illustrated Newspaper* (Oct. 24, 1863, on pp.69-71 and Oct. 31, 1863, on pp.85-87)].

I WAS disappointed—the great actress had not given me what I wanted, and my picture must still remain unfinished for want of a pair of eyes. I knew what they should be, saw them clearly in my fancy, but though they haunted me by night and day I could not paint them, could not find a model who would represent the aspect I desired, could not describe it to any one, and though I looked into every face I met, and visited afflicted humanity in many shapes, I could find no eyes that visibly presented the vacant yet not unmeaning stare of Lady Macbeth in her haunted sleep. It fretted me all most beyond endurance to be delayed in my work so near its completion, for months of thought and labor had been bestowed upon it; the few who had seen it in its imperfect state had elated me with commendation, whose critical sincerity I knew the worth of; and the many not admitted were impatient for a sight of that which others praised, and to which the memory of former successes lent an interest beyond mere curiosity. All was done, and well done, except the eyes; the dimly lighted chamber, the listening attendants, the ghostly figure with wan face framed in hair, that streamed shadowy and long against white draperies, and whiter arms, whose gesture told that the parted lips were uttering that mournful cry—

"Here's the smell of blood still!

All the perfumes of Arabia will not

Sweeten this little hand—"

The eyes alone baffled me, and for want of these my work waited, and my last success was yet unwon.

I was in a curious mood that night, weary yet restless, eager yet impotent to seize the object of my search, and full of haunting images that would not stay to be reproduced. My friend was absorbed in the play, which no longer possessed any charm for me, and leaning back in my seat I fell into a listless reverie, still harping on the one idea of my life; for impetuous and resolute in all things, I had given myself body and soul to the profession I had chosen and followed through many vicissitudes for fifteen years. Art was wife, child, friend, food and fire to me; the pursuit of fame as a reward for my long labor was the object for which I lived, the hope which gave me courage to press on over every obstacle, sacrifice and suffering, for the word "defeat" was not in my vocabulary. Sitting thus, alone, though in a crowd, I slowly became aware of a disturbing influence whose power invaded my momentary isolation, and soon took shape in the uncomfortable conviction that some one was looking at me. Every one has felt this, and at another time I should have cared little for it, but just then I was laboring under a sense of injury, for of all the myriad eyes about me none would give me the expression I longed for; and unreasonable as it was, the thought that I was watched annoyed me like a silent insult. I sent a searching look through the boxes on either hand, swept the remoter groups with a powerful glass, and scanned the sea of heads below, but met no answering glance; all faces were turned stageward, all minds seemed intent upon the tragic scenes enacting there.

Failing to discover any visible cause for my fancy, I tried to amuse myself with the play, but having seen it many times and being in an ill-humor with the heroine of the hour, my thoughts soon wandered, and though still apparently an interested auditor, I heard nothing, saw nothing, for the instant my mind became abstracted the same uncanny sensation returned. A vague consciousness that some stronger nature was covertly exerting its power upon my own; I smiled as this whim first suggested itself, but it rapidly grew upon me, and a curious feeling of impotent resistance took possession of me, for I was indignant with knowing why, and longed to rebel against—I knew not what. Again I looked far and wide, met several inquiring glances from near neighbors, but none that answered my demand by any betrayal of especial interest or malicious pleasure. Baffled, yet not satisfied, I turned to myself, thinking to find the cause of my disgust there, but did not succeed. I seldom drank wine, had not worked intently the day, and except the picture had no anxiety to harass me; yet without any physical or mental cause that I could discover, every nerve seemed jangled out of tune, my temples beat, my breath came short, and the air seemed feverishly close, though I had not perceived it until then. I did not understand this mood and with an impatient gesture took the playbill from my friend's knee, gathered it into my hand and fanned myself like petulant woman, I suspect, for Louis turned and surveyed me with surprise as he asked:

"What is it, Max; you seem annoyed?"

"I am, but absurd as it is, I don't know why except a foolish fancy that someone whom I do not see is looking at me and wishes me to look at him."

Louis laughed—"Of course there is, aren't you used to it yet? And are you so modest as not to know that many eyes take stolen glances at the rising artist, whose ghost and goblins make their hair stand on end so charmingly? I had the mortification to discover some time ago that, young and comely as I take the liberty of thinking myself, the upturned lorgnettes are not levelled at me, but the stern-faced, black-bearded gentleman beside me, for he looks particularly moody and interesting to-night."

"Bah! I just wish I could inspire some of those starers with gratitude enough to set them walking in their sleep for my benefit and their own future glory. Your suggestion has proved a dead failure, the woman there cannot give me what I want, the picture will never get done, and the whole affair will go to the deuce for want of a pair of eyes."

I rose to go as I spoke, and there they were behind me!

What sort of expression my face assumed I cannot tell, for I forgot time and place, and might have committed some absurdity if Louis had not pulled me down with a look that made me aware that I was staring with an utter disregard of common courtesy.

"Who are those people? Do you know them?" I demanded in a vehement whisper.

"Yes, but put down that glass and sit still or I'll call an usher to put you out," he answered, scandalized at my energetic demonstrations.

"Good! then introduce me—now at once—Come on," and I rose again, to be again arrested.

"Are you possessed to-night? You have visited so many fever wards and madhouses in your search that you've unsettled your own wits, Max. What whim has got into your brain now? And why do you want to know those people in such haste?"

"Your suggestion has not proved failure, a woman can give me what I want, the picture will be finished, and nothing will go to the deuce, for I've found the eyes—now be obliging and help me secure them."

Louis stared at me as if he seriously began to think me a little mad, but restrained the explosive remark that rose to his lips and answered hastily, as several persons looked round as if our whispering annoyed them.

"I'll take you in there after the play if you must go, so for heaven's sake behave like a gentleman till then, and let me enjoy myself in peace."

I nodded composedly, he returned to his tragedy, and shading my eyes with my hand, I took a critical survey, feeling more and more assured that my long search was at last ended. Three persons occupied the box, a well-dressed elderly lady dozing behind her fan, a lad leaning over the front absorbed in the play, and a young lady looking straight before her with the aspect I had waited for with such impatience. This figure I scrutinized with the eye of an artist which took in every accessory of outline, ornament and hue.

Framed in darkest hair, rose a face delicately cut, but cold and coloress as that of any statue in the vestibule without. The lips were slightly parted with the long slow breaths that came and went, the forehead was femininely broad and low, the brows straight and black, and underneath them the mysterious eyes fixed on vacancy, full of that weird regard so hard to counterfeit, so impossible to describe; for though absent, it was not expressionless, and through its steadfast shine a troubled meaning wandered, as if soul and body could not be utterly divorced by any effort of the will. She seemed unconscious of the scene about her, for the fixture of her glance never changed, and nothing about her stirred but the jewel on her bosom, whose changeful glitter seemed to vary as it rose and fell. Emboldened by this apparent absorption, I prolonged my scrutiny and scanned this countenance as I had never done a woman's face before. During this examination I had forgotten myself in her, feeling only a strong desire to draw nearer and dive deeper into those two dark wells that seemed so tranquil yet so fathomless, and in the act of trying to fix shape, color and expression in my memory, I lost them all; for a storm of applause broke the attentive hush as the curtain fell, and like one startled from sleep a flash of intelligence lit up the eyes, then a white hand was passed across them, and long downcast lashes hid them from my sight.

Louis stood up, gave himself a comprehensive survey, and walked out, saying, with a nod,

"Now, Max, put on your gloves, shake the hair out of your eyes, assume your best 'deportment,' and come and take an observation which may immortalize your name."

Knocking over a chair in my haste, I followed close upon his heels, as he tapped at the next door; the lad opened it, bowed to my conductor, glanced at me and strolled away, while we passed in. The elderly lady was awake, now, and received us graciously; the younger was leaning on her hand, the plumy fan held between her and the glare of the great chandelier as she watched the moving throng below.

"Agatha, here is Mr. Yorke and a friend whom he wishes to present to you," said the old lady, with a shade of deference in her manner which betrayed the companion, not the friend.

Agatha turned, gave Louis her hand, with a slow smile dawning on her lip, and looked up at me as if the fact of my advent had no particular interest for her, and my appearance promised no great pleasure.

"Miss Eure, my friend Max Erdmann yearned to be made happy by a five minutes audience, and I ventured to bring him without sending an *avant courier* to prepare the way. Am I forgiven?" with which half daring, half apologetic introduction, Louis turned to the chaperone and began to rattle.

Miss Eure bowed, swept the waves of silk from the chair beside her, and I sat down with a bold request waiting at my lips till an auspicious moment came, having resolved not to exert myself for nothing. As we discussed the usual topics suggested by the time and place, I looked often into the face before me and soon found it difficult to look away again, for it was a constant surprise to me. The absent mood had passed and with it the frost seemed to have melted from mien and manner, leaving a living woman in the statue's place. I had thought her melancholy, but her lips were dressed in smiles, and frequent peals of low-toned laughter parted them like pleasant music; I had thought her pale, but in either cheek now bloomed a color deep and clear as any tint my palette could have given; I had thought her shy and proud at first, but with each moment her manner warmed, her speech grew franker and her whole figure seemed to glow and brighten as if a brilliant lamp were lit behind the pale shade she had worn before. But the eyes were the greatest surprise of all—I had fancied them dark, and found them the light, sensitive gray belonging to highly nervous temperaments. They were remarkable eyes; for though softly fringed with shadowly lashes they were not mild, but fiery and keen, with many lights and shadows in them as the pupils dilated, and the irids shone with a transparent lustre which varied with her varying words, and proved the existence of an ardent, imperious nature underneath the seeming snow.

They exercised a curious fascination over me and kept my own obedient to their will, although scarce conscious of it at the time and believing mine to be the controlling power. Wherein the charm lay I cannot tell; it was not the influence of a womanly presence alone, for fairer faces had smiled at me in vain; yet as I sat there I felt a pleasant quietude creep over me, I knew my voice had fallen to a lower key, my eye softened from its wonted cold to an indifference, my manner grown smooth and my demeanor changed to one almost as courtly as my friend's, who well deserved his soubriquet of "Louis the Debonnair."

"It is because my long fret is over," I thought, and having something to gain, exerted myself to please so successfully that, soon emboldened by her gracious mood and the flattering compliments bestowed upon my earlier works, I ventured to tell my present strait and the daring hope I had conceived that she would help me through it. How I made this blunt request I cannot tell, but remember that it slipped over my tongue as smoothly as if I had meditated upon it for a week. I glanced over my shoulder as I spoke, fearing Louis might mar all with apology or reproof; but he was absorbed in the comely duenna, who was blushing like a girl at the half playful, half serious devotion he paid all womankind; and reassured, I waited, wondering how Miss Eure would receive my request. Very quietly; for with no change but a peculiar dropping of the lids, as if her eyes sometimes played the traitor to her will, she answered, smilingly,

"It is I who receive the honor, sir, not you, for genius possesses the privileges of royalty, and may claim subjects everywhere, sure that its choice ennobles and its power extends beyond the narrow bounds of custom, time and place. When shall I serve you, Mr. Erdmann?"

At any other time I should have felt surprised both at her and at myself; but just then, in the ardor of the propitious moment, I thought only of my work, and with many thanks for her great kindness left the day to her, secretly hoping she would name an early one. She sat silent an instant, then seemed to come to some determination, for when she spoke a shadow of mingled pain and patience swept across her face as if her resolve had cost her some sacrifice of pride or feeling.

"It is but right to tell you that I may not always have it in my power to give you the expression you desire to catch, for the eyes you honor by wishing to perpetuate are not strong and often fail me for a time. I have been utterly blind once and may be again, yet have no present cause to fear it, and if you can come to me on such days as they will serve your purpose, I shall be most glad to do my best for you. Another reason makes me bold to ask this favor of you, I cannot always summon this absent mood, and should certainly fail in a strange place; but in my own home, with all familiar things about me, I can more easily fall into one of my deep reveries and forget time by the hour together. Will this arrangement cause much inconvenience or delay? A room shall be prepared for you—kept inviolate as long as you desire it— and every facility my house affords is at your service, for I feel much interest in the work which is to add another success to your life."

She spoke regretfully at first, but ended with a cordial glance as if she had forgotten herself in giving pleasure to another. I felt that it must have cost her an effort to confess that such a dire affliction had ever darkened her youth and might still return to sadden her prime; this pity mingled with my expressions of gratitude for the unexpected interest she bestowed upon my work, and in a few words the arrangement was made, the day and hour fixed, and a great load off my mind. What the afterpiece was I never knew; Miss Eure stayed to please her young companion, Louis stayed to please himself, and I remained because I had not energy enough to go away. For, leaning where I first sat down, I still looked and listened with a dreamy sort of satisfaction to Miss Eure's low voice, as with downcast eyes, still shaded by her fan, she spoke enthusiastically and well of art (the one interesting theme to me) in a manner which proved that she had read and studied more than her modesty allowed her to acknowledge.

We parted like old friends at her carriage door, and as I walked away with Louis in the cool night air I felt like one who had been asleep in a close room, for I was both languid and drowsy, though a curious undercurrent of excitement still stirred my blood and tingled along my nerves. "A theatre is no place for me," I decided, and anxious to forget myself said aloud:

"Tell me all you know about that woman."

"What woman, Max?"

"Miss Agatha Eure, the owner of the eyes."

"Aha! smitten at last! That ever I should live to see our Benedict the victim of love at first sight!"

"Have done with your nonsense, and answer my question. I don't ask from mere curiosity, but that I may have some idea how to bear myself at these promised sittings; for it will never do to ask after her papa if she has none, to pay my respects to the old lady as her mother if she is only the duenna, or joke with the lad if he is the heir apparent."

"Do you mean to say that you asked her to sit to you?" cried Louis, falling back a step and staring at me with undisguised astonishment.

"Yes, why not?"

"Why, man, Agatha Eure is the haughtiest piece of humanity ever concocted; and I, with all my daring, never ventured to ask more than an occasional dance with her, and feel myself especially favored that she deigns to bow to me, and lets me pick up her gloves or carry her bouquet as a mark of supreme condescension. What witchcraft did you bring to bear upon her? and how did she grant your audacious request?"

"Agreed to it at once."

"Like an empress conferring knighthood, I fancy."

"Not at all. More like a pretty woman receiving a compliment to her beauty—though she is not pretty, by the way."

Louis indulged himself in the long, low whistle, which seems the only adequate expression for masculine surprise. I enjoyed his amazement, it was my turn to laugh now, and I did so, as I said:

"You are always railing at me for my avoidance of all womankind, but you see I have not lost the art of pleasing, for I won your haughty Agatha to my will in fifteen minutes, and am not only to paint her handsome eyes, but to do it at her own house, by her own request. I am beginning to find that, after years of effort, I have mounted a few more rounds of the social ladder than I was aware of, and may now confer as well as receive favors; for she seemed to think me the benefactor, and I rather enjoyed the novelty of the thing. Now tell your story of the 'haughtiest piece of humanity' ever known. I like her the better for that trait."

Louis nodded his head, and regarded the moon with an aspect of immense wisdom, as he replied:

"I understand it now; it all comes back to me, and my accusation holds good, only the love at first sight is on the other side. You shall have your story, but it may leave the picture in the lurch if it causes you to fly off, as you usually see fit to do when a woman's name is linked with your own. You never saw Miss Eure before; but what you say reminds me that she has seen you, for one day last autumn, as I was driving with her and old madame—a mark of uncommon favor, mind you—we saw you striding along, with your hat over your eyes, looking very much like a comet streaming down the street. It was crowded, and as you waited at the crossing you spoke to Jack Mellot, and while talking pulled off your hat and tumbled your hair about, in your usual fashion, when very earnest. We were blockaded by cars and coaches for a moment, so Miss Eure had a fine opportunity to feast her eyes upon you, 'though you are not pretty, by the way.' She asked your name, and when I told her she gushed out into a charming little stream of interest in your daubs, and her delight at seeing their creator; all of which was not agreeable to me, for I considered myself much the finer work of art of the two. Just then you caught up a shabby child with a big basket, took them across, under our horses' noses, with never a word for me, though I called to you, and, diving into the crowd, disappeared.'I like that,' said Miss Eure; and as we drove on she asked questions, which I answered in a truly Christian manner, doing you no harm, old lad; for I told all you had fought through, with the courage of a stout-hearted man, all you had borne with the patience of a woman, and what a grand future lay open to you, if you chose to accept and use it, making quite a fascinating little romance of it, I assure you. There the matter dropped. I forgot it till this minute, but it accounts for the ease with which you gained your first suit, and is prophetic of like success in a second and more serious one. She is young, well-born, lovely to those who love her, and has a fortune and position which will lift you at once to the topmost round of the long ladder you've been climbing all these years. I wish you joy, Max."

"Thank you. I've no time for lovemaking, and want no fortune but that which I earn for myself. I am already married to a fairer wife than Miss Eure, so you may win and wear the lofty lady yourself."

Louis gave a comical groan.

"I've tried that, and failed; for she is too cold to be warmed by any flame of mine, though she is wonderfully attractive when she likes, and I hover about her even now like an infatuated moth, who beats his head against the glass and never reaches the light within. No; you must thankfully accept the good the gods bestow. Let Art be your Leah, but Agatha your Rachel. And so, good-night!"

"Stay and tell me one thing—is she an orphan?"

"Yes; the last of a fine old race, with few relatives and few friends, for death has deprived her of the first, and her own choice of the last. The lady you saw with her plays propriety in her establishment; the lad is Mrs. Snow's son, and fills the role of *cavaliere-servente*; for Miss Eure is a Diana toward men in general, and leads a quietly luxurious life among her books, pencils and music, reading and studying all manner of things few women of two-and-twenty care to know. But she has the wit to see that a woman's mission is to be charming, and when she has sufficient motive for the exertion she fulfils that mission most successfully, as I know to my sorrow. Now let me off, and be forever grateful for the good turn I have done you to-night, both in urging you to go to the theatre and helping you to your wish when you got there."

We parted merrily, but his words lingered in my memory, and half unconsciously exerted a new influence over me, for they flattered the three ruling passions that make or mar the fortunes of us all—pride, ambition and self-love. I wanted power, fame and ease, and all seemed waiting for me, not in the dim future but the actual present, if my friend's belief was to be relied upon; and remembering all I had seen and heard that night, I felt that it was not utterly without foundation. I pleased myself for an idle hour in dreaming dreams of what might be; finding that amusement began to grow dangerously attractive, I demolished my castles in the air with the last whiff of my meerschaum, and fell asleep, echoing my own words:

"Art is my wife, I will have no other!"

Punctual to the moment I went to my appointment, and while waiting an answer to my ring took an exterior survey of Miss Eure's house. One of an imposing granite block, it stood in a West End square, with every sign of unostentatious opulence about it. I was very susceptible to all influences, either painful or pleasant, and as I stood there the bland atmosphere that surrounded me seemed most attractive; for my solitary life had been plain and poor, with little time for ease, and few ornaments to give it grace. Now I seemed to have won the right to enjoy both if I would; I no longer felt out of place there, and with this feeling came the wish to try the sunny side of life, and see if its genial gifts would prove more inspiring than the sterner masters I had been serving so long.

The door opened in the middle of my reverie, and I was led through an anteroom, lined with warmhued pictures, to a large apartment, which had been converted into an impromptu studio by some one who understood all the requisites for such a place. The picture, my easel and other necessaries had preceded me, and I thought to have spent a good hour in arranging matters. All was done, however, with a skill that surprised me; the shaded windows, the carefully-arranged brushes, the proper colors already on the palette, the easel and picture placed as they should be, and a deep curtain hung behind a small dais, where I fancied my model was to sit. The room was empty as I entered, and with the brief message, "Miss Eure will be down directly," the man noiselessly departed.

I stood and looked about me with great satisfaction, thinking, "I cannot fail to work well surrounded by such agreeable sights and sounds." The house was very still, for the turmoil of the city was subdued to a murmur, like the far-off music of the sea; a soft gloom filled the room, divided by one strong ray that fell athwart my picture, gifting it with warmth and light. Through a half-open door I saw the green vista of a conservatory, full of fine blendings of color, and wafts of many odors blown to me by the west wind rustling through orange trees and slender palms; while the only sound that broke the silence was the voice of a flame-colored foreign bird, singing a plaintive little strain like a sorrowful lament. I liked this scene, and, standing in the doorway, was content to look, listen and enjoy, forgetful of time, till a slight stir made me turn and for a moment look straight before me with a startled aspect. It seemed as if my picture had left its frame; for, standing on the narrow dais, clearly defined against the dark background, stood the living likeness of the figure I had painted, the same white folds falling from neck to ankle, the same shadowy hair, and slender hands locked together, as if wrung in slow despair; and fixed full upon my own the weird, unseeing eyes, which made the face a pale mask, through which the haunted spirit spoke eloquently, with its sleepless anguish and remorse.

"Good morning, Miss Eure; how shall I thank you?" I began, but stopped abruptly, for without speaking she waved me towards the easel with a gesture which seemed to say "Prove your gratitude by industry."

"Very good," thought I, "if she likes the theatrical style she shall have it. It is evident she has studied her part and will play it well, I will do the same, and as Louis recommends, take the good the gods send me while I may."

Without more ado I took my place and fell to work; but, though never more eager to get on, with each moment that I passed I found my interest in the picture grow less and less intent, and with every glance at my model found that it was more and more difficult to look away. Beautiful she was not, but the wild and woful figure seemed to attract me as no Hebe, Venus or sweet-faced Psyche had ever done. My hand moved slower and slower, the painted face grew dimmer and dimmer, my glances lingered longer and longer, and presently palette and brushes rested on my knee, as I leaned back in the deep chair and gave myself up to an uninterrupted stare. I knew that it was rude, knew that it was a trespass on Miss Eure's kindness as well as a breach of good manners, but I could not help it, for my eyes seemed beyond my control, and though I momentarily expected to see her color rise and hear some warning of the lapse of time, I never looked away, and soon forgot to imagine her feelings in the mysterious confusion of my own.

I was first conscious of a terrible fear that I ought to speak or move, which seemed impossible, for my eyelids began to be weighed down by a delicious drowsiness in spite of all my efforts to keep them open. Everything grew misty, and the beating of my heart sounded like the rapid, irregular roll of a muffled drum; then a strange weight seemed to oppress and cause me to sigh long and deeply. But soon the act of breathing appeared to grow unnecessary, for a sensation of wonderful airiness came over me, and I felt as if I could float away like a thistledown. Presently every sense seemed to fall asleep, and in the act of dropping both palette and brush I drifted away into a sea of blissful repose, where nothing disturbed me but a fragmentary dream that came and went like a lingering gleam of consciousness through the new experience which had befallen me.

I seemed to be still in the quiet room, still leaning in the deep chair with half-closed eyes, still watching the white figure before me, but that had changed. I saw a smile break over the lips, something like triumph flash into the eyes, sudden color flush the cheeks, and the rigid hands lifted to gather up and put the long hair back; then with noiseless steps it came nearer and nearer till it stood beside me. For awhile it paused there mute and intent, I felt the eager gaze searching my face, but it caused no displeasure; for I seemed to be looking down at myself, as if soul and body had parted company and I was gifted with a double life. Suddenly the vision laid a light hand on my wrist and touched my temples, while a shade of anxiety seemed to flit across its face as it turned and vanished. A dreamy wonder regarding its return woke within me, then my sleep deepened into utter oblivion, for how long I cannot tell. A pungent odor seemed to recall me to the same half wakeful state. I dimly saw a woman's arm holding a glittering object before me, whence the fragrance came; an unseen hand stirred my hair with the grateful drip of water, and once there came a touch like the pressure of lips upon my forehead, soft and warm, but gone in an instant. These new sensations grew rapidly more and more defined; I clearly saw a bracelet on the arm and read the Arabic characters engraved upon the golden coins that formed it; I heard the rustle of garments, the hurried breathing of some near presence, and felt the cool sweep of a hand passing to and fro across my forehead. At this point my thoughts began to shape themselves into words, which came slowly and seemed strange to me as I searched for and connected them, then a heavy sigh rose and broke at my lips, and the sound of my own voice woke me, drowsily echoing the last words I had spoken:

"Good morning, Miss Eure; how shall I thank you?"

To my great surprise the well-remembered voice answered quietly:

"Good morning, Mr. Erdmann; will you have some lunch before you begin?"

How I opened my eyes and got upon my feet was never clear to me, but the first object I saw was Miss Eure coming towards me with a glass in her hand. My expression must have been dazed and imbecile in the extreme, for to add to my bewilderment the tragic robes had disappeared, the dishevelled hair was gathered in shining coils under a Venetian net of silk and gold, a white embroidered wrapper replaced the muslins Lady Macbeth had worn, and a countenance half playful, half anxious, now smiled where I had last seen so sorrowful an aspect. The fear of having committed some great absurdity and endangered my success brought me right with a little shock of returning thought. I collected myself, gave a look about the room, a dizzy bow to her, and put my hand to my head with a vague idea that something was wrong there. In doing this I discovered that my hair was wet, which slight fact caused me to exclaim abruptly:

"Miss Eure, what have I been doing? Have I had a fit? been asleep? or do you deal in magic and rock your guests off into oblivion without a moment's warning?"

Standing before me with uplifted eyes, she answered, smiling:

"No, none of these have happened to you; the air from the Indian plants in the conservatory was too powerful, I think; you were a little faint, but closing the door and opening a window has restored you, and a glass of wine will perfect the cure I hope."

She was offering the glass as she spoke. I took it but forgot to thank her, for on the arm extended to me was the bracelet never seen so near by my waking eyes, yet as familiar as if my vision had come again. Something struck me disagreeably, and I spoke out with my usual bluntness.

"I never fainted in my life, and have an impression that people do not dream when they swoon. Now I did, and so vivid was it that I still remember the characters engraved on the trinket you wear, for that played a prominent part in my vision. Shall I describe them as proof of it, Miss Eure?"

Her arm dropped at her side and her eyes fell for a moment as I spoke; then she glanced up unchanged, saying as she seated herself and motioned me to do the same:

"No, rather tell the dream, and taste these grapes while you amuse me."

I sat down and obeyed her. She listened attentively, and when I ended explained the mystery in the simplest manner.

"You are right in the first part of your story. I did yield to a whim which seized me when I saw your picture, and came down *en costume*, hoping to help you by keeping up the illusion. You began, as canvas and brushes prove; I stood motionless till you turned pale and regarded me with a strange expression; at first I thought it might be inspiration, as your friend Yorke would say, but presently you dropped everything out of your hands and fell back in your chair. I took the liberty of treating you like a woman, for I bathed your temples and wielded my vinaigrette most energetically till you revived and began to talk of 'Rachel, art, castles in the air, and your wife Lady Macbeth;' then I slipped away and modernized myself, ordered some refreshments for you, and waited till you wished me 'Good-morning.'"

She was laughing so infectiously that I could not resist joining her and accepting her belief, for curious as the whole affair seemed to me I could account for it in no other way. She was winningly kind, and urged me not to resume my task, but I was secretly disgusted with myself for such a display of weakness, and finding her hesitation caused solely by fears for me, I persisted, and seating her, painted as I had never done before. Every sense seemed unwontedly acute, and hand and eye obeyed me with a docility they seldom showed. Miss Eure sat where I placed her, silent and intent, but her face did not wear the tragic aspect it had worn before, though she tried to recall it. This no longer troubled me, for the memory of the vanished face was more clearly before me than her own, and with but few and hasty glances at my model, I reproduced it with a speed and skill that filled me with delight. The striking of a clock reminded me that I had far exceeded the specified time, and that even a woman's patience has limits; so concealing my regret at losing so auspicious a mood, I laid down my brush, leaving my work unfinished, yet glad to know I had the right to come again, and complete it in a place and presence which proved so inspiring.

Miss Eure would not look at it till it was all done, saying in reply to my thanks for the pleasant studio she had given me—"I was not quite unselfish in that, and owe you an apology for venturing to meddle with your property; but it gave me real satisfaction to arrange these things, and restore this room to the aspect it wore three years ago. I, too, was an artist then, and dreamed aspiring dreams here, but was arrested on the threshold of my career by loss of sight; and hard as it seemed then to give up all my longings, I see now that it was better so, for a few years later it would have killed me. I have learned to desire for others what I can never hope for myself, and try to find pleasure in their success, unembittered by regrets for my own defeat. Let this explain my readiness to help you, my interest in your work and my best wishes for your present happiness and future fame."

The look of resignation, which accompanied her words, touched me more than a flood of complaints, and the thought of all she had lost woke such sympathy and pity in my frosty heart, that I involuntarily pressed the hand that could never wield a brush again. Then for the first time I saw those keen eyes soften and grow dim with unshed tears; this gave them the one charm they needed to be beautiful as well as penetrating, and as they met my own, so womanly sweet and grateful, I felt that one might love her while that mood remained. But it passed as rapidly as it came, and when we parted in the anteroom the cold, quiet lady bowed me out, and the tender-faced girl was gone.

I never told Louis all the incidents of that first sitting, but began my story where the real interest ended; and Miss Eure was equally silent, through forgetfulness or for some good reason of her own. I went several times again, yet though the conservatory door stood open I felt no ill effects from the Indian plants that still bloomed there, dreamed no more dreams, and Miss Eure no more enacted the somnambulist. I found an indefinable charm in that pleasant room, a curious interest in studying its mistress, who always met me with a smile, and parted with a look of unfeigned regret. Louis rallied me upon my absorption, but it caused me no uneasiness, for it was not love that led me there, and Miss Eure knew it. I never had forgotten our conversation on that first night, and with every interview the truth of my friend's suspicion grew more and more apparent to me. Agatha Eure was a strong-willed, imperious woman, used to command all about her and see her last wish gratified; but now she was conscious of a presence she could not command, a wish she dare not utter, and, though her womanly pride sealed her lips, her eyes often traitorously betrayed the longing of her heart. She was sincere in her love for art, and behind that interest in that concealed, even from herself, her love for the artist; but the most indomitable passion given humanity cannot long be hidden. Agatha soon felt her weakness, and vainly struggled to subdue it. I soon knew my power, and owned its subtle charm, though I disdained to use it.

The picture was finished, exhibited and won me all, and more than I had dared to hope; for rumor served me a good turn, and whispers of Miss Eure's part in my success added zest to public curiosity and warmth to public praise. I enjoyed the little stir it caused, found admiration a sweet draught after a laborious year, and felt real gratitude to the woman who had helped me win it. If my work had proved a failure I should have forgotten her, and been an humbler, happier man; it did not, and she became a part of my success. Her name was often spoken in the same breath with mine, her image was kept before me by no exertion of my own, till the memories it brought with it grew familiar as old friends, and slowly ripened into a purpose which, being born of ambition and not love, bore bitter fruit, and wrought out its own retribution for a sin against myself and her.

The more I won the more I demanded, the higher I climbed the more eager I became; and, at last, seeing how much I could gain by a single step, resolved to take it, even though I knew it to be a false one. Other men married for the furtherance of their ambitions, why should not I? Years ago I had given up love of home for love of fame, and the woman who might have made me what I should be had meekly yielded all, wished me a happy future, and faded from my world, leaving me only a bitter memory, a veiled picture and a quiet grave my feet never visited but once. Miss Eure loved me, sympathised in my aims, understood my tastes; she could give all I asked to complete the purpose of my life, and lift me at once and for ever from the hard lot I had struggled with for thirty years. One word would work the miracle, why should I hesitate to utter it?

I did not long—for three months from the day I first entered that shadowy room I stood there intent on asking her to be my wife. As I waited I lived again the strange hour once passed there, and felt as if it had been the beginning of another dream whose awakening was yet to come. I asked myself if the hard healthful reality was not better than such feverish visions, however brilliant, and the voice that is never silent when we interrogate it with sincerity answered, "Yes." "No matter, I choose to dream, so let the phantom of a wife come to me here as the phantom of a lover came to me so long ago." As I uttered these defiant words aloud, like a visible reply, Agatha appeared upon the threshold of the door. I knew she had heard me—for again I saw the soft-eyed, tender girl, and opened my arms to her without a word. She came at once, and clinging to me with unwonted tears upon her cheek, unwonted fervor in her voice, touched my forehead, as she had done in that earlier dream, whispering like one still doubtful of her happiness—

"Oh, Max! be kind to me, for in all the world I have only you to love."

I promised, and broke that promise in less than a year.

We were married quietly, went away till the nine days gossip was over, spent our honeymoon as that absurd month is usually spent, and came back to town with the first autumnal frosts; Agatha regretting that I was no longer entirely her own, I secretly thanking heaven that I might drop the lover, and begin my work again, for I was as an imprisoned creature in that atmosphere of "love in idleness," though my bonds were only a pair of loving arms. Madame Snow and son departed, we settled ourselves in the fine house, and then endowed with every worldly blessing, I looked about me, believing myself master of my fate, but found I was its slave.

If Agatha could have joined me in my work we might have been happy; if she could have solaced herself with other pleasures and left me to my own, we might have been content; if she had loved me less, we might have gone our separate ways, and yet been friends like many another pair; but I soon found that her affection was of that exacting nature which promises but little peace unless met by one as warm. I had nothing but regard to give her, for it was not in her power to stir a deeper passion in me; I told her this before our marriage, told her I was a cold, hard man, wrapt in a single purpose; but what woman believes such confessions while her heart still beats fast with the memory of her betrothal? She said everything was possible to love, and prophesied a speedy change; I knew it would not come, but having given my warning left the rest to time. I hoped to lead a quiet life and prove that adverse circumstances, not the want of power, had kept me from excelling in the profession I had chosen; but to my infinite discomfort Agatha turned jealous of my art, for finding the mistress dearer than the wife, she tried to wean me from it, and seemed to feel that having given me love, wealth and ease, I should ask no more, but play the obedient subject to a generous queen. I rebelled against this, told her that one-half my time should be hers, the other belonged to me, and I would so employ it that it should bring honor to the name I had given her. But, Agatha was not used to seeing her will thwarted or her pleasure sacrificed to another, and soon felt that though I scrupulously fulfilled my promise, the one task was irksome, the other all absorbing; that though she had her husband at her side his heart was in his studio, and the hours spent with her were often the most listless in his day. Then began that sorrowful experience old as Adam's reproaches to Eve; we both did wrong, and neither repented; both were self-willed, sharp tongued and proud, and before six months of wedded life had passed we had known many of those scenes which so belittle character and lessen self-respect.

Agatha's love lived through all, and had I answered its appeals by patience, self-denial and genial friendship, if no warmer tie could exist, I might have spared her an early death, and myself from years of bitterest remorse; but I did not. Then her forbearance ended and my subtle punishment began.

"Away again to-night, Max? You have been shut up all day, and I hoped to have you to myself this evening. Hear how the storm rages without, see how cheery I have made all within for you, so put your hat away and stay, for this hour belongs to me, and I claim it."

Agatha took me prisoner as she spoke, and pointed to the cosy nest she had prepared for me. The room was bright and still; the lamp shone clear; the fire glowed; warm-hued curtains muffled the war of gust and sleet without; books, music, a wide-armed seat and a woman's wistful face invited me; but none of these things could satisfy me just then, and though I drew my wife nearer, smoothed her shining hair, and kissed the reproachful lips, I did not yield.

"You must let me go, Agatha, for the great German artist is here, I had rather give a year of life than miss this meeting with him. I have devoted many evenings to you, and though this hour is yours I shall venture to take it, and offer you a morning call instead. Here are novels, new songs, an instrument, embroidery and a dog, who never can offend by moody silence or unpalatable conversation—what more can a contented woman ask, surely not an absent-minded husband?"

"Yes, just that and nothing more, for she loves him, and he can supply a want that none of these things can. See how pretty I have tried to make myself for you alone; stay, Max, and make me happy."

"Dear, I shall find my pretty wife to-morrow, but the great painter will be gone; let me go, Agatha, and make me happy."

She drew herself from my arm, saying with a flash of the eye—"Max, you are a tyrant!"

"Am I? then you made me so with too much devotion."

"Ah, if you loved me as I loved there would be no selfishness on your part, no reproaches on mine. What shall I do to make myself dearer, Max?"

"Give me more liberty."

"Then I should lose you entirely, and lead the life of a widow. Oh, Max, this is hard, this is bitter, to give all and receive nothing in return."

She spoke passionately, and the truth of her reproach stung me, for I answered with that coldness that always wounded her:

"Do you count an honest name, sincere regard and much gratitude as nothing? I have given you these, and ask only peace and freedom in return. I desire to do justice to you and to myself, but I am not like you, never can be, and you must not hope it. You say love is all-powerful, prove it upon me, I am willing to be the fondest of husbands if I can; teach me, win me in spite of myself, and make me what you will; but leave me a little time to live and labor for that which is dearer to me than your faulty lord and master can ever be to you."

"Shall I do this?" and her face kindled as she put the question.

"Yes, here is an amusement for you, use what arts you will, make your love irresistible, soften my hard nature, convert me into your shadow, subdue me till I come at your call like a pet dog, and when you make your presence more powerful than painting I will own that you have won your will and made your theory good."

I was smiling as I spoke, for the twelve labors of Hercules seemed less impossible than this, but Agatha watched me with her glittering eyes; and answered slowly—

"I will do it. Now go, and enjoy your liberty while you may, but remember when I have conquered that you dared me to it, and keep your part of the compact. Promise this." She offered me her hand with a strange expression—I took it, said good-night, and hurried away, still smiling at the curious challenge given and accepted.

Agatha told me to enjoy my liberty, and I tried to do so that very night, but failed most signally, for I had not been an hour in the brilliant company gathered to meet the celebrated guest before I found it impossible to banish the thought of my solitary wife. I had left her often, yet never felt disturbed by more than a passing twinge of that uncomfortable bosom friend called conscience; but now the interest of the hour seemed lessened by regret, for through varying conversation held with those about me, mingling with the fine music that I heard, looking at me from every woman's face, and thrusting itself into my mind at every turn, came a vague, disturbing self-reproach, which slowly deepened to a strong anxiety. My attention wandered, words seemed to desert me, fancy to be frostbound, and even in the presence of the great man I had so ardently desired to see I could neither enjoy his society nor play my own part well. More than once I found myself listening for Agatha's voice; more than once I looked behind me expecting to see her figure, and more than once I resolved to go, with no desire to meet her.

"It is an acute fit of what women call nervousness; I will not yield to it," I thought, and plunged into the gayest group I saw, supped, talked, sang a song, and broke down; told a witty story, and spoiled it; laughed and tried to bear myself like the lightest-hearted guest in the rooms; but it would not do, for stronger and stronger grew the strange longing to go home, and soon it became uncontrollable. A foreboding fear that something had happened oppressed me, and suddenly leaving the festival at its height I drove home as if life and death depended on the saving of a second. Like one pursuing or pursued I rode, eager only to be there; yet when I stood on my own threshold I asked myself wonderingly, "Why such haste?" and stole in ashamed at my early return. The storm beat without, but within all was serene and still, and with noiseless steps I went up to the room where I had left my wife, pausing a moment at the half open door to collect myself, lest she should see the disorder of both mind and mien. Looking in I saw her sitting with neither book nor work beside her, and after a momentary glance began to think my anxiety had not been causeless, for she sat erect and motionless as an inanimate figure of intense thought; her eyes were fixed, face colorless, with an expression of iron determination, as if every energy of mind and body were wrought up to the achievement of a single purpose. There was something in the rigid attitude and stern aspect of this familiar shape that filled me with dismay, and found vent in the abrupt exclamation,

"Agatha, what is it?"

She sprang up like a steel spring when the pressure is removed, saw me, and struck her hands together with a wild gesture of surprise, alarm or pleasure, which I could not tell, for in the act she dropped into her seat white and breathless as if smitten with sudden death. Unspeakably shocked, I bestirred myself till she recovered, and though pale and spent, as if with some past exertion, soon seemed quite herself again.

"Agatha, what were you thinking of when I came in?" I asked, as she sat leaning against me with half closed eyes and a faint smile on her lips, as if the unwonted caresses I bestowed upon her were more soothing than any cordial I could give. Without stirring she replied,

"Of you, Max. I was longing for you, with heart and soul and will. You told me to win you in spite of yourself, and I was sending my love to find and bring you home. Did it reach you? did it lead you back and make you glad to come?"

A peculiar chill ran through me as I listened, though her voice was quieter, her manner gentler than usual as she spoke. She seemed to have such faith in her tender fancy, such assurance of its efficacy, and such a near approach to certain knowledge of its success, that I disliked the thought of continuing the topic, and answered cheerfully,

"My own conscience brought me home, dear; for, discovering that I had left my peace of mind behind me, I came back to find it. If your task is to cost a scene like this it will do more harm than good to both of us, so keep your love from such uncanny wanderings through time and space, and win me with less dangerous arts."

She smiled her strange smile, folded my hand in her own, and answered, with soft exultation in her voice,

"It will not happen so again, Max; but I am glad, most glad you came, for it proves I have some power over this wayward heart of yours, where I shall knock until it opens wide and takes me in."

The events of that night made a deep impression on me, for from that night my life was changed. Agatha left me entirely free, never asked my presence, never upbraided me for long absences or silence when together.

She seemed to find happiness in her belief that she should yet subdue me, and though I smiled at this in my indifference, there was something half pleasant, half pathetic in the thought of this proud woman leaving all warmer affections for my negligent friendship, the sight of this young wife laboring to win her husband's heart. At first I tried to be all she asked, but soon relapsed into my former life, and finding no reproaches followed, believed I should enjoy it as never before—but I did not. As weeks passed I slowly became conscious that some new power had taken possession of me, swaying my whole nature to its will; a power alien yet sovereign. Fitfully it worked, coming upon me when least desired, enforcing its commands regardless of time, place or mood; mysterious yet irresistible in its strength, this mental tyrant led me at all hours, in all stages of anxiety, repugnance and rebellion, from all pleasures or employments, straight to Agatha. If I sat at my easel the sudden summons came, and wondering at myself I obeyed it, to find her busied in some cheerful occupation, with apparently no thought or wish for me. If I left home I often paused abruptly in my walk or drive, turned and hurried back, simply because I could not resist the impulse that controlled me. If she went away I seldom failed to follow, and found no peace till I was at her side again. I grew moody and restless, slept ill, dreamed wild dreams, and often woke and wandered aimlessly, as if sent upon an unknown errand. I could not fix my mind upon my work; a spell seemed to have benumbed imagination and robbed both brain and hand of power to conceive and skill to execute.

At first I fancied this was only the reaction of entire freedom after long captivity, but I soon found I was bound to a more exacting mistress than my wife had ever been. Then I suspected that it was only the perversity of human nature, and that having gained my wish it grew valueless, and I longed for that which I had lost; but it was not this, for distasteful as my present life had become, the other seemed still more so when I recalled it. For a time I believed that Agatha might be right, that I was really learning to love her, and this unquiet mood was the awakening of that passion which comes swift and strong when it comes to such as I. If I had never loved I might have clung to this belief, but the memory of that earlier affection, so genial, entire and sweet, proved that the present fancy was only a delusion; for searching deeply into myself to discover the truth of this, I found that Agatha was no dearer, and to my own dismay detected a covert dread lurking there, harmless and vague, but threatening to deepen into aversion or resentment for some unknown offence; and while I accused myself of an unjust and ungenerous weakness, I shrank from the thought of her, even while I sought her with the assiduity but not the ardor of a lover.

Long I pondered over this inexplicable state of mind, but found no solution of it; for I would not own, either to myself or Agatha, that the shadow of her prophecy had come to pass, though its substance was still wanting. She sometimes looked inquiringly into my face with those strange eyes of hers, sometimes chid me with a mocking smile when she found me sitting idly before my easel, without a line or tint given though hours had passed; and often, when driven by that blind impulse I sought her anxiously among her friends, she would glance at those about her, saying, with a touch of triumph in her mien, "Am I not an enviable wife to have inspired such devotion in this grave husband?" Once, remembering her former words, I asked her playfully if she still "sent her love to find and bring me home?" but she only shook her head and answered, sadly,

"Oh, no; my love was burdensome to you, so I have rocked it to sleep and laid it where it will not trouble you again."

At last I decided that some undetected physical infirmity caused my disquiet, for years of labor and privation might well have worn the delicate machinery of heart or brain, and this warning suggested the wisdom of consulting medical skill in time. This thought grew as month after month increased my mental malady and began to tell upon my hitherto unbroken health. I wondered if Agatha knew how listless, hollow-eyed and wan I had grown; but she never spoke of it, and an unconquerable reserve kept me from uttering a complaint to her.

One day I resolved to bear it no longer, and hurried away to an old friend in whose skill and discretion I had entire faith. He was out, and while I waited I took up a book that lay among the medical works upon his table. I read a page, then a chapter, turning leaf after leaf with a rapid hand, devouring paragraph after paragraph with an eager eye. An hour passed, still I read on. Dr. L— did not come, but I did not think of that, and when I laid down the book I no longer needed him, for in that hour I had discovered a new world, had seen the diagnosis of my symptoms set forth in unmistakable terms, and found the key to the mystery in the one word— Magnetism. This was years ago, before spirits had begun their labors for good or ill, before ether and hashish had gifted humanity with eternities of bliss in a second, and while Mesmer's mystical discoveries were studied only by the scientific or philosophic few. I knew nothing of these things, for my whole life had led another way, and no child could be more ignorant of the workings or extent of this wonderful power. There was Indian blood in my veins, and superstition lurked there still; consequently the knowledge that I was a victim of this occult magic came upon me like an awful revelation, and filled me with a storm of wrath, disgust and dread.

Like an enchanted spirit who has found the incantation that will free it from subjection, I rejoiced with a grim satisfaction even while I cursed myself for my long blindness, and with no thought for anything but instant accusation on my part, instant confession and atonement on hers, I went straight home, straight into Agatha's presence, and there, in words as brief as bitter, told her that her reign was over. All that was sternest, hottest and most unforgiving ruled me then, and like fire to fire roused a spirit equally strong and high. I might have subdued her by juster and more generous words, but remembering the humiliation of my secret slavery I forgot my own offence in hers, and set no curb on tongue or temper, letting the storm she had raised fall upon her with the suddenness of an unwonted, unexpected outburst.

As I spoke her face changed from its first dismay to a defiant calmness that made it hard as rock and cold as ice, while all expression seemed concentrated in her eye, which burned on me with an unwavering light. There was no excitement in her manner, no sign of fear, or shame, or grief in her mien, and when she answered me her voice was untremulous and clear as when I heard it first.

"Have you done? Then hear me: I knew you long before you dreamed that such a woman as Agatha Eure existed. I was solitary, and longed to be sincerely loved. I was rich, yet I could not buy what is unpurchasable; I was young, yet I could not make my youth sweet with affection; for nowhere did I see the friend whose nature was akin to mine until you passed before me, and I felt at once, 'There is the one I seek!' I never yet desired that I did not possess the coveted object, and believed I should not fail now. Years ago I learned the mysterious gift I was endowed with, and fostered it; for, unblessed with beauty, I hoped its silent magic might draw others near enough to see, under this cold exterior, the woman's nature waiting there. The first night you saw me I yielded to an irresistible longing to attract your eye, and for a moment see the face I had learned to love looking into mine. You know how well I succeeded—you know your own lips asked the favor I was so glad to give, and your own will led you to me. That day I made another trial of my skill and succeeded beyond my hopes, but dared not repeat it, for your strong nature was not easily subdued, it was too perilous a game for me to play, and I resolved that no delusion should make you mine. I would have a free gift or none. You offered me your hand, and believing that it held a loving heart, I took it, to find that heart barred against me, and another woman's name engraved upon its door. Was this a glad discovery for a wife to make? Do you wonder she reproached you when she saw her hopes turn to ashes, and could no longer conceal from herself that she was only a stepping-stone to lift an ambitious man to a position which she could not share? You think me weak and wicked; look back upon the year nearly done and ask yourself if many young wives have such a record of neglect, despised love, unavailing sacrifices, long suffering patience and deepening despair? I had been reading the tear-stained pages of this record when you bid me win you if I could; and with a bitter sense of the fitness of such a punishment, I resolved to do it, still cherishing a hope that some spark of affection might be found. I soon saw the vanity of such a hope, and this hard truth goaded me to redouble my efforts till I had entirely subjugated that arrogant spirit of yours, and made myself master where I would so gladly have been a loving subject. Do you think I have not suffered? have not wept bitter tears in secret, and been wrung by sharper anguish than you have ever known? If you had given any sign of affection, shown any wish to return to me, any shadow of regret for the wrong you had done me, I should have broken my wand like Prospero, and used no magic but the pardon of a faithful heart. You did not, and it has come to this. Before you condemn me, remember that you dared me to do it that you bid me make my presence more powerful than Art—bid me convert you to my shadow, and subdue you till you came like a pet dog at my call. Have I not obeyed you? Have I not kept my part of the compact? Now keep yours."

There was something terrible in hearing words whose truth wounded while they fell, uttered in a voice whose concentrated passion made its tones distinct and deep, as if an accusing spirit read them from that book whose dread records never are effaced. My hot blood cooled, my harsh mood softened, and though it still burned, my resentment sank lower, for, remembering the little life to be, I wrestled with myself, and won humility enough to say, with regretful energy:

"Forgive me, Agatha, and let this sad past sleep. I have wronged you, but I believed I sinned no more than many another man who, finding love dead, hoped to feed his hunger with friendship and ambition. I never thought of such an act till I saw affection in your face; that tempted me, and I tried to repay all you gave me by the offer of the hand you mutely asked. It was a bargain often made in this strange world of ours, often repented as we repent now. Shall we abide by it, and by mutual forbearance recover mutual peace? or shall I leave you free, to make life sweeter with a better man, and find myself poor and honest as when we met?"

Something in my words stung her; and regarding me with the same baleful aspect, she lifted her slender hand, so wasted since I made it mine, that the single ornament it wore dropped into her palm, and holding it up, she said, as if prompted by the evil genius that lies hidden in every heart:

"I will do neither. I have outlived my love, but pride still remains; and I will not do as you have done, take cold friendship or selfish ambition to fill an empty heart; I will not be pitied as an injured woman, or pointed at as one who staked all on a man's faith and lost; I will have atonement for my long-suffering—you owe me this, and I claim it. Henceforth you are the slave of the ring, and when I command you must obey, for I possess charm you cannot defy. It is too late to ask for pity, pardon, liberty or happier life; law and gospel joined us, and as yet law and gospel cannot put us asunder. You have brought this fate upon yourself, accept it, submit to it, for I have bought you with my wealth, I hold you with my mystic art, and body and soul, Max Erdmann, you are mine!"

I knew it was all over then, for a woman never flings such taunts in her husband's teeth till patience, hope and love are gone. A desperate purpose sprung up within me as I listened, yet I delayed a moment before I uttered it, with a last desire to spare us both.

"Agatha, do you mean that I am to lead the life I have been leading for three months—a life of spiritual slavery worse than any torment of the flesh?"

"I do."

"Are you implacable? and will you rob me of all self-control, all peace, all energy, all hope of gaining that for which I have paid so costly a price?"

"I will."

"Take back all you have given me, take my good name, my few friends, my hard-earned success; leave me stripped of every earthly blessing, but free me from this unnatural subjection, which is more terrible to me than death!"

"I will not!"

"Then your own harsh decree drives me from you, for I will break the bond that holds me, I will go out of this house and never cross its threshold while I live—never look into the face which has wrought me all this ill. There is no law, human or divine, that can give you a right to usurp the mastery of another will, and if it costs life and reason I will not submit to it."

"Go when and where you choose, put land and sea between us, break what ties you may, there is one you cannot dissolve, and when I summon you, in spite of all resistance, you must come."

"I swear I will not!"

I spoke out of a blind and bitter passion, but I kept my oath. How her eyes glittered as she lifted up that small pale hand of hers, pointed with an ominous gesture to the ring, and answered:

"Try it."

As she spoke like a sullen echo came the crash of the heavy picture that hung before us. It bore Lady Macbeth's name, but it was a painted image of my wife. I shuddered as I saw it fall, for to my superstitious fancy it seemed a fateful incident; but Agatha laughed a low metallic laugh that made me cold to hear, and whispered like a sibyl:

"Accept the omen; that is a symbol of the Art you worship so idolatrously that a woman's heart was sacrificed for its sake. See where it lies in ruins at your feet, never to bring you honor, happiness or peace; for I speak the living truth when I tell you that your ambitious hopes will vanish as the cloud of dust now rising like a veil between us, and the memory of this year will haunt you day and night, till the remorse you painted shall be written upon heart, and face, and life. Now go!"

Her swift words and forceful gesture seemed to banish me forever, and, like one walking in his sleep, I left her there, a stern, still figure, with its shattered image at its feet.

That instant I departed, but not far—for as yet I could not clearly see which way duty led me. I made no confidante, asked no sympathy or help, told no one of my purpose, but resolving to take no decisive step rashly, I went away to a country house of Agatha's, just beyond the city, as I had once done before when busied on a work that needed solitude and quiet, so that if gossip rose it might be harmless to us both. Then I sat down and thought. Submit I would not, desert her utterly I could not, but I dared defy her, and I did; for as if some viewless spirit whispered the suggestion in my ear, I determined to oppose my will to hers, to use her weapons if I could, and teach her to be merciful through suffering like my own. She had confessed my power to draw her to me, in spite of coldness, poverty and all lack of the attractive graces women love; that clue inspired me with hope. I got books and pored over them till their meaning grew clear to me; I sought out learned men and gathered help from their wisdom; I gave myself to the task with indomitable zeal, for I was struggling for the liberty that alone made life worth possessing. The world believed me painting mimic woes, but I was living through a fearfully real one; friends fancied me busied with the mechanism of material bodies, but I was prying into the mysteries of human souls; and many envied my luxurious leisure in that leafy nest, while I was leading the life of a doomed convict, for as I kept my sinful vow so Agatha kept hers.

She never wrote, or sent, or came, but day and night she called me— day and night I resisted, saved only by the desperate means I used—means that made my one servant think me mad. I bid him lock me in my chamber; I dashed out at all hours to walk fast and far away into the lonely forest; I drowned consciousness in wine; I drugged myself with opiates, and when the crisis had passed, woke spent but victorious. All arts I tried, and slowly found that in this conflict of opposing wills my own grew stronger with each success, the other lost power with each defeat. I never wished to harm my wife, never called her, never sent a baneful thought or desire along that mental telegraph which stretched and thrilled between us; I only longed to free myself, and in this struggle weeks passed, yet neither won a signal victory, for neither proud heart knew the beauty of self-conquest and the power of submission.

One night I went up to the lonely tower that crowned the house, to watch the equinoctial storm that made a Pandemonium of the elements without. Rain streamed as if a second deluge was at hand; whirlwinds tore down the valley; the river chafed and foamed with an angry dash, and the city lights shone dimly through the flying mist as I watched them from my lofty room. The tumult suited me, for my own mood was stormy, dark and bitter, and when the cheerful fire invited me to bask before it I sat there wrapped in reveries as gloomy as the night. Presently the well-known premonition came with its sudden thrill through blood and nerves, and with a revengeful strength never felt before I gathered up my energies for the trial, as I waited some more urgent summons. None came, but in its place a sense of power flashed over me, a swift exultation dilated within me, time seemed to pause, the present rolled away, and nothing but an isolated memory remained, for fixing my thoughts on Agatha, I gave myself up to the dominant spirit that possessed me. I sat motionless, yet I willed to see her. Vivid as the flames that framed it, a picture started from the red embers, and clearly as if my bodily eye rested on it, I saw the well-known room, I saw my wife lying in a deep chair, wan and wasted as if with suffering of soul and body, I saw her grope with outstretched hands, and turn her head with eyes whose long lashes never lifted from the cheek where they lay so dark and still, and through the veil that seemed to wrap my senses I heard my own voice, strange and broken, whispering:

"God forgive me, she is blind!"

For a moment the vision wandered mistily before me, then grew steady, and I saw her steal like a wraith across the lighted room, so dark to her; saw her bend over a little white nest my own hands placed there, and lift some precious burden in her feeble arms; saw her grope painfully back again, and sitting by that other fire—not solitary like my own—lay her pale cheek to that baby cheek and seem to murmur some lullaby that mother-love had taught her. Over my heart strong and sudden gushed a warmth never known before, and again, strange and broken through the veil that wrapped my senses, came my own voice whispering:

"God be thanked, she is not utterly alone!"

As if my breath dissolved it, the picture faded; but I willed again and another rose—my studio, dim with dust, damp with long disuse, dark with evening gloom—for one flickering lamp made the white shapes ghostly, and the pictured faces smile or frown with fitful vividness. There was no semblance of my old self there, but in the heart of the desolation and the darkness Agatha stood alone, with outstretched arms and an imploring face, full of a love and longing so intense that with a welcoming gesture and a cry that echoed through the room, I answered that mute appeal:

"Come to me! come to me!"

A gust thundered at the window, and rain fell like stormy tears, but nothing else replied; as the bright brands dropped the flames died out, and with it that sad picture of my deserted home. I longed to stir but could not, for I had called up a power I could not lay, the servant ruled the master now, and like one fastened by a spell I still sat leaning forward intent upon a single thought. Slowly from the gray embers smouldering on the hearth a third scene rose behind the smoke wreaths, changeful, dim and strange. Again my former home, again my wife, but this time standing on the threshold of the door I had sworn never to cross again. I saw the wafture of the cloak gathered about her, saw the rain beat on her shelterless head, and followed that slight figure through the deserted streets, over the long bridge where the lamps flickered in the wind, along the leafy road, up the wide steps and in at the door whose closing echo startled me to the consciousness that my pulses were beating with a mad rapidity, that a cold dew stood upon my forehead, that every sense was supernaturally alert, and that all were fixed upon one point with a breathless intensity that made that little span of time as fearful as the moment when one hangs poised in air above a chasm in the grasp of nightmare. Suddenly I sprang erect, for through the uproar of the elements without, the awesome hush within, I heard steps ascending, and stood waiting in a speechless agony to see what shape would enter there.

One by one the steady footfalls echoed on my ear, one by one they seemed to bring the climax of some blind conflict nearer, one by one they knelled a human life away, for as the door swung open Agatha fell down before me, storm-beaten, haggard, spent, but loving still, for with a faint attempt to fold her hands submissively, she whispered:

"You have conquered, I am here!" and with that act grew still forever, as with a great shock I woke to see what I had done.

ഇ)ര

Ten years have passed since then. I sit on that same hearth a feeble, white-haired man, and beside me, the one companion I shall ever know, my little son—dumb, blind and imbecile. I lavish tender names upon him, but receive no sweet sound in reply; I gather him close to my desolate heart, but meet no answering caress; I look with yearning glance, but see only those haunting eyes, with no gleam of recognition to warm them, no ray of intellect to inspire them, no change to deepen their sightless beauty; and this fair body moulded with the Divine sculptor's gentlest grace is always here before me, an embodied grief that wrings my heart with its pathetic innocence, its dumb reproach. This is the visible punishment for my sin, but there is an unseen retribution heavier than human judgment could inflict, subtler than human malice could conceive, for with a power made more omnipotent by death Agatha still calls me. God knows I am willing now, that I long with all the passion of desire, the anguish of despair to go to her, and He knows that the one tie that holds me is this aimless little life, this duty that I dare not neglect, this long atonement that I make. Day and night I listen to the voice that whispers to me through the silence of these years; day and night I answer with a yearning cry from the depths of a contrite spirit; day and night I cherish the one sustaining hope that Death, the great consoler, will soon free both father and son from the inevitable doom a broken law has laid upon them; for then I know that somewhere in the long hereafter my remorseful soul will find her, and with its poor offering of penitence and love fall down before her, humbly saying:

"You have conquered, I am here!"

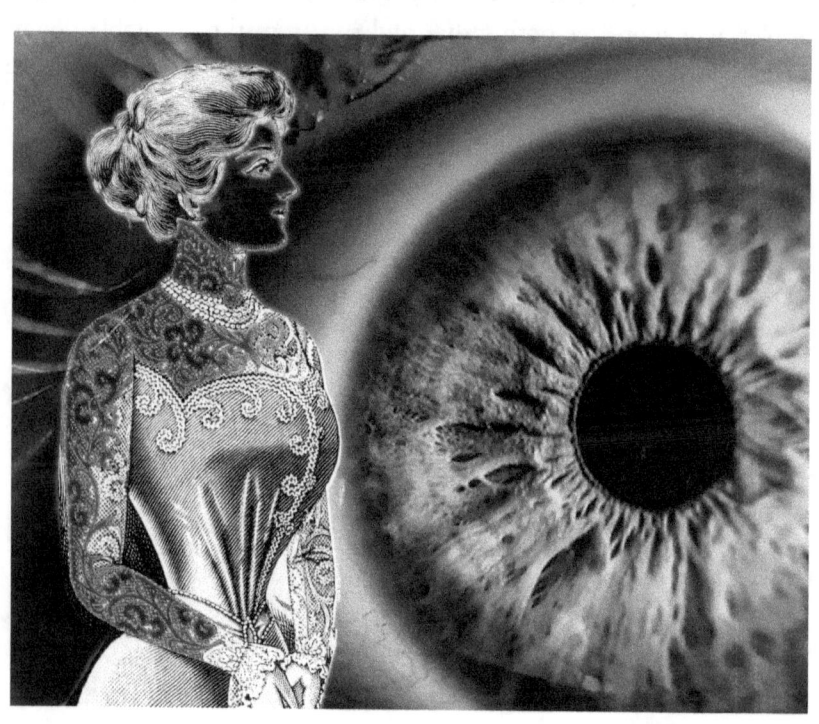

A Scientific Revenge

By Marie Madison

"Do you remember the murder of the banker Halliday, about seven years ago? It has always remained shrouded in mystery. The best detectives were detailed on the case. Every clue, however slight, was investigated to the fullest extent; but nothing came of them. The police were compelled to confess themselves baffled. To this day they are as much in the dark regarding it as ever. It is not a mystery to me, however, but I can't go with my story to the authorities. They would laugh at me and ask for proof, which is beyond my reach."

I must confess that I was playing the part of an eavesdropper, and that these words were not spoken for my benefit. If this reaches the eye of the gentleman who uttered them, I am sure he will be as much surprised as I was on hearing the story which followed this introduction.

I was seated at a table in the cafe of the Manhattan Club, sipping a delicious claret punch, when the above startling words reached my ear. I turned and looked at the speaker and his companions. The latter awoke no interest within me—they were ordinary men about town—but the one who had spoken at once brought to life every inquisitive instinct of my nature. He was a man long past his prime, yet younger in mind and heart, by far, than the two blasé, worn out individuals who sat with him. He looked like one who had stored up his vitality, who had not wasted one hour of his time, either in useless thought or more useless dissipation, and, as I studied his striking face more closely, through the clouds of smoke from my cigar, I felt a double interest in his words and prepared myself the more successfully to play the eavesdropper by changing the position of my chair, and while apparently absorbed in the enjoyment of my claret punch, drank in every word of the following story:

"There has been a great deal said of late in the New York papers about hypnotism, but I doubt if many people who read of the various tests have much faith in them. To show you what a dangerous weapon may be made of hypnotism, I'll relate to you an incident which came under my own observation, and which is closely connected with the Halliday mystery. Indeed, I may say I played a part in the drama, the leading character of which was a woman.

"Halliday had an only child, a daughter, just budding into womanhood at the time of his death. Being an intimate friend of the family, I often called at his home, when I had ample opportunity to study the girl. I first met her after her return from abroad, where she had been attending school. She was not particularly beautiful, but there was a subtle charm about her that rivalled beauty and in spite of myself I would find my glance wandering toward her whenever she was present. There was a peculiar look in her soft grey eyes that puzzled me, and I became fascinated with something in her manner that I could not analyse. She was a slight, delicate girl, yet every move, turn, and glance suggested power, but I was confident that it was a power of which even she herself was not cognizant. Owing to my studies of the occult forces and hypnotism I was as great a curiosity to the girl as she was to me, for whenever I looked toward her I invariably found her glance bent upon me in a searching, inquiring way. Whenever we were alone she fell to questioning me about some scientific problem that would not have interested many men. Halliday was a man of wonderful mental vigor, and I was not surprised to find the girl uncommonly bright, though her choice of subjects for study and conversation astonished me. You would have said that there was something uncanny about her.

"Do you remember anything about the murder? Halliday was found seated at his desk, his head lying on his outstretched arms, shot through the head with his own revolver. It was after hours, but he often remained alone in the bank when he went over the books, keeping everything securely locked meanwhile. He was a most pains-taking worker, superintending most of the business of the bank himself. He went over the books periodically to see that there were no deficiencies; investigated doubtful securities—indeed, it was to his indefatigable industry that the firm owed its reputation and stood solid during the panic, eight years ago, when so many banks went under. He was quiet and cautious, and never made any display of his habits. Judging from the appearance of the bank, no one would have dreamed that Halliday was sitting in his office, pouring over accounts, and keeping track of his millions—except the murderer.

"Truly whoever committed that crime was familiar with the habits of the banker. Robbery seemed to be the motive, for a large amount of money was stolen from the dead man's pockets, though the vaults and safes were untouched. It is believed that the robber was frightened away by the watchman, for Halliday had not been dead more than five minutes when he was found lying across his desk, his head resting upon an open journal and ledger, which were saturated with the life blood that poured from a bullet hole in his temple.

"The crime created the greatest sensation of the year. The murdered man had been popular, both in business and society, and had always been charitable and just. So far as was known he had not an enemy on earth. Though large rewards were offered for a clue to the murderer, the case became one of the great mysteries of New York, and finally people ceased to speak of it. I doubt if one person out of a hundred will even remember it.

"As soon as possible after the death of her husband Mrs. Halliday and her daughter Helen sailed for Europe. They were about three years absent, and when they again returned to America I received an invitation to attend a reception to be given in honor of Helen, who on that occasion was to make her formal debut into society.

"When I entered the drawing-room, and again stood before my interesting young friend, I was both surprised and delighted. She had developed into a tall, stately woman. There was something in her attitude, her stride, her whole appearance, that suggested the tragedy queen, and I knew that the 'old power' which I had discovered in the girl had developed in the woman, till I felt almost sure that she must be aware of its existence.

"She was above the usual height of woman, and her figure had filled out in what artists term 'curves of grace.' A calico gown would have hung in regal folds from those shoulders, and it needed little imagination to change the fan she bore into a sceptre, so royally did she wield it. During the course of the evening I offered her my arm, and requested the pleasure of a few moments' social chat—as in the old days. I suggested that we seek the wide veranda, which had been so profusely decorated with palms and flowers as to present the appearance of some tropical garden.

"'You know I don't dance,' I said, 'but if you will honor an old cavalier with a few moments' conversation, he will try to dream that he is young again.'

"She declared herself glad of an opportunity to rest awhile, and, as she said, 'to renew some of the old subjects which were so fascinating to me when I was too young to enjoy them to the full.'

"I led the way to the coolest spot, and for a few moments we sat speechless under the palms, looking out on the scene before us, where the garden surrounding the house had been decorated with Japanese and Chinese lanterns that swayed in the soft breeze, flickering and sputtering, and threatening to become extinguished at every stronger gust of wind.

"I broke the silence, saying—'I hear you have become a famous horsewoman since you went abroad.'

"'Yes?' There was a peculiar smile on her lips as she said this word, in a half assertive, half questioning tone. 'I love horses, and they—well, if they don't love me they obey me.'

"'Obey!' She had struck the keynote of her power.

"'I believe it,' I said. 'Few living creatures could look into your eyes and not obey you.'

"'What do you mean?' There was something almost of suspense in the way she spoke those words, and I could not but feel surprised.

"'I mean that you have great power, though you may not know it. You have heard of Mesmer—?'

"'Have I heard of Mesmer? Then I have hypnotic power, you mean?'

"'To a wonderful degree, and I thank heaven, for that reason, that you are a good woman.'

"'But I have never hypnotised anyone.'

"'That is because your power is undeveloped. You do not know how to control it yourself. If you wish to become my pupil I will teach you how to use it, and you may be able to do a great deal of good.'

"'No, no.' I saw her recoil at the thought. 'I should be afraid. I am not always good. If anyone wrongs me I want to be revenged. I don't think it would be safe!' These last words were spoken in a light tone, and ended with a laugh, but I felt there was more in them than appeared from her manner at that moment.

"'But,' she added, more seriously, 'there is one gift which I possess that I have cultivated. I say nothing to my friends about it, for they, will laugh at me. But you will not, professor; you understand me. I found out by accident that I was capable of reading what was in another's mind. At first I was surprised to find, during conversation with someone, that I occasionally was about to speak the very words they uttered, or would speak them in unison. This happened so often that I began to question myself the meaning of it, and to experiment, until at last I seemed to be able to read the thoughts of those about me; but I have left every one in the dark as to how I have learned much that I know, from the dread of being laughed at.'

"'You must be a martyr and endure the ridicule of the ignorant for the sake of science,' I said. 'However, if you will agree to a plan I have in mind, I will arrange a way in which you can give a test of your powers without running the risk of being laughed at.'

"'You mean that you will apparently be the controlling spirit, and thus cloak my art, or whatever you would call it, under your own science. You would feign to hypnotise me, and thus allow me to read the mind of a subject without arousing suspicion toward myself.'

"I looked up in astonishment. She had read my thought as plainly as if it were written in legible characters.

"'You are right. That is my plan, and you have either a very keen insight into the methods of a man or you are a marvel in the science of mind reading.'

"We agreed upon a plan, and returned to the drawing-room. In a short time a little group that had formed about the attractive debutante was plunged into an animated discussion of the occult forces, and especially hypnotism. I had adroitly led them into that channel, and finally volunteered to give an exhibition of the power of mind over matter. Soon the large room was filled with expectant guests, all ready for an impromptu entertainment. I gave several amusing tests then, turning to my young friend Helen, said:

"'I will now give you a slight idea of the use of hypnotism in the science of mind reading. Miss Helen, will you assist me?'

"Without hesitation the young girl came forward and seated herself before me. I made several passes before her face, then looked steadily into her eyes, as though placing her under a spell. Strong as my power is I found it drifting away from me as I gazed into those deep grey orbs. I whispered to Helen to obey me implicitly and to pretend to be under my influence. Then, turning to our audience, I looked about for a suitable subject. Seated near in a languid attitude, with a sceptical smile on his face, was Bruce Halliday, a second cousin of Helen's whose good looks and quiet ways had made him a universal favorite with the gentler sex, and I heard that night, through the gossip of the quests, that he was desperately in love with his fair cousin.

"I had never liked Bruce Halliday. His lazy, indolent air exasperated me. Whenever I saw him I felt I would like to shake some life into him. His manner at that supreme moment was almost maddening to a sensitive person. He seemed so sure of himself—so doubtful of others. Nothing was sacred to him, science nor religion, and as I saw the supercilious smiles which curved his lip I hated him intensely.

"'I will teach you a lesson, my friend,' I said mentally, then aloud:

"'Mr. Halliday, I believe you are sufficient of a sceptic to make an excellent subject for I, the young lady. Will you come forward?'"

"He arose and advanced toward me with a manner that said as plainly as words:

"'Watch me show this old fraud up.'

"In spite of herself, Helen smiled faintly when Bruce came toward her, and I placed her hand upon his wrist. I smiled also; it suggested a betrothal, and I believe many of the guests thought the same thing, for there was a suppressed titter among them.

"To all but myself Helen was in a hypnotic sleep, and I watched her eagerly, waiting to hear what she would say to verify my belief in her.

"A moment passed. I saw a look of annoyance come over Bruce's face, followed by one of dismay, and he endeavored to draw his hand away from the detaining grasp of his cousin. I looked quickly at Helen.

"'What do you read in this man's mind?' I asked, but instead of speaking the girl gave a quick, sharp gasp, and, opening her eyes, looked up into the startled face of young Halliday with such an expression of horror and doubt that it seemed to justify my hatred for the man, then, throwing his hand from her, she sprang to her feet and dashed away out of the room.

"It is needless to say that her action created a sensation, till some bright wit suggested that this was part of the performance, and that I was very clever to find such a way out of a failure. It had all been fixed up beforehand.

"I did not mind having the laugh on me. I was too anxious about Helen to pay any attention to the remarks of the jokers. I suggested to Mrs. Halliday that she had best follow her daughter, and learn if any harm had come to her. She did as I bade, and in a few moments a servant announced that Miss Helen would have to be excused from again returning to the drawing-room that evening, as she was very ill.

"That broke up the festivities for the night. I afterwards learned from Mrs. Halliday that on going upstairs she had found Helen lying in a dead faint across the threshold of her boudoir.

"About a week after the reception I was seated in my study when the bell rang, and a moment later Helen entered the room. She had recovered from her indisposition, but still looked somewhat pale.

"I motioned her to a chair, but stood before her, with my elbow on the mantel, and studied her face.

"'You gave us quite a scare the other night,' said I.

"'Foolish of me, wasn't it?' she answered.

"'No, it is easily explained, I assure you. It often happens that mind readers fall into a state of catelepsy while under intense strain.'

"'And you think that is all that ailed me?'

"'Undoubtedly. You must not overdo yourself. Your subject was too strong, but that was my fault. If I had allowed you to choose someone for yourself you probably would not have made that mistake.'

"For, after several hours' puzzling thought over the strange turn affairs had taken on the night of her debut, I had arrived at this decision.

"'I am glad you think that is all that ailed me,' said Helen, seeming relieved. 'And now, I am going to accept your proposition. I want to become your pupil. Teach me to be a hypnotist.'

"But you told me you did not wish to develop your power; you were afraid of yourself.'

"'I have changed my mind. I have come to the conclusion that if I have power enough to control the will of others, I ought surely to be able to control my own when it leads me in the wrong direction.'

"'True, and will you?'

"'Of course. When will we begin?'

"'To-morrow?'

"'Yes.'

"'That will suit me.'

"'Thanks. I will be here at eleven.'"

"True to her word, and punctual to the moment, Helen rang my bell.

"I took great pleasure in teaching her the methods of the different masters with whom I was familiar. I had not made a mistake in her. She had the strongest will I had ever found in a woman, and I thanked heaven, as I saw it develop under my instruction, that she was a pure, noble-minded girl.

"In three months she was my master, but before that three months were over she became engaged to her cousin Bruce. I was pained when I heard of the betrothal, for I thought her worthy of a far better man, but she declared that she loved him, and against the wishes of all—even of her mother— she had promised to become his wife. The wedding was to take place eight months from the time she had given him her word. It was to be on the anniversary of her debut into society. I was glad, at any rate, that there was to be no hurried marriage, and secretly hoped that something would occur to prevent it before the time had elapsed.

"About five months after the betrothal I passed the evening at Mrs. Halliday's. It was a rainy night. I always chose bad weather in which to make my calls on the Hallidays, in hopes of finding them alone. On this evening only Bruce and a friend of Helen's were present. I had not seen young Halliday since his betrothal, and was surprised to find him quite changed. A spirit of unrest seemed to have taken possession of him. His eyes were dark and sunken, his cheeks pale and so drawn that the cheek bones showed with ghastly prominence. He had lost that supercilious air that so exasperated me, and seemed to be suffering. Much as I disliked him, I could not but feel sorry for him.

"Helen seemed to partake of the indisposition of her lover, for her face had grown thinner, and a weary look about the mouth told of sleepless nights. To me she gave the idea of one supported only by her will. During the evening Mrs. Halliday spoke of the changed appearance of her son-in-law to be. She told me she believed the marriage would never take place, for Bruce seemed to be in decline. He had become a victim of melancholia, and she would not be surprised if it developed into insanity. I felt that I had read the young man's character aright, and said to myself that this change was the result of dissipation, and I feared that Helen, with her ability to read the mind, was aware of the truth.

"A month later Bruce Halliday was dead—a suicide.

"The papers were full of the case. They spoke of the young man's family, his betrothal to the heiress, his good looks, his decline, and finally of the mad act which ended his life, making much of the fact that he was found in the same attitude as Helen's father—his arms extended over his desk and his life blood staining the pages of a book upon which his head was resting—that book the Bible, which lay open at the Ten Commandments, while the index finger of his left hand pointed to the sentence: 'Thou shalt not kill.'

"Little was seen of Helen after that. I called to express my regrets, but she was not at home. Later I heard that she was going to Europe again, and went to bid her good-bye. She had grown much paler and thinner since I had last seen her, and I felt that grief for her betrothed, though not made manifest, was wearing her life away.

"After a short call I bade the mother and daughter good-bye and left, wondering if I should ever see my interesting pupil again.

"I sat musing on the strange fate that had robbed this young girl of the man she loved, in the very dawning of their life, when I was surprised to suddenly find her standing before me.

"Her face was even paler than usual, and her eyes moved restlessly to and fro as she stood waiting for me to speak.

"'Miss Halliday,' I exclaimed, as soon as I recovered sufficiently from my surprise to find my voice. 'What is it? You look ill. Has anything happened?'

"I seized her arm, and placed her gently in the chair from which I had arisen. She did not reply for a moment, but, fixing her dark eyes upon mine, looked at me in a strange, reproachful manner. Suddenly she startled me by saying—

"'Never teach a woman the power of hypnotism again. You place a dangerous weapon in the hands of the most irresponsible possessors in the world—not unscrupulous, but impulsive. None should know it save those who value earth's possessions lightly—who harbor no revenge. You are not to blame that I became your pupil, for I promised you sacredly that I would do no harm, but listen till I tell you what I have done.'

"'You remember the night I made my debut? You also remember our experience in mind reading? I rushed out of the drawing-room and fell in a faint on the threshold of my own room. You said it was the strain. No, it was not. It was what I read in Bruce Halliday's mind. When I took his hand he was thinking of his love for me, but, suddenly, the current of his thought changed, and I saw a picture in his mind that drove the blood out of my heart. I saw my father seated at his desk in the banking office, going over his books—they were, however, the books Bruce kept at the bank. I read down the page with him. I saw deficiencies that were there to cover systematic robberies committed by my cousin in my father's bank. I saw the guilt of the theft in Bruce's mind, and I saw him, look furtively back at my father, as he left with the other clerks, and Banker Halliday was alone. Then, I saw him return, unseen. I saw him as he demanded the books of my father; a stormy scene ensued; Bruce tried forcibly to gain possession of those tell-tale books; he was choking my father into insensibility, when father drew his revolver from the desk drawer and endeavored to turn it upon the wretched thief. Bruce wrested it from him and shot him through the head. My father fell back in his chair, dying, the red blood pouring from a wound in his temple. Bruce saw that he was dying, and he laid him across the desk as he was found shortly afterwards, arranging his head in such a position that the life blood would obliterate the evidence of guilt in the books which lay open on the desk. He dare not destroy them; that would place the suspicion of murder upon him; and to further prevent this, he robbed the pockets of the dying man as he breathed his last, and then made his escape. That is what I saw in Bruce Halliday's mind. That is why I promised to be his wife. That is why I wished to develop my hypnotic powers. I have had my revenge. I killed Bruce Halliday as he killed my father. You look at me as if you thought I was mad. Don't you understand me? I killed him by my will. From the moment I learned how to use my mesmeric power I began to torture him with the memory of his crime, of which hitherto he seemed to be utterly indifferent. I put the idea in his mind to take his own life. You see how I have succeeded. No one can convict me, yet I am a murderess—no, perhaps I am an executioner. You look horrified, my friend. Perhaps you think I may have made a mistake. Here, are proofs that I did not! Here is a confession Bruce Halliday left, in which he describes the cowardly murder of my father just as I saw it, so I know that I was right. And now good-bye, professor. I am going to France and shall probably never return to America.'

"'And what became of her?'

"She still lives in her adopted country. At last accounts she was studying for the medical profession, and wrote me that she believed that in that calling she would find opportunity to put her hypnotic power to use in doing good."

The Burglar's Blunder
By Richard Marsh

"That's done the trick! Now for the swag!"

As Mr. Bennett made this observation to himself, he slipped the window up and stepped into the room. He stood for a moment listening. Within, all was still; without, not a sound disturbed the silence of the night.

"I think it's all serene."

It is probable that Mr. Bennett smiled. He was engaged in the exercise of his profession, and it consoled him to perceive that, on this occasion, the stars seemed to be fighting on his side. He drew down the window softly, and replaced the blind. It was a principle of his never to leave anything which might give a hint to the outside public of what was going on within. The room, with the blind down, was intensely dark. He put his hand into his pocket, and drew out a little shaded lantern. Cautiously removing the shutter about half an inch, a pencil of light gleamed across the room. He was apparently content with this illumination. By its aid he carefully examined floor, walls, and ceiling.

"Early English. I thought so."

This remark referred to the upholstering of the room, which was in the Early English style. Stooping down, he drew a pair of list slippers over his indiarubber shoes. With swift, cat-like steps he strode across the floor, and left the room. He was evidently familiar with his ground. The burglar's profession, to be profitably practised, entails no inconsiderable labour. It is quite an error to suppose that the burglar has only to stroll along the street and break into the first house which catches his eye. Not at all. Such a course is altogether unprofessional. Persons who do that kind of thing get what they deserve—"stir," and plenty of it. A really professional man, an artist—such, for example, as Mr. Bennett—works on entirely different lines. He had had this little job in his mind's eye for the last three months. Acacia Villa presented an almost ideal illustration of *the* promising crib to crack. Did he rush at it on that account? Quite the other way. He prepared his ground. He discovered, what all the world—in that neighbourhood—knew already, that it was occupied by a single lady and a solitary maid. That fact alone would have induced some men to make a dash at it before unscrupulous competitors had had an opportunity to take the bread out of their mouths. But Mr. Bennett was made of other stuff.

It was situated in a lonely suburb, and in a lonely portion of the lonely suburb. It stood in its own grounds. There was not a dog about the place. There was not a shutter to a window. There was no basement to the house—you had only to step from the ground to the window-sill, and from the window-sill into the house. These facts would have been so many extra inducements to the average burglar to "put up" the place at once.

But Mr. Bennett looked at the matter from a different standpoint. He did not ask if he could crack the crib—he had never yet encountered one which had mastered him—but whether the crib was really worth the cracking. The very defencelessness of the place was against it—in his eyes, at any rate—at first. People who have anything very well worth stealing do not, as a rule, leave it at the mercy of the first individual who passes by—though there are exceptions to the rule. Mr. Bennett discovered that there was one, and the discovery revealed the *artist* in the man.

The occupant of Acacia Villa was a Miss Cecilia Jones. Mr. Bennett had never seen Miss Cecilia Jones. Nobody—or hardly anybody—ever had. There appeared to be a mystery about Miss Cecilia Jones. But Mr. Bennett had seen the maid, and not only seen her, but promised to marry her as well. This was a promise which he never made to any woman unless actually compelled: the present had been a case of actual compulsion.

The maid's name was Hannah—Miss Hannah Welsh. She was not young, and she was not good-looking. Mr. Bennett was partial to both youth and beauty. It went against the grain to court Miss Welsh. But he found that courtship was an absolutely indispensable preliminary. After he had encircled her waist a few times with his arm, and tasted the nectar of her lips—also a few times—Miss Welsh began gradually to unbend. But the process was very gradual. She was the most reticent of maids. He had not only to present her with several presents—the proceeds of the exercise of his profession—he had not only to promise to marry her, he had not only to name the day, but he had even to buy—or steal: the words were synonymous with him—the wedding-ring, before all the tale was told.

When he had actually tried the ring on Miss Welsh's finger—to see if it would fit—then, and only then, he heard all there was to hear.

Miss Jones was queer—not mad exactly, but peculiar. She had quarrelled with all her relatives. She was rich. She was full of crotchets. She distrusted all the world, particularly bankers. To such a length had she carried her want of confidence that she had realised all her fortune, turned it into specie, and kept it in the house. It was at this point that Miss Welsh's conversation became interesting to Mr. Bennett.

"Keeps it in the house, does she? In notes, I suppose?"

"Then you suppose wrong. She won't have nothing to do with notes— trust her. It's all in gold and diamonds."

"Diamonds? How do you know they're diamonds?"

Miss Welsh glanced at him out of the corner of her eyes. The conversation was carried on in the back garden at Acacia Villa, which was extensive and secluded. The time was evening, that season which is popularly supposed to be conducive to sentimental intercourse.

"Perhaps I know as much about diamonds as here and there a few."

Her tone was peculiar, almost suggestive. For an instant Mr. Bennett meditated making a clean breast of it, and asking Miss Welsh to come in on sharing terms. But he had an incurable objection to collaboration. Besides, in this case sharing terms would probably mean that he would have to go through the form, at any rate, of making her his wife.

"Where does she keep them? In a safe, I hope."

He did not hope so, though he said he did. At the very best, a safe, to a professional man, means the wasting of valuable time.

"She keeps them in her bedroom, in the chest of drawers, in a red leather box, in the little top drawer on the left-hand side."

Mr. Bennett felt a glow steal all over him. He began to conceive quite a respect for Miss Cecilia Jones.

"And the gold—where does she keep that?"

"In tin boxes. There are ten of them. There are a thousand sovereigns in each. There are five boxes on each side of the chest of drawers." Mr. Bennett possessed considerable presence of mind, but he almost lost it then. Ten thousand pounds in sovereigns! He would never regret the affection he had lavished on Miss Welsh—never, to his dying day. *Would* it be a bad speculation to marry her? But no; the thought was rash. He would reward her, but in quite a different way. He made a rapid calculation. Ten thousand sovereigns would weigh, roughly, about a hundred and thirty pounds avoirdupois. He might turn them into a sack—fancy, a sackful of money! But a hundred and thirty pounds was no light weight to carry far. He must have a vehicle at hand. What a convenience a "pal" would be! But he had worked single-handed so far, and he would work single-handed to the end.

When he had ascertained his facts he acted on them at once, thus revealing the artist again. Spare no pains in making sure that the crib is worth the cracking, *then* crack it at once. On the night following this conversation the crib was cracked: he had arranged for the marriage to take place on the next day but one—or Miss Welsh thought he had—so that if he wished to avoid a scandal he really had no time to lose. We have seen him enter the house. Now we understand how it was he knew his ground.

He paused for an instant outside the drawing-room door: it was through the drawing-room window he had effected an entrance. All was still. He moved up the staircase two steps at a time. There was not a stair that creaked. At the top he paused again. From information received, to adopt a phrase popular in an antagonistic profession, he was aware that Miss Jones slept in the front bedroom.

"There's three bedrooms on the first floor. When you gets to the top of the stairs, you turns to the left; and if you goes straight on, you walks right into Miss Jones's room."

Mr. Bennett turned to the left. He went straight on. Outside Miss Jones's door he paused again. The critical moment had arrived. He felt that all his properties were in order—a bottle and a sponge in his right-hand pocket, a revolver in his left, a stout canvas bag fastened round his body beneath his coat. The lantern was shut. He opened it sufficiently to enable him to see what sort of handle there was on the door. Having satisfied himself on that point, he closed it again. Then he proceeded to effect an entrance into Miss Jones's bedroom.

He took the handle firmly in his hand. It turned without the slightest sound. The door yielded at once.

"Not locked," said Mr. Bennett beneath his breath. "What a stroke of luck!"

Noiselessly the door moved on its hinges. He opened it just wide enough to enable him to slip inside. When he was in he released the handle. Instantly the door moved back and closed itself without a sound.

"Got a spring upon the door," Mr. Bennett told himself—always beneath his breath. "Uncommonly well oiled they must keep it, too."

The room was pitchy dark. He listened acutely. All was still as the grave. He strained his ears to catch Miss Jones's breathing.

"A light sleeper!"

A very light sleeper. Strain his ears as he might, he could not catch the slightest sound. Mr. Bennett hesitated. As an artist he was averse to violence. In cases of necessity he was quite equal to the occasion, but in cases where it was not necessary he preferred the gentler way. And where a woman was in question, under hardly any provocation would he wish to cut her throat. He had chloroform in his pocket. If Miss Jones was disagreeable, he could make his peace with that. But if she left him unmolested, should he stupify her still? He decided that while she continued to sleep she should be allowed to sleep, only it would be well for her not to wake up too soon.

He moved across the room. Instinctively, even in the thick darkness, he knew the position of the chest of drawers. He reached it. He quickly discovered the little top drawer on the left-hand side.

In a remarkably short space of time he had it open. Then he began to search for the red leather box. He gleamed the lantern into the drawer, so that its light might assist his search.

While he was still engaged in the work of discovery, suddenly the room was all ablaze with light.

"Thank you. I thought it was you."

A voice, quite a musical voice, spoke these words behind his back. Mr. Bennett was, not unnaturally, amazed. The sudden blaze of light dazzled his eyes. He turned to see who the speaker was.

"Don't move, or I fire. You will find I am a first-rate shot."

He stared. Indeed, he had cause to stare. A young lady—a distinctly pretty young lady—was sitting up in bed, holding a revolver in her hand, which she was pointing straight at him.

"This room is lighted by electricity. I have only to press a button, it all goes out." And, in fact, it all went out; again the room was dark as pitch. "Another, it is alight again." As it was—and that with the rapidity of a flash of lightning.

Mr. Bennett stood motionless. For the first time in his professional career he was at a loss, not only as to what he ought to say, but as to what he ought to do. The young lady was so pretty. She had long, fair hair, which ranged loose upon her shoulders; a pair of great big eyes, which had a very curious effect on Mr. Bennett as they looked at him; a sweet mouth; through her rosy lips gleamed little pearl-like teeth; and a very pretty—and equally determined—nose and chin. She had on the orthodox nightdress, which, in her case, was a gorgeous piece of feminine millinery, laced all down the front with the daintiest pink bows. Mr. Bennett had never seen such a picture in his life.

"I am Miss Cecilia Jones. You are Mr. Bennett, I presume—George Bennett—'My George,' as Hannah says. Hannah is a hypnotic subject. When I am experimenting on her, the poor dear creature tells me everything, you know. I wonder if I could hypnotise you."

Mr. Bennett did not know what she meant. He was only conscious of the most singular sensation he had ever experienced. To assist his understanding, possibly, Miss Jones gave a practical demonstration of her meaning. With her disengaged hand she made some slight movements in the air, keeping her eyes fixed on Mr. Bennett all the while. Mr. Bennett in vain struggled to escape her gaze. Suddenly he was conscious that, as it were, something had gone from him—his resolution—his freedom of will—he knew not what.

Miss Jones put down her hand.

"I think that you will do. How do you feel?"

"Very queer."

Mr. Bennett's utterance was peculiar. He spoke as a man might speak who is under the influence of a drug, or as one who dreams—unconsciously, without intention, as it were.

"Oh, they always do feel like that at first. Are you considered a good burglar, as a rule?"

"As a rule."

Mr. Bennett hesitatingly put up his hand and drew it across his brow. It was the hand which held the lantern. When the lantern touched his skin he found that it was hot. He let it fall from his hand with a clatter to the floor. Miss Jones eyed him keenly all the time.

"I see you are not quite subjective yet; but I think that you will do. And of course I can always complete the influence if I will. It only illustrates what I have continually said—that it is not necessarily the lowest mental organisations that traffic in crime. I should say that yours was above, rather than below, the average. Have you yourself any ideas upon that point?"

As he answered, Mr. Bennett faintly sighed.

"None!"

Miss Jones smiled, and as she smiled he smiled too. Though there was this feature about Mr. Bennett's smile—there was not in it any sense of mirth. Miss Jones seemed to notice this, for she smiled still more. Immediately Mr. Bennett's smile expanded into a hideous grin. Then she burst into laughter. Mr. Bennett laughed out too.

"After all, you are more subjective than I thought you were. I don't think I ever had a subject laugh quite so sympathetically before."

As Miss Jones said this—which she did when she had done laughing— she turned and adjusted the pillows so as to form a support to her back. Against this she reclined at ease. She placed the revolver on the bolster at her side. From a receptacle in the nature of a tidy, which was fastened to the wall above her head, she drew a small leather case. From this she took a cigarette and a match. With the most charming air imaginable, she proceeded to light the cigarette, and smoke.

Mr. Bennett watched all her movements, feeling that he must be playing a part in a dream. It was a perceptible relief when she removed her eyes from his face, though they were such pretty eyes. Yet, although she was not looking at him, he felt that she saw him all the time—he had a hideous impression that she even saw what was passing in his mind.

"I wouldn't think about my revolver. You won't be able to fire it, you know."

He had been thinking about his revolver: a faint notion had been growing up in his mind that he would like to have just one shot at her. Miss Jones made this remark in the most tranquil tone of voice, as she was engaged in extinguishing the match with which she had lighted her cigarette.

"And I wouldn't worry about that chloroform—it is chloroform, isn't it?—in the right-hand pocket of your coat."

As she said this, Miss Jones threw the extinguished match from her on to the bedroom floor. A great cloud of horror was settling down on Mr. Bennett's brain. Was this fair creature a thing of earth at all? Was she a witch, or a fairy queen? Mr. Bennett was a tolerably well-educated man, and he had read of fairy queens. He gave a sudden start. Miss Jones had lighted the cigarette to her satisfaction, and had fixed her eyes upon his face again.

"I suppose you were hardly prepared for this sort of thing?"

"Hardly."

The word came from Mr. Bennett's stammering lips.

"When you heard about the defencelessness of Acacia Villa, and about Miss Jones—who was peculiar—and that sort of thing, you doubtless took it for granted that it was to be all plain sailing?"

"Something of the kind."

Not the least odd part of the affair was that Mr. Bennett found himself answering Miss Jones without the least intention of doing anything of the sort.

"Those diamonds you were looking for are at the bottom of the drawer—at the back. Just get them out and bring them here. In a red leather case, you know."

Mechanically Mr. Bennett did as he was told. When his back was turned to the lady, and he ceased to be compelled to meet her eyes, quite a spasm of relief went over him. A faint desire was again born within his breast to assert his manhood. The lady's quiet voice immediately interposed.

"I wouldn't worry myself with such thoughts if I were you. You are quite subjective."

He was subjective—though still Mr. Bennett had not the faintest notion what she meant. He found the red leather box. He brought it to her on the bed. He came so close to her that she puffed the smoke between her rosy lips up into his face.

"It is not locked. It opens with a spring, like this."

She stretched out her hand. As she did so, she grazed slightly one of his. He trembled at her touch. She pressed some hidden spring in the box, and the lid flew open. It was full of diamonds, which gleamed and sparkled like liquid light.

"Not bad stones, are they? There's a hundred thousand pounds' worth at the least. There are the tin boxes, you see. Five on either side the chest of drawers." Mr. Bennett followed the direction of Miss Jones's hand—he saw them plainly enough. "A hundred thousand pounds' worth of diamonds in your hand, ten thousand pounds in front of you—not bad plunder for a single night's work. And only a young woman to reckon with—it is not twelve months since I turned twenty-one. Yet I don't think you will get much out of this little job—do you?"

The tears actually stood in Mr. Bennett's eyes.

"I don't think I shall," he moaned.

"And yet there is no magic about it—not the least. It is simply an illustration of the latest phase in scientific development." Miss Jones leaned back against the pillows, enjoying her cigarette with the etherealised satisfaction of the true lover of the weed. With her left hand—what a little white and dainty hand it was!—she toyed with her long, fair hair. "At an extremely early age I discovered that I could exercise at will remarkable powers over my fellow creatures. I lost no opportunity to develop those powers. At twenty-one I became my own mistress. I realised my fortune—as Hannah told you—and retired to Acacia Villa. You understand I had ideas of my own. I was peculiar, if you choose to have it so. I continued to develop my powers. I experimented upon Hannah. Now I am experimenting upon you. I am enjoying this experiment very much indeed. I hope you are enjoying it a quarter as much as I am—are you?" Some slightly inarticulate remark dropped from Mr. Bennett, which was apparently to the effect that he was not.

"I am sorry to hear that. Perhaps you will enjoy it more a little later on. Now, what shall I do with you? I know."

Miss Jones pressed a little ivory button, which was one of a row set in a frame of wood against the wall.

"That rings an electric bell in Hannah's room. I often ring her down in the middle of the night to be experimented on. She comes directly. Here she is, you see."

There was a slight tapping against the bedroom door.

"Come in!" exclaimed Miss Jones.

The door opened and Miss Welsh came in. She was not exactly in full dress—in fact, rather the other way. Mr. Bennett, who through it all was conscious in a horrid, nightmare sort of way, thought that he had never seen anyone look so extremely unprepossessing as Miss Welsh looked in disarray. The instant she was inside the room Miss Jones raised her hand. Miss Welsh stood still. Miss Jones turned to Mr. Bennett.

"I have her entirely under control. Some of the results I have obtained with her are really quite remarkable. But you shall see for yourself, and judge." The young lady addressed Miss Welsh.

"Well, Hannah, here is Mr. Bennett, you see."

It was evident that Miss Welsh did see. She seemed struggling to give expression to her feelings in speech. Miss Jones went calmly on:

"He is here on business—he is committing burglary, in fact. You were right in supposing that was his profession. The mistake you made was in imagining that he would have shared the spoil with you. I think, Mr. Bennett, I am right in saying that you would not have given Hannah much?"

"Not a sou."

"Probably you did not even intend to marry her?"

"I would have seen her hung first."

Mr. Bennett made this plain statement with quite curious ferocity. Miss Welsh rubbed her eyes with the sleeve of what we will suppose, for courtesy's sake, was her nightdress.

"That makes nine of 'em," she said.

"That makes nine of them, as Hannah says. Hannah, Mr. Bennett, is a woman of experience. She has had nine promises of marriage, but not one of them came off. But I don't think, Hannah, that you ever had a promise from a burglar before?"

"Never before."

"Then, at least, that is a new experience; and a new experience is so precious. Is there any remark you would like to make, Hannah, appropriate to the occasion?"

For a moment it did not appear as though there were. Then it seemed that there at least was one.

"I should like to scratch his eyes out," observed the damsel—aetat forty-five or so.

Miss Cecilia smiled. Mr. Bennett immediately smiled too. But there was this difference—that while the lady's smile was a thing of beauty, the gentleman's was a peculiar ghastly grin. Miss Jones remarked Mr. Bennett's facial contortions with an appearance of considerable interest.

"I never had them smile quite so sympathetically before. In that respect, Mr. Bennett, you are unique. Charmed to have met you, I am sure." The young lady knocked the ash off her cigarette with her dainty finger, and turned her attention to Miss Welsh. "I don't think, Hannah, that we will have any scratching out of eyes."

When she had thus delivered herself, Miss Jones reclined in silence for some moments on her pillows, discharging the smoke of her cigarette through her delicate pink nostrils. When she spoke again, it was to the gentleman she addressed herself.

"Mr. Bennett, would you mind closing that box of diamonds, and replacing them in the drawer?"

Mr. Bennett shut the box with a little snap, and carried it across the room. There was something odd about his demeanour as he did this—an appearance as though he were not engaged in the sort of labour which physics pain. Miss Welsh, standing as though rooted to the ground, followed him with her eyes. The expression of her countenance was one of undisguised amazement. Her face was eloquent with a yearning to relieve herself with words. When Mr. Bennett put the box back where he had found it, and shut the drawer, she gave a kind of gasp. From Mr. Bennett there came a distinctly audible groan. "Turn round, Mr. Bennett, and look at me." Mr. Bennett did as he was bidden. He was not altogether a bad-looking young man—his chief fault, from the physiognomist's point of view, lay in the steely tint of his clear blue eyes. Miss Jones's great big orbs seemed to rest upon him with a certain degree of pleasure. "I need scarcely point out to you that the burglary is a failure. The principal cause of failure is that you are too subjective. You have quite one of the most subjective organisations I have yet encountered. The ideal criminal must keep himself abreast with the advance of science. In failing to do so, Mr. Bennett, you have been guilty of a blunder which, in your case, is certainly worse than crime. You are a dreadful example of the burglar's blunder. I might label you, preserve you in your hypnotic state, and use you as an illustration of a lecture I am now preparing. But I have other views, and it is not impossible I may encounter you again. Go to my writing-table. You will find a sheet of foolscap paper. Write what I dictate."

Mr. Bennett went to the writing-table. He found the sheet of foolscap paper. "Write, in good, bold characters—

'I AM GEORGE BENNETT,

The Burglar.

For further particulars apply at Acacia Villa.'

Mr. Bennett wrote as she dictated, displaying the above legend in a striking, round hand right across the sheet of paper. Miss Jones addressed Miss Welsh:

"Hannah, in my workbasket you will find a needle and some good stout thread. Get it out." Miss Welsh got it out. "Mr. Bennett, take off that sack which you have wound round your body beneath your coat." Mr. Bennett took it off. "Button up your coat again." Mr. Bennett buttoned it up. "Hannah, take that sheet of foolscap paper on which Mr. Bennett has written at my dictation, and sew it firmly to the front of his buttoned-up coat."

Miss Welsh took the sheet of foolscap paper. She approached Mr. Bennett, holding it in her hand. Mr. Bennett's hands dropped to his sides. He regarded her with a look which was the reverse of amiable. She eyed him with what were doubtless intended to be soft, pleading glances. When she reached him she placed her hand timidly against his chest. Mr. Bennett looked particularly glum. She raised the other hand which held the sheet of foolscap paper, and spread it out upon his breast. It was legible at quite a considerable distance:

"I AM GEORGE BENNETT,

The Burglar.

For further particulars apply at Acacia Villa."

It was hardly the sort of inscription a chivalrous spirit would wish to have displayed upon his breast by the object of his heart's desire, or even by the woman he had promised to marry in the course of the following morning. Miss Welsh, who seemed to feel the truth of this, looked at him with sad, beseeching eyes. But Mr. Bennett's glumness perceptibly increased. Then Miss Welsh proceeded to sew the inscription on. It must be owned that it was a conscientious piece of sewing. She first tacked it round the edges; then she sewed it up and down, and across, from corner to corner, with a hundred careful stitches, in such a way that he would have had to tear it to fragments, piecemeal, in order to get it off. It would have been quite impossible to unbutton his coat while he had that inscription on. The process seemed to make Miss Welsh extremely sad. It made Mr. Bennett sadder still. When she had finished her conscientious piece of work, she crossed her hands meekly in front of her, and looked up at him with a rapturous gaze. Mr. Bennett did not seem to feel rapturous at all.

"Now, Hannah, take the sack which Mr. Bennett wore beneath his coat, and hold it open for him, and enable him to step inside."

The sack was lying on the floor. Miss Welsh, with a half-uttered sigh, picked it up, and held the mouth wide open. Mr. Bennett scowled first at the lady, then at the bag. He raised his left foot gingerly, and placed it in the opening. Miss Welsh assisted him in thrusting his leg well home. Then there was a pause.

"Perhaps, Mr. Bennett, you had better put your arms round Hannah's neck," observed Miss Jones. She was engaged in lighting a second cigarette at the ashes of the first.

Mr. Bennett put his arms about Miss Welsh's neck, and thrust his other leg into the sack.

"Draw it up about his waist," remarked Miss Jones. By now the second cigarette was well alight.

Miss Welsh drew it up about his waist. It was a good-sized sack, so that, although a man of at least the average height, being drawn up it reached his loins. "Mr. Bennett, hold the sack in that position with both your hands." Mr. Bennett held the sack in that position with both his hands. "Hannah, in the bottom of the hanging cupboard you will find some cord. Get it out."

In a mechanically melancholy way Miss Welsh did as she was told. The cord, being produced, took the shape of a coil of rope, about the thickness of one's middle finger.

"Make two holes in the front of the sack, and pass the cord through them." With the same sad air Miss Welsh acted on Miss Jones's fresh instructions. She made two holes in the front of the sack, and passed the two ends of the cord through them.

"Now pass the cord over his shoulders, make two holes in the back of the sack, pass the cord through them, then draw it tight."

Again Miss Welsh obeyed, dolefully, yet conscientiously withal. The result was that when the rope was tightened—and Miss Welsh, in the most conscientious manner, drew it as tight as she possibly could—Mr. Bennett's lower portions were imprisoned in the sack in a manner which was hardly dignified. He might have been about to engage in a sack-race, only he did not appear to be in a sack-racing frame of mind. Miss Welsh seemed to feel that she was hardly treating him in the way in which one would wish to treat one's best young man. It was evident that Mr. Bennett had not the slightest doubt but that he was being used very badly indeed.

"Take the bottle and sponge, which you will find in his right-hand pocket, and the revolver, which you will find in his left, and place them on the bed." Miss Welsh did as her mistress told her. "Now tie him up with the cord so as to render him incapable of moving a limb. There are thirty-two yards of it. With that quantity, and the exercise of a little skill, you should be able to make him tolerably secure."

As Miss Jones said this, it almost seemed that Miss Welsh started. Mr. Bennett certainly did. Miss Welsh looked at him with such piteous eyes; Mr. Bennett favoured her with an unmistakable scowl—a scowl, indeed, of singular malignity. Then she proceeded to tie him up. In doing so, she showed considerable skill, and conscientiousness to boot. She first passed the rope two or three times right round him, so as to pinion his arms to his sides. Then, putting her foot up against his side, so as to enable her to use it as a lever, she hauled the rope as tight as she could. She did not seem to enjoy the hauling part of it—nor did Mr. Bennett, for the matter of that. She was a woman of undeniable strength; it was a wonder that she did not cut in two the man she had promised to marry. When the rope was at its utmost tension, she made a most dexterous knot. He would have been tolerably secure had she done no more. But she did a great deal more; in that conscientious way she had, she ran the rope about his legs, hauling it fast with the same ingenuity of method—with such energy, in fact, that she hauled him off his legs, and both he and she fell flat upon the floor.

"Pick yourself up, Hannah; and you had better continue to tie Mr. Bennett where he lies—you will find it more convenient, perhaps."

Miss Welsh acted on Miss Jones's hint. But, however it may have added to her convenience, so far as Mr. Bennett was concerned it made the matter worse. She performed her task in such a very conscientious way; she rolled him over and over, she knelt on him—to give her leverage in hauling, she even stood on him—she stood him on his feet, and on his head. It certainly was not a favourable example of the way in which a young woman should use her best young man.

"Now, Hannah, you can stand Mr. Bennett on his feet," remarked Miss Jones, when she saw that Miss Welsh had completed her task. "If Mr. Bennett is unable to stand, you had better prop him up with his back against the wall."

Miss Welsh propped Mr. Bennett up with his back against the wall: he would have certainly been unable to stand alone. Miss Jones addressed herself to him:

"You see, Mr. Bennett, how entirely I have Hannah under my control. She is beautifully subjective. As I pointed out to you before, I assure you I have obtained some really remarkable results with Hannah. I hope that you have enjoyed all that you have seen—have you?"

Mr. Bennett feebly shook his head. He did not seem to have sufficient energy left to enable him to say he hadn't. He was too much tied up. Miss Jones went on:

"Before we part—and we are about to part; for the present, at least—I should like to address to you a few appropriate remarks. Burglary, I need not point out to you, Mr. Bennett, is criminal, and not only criminal, but cowardly. You choose, as a rule, the night. You choose, preferentially, a house in which the inhabitants are helpless. You steal upon them unawares, prepared, if necessary, to take their lives at the moment when they are least able to defend them. You yourself are a coward of the most despicable sort, or you would never have come, in the dead of the night, certainly to rob, and perhaps to kill, an unprotected woman. I cannot describe to you the satisfaction which I feel when I consider that this is a case of the biter bit. When I think how conscious you yourself must be of how completely the tables have been turned, I assure you that I am ready to dance about the room with joy. I trust, Mr. Bennett, that you will perceive and allow that these few remarks point a moral and adorn a tale. What I am now about to do with you is this. You brought that chloroform to stupify me. On the contrary, with it Hannah shall stupify you. When you are stupified she will open the window, she will drag you to it, and she will drop you out. There is only a drop of about twelve feet. There is a flower-bed beneath. I hope you will not fall hard. You will damage the flowers, I am afraid; but, under the circumstances, I will excuse you that. You will lie there through the night. In the morning I will take care that a policeman finds you there. He will see the inscription written by yourself, and sewn on your breast by Hannah. He will see that you are George Bennett, the burglar, and he will act on the hint contained in the last line—he will make further inquiries at Acacia Villa. I assure you I will answer them. I will prosecute you with the utmost rigour of the law. You have doubtless, in the course of your career, been guilty of multitudinous crimes. I think I know a means of bringing every one of them home to you. You will be sentenced to a long term of penal servitude. For a considerable time to come I shall know where to find you should I desire to subject you to further experiment."

As Miss Jones made these observations, which she did in the sweetest and most musical of voices, she continued to enjoy her cigarette. A fairer picture of feminine indulgence in the nicotian weed, it is not improbable, was never seen. But neither Mr. Bennett nor Miss Welsh seemed to appreciate the opportunity they had of observing the fair picture under circumstances of such exceptional advantage—the gentleman even less than the lady. After a short pause, the beautiful young smoker gave a few instructions to Miss Welsh:

"Hannah, take that bottle of chloroform and that sponge. Empty the contents of the bottle on to the sponge; then press the sponge against Mr. Bennett's mouth and nose, and hold it there."

As Miss Jones said this, an expression of great agony struggled through the stupor which was the prevailing characteristic of Mr. Bennett's face. It seemed as though he struggled to speak. But tongue was mute. Miss Welsh, too, seemed unutterably sad. At the same time, she did as her mistress bade. She drew the cork out of the bottle, and emptied the contents on to the sponge. As she did so, Mr. Bennett's eyes passed from Miss Welsh to Miss Jones, and from Miss Jones to Miss Welsh, with something of that look of dumb agony which it is so painful to see at times upon the face of a dog. Miss Welsh emptied the bottle to its latest drop. She advanced towards Mr. Bennett, labelled, tied, and propped up against the wall. He made a perceptible effort to give expression to his agony in speech. But Miss Welsh gave him no time. She clapped the sponge upon his mouth and nose, pressing his head with all her force against the wall. He shivered, gave a sort of sigh, and fell, lying where he had fallen. Under Miss Welsh's forcible manipulation, the anaesthetic had quickly done its work.

"Open the window wide!" Miss Welsh opened the window wide. "Pick Mr. Bennett up!" Miss Welsh picked him up. "Carry him to the window!" She carried him to the window. It was a curious spectacle to see her bearing all that was near and dear to her to his ignominious doom. "Throw him out!"

She threw him out. There was a momentary silence. Then came the sound of a thud. Mr. Bennett had fallen on the flower-bed beneath. "Shut the window down!" Miss Welsh shut the window down. "Go to the door, turn round, and look at me!" Miss Welsh did as she was bidden. She shuddered when her eyes encountered her mistress's glorious orbs.

The young smoker, raising her exquisitely-shaped hand, made a slight movement with it in the air.

"Leave the room, and go to bed!" she said. Miss Welsh left the room and disappeared.

When she was left alone, Miss Cecilia Jones carefully extinguished her cigarette, placing the unconsumed fragment in a little ash-tray which was fastened to the wall above her head. She replaced the pillows in their former position; under one of them she placed her revolver, on it she placed her head. Touching one of the ivory buttons, which she could easily do from where she lay, instantly the room was dark. In the darkness, having made herself comfortable between the sheets, she set herself to woo sweet sleep.

The Facts in the Ratcliff Case
By Edward Page Mitchell

I.

I first met Miss Borgier at a tea party in the town of R—, where I was attending medical lectures. She was a tall girl, not pretty; her face would have been insipid but for the peculiar restlessness of her eyes. They were neither bright nor expressive, yet she kept them so constantly in motion that they seemed to catch and reflect light from a thousand sources. Whenever, as rarely happened, she fixed them even for a few seconds upon one object, the factitious brilliancy disappeared, and they became dull and somnolent. I am unable to say what was the color of Miss Borgier's eyes.

After tea I was one of a group of people whom our host, the Reverend Mr. Tinker, sought to entertain with a portfolio of photographs of places in the Holy Land. While endeavoring to appear interested in his descriptions and explanations, all of which I had heard before, I became aware that Miss Borgier was honoring me with steady regard. My gaze encountered hers and I found that I could not, for the life of me, withdraw my own eyes from the encounter. Then I had a singular experience, the phenomena of which I noted with professional accuracy. I felt the slight constriction of the muscles of my face, the numbness of the nerves that precedes physical stupor induced by narcotic agency. Although I was obliged to struggle against the physical sense of drowsiness, my mental faculties were more than ordinarily active. Her eyes seemed to torpify my body while they stimulated my mind, as opium does. Entirely conscious of my present surroundings, and particularly alert to the Rev. Mr. Tinker's narrative of the ride from Joppa, I accompanied him on that journey, not as one who listens to a traveler's tale, but as one who himself travels the road. When, finally, we reached the point where the Rev. Mr. Tinker's donkey makes the last sharp turn around the rock that has been cutting off the view ahead, and the Rev. Mr. Tinker beholds with amazement and joy the glorious panorama of Jerusalem spread out before him, I saw it all with remarkable vividness. I saw Jerusalem in Miss Borgier's eyes.

I tacitly thanked fortune when her eyes resumed their habitual dance around the room, releasing me from what had become a rather humiliating captivity. Once free from their strange influence, I laughed at my weakness. "Pshaw!" I said to myself. "You are a fine subject for a young woman of mesmeric talents to practice upon."

"Who is Miss Borgier?" I demanded of the Rev. Mr. Tinker's wife, at the first opportunity.

"Why, she is Deacon Borgier's daughter," replied that good person, with some surprise.

"And who is Deacon Borgier?"

"A most excellent man; one of the pillars of my husband's congregation. The young people laugh at what they call his torpidity, and say that he has been walking about town in his sleep for twenty years; but I assure you that there is not a sincerer, more fervent Chris—"

I turned abruptly around, leaving Mrs. Tinker more astonished than ever, for I knew that the subject of my inquiries was looking at me again. She sat in one corner of the room, apart from the rest of the company. I straightway went and seated myself at her side.

"That is right," she said. "I wished you to come. Did you enjoy your journey to Jerusalem?"

"Yes, thanks to you."

"Perhaps. But you can repay the obligation. I am told that you are Dr. Mack's assistant in surgery at the college. There is a clinic to-morrow. I want to attend it."

"As a patient?" I inquired.

She laughed. "No, as a spectator. You must find a way to gratify my curiosity."

I expressed, as politely as possible, my astonishment at so extraordinary a fancy on the part of a young lady, and hinted at the scandal which her appearance in the amphitheatre would create. She immediately offered to disguise herself in male attire. I explained that the nature of the relations between the medical college and the patients who consented to submit to surgical treatment before the class were such that it would be a dishonorable thing for me to connive at the admission of any outsider, male or female. That argument made no impression upon her mind. I was forced to decline peremptorily to serve her in the affair. "Very well," she said. "I must find some other way."

At the clinic the next day I took pains to satisfy myself that Miss Borgier had not surreptitiously intruded. The students of the class came in at the hour, noisy and careless as usual, and seated themselves in the lower tiers of chairs around the operating table. They produced their note-books and began to sharpen lead pencils. Miss Borgier was certainly not among them. Every face in the lecture-room was familiar to me. I locked the door that opened into the hallway, and then searched the anteroom on the other side of the amphitheatre. There were a dozen or more patients, nervous and dejected, waiting for treatment and attended by friends hardly less frightened than themselves. But neither Miss Borgier nor anybody resembling Miss Borgier was of the number.

Dr. Mack now briskly entered by his private door. He glanced sharply at the table on which his instruments were arranged, ready for use, and, having assured himself that everything was in its place, began the clinical lecture. There were the usual minor operations—two or three for strabismus, one for cataract, the excision of several cysts and tumors, large and small, the amputation of a railway brakeman's crushed thumb. As the cases were disposed of I attended the patients back to the anteroom and placed them in the care of their friends.

Last came a poor old lady named Wilson, whose leg had been drawn up for years by a rheumatic affection, so that the joint of the knee had ossified. It was one of those cases where the necessary treatment is almost brutal in its simplicity. The limb had to be straightened by the application of main force. Mrs. Wilson obstinately refused to take advantage of anesthesia. She was placed on her back upon the operating table, with a pillow beneath her head. The geniculated limb showed a deflection of twenty or twenty-five degrees from a right line. As already remarked, this deflection had to be corrected by direct, forcible pressure downward upon the knee.

With the assistance of a young surgeon of great physical strength, Dr. Mack proceeded to apply this pressure. The operation is one of the most excruciating that can be imagined. I was stationed at the head of the patient, in order to hold her shoulders should she struggle. But I observed that a marked change had come over her since we established her upon the table. Very much agitated at first, she had become perfectly calm. As she passively lay there, her eyes directed upward with a fixed gaze, the eyelids heavy as if with approaching slumber, the face tranquil, it was hard to realize that this woman had already crossed the threshold of an experience of cruel pain.

I had no time, however, to give more than a thought to her wonderful courage. The harsh operation had begun. The surgeon and his assistant were steadily and with increasing force bearing down upon the rigid knee. Perhaps the Spanish Inquisition never devised a method of inflicting physical torture more intense than that which this woman was now undergoing, yet not a muscle of her face quivered. She breathed easily and regularly, her features retained their placid expression, and, at the moment when her sufferings must have been the most agonizing, I saw her eyes close, as if in peaceful sleep.

At the same instant the tremendous force exerted upon the knee produced its natural effect. The ossified joint yielded, and, with a sickening noise—the indescribable sound of the crunching and gritting of the bones of a living person, a sound so frightful that I have seen old surgeons, with sensibilities hardened by long experience, turn pale at hearing it—the crooked limb became as straight as its mate.

Closely following this horrible sound, I heard a ringing peal of laughter.

The operating table, in the middle of the pit of the amphitheatre, was lighted from overhead. Directly above the table, a shaft, five or six feet square, and closely boarded on its four sides, led up through the attic story of the building to a skylight in the roof. The shaft was so deep and so narrow that its upper orifice was visible from no part of the room except a limited space immediately around the table. The laughter which startled me seemed to come from overhead. If heard by any other person present, it was probably ascribed to a hysterical utterance on the part of the patient. I was in a position to know better. Instinctively I glanced upward, in the direction in which the eyes of Mrs. Wilson had been so fixedly bent.

There, framed in a quadrangle of blue sky, I saw the head and neck of Miss Borgier. The sash of the skylight had been removed, to afford ventilation. The young woman was evidently lying at full length upon the flat roof. She commanded a perfect view of all that was done upon the operating table. Her face was flushed with eager interest and wore an expression of innocent wonder, not unmingled with delight. She nodded merrily to me when I looked up and laid a finger against her lips, as if to warn me to silence. Disgusted, I withdrew my eyes hastily from hers. Indeed, after my experience of the previous evening, I did not care to trust my self-control under the influence of her gaze.

As Dr. Mack with his sharp scissors cut the end of a linen bandage, he whispered to me: "This is without a parallel. Not a sign of syncope, no trace of functional disorder. She has dropped quietly into healthy sleep during an infliction of pain that would drive a strong man mad."

As soon as released from my duties in the lecture room, I made my way to the roof of the building. As I emerged through the scuttleway, Miss Borgier scrambled to her feet and advanced to meet me without manifesting the slightest discomposure. Her face fairly beamed with pleasure.

"Wasn't it beautiful?" she asked with a smile, extending her hand. "I heard the bones slowly grinding and crushing!"

I did not take her hand. "How came you here?" I demanded, avoiding her glance.

"Oh!" said she, with a silvery laugh. "I came early, about sunrise. The janitor left the door ajar and I slipped in while he was in the cellar. All the morning I spent in the place where they dissect; and when the students began to come in downstairs I escaped here to the roof."

"Are you aware, Miss Borgier," I asked, very gravely, "that you have committed a serious indiscretion, and must be gotten out of the building as quickly and privately as possible?"

She did not appear to understand. "Very well," she said. "I suppose there is nothing more to see. I may as well go."

I led her down through the garret, cumbered with boxes and barrels of unarticulated human bones; through the medical library, unoccupied at that hour; by a back stairway into and across the great vacant chemical lecture-room; through the anatomical cabinet, full of objects appalling to the imagination of her sex. I was silent and she said nothing; but her eyes were everywhere, drinking in the strange surroundings with an avidity which I could feel without once looking at her. Finally we came to a basement corridor, at the end of which a door, not often used, gave egress by an alleyway to the street. It was through this door that subjects for dissection were brought into the building. I took a bunch of keys from my pocket and turned the lock. "Your way is clear now," I said.

To my immense astonishment, Miss Borgier, as we stood together at the end of the dark corridor, threw both arms around my neck and kissed me.

"Good-by," she said, as she disappeared through the half-opened door.

When I awoke the next morning, after sleeping for more than fifteen hours, I found that I could not raise my head from the pillow without nausea. The symptoms were exactly like those which mark the effects of an overdose of laudanum.

II.

I have thought it due to myself and to my professional reputation to recount these facts before briefly speaking of my recent testimony as an expert, in the Ratcliff murder trial, the character of my relations with the accused having been persistently misrepresented.

The circumstances of that celebrated case are no doubt still fresh in the recollection of the public. Mr. John L. Ratcliff, a wealthy, middle-aged merchant of Boston, came to St. Louis with his young bride, on their wedding journey. His sudden death at the Planters' Hotel, followed by the arrest of his wife, who was entirely without friends or acquaintances in the city, her indictment for murder by poisoning, the conflict of medical testimony at the trial, and the purely circumstantial nature of the evidence against the prisoner, attracted general attention and excited public interest to a degree that was quite extraordinary.

It will be remembered that the state proved that the relations of Mr. and Mrs. Ratcliff, as observed by the guests and servants of the hotel, were not felicitous; that he rarely spoke to her at table, habitually averting his face in her presence; that he wandered aimlessly about the hotel for several days previous to his illness, apparently half stupefied, as if by the oppression of some heavy mental burden, and that when accosted by anyone connected with the house he started as if from a dream, and answered incoherently if at all.

It was also shown that, by her husband's death, Mrs. Ratcliff became the sole mistress of a large fortune.

The evidence bearing directly upon the circumstances of Mr. Ratcliff's death was very clear. For twenty-four hours before a physician was summoned, no one had access to him save his wife. At dinner that day, in response to the polite inquiry of a lady neighbor at table, Mrs. Ratcliff announced, with great self-possession, that her husband was seriously indisposed. Soon after eleven o'clock at night, Mrs. Ratcliff rang her bell, and, without the least agitation of manner, remarked that her husband appeared to be dying, and that it might be well to send for a physician.

Dr. Culbert, who arrived within a very few minutes, found Mr. Ratcliff in a profound stupor, breathing stertorously. He swore at the trial that when he first entered the room the prisoner, pointing to the bed, coolly said, "I suppose that I have killed him."

Dr. Culbert's testimony seemed to point unmistakably to poisoning by laudanum or morphine. The unconscious man's pulse was full but slow; his skin cold and pallid; the expression of his countenance placid, yet ghastly pale; lips livid. Coma had already supervened, and it was impossible to rouse him. The ordinary expedients were tried in vain. Flagellation of the palms of his hands and the soles of his feet, electricity applied to the head and spine, failed to make any impression on his lethargy. The eyelids being forcibly opened, the pupils were seen to be contracted to the size of pinheads, and violently turned inward. Later, the stertorous breathing developed into the ominously loud rattle of mucous in the trachea; there were convulsions, attended by copious frothings at the mouth; the under jaw fell upon the breast; and paralysis and death followed, four hours after Dr. Culbert's arrival.

Several of the most eminent practitioners of the city, put upon the stand by the prosecution, swore that, in their opinion, the symptoms noted by Dr. Culbert not only indicated opium poisoning, but could have resulted from no other cause.

On the other hand, the state absolutely failed to show either that opium in any form had been purchased by Mrs. Ratcliff in St. Louis, or that traces of opium in any form were found in the room after the event. It is true that the prosecuting attorney, in his closing argument, sought to make the latter circumstance tell against the prisoner. He argued that the disappearance of any vessel containing or having contained laudanum, in view of the positive evidence that laudanum had been employed, served to establish a deliberate intention of murder and to demolish any theory of accidental poisoning that the defense might attempt to build; and he propounded half a dozen hypothetical methods by which Mrs. Ratcliff might have disposed, in advance, of this evidence of her crime. The court, of course, in summing up, cautioned the jury against attaching weight to these hypotheses of the prosecuting attorney.

The court, however, put much emphasis on the medical testimony for the prosecution, and on the calm declaration of Mrs. Ratcliff to Dr. Culbert, "I suppose that I have killed him."

Having conducted the autopsy, and afterward made a qualitative analysis of the contents of the dead man's stomach, I was put upon the stand as a witness for the defence.

Then I saw the prisoner for the first time in more than five years. When I had taken the oath and answered the preliminary questions, Mrs. Ratcliff raised the veil which she had worn since the trial began, and looked me in the face with the well-remembered eyes of Miss Borgier.

I confess that my behavior during the first few moments of surprise afforded some ground for the reports that were afterward current concerning my relations with the prisoner. Her eyes chained not only mine, but my tongue also. I saw Jerusalem again, and the face framed in blue sky peering down into the amphitheatre of the old medical college. It was only after a struggle which attracted the attention of judge, jury, bar, and spectators that I was able to proceed with my testimony.

That testimony was strong for the accused. My knowledge of the case was wholly postmortem. It began with the autopsy. Nothing had been found that indicated poisoning by laudanum or by any other agent. There was no morbid appearance of the intestinal canal; no fullness of the cerebral vessels, no serous effusion. Every appearance that would have resulted from death by poison was wanting in the subject. That, of course, was merely negative evidence. But, furthermore, my chemical analysis had proved the absence of the poison in the system. The opium odor could not be detected. I had tested for morphine with nitric acid, permuriate of iron, chromate of potash, and, most important of all, iodic acid. I had tested again for meconic acid with the permuriate of iron. I had tested by Lassaigne's process, by Dublanc's, and by Flandin's. As far as the resources of organic chemistry could avail, I had proved that, notwithstanding the symptoms of Mr. Ratcliff's case before death, death had not resulted from laudanum or any other poison known to science.

The questions by the prosecuting counsel as to my previous acquaintance with the prisoner, I was able to answer truthfully in a manner that did not shake the force of my medical testimony. And it was chiefly on the strength of this testimony that the jury, after a short deliberation, returned a verdict of not guilty.

Did I swear falsely? No, for science bore me out in every assertion. I knew that not a drop of laudanum or a grain of morphine had passed Ratcliff's lips. Ought I to have declared my belief regarding the true cause of the man's death, and told the story of my previous observations of Miss Borgier's case? No, for no court of justice would have listened to that story for a single moment. I knew that the woman did not murder her husband. Yet I believed and knew—as surely as we can know anything where the basis of ascertained fact is slender and the laws obscure—that she poisoned him, *poisoned him to death with her eyes.*

I think that it will be generally conceded by the profession that I am neither a sensationalist nor prone to lose my self-command in the mazes of physico-psychologic speculation. I make the foregoing assertion deliberately, fully conscious of all that it implies.

What was the mystery of the noxious influence which this woman exerted through her eyes? What was the record of her ancestry, the secret of predisposition in her case? By what occult process of evolution did her glance derive the toxical effect of the *papaver somniferum?* How did she come to be a Woman-Poppy? I cannot yet answer these questions. Perhaps I shall never be able to answer them.

But if there is need of further proof of the sincerity of my denial of any sentiment on my part which might have led me to shield Mrs. Ratcliff by perjury, I may say that I have now in my possession a letter from her, written after her acquittal, proposing to endow me with her fortune and herself; as well as a copy of my reply, respectfully declining the offer.

Suggestion

(Translated from *Le Petit Journal*, of Paris by Edyth Kirkwood)

"What do you think of it, doctor?" asked the prisoner's counsel.

The physician, a celebrated specialist and authority on mental diseases, shook his head gravely in a non-committal sort of way.

"You followed up the clue I gave you?" persisted the lawyer.

"Yes."

"And you think——?"

"I shall examine him again to-day," replied the doctor. "I have seen several experts in the new science and they all agree that poor Julian is an impressionable subject, a ready-made victim to any one who might have wished this deed done by proxy; but the motive? Probably some lover's quarrel, some revenge; they say the girl was pretty and coquettish. There is something baffling about the affair," added the doctor with a slight relaxation of his professional caution. "While I have never had too much confidence in this idea of 'suggestion,' I am not prepared to say there is nothing in it."

"Let me go with you to-day, doctor. I will slip in without speaking, listen to the story he relates, and one of us may chance on some word or idea to give us the indication we seek."

So it was agreed.

"How do you feel to-day?" asked the doctor kindly, as they entered the prisoner's cell.

The man was lying on his hard bed, staring in front of him, with hollow, vacant eyes.

"My thoughts," he replied, "flutter about aimlessly; sad, oh! sad as long snow-covered plains under the light of the moon. I have worn myself out with walking to and fro. My limbs ache as if I had been beaten. I feel very cold, but the palms of my hands are burning with fever, and I have a dull pain at the base of my brain."

The physician nodded gravely and said a few soothing words, then requested the patient to relate all he could remember about the crime.

"But, doctor," objected Julian, "I have already told you twenty times and more. It will be monotonous to go over all that again, though, to be sure, there is nothing better to do here... Well then, place yourself there, opposite to me, so that you will hide that white wall; it looks to me like a canvas on which is painted that unfading image; the coffer with the head upon it! When you go away my terror will return. If they would only soil that wall a little; it seems to me the slightest stain would obviate this fancy... I tried to soil it, and the jailer scolded me as if I had been a schoolboy."

"Go on with your story," said the doctor quietly.

"I was walking along aimlessly when from a long, dark, narrow street I emerged on the thoroughfare. Lights were shining here and there under the trees like great flowers of flame. The yelling of showmen, the music and bells of the merry-go-rounds, the trumpets and drums, hurdy-gurdys and squeaking playthings of the children made a most horrible din, for the annual festival was in full tide.

"Cornered by a group of curious people, I was crowded and crushed, raised off my feet and carried along before a booth. Above the door I read the word: *Metempsychosis*.

"A fat man was selling tickets; he was pitted by small-pox and had one eye smaller than the other.

"Inside it was very, almost quite, dark.

"Before us a square of light opened in the canvas which was stretched at the further end of the booth. Within this frame appeared a table with a gauze screen separating it from the spectators.

"The fat man passed around a pasteboard head such as milliners use for bonnets. When it had gone from hand to hand and was acknowledged to be truly what it appeared to be, he placed it on the table and fastened the gauze screen. The light brightened; by transitions impossible to catch, without anything seeming to move, as the man announced a transformation the pasteboard head turned into a vase full of flowers, then into a cage full of birds, after that into a death's head which became the mask of celebrated statues representing successively Venus, Juno, Cleopatra, Anne of Austria, Marie Antoinette, and so on and on, until the showman said: 'Instead of pasteboard and stucco you shall now see living flesh.'

"Slowly the face dislocated, the features became hazy, confused, to form again little by little and appear distinct, animated, *humanized.*

"'An ingenious trick,' I thought; 'I don't even care to know if it is accomplished by the aid of mirrors.'

"The head of a young girl, sweet and fair, had formed behind the gauze. She opened her great black eyes, which, without definite expression, followed me with the strange fixity of a portrait, while across her face flitted the rather silly smile of the antique statues.

"This steady stare seemed to turn me to stone. My limbs grew rigid. I felt very strangely, though it was neither fatigue nor pain, and there was something oddly familiar about the head. Where I could have seen it before under different circumstances and in different attire I can no more remember now than I could then.

"When the crowd of spectators left, I remained. The showman seemed surprised, but sold me another ticket." I remained through another representation. When the young girl appeared in the last act I experienced the same singular sensation of torpor, and could not move hand or foot until she vanished from the square.

"The showman walked toward the door and I followed him.

"'Why,' I asked, 'did you write *Metempsychosis* on your sign instead of *Metamorphosis?*'

"'Then I must have been mistaken!' he said. 'Bah! never mind; very few will know the difference.'

Profiting by a push of the crowd, I slipped behind him and hid against the canvas. He went out saying:

"'Don't be impatient, Milie; I am going out to get something for supper.'

"I raised the canvas. On a large coffer, covered with some Algerian stuff and ornamented with copper nails, I saw the pasteboard head. A young girl, tall and thin, dressed in a gray wrapper, was combing the long hair that fell over her face. She threw back her hair as she heard my step and recoiled so that the floor of the booth rattled. It seemed to me as if she was trying to break through the boards to escape from me. She looked pale, supernaturally pale. It might have been an effect of light, for the gas was directly above her head.

"I gazed alternately at her bloodless face and at the white face of the manikin; they seemed to grow confused in my mind.

"The girl's eyes shone, haggard and dilated like those of a somnambulist. Her pallid lips moved:

"'You have come to kill me?'

"'Kill you? Nonsense! What weapon could I use?' I remember, laughing as I said these words, ... and that is all...."

"Collect your mind. Force your memory to obey you," said the doctor anxiously.

"That is all I can remember. The next thing I recall is that a man's hands closed around my throat and the man was shrieking with sorrow. His grasp must have been furious, yet I felt nothing.

"Over his shoulder I peered about to see the coffer without trying at all to free myself. The coffer was still in the corner, and the head was still on top of it. There was blood on the floor. The head looked like the pale young girl. Beside it lay a shining sword of curious shape, like an African weapon."

"'The sword was in the booth," explained the physician; "you took it to cut off the girl's head. Then you substituted her head for that of the manikin. All that was accomplished with a strength and rapidity only explicable by vertigo—temporary insanity—aberration, call it what you please."

"Decidedly, you insist upon it as firmly as the examining magistrate," said Julian. "Yet I can never admit myself guilty of an act I am unconscious of having done."

"You were out of your mind," said the doctor. "What happened next?"

"I remember gendarmes with drawn swords... A walk past the booths of the showmen. And I think they hooted and jeered. All the clamor mingled and confounded and became one great sound of rushing waves, then that noise resolved itself into a harmonious concert with dominating chords of deep, sweet sound. After that I found myself here, and you know the rest. You, doctor, felt my pulse, my forehead, and questioned me searchingly; but without succeeding in establishing my irresponsibility. I have never been subject to epilepsy, nor to somnambulism, and my brain is not diseased. My own opinion? I have given it and been laughed at. Yet if I really did this hideous thing I am accused of, the very thought of which freezes the blood in my veins, then I have been the instrument of another's crime, a victim of *suggestion*. I am excessively nervous and susceptible to hypnotic influence, and have submitted to experiments until I have become a 'good subject.' I have no hope of this theory being accepted. I offer it merely as my own conviction."

"Have you arrived at any conclusion?" asked the lawyer three days after, as he entered the doctor's office with a curious expression on his keen face, and a certain pallor and subdued excitement that at once attracted the physician's attention.

"Why no; I am just where I was," replied the latter. "I can make nothing of it. And you? You have found some solution?"

"The solution—the motive—all," said the prisoner's counsel, unfolding a package of manuscript. "The girl had been insane, melancholy, suicidal mania, and all that; but had been cured, as it was supposed, and was not considered dangerous. The *idée fixe*, however, still enthralled her brain, and, like all demented women, the more fantastic the *mise en scène* of the crime, the better it would please her warped imagination. She conceived the idea of employing hypnotism, attended lectures and *séances*, and became an expert pupil. At one of these pseudo scientific gatherings, which were frequented by some medical students of the Latin quarter, she met Julian and—incredible as it seems—hypnotized him and suggested her own murder. This MS., found a few hours ago among her effects, contains a calm statement of the facts, and completely exonerates the prisoner."

One Woman's Will
By G.F.G.

My health was never very robust, and the stress of professional duties that had of late been imposed upon my shoulders completely broke me down. I was half glad, half sorry when my doctor advised me to take a long rest, and try change of air and scene—glad, because I longed for a rest, and sorry because it would entail separation for at least a few weeks from my fiancée, Lydia Atherton.

Lydia came to Charing Cross to "see me off." I watched her from the carriage window as long a she was in sight, and when the distance hid from my eyes the fluttering handkerchief with which she waved her adieux, I fell back into my seat with a sigh. Little did I know what was to happen before I saw her again.

Two days later I was in Mentone, in the rooms of my old college chum, Jack Prendergast, overlooking the sapphire waters of the Mediterranean. The tranquil surface of the bay was flecked with white sails, to which the rays of the sun gave a golden tinge. On each side rose the hills, clad with olive trees in full bloom.

"This is all very pleasant," Jack said, one morning at breakfast, "but I prefer a little more excitement. What do you say if we run over to Monte Carlo to-day?"

"If you want to have a spectator of your losings, Jack, I'll go; but I shan't stake anything myself."

So that afternoon saw us both ascend the rocky slope from the shore and enter the Casino at Monte Carlo, where "business" was in full swing.

The rattle of gold as it was staked or raked in was mingled with the subdued murmur of the throng that crowded round the tables.

Above all could be heard the harsh tones of the croupiers—"*Le jeu est fait; messieurs, faites votre jeu!*"

Jack staked the modest sum he was willing to lose, and, as he expected, lost it. When we entered, a little crowd had begun to collect at an adjoining table, and it was considerably augmented when Jack ceased play.

A tall, dark young lady—Spanish or Italian, I fancied—sat at the further end of a roulette table. A big pile of gold, every minute increasing in size, was at her elbow, and Dame Fortune was evidently directing affairs in her favour. This was plain, too, from the croupier's words, as, like the voice of Fate, he called out the numbers.

Over and over again the young lady won.

And so, every two minutes, with unvarying regularity, the stakes were swept to her side, and went to swell the heap already accumulated there.

"Did you ever see such luck?" inquired Jack of me, in a whisper. "I shall soon begin to believe in the truth of the saying, 'a run of luck,' if only from experience of its opposite."

"And that you most certainly have had," I replied, with a laugh. "But just look at those two men on the other side; what ill-favoured fellows they are."

"I have been noticing them for some time past," responded Jack, "and assuredly their faces would be a first-rate passport to the guillotine. They're hatching some pretty plot even now, if one may judge from appearances. I've no doubt they envy the lady's luck and would run some risk to have a share of its proceeds."

He had scarcely finished speaking when the young lady referred to rose from her seat, and prepared to quit the *salon*.

"Surely she is not going to leave the casino with all that money on her person, and without a protector," exclaimed Jack, as she thrust the money into her satchel.

Calm and self-possessed, without betraying the least sign of the agitation which is subdued with difficulty even by the most hardened gamester, she walked the whole length of the *salon* and passed out into the hall, and into the night.

"She has nerve enough for a regiment," said Jack, turning to me. "Yet she's not the sort of young lady I should care to be entangled with; there's too much self-will concealed under her cold exterior. However, it is not— By Jove! Those fellows are following her."

"I don't like to play the spy," I replied to Jack's whisper, as the two men lounged leisurely to the door, "but there are times when it is advisable to do so. And this, I think, is one of them. Let us follow, Jack."

We kept them in sight for ten or twenty minutes, or more. Till they were clear of the grounds and villas they walked slowly, but when once beyond Monte Carlo their steps quickened at times almost to a run. In the bend of a narrow street leading to the Condamine, they made a sudden rush forward, and a shrill scream, instantly stifled, broke on the silent air. Jack hurried forward.

One of the ruffians had his arms tightly clasped round the form of the lady we had seen in the casino, rendering her powerless; whilst the second man, pressing one hand firmly on her mouth to prevent any outcry, seized the satchel.

The lady struggled violently, and succeeded in shaking off the rough grasp of her assailants. With an oath, one of them lifted the heavy stick he carried.

"You cur," cried Jack, as, rushing forward, he received the blow upon his outstretched arm.

Next moment both the stick and its owner were sent flying into the gutter with a well-directed blow from Jack's fist.

The fellow I attacked was a tall, burly Frenchman, for whom I was no match; and the struggle would have gone ill with me had not Jack, having, as he thought, disposed of his adversary, hastened to my assistance.

Between us we managed to bring the scoundrel to his knees, when the other dealt Jack a blow that would have smashed in his skull if the stick had fallen upon it. As it was, however, the blow only took effect on his shoulder. Even then, Jack reeled under it.

My opponent saw the chance this unexpected diversion gave him, and, shaking himself free, he took to his heels, an example quickly followed by his sinister comrade.

"Why, where is the lady in distress, for whom we, like the gallant knights we are, have ventured our lives?" Jack said, rubbing his shoulder, ruefully. "Vanished, apparently."

"Like a sensible woman!" I replied. "She has taken advantage of the fray to seek a place of shelter and safety. I don't blame her."

"Nor I," added Jack, as we walked back to our hotel. "Still, it seems hard that we should have no reward whatever for our trouble; not even the miserable pleasure of seeing her safely home. Catch me acting the knight-errant again!"

I laughed at his lugubrious tones and the mock-mournful air he put on.

"This first expedition has not ended very romantically," I said. "What was to have been a battle-royal, when we were engaged in it, has assumed the phase of an inglorious fracas, now it is ended. Not very encouraging to chivalric natures, I must confess!"

A month later I was again in England.

I might have delayed my departure from the Riviera another couple of months with advantage to my health; but after Jack left, the place began to pall on me. And moreover, I was induced to return by another and stronger reason, which only those who have been in love themselves can thoroughly appreciate.

I was, therefore, greatly chagrined, on arriving in Paris, to find a telegram from Lydia awaiting me. It informed me that she had been unexpectedly called away from town to the bedside of a dying relative in the north of England. This necessarily prevented our meeting for a week or two longer, and the interval I proposed to spend at Sir Reginald Titherby's, in Berkshire, whither Jack had previously gone.

"Who do you think is here?" said he, as soon as we got together after my arrival. "None other than Inez de Lara."

"Inez de Lara! And who may Inez de Lara be?"

"Oh, I forgot! Of course, you don't know her name. If you will just look here," pointing out of the window, "perhaps you will be able to recall when and where you first saw her."

Coming slowly across the lawn, her dark eyes, bent upon the ground, grave and silent, a striking contrast to the group of laughing guests whom she preceded, was the siren of the gaming-tables of Monte Carlo.

"She did not recognise me," Jack continue; "or, at least, she did not appear to do so."

"You surely don't expect her to acknowledge such an informal introduction as ours was, Jack? In fact, I question if she saw us at all."

"Perhaps not," answered Jack; "and yet why did she look at me so curiously if she did not? By the way, what a penetrating glance she does give one! It goes through and through you like a dirk, and makes you feel more uncomfortable, especially if one is at all nervous, as I am."

"Well, well," I said, laughing, "looks can do no harm physically, though they may make sad havoc with the heart, metaphorically. Beware, Jack!"

"Thanks for the caution, Allan, but I'm quite safe in that direction. She may have a great deal of what is known as 'will power,' but not enough to make a dent in my pachydermatous hide. Now, with yourself it might be different. You are in what doctors call a 'very low state,' and consequently just the person upon whom the said 'will power' would make the greatest impression. But here they come."

In the course of the next few days I saw Miss de Lara frequently. Her society possessed for me an infatuation for which I am utterly unable to account; some sort of magnetic influence, subtle, yet powerful, seemed always exercising its sway to draw me to her side.

A glance from her eyes, a gesture of her hand, even the tone of her voice, conveyed to me the meanings hidden from, and imperceptible to, others—meanings which, often in opposition to my inclination, I was compelled to understand and obey.

It is true, at first I did not struggle against the strange power Inez wielded over me. The companionship of a pretty and unconventional woman is always pleasurable, and doubly so in a country house, where the hours often hang wearily upon one's hands, no matter how cheery and full of resources the host may be.

Do not imagine that I fell in love with Inez. My affections were already engaged elsewhere, and the strong, pure love I had for Lydia owned nothing in common with the singular fascination Inez exerted over me.

The former was given with my whole soul and being, while I yielded to the latter against my will and better judgment. But I could not combat it—I was as powerless against it as is the fly to extricate itself from the toils of a spider's web.

"Have you ever studied hypnotism?" she asked me, rather abruptly, one day, when we stood watching a lively game of tennis.

"No. It is rather outside the range of my usual studies. Besides, I have always looked upon hypnotism, mesmerism, will-power, and thought-reading as unworthy of attention; in fact, only as so many means by which the charlatan and quack may gull unthinking audiences."

"Oh, that is your opinion, is it?" she answered, with a sarcastic little laugh. "You think there is no wisdom beyond that contained in black-letter law books and modern statutes?"

"You are unfair, Miss de Lara, to construe my words in that sense. I ought to have been more guarded in my answer, for I presume, from your question, that you are not so ignorant as I am of the subject."

"I have paid some attention to it," she replied. "Of course, I do not claim to be an adept, yet I fancy I have made one or two discoveries in the science that were hitherto unknown."

"You have?" I cried, in surprise.

"Yes. Why not?" she asked, arching her eyebrows. "For instance, it is generally supposed that the hypnotic subject advances through successive stages, during which he reaches the ultimate stage, in which he acts entirely according to the will and suggestion of the operator; in other words, he acts unconsciously and automatically. Now, I have found out a method by which a suitable subject may be made to act under suggestion while still retaining his own conscious identity—to act as though by his own free will, and yet really under compulsion."

"What a strange woman you are, Miss de Lara!" I said, as a feeling of repulsion, almost of loathing, came over me.

"So I have often been told. But when people know more about these so-called mysteries, they will find nothing stranger or more unnatural in them than in chemistry or electricity. The knowledge will alter our ideas of many things, no doubt; good and ill-luck will have no meaning."

"How! Have no meaning?"

"Ah, ah!" she laughed. "That's another of my discoveries. Good and ill-luck, chance, fate, or whatever you like to call it, is not so independent of human will as is supposed. Within certain limits it is controllable by those who possess the secret. By the bye, I think you have seen a sample of my skill in this respect."

"You mean at Monte Carlo?"

"Yes." Then, after a pause, "I must apologize for not thanking you and your friend for the great service you did me that night. It was not ingratitude that withheld me from thanking you before, but the desire to conceal the circumstances from the guests here. One must attend sometimes to the conventional opinions of society, and I am afraid, in that matter, they would tell against me."

"But neither Mr. Pendergast nor myself could understand why you disappeared so suddenly after our encounter with the rascals in the lane."

"For the reason I have just mentioned, I did not want the friends with whom I was staying to know of my unladylike escapade. But here comes Mr. Prendergast," she added, with something like a frown in Jack's direction. "I will leave you to him."

"Well," was Jack's greeting, as Inez walked over and joined Sir Reginald, "whose caution was the more necessary, Allan—yours or mine? I warned you against the charms of Miss de Lara, and here you have been ever since constantly with her—and you almost as good as married to Miss Atherton. Oh, you sad dog!"

"When the cat's away, Jack, you know."

"That is complimentary to your future wife anyhow."

"Well, I go back to town to-morrow," I said, ignoring his remark. "You will understand at once that there can be nothing under the surface."

"You go back to-morrow!" he exclaimed. "Why this sudden resolution?"

"Work, Jack, work! I have had too long a holiday already."

From terrible experience, I know that the baleful influence of Inez was strong in inverse ratio to the distance between us, and I had little fear that it would reach me when fifty miles divided us.

So I set to work early next morning to pack my luggage, intending to leave Sir Reginald's immediately after breakfast.

But all the time during which I was thus engaged, the inward working I so dreaded, which paralyzed my will, and rendered me an object of contempt to myself, was ever present.

I knew that Inez wanted to see me, that she was exerting all her energies for that purpose.

I set my teeth firmly, and clenched my hands with determination, but I felt my resistance gradually oozing away before her superior power.

And when I heard footsteps on the stairs—footsteps I recognised with dread—and became aware that she was coming nearer—nearer—I felt that I must comply.

I made one last effort—one vain, despairing effort, and then rushed out to the gallery. I met her face to face.

"Good morning, Mr. Ashley," she said, meeting my gaze with a cynical smile. "You have not been out for your usual morning's stroll to-day."

"I—I am leaving Sir Reginald's to-day, and was packing up my things," I said, summoning up all the courage I had left. "I always prefer to pack my kit myself."

"Leaving!" Inez cried. "You surely cannot mean it. You must have forgotten that we are matched against Mr. Prendergast and Lady Calesford for a set of tennis to-morrow. You must stay for that."

My resolution faded away before the cool look of her hazel eyes and the mysterious emotion her presence stirred within me.

"Well, perhaps—yes, I will stay over to-morrow.'

"I thought you would not desert us so unceremoniously," she replied, as she walked on. "We shall be sure to win."

Ashamed of my feebleness and indecision, crestfallen and wretched, I went sullenly down to breakfast.

As I entered the breakfast-room, Sir Reginald was holding forth to Jack on the great bugbear of his existence—the great havoc done among his pheasants by poachers.

"The rascally fellows are simply decimating the birds," he was saying. "They are so cautious and cunning in their depredations that, in spite of the keepers, they'll soon make a clean sweep of the lot."

"And so you think of undertaking the role of amateur keeper yourself?" replied Jack, with a shrug of his shoulder.

"Yes; I am going out with Hodgson and the under-keepers before dark to try if I cannot surprise the poachers at work. It is my impression that most of the damage, if not all of it, is done not after dark, when the keepers are most wide-awake, but at dusk, when they are less vigilant."

The conversation was here dropped, as half a dozen new-comers trooped in. At the first opportunity I made my way out of the room; the thoughts that racked my brain did not make me desirous of companionship, and I was glad to be alone.

I did not see anything more of Inez that morning; but after dinner (which was early) I found myself—I know not how I got there—walking by her side in the park.

Fettered in the bonds of this enchantress—this nineteenth-century Venus—powerless to shield myself from her wiles and sorceries, how I felt the degradation of my own will! I thought of Lydia, and shuddered at the fancies her image brought before me. How she would despise me, could she see me now!

Ah, a sudden idea struck me! Why not tell Inez of my love for Lydia, and trust to her sense of justice and propriety to release me from the chains that so galled me?

As a drowning man clutches at a straw, so did I cling to this new thought, and wait for a favourable moment to bring it into play.

"I am sorry to hear," Inez said, as we proceeded, "that Mr. Prendergast has become engaged to Lady Calesford."

"Sorry?" I cried, in astonishment. "Why sorry?"

"In my opinion they are unsuited to each other,"—looking straight into my eyes with a penetrating gaze that made me quiver. "Do you think they are?"

"They are evidently in love with one another," I replied, evasively.

"But that is not all that is requisite for a happy union. There are feelings and emotions stronger and more stable than those of love."

Was my last lingering hope, then, to be dashed to the ground? Had this woman no sense of the sacredness of the affection which binds two congenial souls together? My heart sank despairingly as I listened to her.

"Yes," she continued, "unless they possess that magnetic sympathy of heart—that refined intercourse of mind with mind, of thought with thought, far different from mere love, their lives will be empty, purposeless, and miserable. It were better they had never met. But if they do possess these communions of nature, nothing can separate them; neither prejudice, class, nor religion—not love itself. If the woman alone is conscious of this affinity, she must confess it; if both, then the man, against his will or with it, must perforce—"

"Ask the woman to be his wife?"

"Exactly."

I asked the question, knowing there could be but one answer to it from her; and the symptoms I experienced confirmed her words. I grew hot and cold by turns, my head swam, my muscles relaxed; I reeled, and had to catch at the bole of a tree to support myself. But I saw no pity, not the least sign of compassion in the dark eyes fixed so steadfastly upon me.

"Have pity!" I groaned. "Have pity! You are—"

A loud cry interrupted me. It was succeeded by the sound of a shot, and three men, rough and ill-kempt, crashed through the thicket that surrounded the neighbouring plantation. They paused for a moment on seeing us.

"Ding it!" shouted one of them, raising the air-gun he carried; "here's another of 'em!"

I heard a metallic click; a pain shot across my shoulders as if I had been struck a sharp blow; a low cry from Inez, and I remember no more.

When I recovered from the fever into which this event had thrown me, I was lying in my own room at Sir Reginald's.

A gentle hand was laid upon mine, and soft, silky hair swept over it. I opened my eyes to see—Lydia.

"Hush, Allan!" she said, as I was about to speak. "The doctor says you must be kept quiet and free from all excitement. If you insist upon talking, I shall leave the room."

"But, tell me, is Miss de Lara—"

"The Spanish lady is dead. The shot glanced from your shoulder, and struck her on the temple. Mr. Prendergast, who was with you at the time, has told me all."

What a load was lifted from my mind!

Once more—the first time for days—I breathed freely. It would be hypocritical to say that I felt the least tinge of sorrow. Inez had tried to spoil my life and the life of one dearer to me than my own. She had no pity for me, and I could not pity her.

To Jack I was grateful for the construction he had led Lydia to put upon the incident—that we were all three together, Inez, Jack, and myself, when the fatal shot was fired—and if ever a "white lie" was justified, surely it was in this case.

It was many weeks before I was sufficiently recovered to leave Sir Reginald's house.

Then a couple of months in Italy set me to rights, and enabled me to look back upon the events connected with my stay in Berkshire as the most hideous of all hideous nightmares.

On my return to England, Lydia became my wife, and on the same day Jack was married to Lady Calesford.

Woman attempting to hypnotize a friend
(Minnesota Historical Society Collection)

Suggested Suicide

By Erckmann-Chatrian

I.

At that time—said Christian—I was as poor as a church mouse, and had taken refuge in the gable end of an old house on the Strasse Minnesinger at Nuremberg.

I dwelt in the angle of the slated roof, and could only stand upright in the middle of my room with its sloping walls. To reach my window I had to walk over my straw pallet, but this window had a magnificent unbroken view of city and country. I could see the cats gravely promenading in the gutters, the swans on the distant river bringing food to their devouring young, the pigeons with their tails spread like fans whirling to the depths of the street below, and when the Angelus bell called the world to prayer they would come and perch on my roof crooning their melancholy song. I could see the good burghers sitting before their doors, smoking their pipes, and the young girls in their short red petticoats with their pitchers on their arms, laughing and talking around the fountain. I would watch the windows of the city light up, one by one; then gradually all would fade away, the shadow queen, Night, would lay her mantle on the earth and sky, the bats come flitting from their hiding places, and I would go to sleep in sweet solitude.

The old second-hand dealer, Toubac, knew the way to my garret as well as I knew it myself. He was not afraid to climb my ladder, and every week his goat-like head, surmounted by a reddish wig, would peer through my trap-door, his fingers clinging to the edge of my loft, as he said, "Ach Himmel, Master Christian, have you anything new?"—to which I would reply, "Come in, come in; I am about finishing a little landscape for you. Then with a silent laugh his great lank body would lengthen, lengthen, until he touched the roof.

To do Toubac justice, he never chaffered with me. He bought all my sketches, one with another, at fifteen florins, and sold them for forty. Oh! he was an honest Jew.

This kind of life pleased me. I was happy and content, when one day the whole city of Nuremberg was startled by a strange, mysterious event. Not far from my dormer window, a little to the left, was the Inn of the Boeuf-Gras, an old inn very renowned throughout the country. There were always three or four wagons standing before the door, loaded with sacks and barrels. The country people on their way to market all stopped at the Boeuf-Gras for their tipple of beer.

The gable end of this inn was remarkable for its peculiar form. It was very narrow and pointed; the sides were cut in saw-teeth, and grotesque carving—intertwined serpents—ornamented the cornice and windows. But what was more remarkable, the house facing it had exactly the same carving, the same ornaments, even the same iron rod for the sign board. You could almost imagine that these two old dwellings reflected each other, only behind the inn a great oak spread its shadowing leaves above the roof, while the roof of the other house was clearly outlined against the sky. Again, as the Boeuf-Gras was gay and animated, the other house was dark and silent. On one side, crowds of drinkers were incessantly coming and going, shouting, singing, and cracking their whips, on the other side, were silence and solitude. Only once or twice a day, the heavy door would open to let an old woman pass through, her back bent like a bow, her chin long and pointed, her robe clinging to her hips, and an enormous basket on her arm.

The physiognomy of this old woman struck me forcibly; her little green eyes, her thin sharp nose, her great flowered shawl, which seemed at least a hundred years old, the lace on her bonnet falling down to her eyebrows, all seemed so fantastic that she interested me in spite of myself. I wanted to know what this lonely old woman was doing in that great, deserted house. I imagined she lived a life of good works and pious meditations.

But one day I stopped in the street a moment to look at her; she suddenly turned and gave me a glance so horrible in expression, distorting her face with such hideous grimaces, that I fairly shuddered. Then walking off, shaking her trembling head, and drawing her great shawl about her, she disappeared behind the heavy door. "She is mad," I said, "a wicked old madwoman. I was stupid to interest myself about her. But truly, I should like to catch that expression. Toubac would willingly give me forty francs for it."

This jesting did not reassure me. The horrible glance of that old woman pursued me everywhere. When I climbed the perpendicular ladder to my garret, I imagined that she was crouching somewhere in the darkness, waiting to catch me by my coat tails and pull me backward.

I related these fancies to Toubac, who, far from laughing, gravely said, "Take care, Master Christian. Beware of this old woman. Her teeth are sharp, pointed, and of marvellous whiteness, which is not natural at her age. They say she has the evil eye, the children fly from her, and the people call her the Flittermouse, or bat."

I admired the perspicacity of the Jew, and his words gave me food for reflection. But after some weeks, having frequently met the Flittermouse without any evil consequences, my fears disappeared, and I thought no more about her.

Well, one evening when I was sleeping a heavy, dreamless sleep, I was awakened by a strange harmony, a sweet melodious vibration, like the breeze sighing among the leaves. I listened a long time, almost breathless, afraid to move for fear of losing this tremulous musical sound. Finally I turned toward my window, and saw two wings beating against the glass. At first I thought it was a bat caught in my room; then the moonbeams gleaming on the transparent filigree of the wings showed me a magnificent "butterfly of the night." Sometimes the vibrations were so rapid that I could scarcely distinguish them, then the rhythmic movement would cease and the creature would repose upon the glass like a delicate tracery of lace.

This aerial apparition in the silence of the night thrilled my heart with sweet emotions. It seemed to me some pitying angel, touched by my solitude, come to soothe my loneliness, and the thought softened me to tenderness and tears.

"Rest tranquil, sweet captive," I said, "I will not retain thee against thy will. Return to liberty and Heaven." I opened my little window. The night was calm, millions of stars sparkled in the sky. One instant I contemplated this sublime spectacle, the words of prayer naturally trembling on my lips, when, imagine my amazement and horror, on lowering my eyes, I saw a man hanged to the rod which supported the sign of the Boeuf-Gras, his straggling hair, stiff arms, and legs stretched to a point, casting a gigantic shadow on the street below.

The immobility of that figure in the cold moonlight was something frightful. I tried to cry out, my tongue seemed frozen in my mouth, my teeth clashed against each other. I do not know what mysterious power drew my eyes to the shadowy depths beyond, where I dimly saw the old woman crouching at her window contemplating the hanged man with diabolical satisfaction.

I was seized with terror. All my strength failed me, and I recoiled against the wall and fell on my bed unconscious. How long I remained in this death-like sleep I do not know. When I came to myself, it was broad day, and my hair was wet with the dews of the night. A confused noise came up from the street below. I looked out. The burgomaster and his secretary were standing before the door of the inn. People were coming and going; some would stop a moment to look, then continue on their way. The good women of the neighborhood, sweeping before their doors, gazed up and down the street, and talked among themselves. At last a litter, and upon that litter a body covered by a woollen cloth, came out of the inn, borne by two men. As they went down the street, the children ran behind them. Then the crowd dispersed, and all was quiet.

The window of the inn in front of me was still open. A bit of rope hung from the rod of the sign board. It was not a dream. I had seen the "butterfly of the night"—the hanged man—and the old woman crouching at her window.

Toubac made me a visit that day. As soon as his great nose was on a level with my floor, he cried out, "Master Christian, have you anything for me?"

Seated upon my only chair, my hands on my knees, my eyes fixed on vacancy, I paid no attention to him. Surprised at my silence, Toubac called still louder, "Master Christian!" Then striding across my loft, he slapped me on the shoulder: "Ach Himmel! What's the matter with you?"

"Ah! Is that you, Toubac?"

"Well, I should think so. Are you sick?"

"No, I am thinking."

"What in the devil are you thinking of?"

"Of the hanged man."

"Ah! ah!" cried the old second-hand dealer, "then you saw him. Poor boy, what a strange story; the third one in the same place!"

"How? The third?" I exclaimed.

"Yes. I should have told you, but it is time enough yet; there will be the fourth to follow his example."

As Toubac spoke, he seated himself on the edge of my chest, and lighting his pipe sent trailings of blue smoke along the bare walls.

"Mein Gott!" he continued; "I am not a coward, but before I would pass a night in that room, I would go and hang myself elsewhere. Just think of it, Master Christian; nine or ten months ago, a good man from Terbingen, fat and jolly, a dealer in furs, stopped at the Boeuf-Gras, demanding supper and lodging. He ate well, drank well; they put him to sleep in that chamber, the green chamber, as they call it. Next morning he was found hanged to the rod of the sign board. Well, if he were the only one, there would be little more to tell. The coroner was summoned, and they buried him in the strangers' grave at the end of the garden.

"But about six weeks afterward, a brave soldier from Neustadt came along. He had his definite discharge in his pocket, and was so happy at the thought of seeing his native village again. All the evening as he emptied his beer glass he talked of nothing but his home, and the dear little cousin waiting to marry him. At last they put this brave man to bed, and that same night, as the watchman passed along the Minnesinger, he perceived something on the rod of the sign board. He raised his lantern, and there hung this brave soldier, his definite discharge in his pocket, his hands pressed close to his thighs as if he were on parade.

"' Bless my soul,' said the burgomaster. 'This is extraordinary. What can it mean?'

"They examined the chamber, replastered the walls, and sent a mortuary report to Neustadt of 'sudden death.' All Nuremburg was indignant against the innkeeper. Some wanted to force him to take down his iron rod, saying it inspired people with dangerous ideas. But old Nikel Schmidt would not hear of it.

"'That rod,' said he,' was put up there by my grandfather. It has carried the sign of the Boeuf-Gras for more than a hundred years. It has done no harm to any one, not even to the hay wagons that pass under it. All those who don't want to look at it can turn their heads.'

"Well, the excitement passed away, and for many months there was nothing new. Unhappily a student from Heidelberg, on his way from the University, stopped at the Boeuf-Gras day before yesterday. He was the son of a pastor. Now do you suppose the son of a pastor would think of hanging himself on the rod of a sign board, just because a great Meinherr and a brave soldier had hanged themselves there? You must acknowledge. Master Christian, it is not reasonable. Ah, well—"

"Stop! stop!" I cried. "There is some frightful mystery under all this. It is not the rod, it is not the chamber."

"What! do you suspect the innkeeper, one of the most honest men in the world, belonging to one of the oldest families of Nuremberg?"

"No. God preserve me from unjust suspicions, but there are depths of darkness we cannot fathom."

"You are right," said Toubac, astonished at my excitement. "Let us talk of something better, Master Christian,—of our landscape."

This brought me back to reality, the affair was soon arranged, and Toubac descended the ladder very well satisfied, charging me to think no more of the student of Heidelberg. I would most willingly have followed his counsel, but when the devil mixes himself up in our affairs, it is not easy to be rid of him.

II.

Alone in the solitude of my room, this strange story returned to my mind with frightful pertinacity.

"The old woman," I said, "is the cause of all this. She alone has conceived and consummated these crimes. But by what means? Has she resorted to artifice, or the assistance of supernatural powers?"

I walked up and down my narrow loft, a voice within me crying out: "It was not in vain that Heaven permitted you to see the Flittermouse contemplating the agony of her victim. It was not in vain that the soul of the poor young man came to you in the form of a butterfly of the night. No, it was not in vain. Heaven has imposed a terrible task upon you, Christian, and if you do not accomplish it, take care! You will fall into the toils of the old woman yourself. Perhaps at this moment she is weaving her net in the shadowy darkness."

For many days these frightful thoughts pursued me without ceasing. I could not sleep. It was impossible to work; the brush fell from my hand, and—horrible to say—I frequently found myself viewing the iron rod with complacency.

At last I could stand it no longer. One evening I leaped down my ladder, four steps at a time, ran out into the street, and crouched behind the door of Flittermouse to surprise her fatal secret.

From this time, there was not a day that I was not in the streets, watching the old woman, never letting her out of my sight; but she was so crafty, and had such subtle instincts, that, without turning her head, she knew when I was following her and caught me at all my schemes. Nevertheless she pretended not to see me, would go and return from the market like any good woman, only now and then she would hasten her steps, and mutter confused words to herself.

At the end of a month, I saw that it was impossible to attain my end by this means, and the conviction filled me with inexpressible sadness.

"What must I do? The old woman divines my projects; she is always on guard; everything fails me; the old vixen already believes that I am at the end of my rope. What must I do?"

As I asked myself this question, a bright thought came into my head. My attic overlooked the dwelling of the Flittermouse, but there was no window on that side of my room. I lightly raised one of the slates of my roof, and could scarcely contain my joy; the whole interior of the old building was open to my view. "At last I have you," I cried; "you cannot escape me now. From here I can see all your movements, the habits of the fox in his den. You will not suspect this invisible eye, this eye that will surprise your crime at the moment of consummation. Oh, justice marches slowly, but surely."

Nothing could be more sinister than the interior of this old building. A dark court, paved with greenish mouldy slabs; in one corner a pool of sickening, stagnant water; a rickety stairway leading to a gallery with a wooden railing; on this railing old clothes, rags, and the empty case of a worn mattress. On the first floor to the left was a stone sink, indicating the kitchen; on the right, were high windows looking upon the street, with some pots of withered flowers on the sills. Everything was gloomy, dilapidated, and mouldering. The sun never penetrated the depths of this court, never brightened the old cracked walls, the worm-eaten gallery, or dust-tarnished windows. It was truly an asylum for bats. Flittermouse must have been well pleased.

I had scarcely finished these observations when the old woman entered. She had returned from the market. I heard the heavy door grind on its hinges, then Flittermouse appeared with her basket. She seemed fatigued, and out of breath; and she held to the banisters as she climbed the stairs.

It was suffocatingly hot, and one of those days when the insects come out of their hiding-places and fill the air with their rasping sounds. The old woman softly crossed the gallery like a ferret. Spying a struggling fly, she caught and delicately presented it to a bloated spider squatting in a corner of the gallery, then passed into the kitchen, returned in a few minutes, shook out the old clothes on the railing, made a few strokes with her broom on the steps, then suddenly raised her head, her green eyes searchingly scanning my roof.

By what strange intuition did she suspect something? I could not tell, but I softly lowered the slate, and gave up the position of spy for that day.

For six weeks I could discover nothing singular in the Flittermouse; sometimes she would peel her potatoes, sometimes spread her linen on the railing, sometimes spin a little; but she never sang, as is the custom of good old women, whose quavering voices blend so well with the buzzing of the wheel.

Silence reigned around her; not a sparrow came to light on her window sill; the pigeons in flying over her court seemed to spread their wings with greater velocity. Everything shunned her. Only the spider seemed pleased in her society.

You cannot conceive of my patience in these long hours of watching; nothing escaped me; at the least noise I would raise my slate, stimulated by curiosity and indefinable fear.

In the mean time Toubac complained:

"Master Christian, how in the devil do you pass your time? In other days you gave me something every week. Now it is scarcely one a month. Ah, these painters! It is a true saying, 'Idle as a painter.' As soon as they get a few kreutzers in their pocket, they go to sleep."

I began to lose courage myself. In spite of all my spying and watching, I could discover nothing extraordinary. I said, "The old woman can't be so very dangerous after all. Perhaps I am wrong to suspect her." I found myself making many excuses for her, when one evening with my eye to my hole I abandoned all these benevolent reflections.

The scene suddenly changed. Flittermouse passed across the gallery like a flash. She was no longer the same. Her back was straight, her head erect, her jaws were firmly set, she walked with a quick step, her gray hair floating behind her. "Oh, ho," I said, "something has happened."

That night, when the noise of the city had died away, when silence and mystery had settled on the old dwelling, I threw myself on my pallet and suddenly saw that the window in front of me was lighted; a traveller occupied the green chamber, the chamber of the hanged. Then all my fears returned; the agitation of Flittermouse was explained; she scented a victim.

I slept no more that night; the rustling of a straw, the nibbling of a mouse under the floor, made me shiver. I got up, perched myself at my window, and listened. The light in front of me was finally extinguished, but a moment before, whether it were reality or illusion, I thought I saw the old vixen also waiting and listening. I watched through the long hours until the gray dawn lay on city and distant hill. Then, worn out with fatigue and excitement, I slept, but my sleep was short; by eight o'clock I was at my post of observation.

It appeared that the night of Flittermouse had not been more peaceful than mine. When she opened the door on the gallery, a livid pallor covered her face and meagre neck; she had on only her chemise and a woolen petticoat, and her gray hair was tumbling on her shoulders. She looked over to my side with a dreamy air, but saw nothing; she was thinking of other things. Suddenly she descended, leaving her old shoes at the top of the stairs, no doubt to assure herself that the lower door was securely fastened; she quickly ascended the stairs, leaping three or four steps at a time—it was frightful. She darted into a neighboring room, I heard something like the opening of a great chest, then Flittermouse appeared on the gallery dragging a manikin behind her—and the manikin was dressed like the student of Heidelberg.

The old woman with surprising dexterity suspended this frightful object to a beam overhead, then she descended to contemplate her work from the court. A peal of abrupt laughter escaped her lips. She ascended and descended again and again like a maniac, every time uttering new cries and fresh bursts of laughter.

A noise was heard in the street; the old woman bounded forward, unhooked the manikin, carried it away, returned, and, leaning on the banister, her neck stretched, her eyes gleaming, she listened intently. The noise passed by, the muscles of her face relaxed, she drew a sigh of relief. It was only a passing carriage. Evidently the old vixen was frightened. Then she re-entered the chamber, and I heard the lid of the chest closed.

This strange scene amazed me. What did the manikin mean? I became more watchful than ever.

Soon after this Flittermouse went out with her basket. I watched her to the turn of the street. She had retaken her air of trembling old age, walked with tottering steps, turning from time to time to see if any one noticed her.

She remained out five long hours, while I restlessly tramped up and down my loft. To me the time was insupportable; the sun beating down on my roof seemed to scorch my brain.

I saw the good man who occupied the fatal chamber sitting at his window, calmly smoking his pipe. He was a good-natured looking peasant from Nassau, with a three-cornered hat and a scarlet waistcoat, and evidently had no thought of harm. I wanted to cry out, "Take care, my good man; beware of the old woman."

But he would not have understood me.

In about two hours Flittermouse returned. I heard the closing of the great heavy door. Then she appeared in the court, seated herself on the lower step of the stairs, and placed her enormous basket before her. At first she drew out some packages of herbs and vegetables, then a scarlet waistcoat, a folded three-cornered hat, plush breeches, a pair of long woollen stockings—the exact costume of the peasant from Nassau.

I had a revelation, flames actually passed before my eyes. I recalled those precipices which draw you with irresistible power, wells you feel forced to throw yourself into, depths of darkness you dare not gaze upon for fear of being drawn into their rayless gloom. I remembered the contagion of suicide and murder, the fantastic allurement of example, which makes you yawn when others yawn, suffer when you see others suffer, and take your life because you see another take his life. My hair stood on end with horror.

How the Flittermouse, this low, degraded creature, had been able to divine this profound law of nature, I could not conceive. How she had found means to make it subservient to her sanguinary instincts, I could not understand. Without reflecting any further upon this strange mystery, I determined to turn this fatal law against herself, to draw the old vixen into her own trap; so many innocent victims were crying for vengeance.

I immediately started to carry out my plans, ran to all the old clothes dealers of Nuremberg, and late that evening arrived at the Boeuf Gras with a great bundle under my arm.

Nickel Schmidt knew me well. I had painted the portrait of his wife.

"Ah, Master Christian; what happy circumstance has procured me the pleasure of seeing you?"

"Well, to tell the truth, Master Schmidt, I have a desire to pass a night in that chamber." As we were standing at the door of the inn, I pointed above to the green room. The good man gave me a suspicious glance.

"Do not be afraid," I said, "I have no thought of hanging myself."

"Ah, that is well. It would be a great pity to lose a painter of your talents. When do you want the room, Master Christian?"

"To-night."

"It is impossible; it is occupied."

"The gentleman can have it immediately," said a voice behind us; "I don't want it any longer."

We turned around much surprised. It was the peasant from Nassau, his great three-cornered hat on the back of his head, his bundle on the end of his stick. He had heard the story of the three suicides, and was fairly trembling with rage.

"Rooms like yours" he stammered, "ought to—ought to—it's murder—assassination—you deserve to be sent to the galleys."

"Come, come; be quiet," said the innkeeper. "It has not prevented you from sleeping well."

"No, thank God! I said my prayers last night; if it had not been for that, where would I be? Where would I be?" and he went off holding up his hands to heaven.

"Ah, well," said Master Schmidt, very much astonished, "the chamber is vacant, but you are not going to play me a bad trick, I hope."

"It would be worse for me than for you, my dear sir."

I handed my package to the servant and took my place among the drinkers. I had not felt so calm and happy for a long time. After so much anxiety, I seemed to be nearing the end, the clouds were breaking, some invisible power seemed upholding me.

I lighted my pipe, emptied my glass of beer, and leaning my elbow on the table listened to a band playing in the Strasse. Lost in a kind of dreamy wakefulness, I would every now and then note the hour, and ask myself if the weary past was not a dream. But when the watchman warned us that it was time to leave the hall, other and more serious thoughts filled my mind, as I followed the little maid who preceded me with a lighted candle.

III.

We ascended to the third story. Placing the light in my hand, she pointed to a door, saying "There it is," and hastily descended the stairs.

Opening the door, I found the green room like all other rooms of an inn, the ceiling very low, the bed very high. I explored it at a glance, and glided to the window. Nothing was yet to be seen at the house of Flittermouse, only in a long obscure chamber a dim light was burning.

"That is well," said I, closing the curtains. "I have sufficient time."

I opened my package, took out a woman's bonnet with deep hanging lace, and put it on, and placing myself before the glass I began with a sharp-pointed brush to trace my face with wrinkles. This took me nearly an hour, and when I put on the robe and great flowered shawl, I was actually afraid of myself. There was Flittermouse looking at me from the depths of the glass.

Just then the watchman cried, "Eleven o'clock!" I quickly took out the manikin I had brought, dressed it in the costume of the old woman, and placed it near the window.

After all I had seen of the old vixen's craftiness, her infernal cunning, and artful deviltry, nothing would have surprised me. I parted the curtains and waited in some trepidation.

The dim light I had noticed in that long, dismal chamber cast its yellowish rays on the manikin of the Nassau peasant. It was cowering at the foot of the bed, the head hanging upon the breast, the three-cornered hat drawn over the face, the arms dragging as if plunged in the depths of despair.

The light was managed with such diabolical skill that only part of the figure appeared, but the red waistcoat with its great buttons was plainly visible. This motionless, pathetic figure in the silence of night struck the imagination with wonderful power. Even I, although forewarned, felt cold shivers down my back. How then would it be with a poor countryman, unexpectedly confronted with this dismal spectre? He would become so terrified that he would lose all self-control, and the spirit of imitation would do the rest.

I could see Flittermouse crouching in the shadowy darkness, but was careful not to let her see me. Softly opening the curtains, I raised the manikin and made it appear as if it were advancing toward her. Then suddenly, seizing a light, I threw the window wide open and stood in full view of the old vixen, *the living image of herself.*

In her amazement she dropped the manikin of the peasant and looked at me in stupefied terror. A horrible pantomime commenced. She extended her finger—I extended mine; her lips trembled—I made mine tremble; she leaned forward—I did the same. I cannot describe this frightful scene. It was like the madness of delirium and insanity. It was a struggle between two wills, two minds, two souls, which should conquer the other, and in that struggle I had the advantage, for the poor victims in shapes of horror aided me.

After imitating the movements of Flittermouse for a few moments, I drew a rope from under my petticoat, and fastened it to the rod of the sign board.

The old woman watched me with gaping mouth as I passed the rope around my neck, her wild-beast eyes gleaming, her features convulsed.

"No, no," she cried in a stifled voice.

I continued with the coolness of an executioner.

Then she was seized with a fit of rage; clinching the window-sill with her hands, she howled:

"Old fool—old fool."

I did not give her time to finish; suddenly extinguishing my light, I bent down like one about to take a sudden leap, and seizing the manikin I had already prepared, I dashed it into space.

A terrible cry from across the street, then all was silent.

I listened a long time, great drops of sweat beading my brow; then I heard far, far away in the distance the voice of the watchman crying: "Past twelve o'clock!"

"Now justice is done," I murmured; "the three victims are avenged. God pardon me!"

Just a moment after the cry of the watchman I had seen the old woman leap from her window, a rope around her neck, and hang suspended from the iron rod, her body writhing in the contortions of death. And the calm, silent moon, looking over the high, pointed roof, cast her cold, pale rays on the distorted face and long, floating hair.

Just as I saw the poor young man, I now saw the Flittermouse.

Next day all Nuremberg knew the bat had hanged herself. It was the last event of that kind on the Strasse Minnesinger.

John Barrington Cowles
By Arthur Conan Doyle

I.

It might seem rash of me to say that I ascribe the death of my poor friend, John Barrington Cowles, to any preternatural agency. I am aware that in the present state of public feeling a chain of evidence would require to be strong indeed before the possibility of such a conclusion could be admitted.

I shall therefore merely state the circumstances which led up to this sad event as concisely and as plainly as I can, and leave every reader to draw his own deductions. Perhaps there may be some one who can throw light upon what is dark to me.

I first met Barrington Cowles when I went up to Edinburgh University to take out medical classes there. My landlady in Northumberland Street had a large house, and, being a widow without children, she gained a livelihood by providing accommodation for several students.

Barrington Cowles happened to have taken a bedroom upon the same floor as mine, and when we came to know each other better we shared a small sitting-room, in which we took our meals. In this manner we originated a friendship which was unmarred by the slightest disagreement up to the day of his death.

Cowles' father was the colonel of a Sikh regiment and had remained in India for many years. He allowed his son a handsome income, but seldom gave any other sign of parental affection—writing irregularly and briefly.

My friend, who had himself been born in India, and whose whole disposition was an ardent tropical one, was much hurt by this neglect. His mother was dead, and he had no other relation in the world to supply the blank.

Thus he came in time to concentrate all his affection upon me, and to confide in me in a manner which is rare among men. Even when a stronger and deeper passion came upon him, it never infringed upon the old tenderness between us.

Cowles was a tall, slim young fellow, with an olive, Velasquez-like face, and dark, tender eyes. I have seldom seen a man who was more likely to excite a woman's interest, or to captivate her imagination. His expression was, as a rule, dreamy, and even languid; but if in conversation a subject arose which interested him he would be all animation in a moment. On such occasions his colour would heighten, his eyes gleam, and he could speak with an eloquence which would carry his audience with him.

In spite of these natural advantages he led a solitary life, avoiding female society, and reading with great diligence. He was one of the foremost men of his year, taking the senior medal for anatomy, and the Neil Arnott prize for physics.

How well I can recollect the first time we met her! Often and often I have recalled the circumstances, and tried to remember what the exact impression was which she produced on my mind at the time. After we came to know her my judgment was warped, so that I am curious to recollect what my unbiased instincts were. It is hard, however, to eliminate the feelings which reason or prejudice afterwards raised in me.

It was at the opening of the Royal Scottish Academy in the spring of 1879. My poor friend was passionately attached to art in every form, and a pleasing chord in music or a delicate effect upon canvas would give exquisite pleasure to his highly-strung nature. We had gone together to see the pictures, and were standing in the grand central salon, when I noticed an extremely beautiful woman standing at the other side of the room. In my whole life I have never seen such a classically perfect countenance. It was the real Greek type—the forehead broad, very low, and as white as marble, with a cloudlet of delicate locks wreathing round it, the nose straight and clean cut, the lips inclined to thinness, the chin and lower jaw beautifully rounded off, and yet sufficiently developed to promise unusual strength of character.

But those eyes—those wonderful eyes! If I could but give some faint idea of their varying moods, their steely hardness, their feminine softness, their power of command, their penetrating intensity suddenly melting away into an expression of womanly weakness—but I am speaking now of future impressions!

There was a tall, yellow-haired young man with this lady, whom I at once recognised as a law student with whom I had a slight acquaintance.

Archibald Reeves—for that was his name—was a dashing, handsome young fellow, and had at one time been a ringleader in every university escapade; but of late I had seen little of him, and the report was that he was engaged to be married. His companion was, then, I presumed, his *fiancée*. I seated myself upon the velvet settee in the centre of the room, and furtively watched the couple from behind my catalogue.

The more I looked at her the more her beauty grew upon me. She was somewhat short in stature, it is true; but her figure was perfection, and she bore herself in such a fashion that it was only by actual comparison that one would have known her to be under the medium height.

As I kept my eyes upon them, Reeves was called away for some reason, and the young lady was left alone. Turning her back to the pictures, she passed the time until the return of her escort in taking a deliberate survey of the company, without paying the least heed to the fact that a dozen pair of eyes, attracted by her elegance and beauty, were bent curiously upon her. With one of her hands holding the red silk cord which railed off the pictures, she stood languidly moving her eyes from face to face with as little self-consciousness as if she were looking at the canvas creatures behind her. Suddenly, as I watched her, I saw her gaze become fixed, and, as it were, intense. I followed the direction of her looks, wondering what could have attracted her so strongly.

John Barrington Cowles was standing before a picture—one, I think, by Noel Paton—I know that the subject was a noble and ethereal one. His profile was turned towards us, and never have I seen him to such advantage. I have said that he was a strikingly handsome man, but at that moment he looked absolutely magnificent. It was evident that he had momentarily forgotten his surroundings, and that his whole soul was in sympathy with the picture before him. His eyes sparkled, and a dusky pink shone through his clear olive cheeks. She continued to watch him fixedly, with a look of interest upon her face, until he came out of his reverie with a start, and turned abruptly round, so that his gaze met hers. She glanced away at once, but his eyes remained fixed upon her for some moments. The picture was forgotten already, and his soul had come down to earth once more.

We caught sight of her once or twice before we left, and each time I noticed my friend look after her. He made no remark, however, until we got out into the open air, and were walking arm-in-arm along Princes Street.

"Did you notice that beautiful woman, in the dark dress, with the white fur?" he asked.

"Yes, I saw her," I answered.

"Do you know her?" he asked eagerly. "Have you any idea who she is?"

"I don't know her personally," I replied. "But I have no doubt I could find out all about her, for I believe she is engaged to young Archie Reeves, and he and I have a lot of mutual friends."

"Engaged!" ejaculated Cowles.

"Why, my dear boy," I said, laughing, "you don't mean to say you are so susceptible that the fact that a girl to whom you never spoke in your life is engaged is enough to upset you?"

"Well, not exactly to upset me," he answered, forcing a laugh. "But I don't mind telling you, Armitage, that I never was so taken by any one in my life. It wasn't the mere beauty of the face—though that was perfect enough—but it was the character and the intellect upon it. I hope, if she is engaged, that it is to some man who will be worthy of her."

"Why," I remarked, "you speak quite feelingly. It is a clear case of love at first sight, Jack. However, to put your perturbed spirit at rest, I'll make a point of finding out all about her whenever I meet any fellow who is likely to know."

Barrington Cowles thanked me, and the conversation drifted off into other channels. For several days neither of us made any allusion to the subject, though my companion was perhaps a little more dreamy and distraught than usual. The incident had almost vanished from my remembrance, when one day young Brodie, who is a second cousin of mine, came up to me on the university steps with the face of a bearer of tidings.

"I say," he began, "you know Reeves, don't you?"

"Yes. What of him?"

"His engagement is off."

"Off!" I cried. "Why, I only learned the other day that it was on."

"Oh, yes—it's all off. His brother told me so. Deucedly mean of Reeves, you know, if he has backed out of it, for she was an uncommonly nice girl."

"I've seen her," I said; "but I don't know her name."

"She is a Miss Northcott, and lives with an old aunt of hers in Abercrombie Place. Nobody knows anything about her people, or where she comes from. Anyhow, she is about the most unlucky girl in the world, poor soul!"

"Why unlucky?"

"Well, you know, this was her second engagement," said young Brodie, who had a marvellous knack of knowing everything about everybody. "She was engaged to Prescott—William Prescott, who died. That was a very sad affair. The wedding day was fixed, and the whole thing looked as straight as a die when the smash came."

"What smash?" I asked, with some dim recollection of the circumstances.

"Why, Prescott's death. He came to Abercrombie Place one night, and stayed very late. No one knows exactly when he left, but about one in the morning a fellow who knew him met him walking rapidly in the direction of the Queen's Park. He bade him good night, but Prescott hurried on without heeding him, and that was the last time he was ever seen alive. Three days afterwards his body was found floating in St. Margaret's Loch, under St. Anthony's Chapel. No one could ever understand it, but of course the verdict brought it in as temporary insanity."

"It was very strange," I remarked.

"Yes, and deucedly rough on the poor girl," said Brodie. "Now that this other blow has come it will quite crush her. So gentle and ladylike she is too!"

"You know her personally, then!" I asked.

"Oh, yes, I know her. I have met her several times. I could easily manage that you should be introduced to her."

"Well," I answered, "it's not so much for my own sake as for a friend of mine. However, I don't suppose she will go out much for some little time after this. When she does I will take advantage of your offer."

We shook hands on this, and I thought no more of the matter for some time.

The next incident which I have to relate as bearing at all upon the question of Miss Northcott is an unpleasant one. Yet I must detail it as accurately as possible, since it may throw some light upon the sequel. One cold night, several months after the conversation with my second cousin which I have quoted above, I was walking down one of the lowest streets in the city on my way back from a case which I had been attending. It was very late, and I was picking my way among the dirty loungers who were clustering round the doors of a great gin-palace, when a man staggered out from among them, and held out his hand to me with a drunken leer. The gaslight fell full upon his face, and, to my intense astonishment, I recognised in the degraded creature before me my former acquaintance, young Archibald Reeves, who had once been famous as one of the most dressy and particular men in the whole college. I was so utterly surprised that for a moment I almost doubted the evidence of my own senses; but there was no mistaking those features, which, though bloated with drink, still retained something of their former comeliness. I was determined to rescue him, for one night at least, from the company into which he had fallen.

"Holloa, Reeves!" I said. "Come along with me. I'm going in your direction."

He muttered some incoherent apology for his condition, and took my arm. As I supported him towards his lodgings I could see that he was not only suffering from the effects of a recent debauch, but that a long course of intemperance had affected his nerves and his brain. His hand when I touched it was dry and feverish, and he started from every shadow which fell upon the pavement. He rambled in his speech, too, in a manner which suggested the delirium of disease rather than the talk of a drunkard.

When I got him to his lodgings I partially undressed him and laid him upon his bed. His pulse at this time was very high, and he was evidently extremely feverish. He seemed to have sunk into a doze; and I was about to steal out of the room to warn his landlady of his condition, when he started up and caught me by the sleeve of my coat.

"Don't go!" he cried. "I feel better when you are here. I am safe from her then."

"From her!" I said. "From whom?"

"Her! her!" he answered peevishly. "Ah! you don't know her. She is the devil! Beautiful—beautiful; but the devil!"

"You are feverish and excited," I said. "Try and get a little sleep. You will wake better."

"Sleep!" he groaned. "How am I to sleep when I see her sitting down yonder at the foot of the bed with her great eyes watching and watching hour after hour? I tell you it saps all the strength and manhood out of me. That's what makes me drink. God help me—I'm half drunk now!"

"You are very ill," I said, putting some vinegar to his temples; "and you are delirious. You don't know what you say."

"Yes, I do," he interrupted sharply, looking up at me. "I know very well what I say. I brought it upon myself. It is my own choice. But I couldn't—no, by heaven, I couldn't—accept the alternative. I couldn't keep my faith to her. It was more than man could do."

I sat by the side of the bed, holding one of his burning hands in mine, and wondering over his strange words. He lay still for some time, and then, raising his eyes to me, said in a most plaintive voice—

"Why did she not give me warning sooner? Why did she wait until I had learned to love her so?"

He repeated this question several times, rolling his feverish head from side to side, and then he dropped into a troubled sleep. I crept out of the room, and, having seen that he would be properly cared for, left the house. His words, however, rang in my ears for days afterwards, and assumed a deeper significance when taken with what was to come.

My friend, Barrington Cowles, had been away for his summer holidays, and I had heard nothing of him for several months. When the winter session came on, however, I received a telegram from him, asking me to secure the old rooms in Northumberland Street for him, and telling me the train by which he would arrive. I went down to meet him, and was delighted to find him looking wonderfully hearty and well.

"By the way," he said suddenly, that night, as we sat in our chairs by the fire, talking over the events of the holidays, "you have never congratulated me yet!"

"On what, my boy?" I asked.

"What! Do you mean to say you have not heard of my engagement?"

"Engagement! No!" I answered. "However, I am delighted to hear it, and congratulate you with all my heart."

"I wonder it didn't come to your ears," he said. "It was the queerest thing. You remember that girl whom we both admired so much at the Academy?"

"What!" I cried, with a vague feeling of apprehension at my heart. "You don't mean to say that you are engaged to her?"

"I thought you would be surprised," he answered. "When I was staying with an old aunt of mine in Peterhead, in Aberdeenshire, the Northcotts happened to come there on a visit, and as we had mutual friends we soon met. I found out that it was a false alarm about her being engaged, and then—well, you know what it is when you are thrown into the society of such a girl in a place like Peterhead. Not, mind you," he added, "that I consider I did a foolish or hasty thing. I have never regretted it for a moment. The more I know Kate the more I admire her and love her. However, you must be introduced to her, and then you will form your own opinion."

I expressed my pleasure at the prospect, and endeavoured to speak as lightly as I could to Cowles upon the subject, but I felt depressed and anxious at heart. The words of Reeves and the unhappy fate of young Prescott recurred to my recollection, and though I could assign no tangible reason for it, a vague, dim fear and distrust of the woman took possession of me. It may be that this was foolish prejudice and superstition upon my part, and that I involuntarily contorted her future doings and sayings to fit into some half-formed wild theory of my own. This has been suggested to me by others as an explanation of my narrative. They are welcome to their opinion if they can reconcile it with the facts which I have to tell.

I went round with my friend a few days afterwards to call upon Miss Northcott. I remember that, as we went down Abercrombie Place, our attention was attracted by the shrill yelping of a dog—which noise proved eventually to come from the house to which we were bound. We were shown upstairs, where I was introduced to old Mrs. Merton, Miss Northcott's aunt, and to the young lady herself. She looked as beautiful as ever, and I could not wonder at my friend's infatuation. Her face was a little more flushed than usual, and she held in her hand a heavy dog-whip, with which she had been chastising a small Scotch terrier, whose cries we had heard in the street. The poor brute was cringing up against the wall, whining piteously, and evidently completely cowed.

"So Kate," said my friend, after we had taken our seats, "you have been falling out with Carlo again."

Only a very little quarrel this time," she said, smiling charmingly. "He is a dear, good old fellow, but he needs correction now and then." Then, turning to me, "We all do that, Mr. Armitage, don't we? What a capital thing if, instead of receiving a collective punishment at the end of our lives, we were to have one at once, as the dogs do, when we did anything wicked. It would make us more careful, wouldn't it?"

I acknowledged that it would.

"Supposing that every time a man misbehaved himself a gigantic hand were to seize him, and he were lashed with a whip until he fainted"—she clenched her white fingers as she spoke, and cut out viciously with the dog-whip—"it would do more to keep him good than any number of high-minded theories of morality."

"Why, Kate," said my friend, "you are quite savage today."

"No, Jack," she laughed. "I'm only propounding a theory for Mr. Armitage's consideration."

The two began to chat together about some Aberdeenshire reminiscence, and I had time to observe Mrs. Merton, who had remained silent during our short conversation. She was a very strange-looking old lady. What attracted attention most in her appearance was the utter want of colour which she exhibited. Her hair was snow-white, and her face extremely pale. Her lips were bloodless, and even her eyes were of such a light tinge of blue that they hardly relieved the general pallor. Her dress was a grey silk, which harmonised with her general appearance. She had a peculiar expression of countenance, which I was unable at the moment to refer to its proper cause.

She was working at some old-fashioned piece of ornamental needlework, and as she moved her arms her dress gave forth a dry, melancholy rustling, like the sound of leaves in the autumn. There was something mournful and depressing in the sight of her. I moved my chair a little nearer, and asked her how she liked Edinburgh, and whether she had been there long.

When I spoke to her she started and looked up at me with a scared look on her face. Then I saw in a moment what the expression was which I had observed there. It was one of fear—intense and overpowering fear. It was so marked that I could have staked my life on the woman before me having at some period of her life been subjected to some terrible experience or dreadful misfortune.

"Oh, yes, I like it," she said, in a soft, timid voice; "and we have been here long—that is, not very long. We move about a great deal." She spoke with hesitation, as if afraid of committing herself.

"You are a native of Scotland, I presume?" I said.

"No—that is, not entirely. We are not natives of any place. We are cosmopolitan, you know." She glanced round in the direction of Miss Northcott as she spoke, but the two were still chatting together near the window. Then she suddenly bent forward to me, with a look of intense earnestness upon her face, and said—

"Don't talk to me any more, please. She does not like it, and I shall suffer for it afterwards. Please, don't do it."

I was about to ask her the reason for this strange request, but when she saw I was going to address her, she rose and walked slowly out of the room. As she did so I perceived that the lovers had ceased to talk and that Miss Northcott was looking at me with her keen, grey eyes.

"You must excuse my aunt, Mr. Armitage," she said; "she is odd, and easily fatigued. Come over and look at my album."

We spent some time examining the portraits. Miss Northcott's father and mother were apparently ordinary mortals enough, and I could not detect in either of them any traces of the character which showed itself in their daughter's face. There was one old daguerreotype, however, which arrested my attention. It represented a man of about the age of forty, and strikingly handsome. He was clean shaven, and extraordinary power was expressed upon his prominent lower jaw and firm, straight mouth. His eyes were somewhat deeply set in his head, however, and there was a snake-like flattening at the upper part of his forehead, which detracted from his appearance. I almost involuntarily, when I saw the head, pointed to it, and exclaimed—

"There is your prototype in your family, Miss Northcott."

"Do you think so?" she said. "I am afraid you are paying me a very bad compliment. Uncle Anthony was always considered the black sheep of the family."

"Indeed," I answered; "my remark was an unfortunate one, then."

"Oh, don't mind that," she said; "I always thought myself that he was worth all of them put together. He was an officer in the Forty-first Regiment, and he was killed in action during the Persian War—so he died nobly, at any rate."

"That's the sort of death I should like to die," said Cowles, his dark eyes flashing, as they would when he was excited; "I often wish I had taken to my father's profession instead of this vile pill-compounding drudgery."

"Come, Jack, you are not going to die any sort of death yet," she said, tenderly taking his hand in hers.

I could not understand the woman. There was such an extraordinary mixture of masculine decision and womanly tenderness about her, with the consciousness of something all her own in the background, that she fairly puzzled me. I hardly knew, therefore, how to answer Cowles when, as we walked down the street together, he asked the comprehensive question—

"Well, what do you think of her?"

"I think she is wonderfully beautiful," I answered guardedly.

"That, of course," he replied irritably. "You knew that before you came!"

"I think she is very clever too," I remarked.

Barrington Cowles walked on for some time, and then he suddenly turned on me with the strange question—

"Do you think she is cruel? Do you think she is the sort of girl who would take a pleasure in inflicting pain?"

"Well, really," I answered, "I have hardly had time to form an opinion."

We then walked on for some time in silence.

"She is an old fool," at length muttered Cowles. "She is mad."

"Who is?" I asked.

"Why, that old woman—that aunt of Kate's—Mrs. Merton, or whatever her name is."

Then I knew that my poor colourless friend had been speaking to Cowles, but he never said anything more as to the nature of her communication.

My companion went to bed early that night, and I sat up a long time by the fire, thinking over all that I had seen and heard. I felt that there was some mystery about the girl—some dark fatality so strange as to defy conjecture. I thought of Prescott's interview with her before their marriage, and the fatal termination of it. I coupled it with poor drunken Reeves' plaintive cry, "Why did she not tell me sooner?" and with the other words he had spoken. Then my mind ran over Mrs. Merton's warning to me, Cowles' reference to her, and even the episode of the whip and the cringing dog.

The whole effect of my recollections was unpleasant to a degree, and yet there was no tangible charge which I could bring against the woman. It would be worse than useless to attempt to warn my friend until I had definitely made up my mind what I was to warn him against. He would treat any charge against her with scorn. What could I do? How could I get at some tangible conclusion as to her character and antecedents? No one in Edinburgh knew them except as recent acquaintances. She was an orphan, and as far as I knew she had never disclosed where her former home had been. Suddenly an idea struck me. Among my father's friends there was a Colonel Joyce, who had served a long time in India upon the staff, and who would be likely to know most of the officers who had been out there since the Mutiny. I sat down at once, and, having trimmed the lamp, proceeded to write a letter to the Colonel. I told him that I was very curious to gain some particulars about a certain Captain Northcott, who had served in the Forty-first Foot, and who had fallen in the Persian War. I described the man as well as I could from my recollection of the daguerreotype, and then, having directed the letter, posted it that very night, after which, feeling that I had done all that could be done, I retired to bed, with a mind too anxious to allow me to sleep.

Part II.

I got an answer from Leicester, where the Colonel resided, within two days. I have it before me as I write, and copy it verbatim.

"DEAR BOB," it said, "I remember the man well. I was with him at Calcutta, and afterwards at Hyderabad. He was a curious, solitary sort of mortal; but a gallant soldier enough, for he distinguished himself at Sobraon, and was wounded, if I remember right. He was not popular in his corps—they said he was a pitiless, cold-blooded fellow, with no geniality in him. There was a rumour, too, that he was a devil-worshipper, or something of that sort, and also that he had the evil eye, which, of course, was all nonsense. He had some strange theories, I remember, about the power of the human will and the effects of mind upon matter.

"How are you getting on with your medical studies? Never forget, my boy, that your father's son has every claim upon me, and that if I can serve you in any way I am always at your command.—Ever affectionately yours,

"EDWARD JOYCE.

"P.S.—By the way, Northcott did not fall in action. He was killed after peace was declared in a crazy attempt to get some of the eternal fire from the sun-worshippers' temple. There was considerable mystery about his death."

I read this epistle over several times—at first with a feeling of satisfaction, and then with one of disappointment. I had come on some curious information, and yet hardly what I wanted. He was an eccentric man, a devil-worshipper, and rumoured to have the power of the evil eye. I could believe the young lady's eyes, when endowed with that cold, grey shimmer which I had noticed in them once or twice, to be capable of any evil which human eye ever wrought; but still the superstition was an effete one. Was there not more meaning in that sentence which followed—"He had theories of the power of the human will and of the effect of mind upon matter"? I remember having once read a quaint treatise, which I had imagined to be mere charlatanism at the time, of the power of certain human minds, and of effects produced by them at a distance. Was Miss Northcott endowed with some exceptional power of the sort? The idea grew upon me, and very shortly I had evidence which convinced me of the truth of the supposition.

It happened that at the very time when my mind was dwelling upon this subject, I saw a notice in the paper that our town was to be visited by Dr. Messinger, the well-known medium and mesmerist. Messinger was a man whose performance, such as it was, had been again and again pronounced to be genuine by competent judges. He was far above trickery, and had the reputation of being the soundest living authority upon the strange pseudo-sciences of animal magnetism and electro-biology. Determined, therefore, to see what the human will could do, even against all the disadvantages of glaring footlights and a public platform, I took a ticket for the first night of the performance, and went with several student friends.

We had secured one of the side boxes, and did not arrive until after the performance had begun. I had hardly taken my seat before I recognised Barrington Cowles, with his *fiancée* and old Mrs. Merton, sitting in the third or fourth row of the stalls. They caught sight of me at almost the same moment, and we bowed to each other. The first portion of the lecture was somewhat commonplace, the lecturer giving tricks of pure legerdemain, with one or two manifestations of mesmerism, performed upon a subject whom he had brought with him. He gave us an exhibition of clairvoyance too, throwing his subject into a trance, and then demanding particulars as to the movements of absent friends, and the whereabouts of hidden objects all of which appeared to be answered satisfactorily. I had seen all this before, however. What I wanted to see now was the effect of the lecturer's will when exerted upon some independent member of the audience.

He came round to that as the concluding exhibition in his performance. "I have shown you," he said, "that a mesmerised subject is entirely dominated by the will of the mesmeriser. He loses all power of volition, and his very thoughts are such as are suggested to him by the master-mind. The same end may be attained without any preliminary process. A strong will can, simply by virtue of its strength, take possession of a weaker one, even at a distance, and can regulate the impulses and the actions of the owner of it. If there was one man in the world who had a very much more highly-developed will than any of the rest of the human family, there is no reason why he should not be able to rule over them all, and to reduce his fellow-creatures to the condition of automatons. Happily there is such a dead level of mental power, or rather of mental weakness, among us that such a catastrophe is not likely to occur; but still within our small compass there are variations which produce surprising effects. I shall now single out one of the audience, and endeavour 'by the mere power of will' to compel him to come upon the platform, and do and say what I wish. Let me assure you that there is no collusion, and that the subject whom I may select is at perfect liberty to resent to the uttermost any impulse which I may communicate to him."

With these words the lecturer came to the front of the platform, and glanced over the first few rows of the stalls. No doubt Cowles' dark skin and bright eyes marked him out as a man of a highly nervous temperament, for the mesmerist picked him out in a moment, and fixed his eyes upon him. I saw my friend give a start of surprise, and then settle down in his chair, as if to express his determination not to yield to the influence of the operator. Messinger was not a man whose head denoted any great brain-power, but his gaze was singularly intense and penetrating. Under the influence of it Cowles made one or two spasmodic motions of his hands, as if to grasp the sides of his seat, and then half rose, but only to sink down again, though with an evident effort. I was watching the scene with intense interest, when I happened to catch a glimpse of Miss Northcott's face. She was sitting with her eyes fixed intently upon the mesmerist, and with such an expression of concentrated power upon her features as I have never seen on any other human countenance. Her jaw was firmly set, her lips compressed, and her face as hard as if it were a beautiful sculpture cut out of the whitest marble. Her eyebrows were drawn down, however, and from beneath them her grey eyes seemed to sparkle and gleam with a cold light.

I looked at Cowles again, expecting every moment to see him rise and obey the mesmerist's wishes, when there came from the platform a short, gasping cry as of a man utterly worn out and prostrated by a prolonged struggle. Messinger was leaning against the table, his hand to his forehead, and the perspiration pouring down his face. "I won't go on," he cried, addressing the audience. "There is a stronger will than mine acting against me. You must excuse me for to-night." The man was evidently ill, and utterly unable to proceed, so the curtain was lowered, and the audience dispersed, with many comments upon the lecturer's sudden indisposition.

I waited outside the hall until my friend and the ladies came out. Cowles was laughing over his recent experience.

"He didn't succeed with me, Bob," he cried triumphantly, as he shook my hand. "I think he caught a Tartar that time."

"Yes," said Miss Northcott, "I think that Jack ought to be very proud of his strength of mind; don't you! Mr. Armitage?"

"It took me all my time, though," my friend said seriously. "You can't conceive what a strange feeling I had once or twice. All the strength seemed to have gone out of me—especially just before he collapsed himself."

I walked round with Cowles in order to see the ladies home. He walked in front with Mrs. Merton, and I found myself behind with the young lady. For a minute or so I walked beside her without making any remark, and then I suddenly blurted out, in a manner which must have seemed somewhat brusque to her—

"You did that, Miss Northcott."

"Did what?" she asked sharply.

"Why, mesmerised the mesmeriser—I suppose that is the best way of describing the transaction."

"What a strange idea!" she said, laughing. "You give me credit for a strong will then?"

"Yes," I said. "For a dangerously strong one."

"Why dangerous?" she asked, in a tone of surprise.

"I think," I answered, "that any will which can exercise such power is dangerous—for there is always a chance of its being turned to bad uses."

"You would make me out a very dreadful individual, Mr. Armitage," she said; and then looking up suddenly in my face—"You have never liked me. You are suspicious of me and distrust me, though I have never given you cause."

The accusation was so sudden and so true that I was unable to find any reply to it. She paused for a moment, and then said in a voice which was hard and cold—

"Don't let your prejudice lead you to interfere with me, however, or say anything to your friend, Mr. Cowles, which might lead to a difference between us. You would find that to be very bad policy."

There was something in the way she spoke which gave an indescribable air of a threat to these few words.

"I have no power," I said, "to interfere with your plans for the future. I cannot help, however, from what I have seen and heard, having fears for my friend."

"Fears!" she repeated scornfully. "Pray what have you seen and heard. Something from Mr. Reeves, perhaps—I believe he is another of your friends?"

"He never mentioned your name to me," I answered, truthfully enough. "You will be sorry to hear that he is dying." As I said it we passed by a lighted window, and I glanced down to see what effect my words had upon her. She was laughing—there was no doubt of it; she was laughing quietly to herself. I could see merriment in every feature of her face. I feared and mistrusted the woman from that moment more than ever.

We said little more that night. When we parted she gave me a quick, warning glance, as if to remind me of what she had said about the danger of interference. Her cautions would have made little difference to me could I have seen my way to benefiting Barrington Cowles by anything which I might say. But what could I say? I might say that her former suitors had been unfortunate. I might say that I believed her to be a cruel-hearted woman. I might say that I considered her to possess wonderful, and almost preternatural powers. What impression would any of these accusations make upon an ardent lover—a man with my friend's enthusiastic temperament? I felt that it would be useless to advance them, so I was silent.

And now I come to the beginning of the end. Hitherto much has been surmise and inference and hearsay. It is my painful task to relate now, as dispassionately and as accurately as I can, what actually occurred under my own notice, and to reduce to writing the events which preceded the death of my friend.

Towards the end of the winter Cowles remarked to me that he intended to marry Miss Northcott as soon as possible—probably some time in the spring. He was, as I have already remarked, fairly well off, and the young lady had some money of her own, so that there was no pecuniary reason for a long engagement. "We are going to take a little house out at Corstorphine," he said, "and we hope to see your face at our table, Bob, as often as you can possibly come." I thanked him, and tried to shake off my apprehensions, and persuade myself that all would yet be well.

It was about three weeks before the time fixed for the marriage, that Cowles remarked to me one evening that he feared he would be late that night. "I have had a note from Kate," he said, "asking me to call about eleven o'clock to-night, which seems rather a late hour, but perhaps she wants to talk over something quietly after old Mrs. Merton retires."

It was not until after my friend's departure that I suddenly recollected the mysterious interview which I had been told of as preceding the suicide of young Prescott. Then I thought of the ravings of poor Reeves, rendered more tragic by the fact that I had heard that very day of his death. What was the meaning of it all? Had this woman some baleful secret to disclose which must be known before her marriage? Was it some reason which forbade her to marry? Or was it some reason which forbade others to marry her? I felt so uneasy that I would have followed Cowles, even at the risk of offending him, and endeavoured to dissuade him from keeping his appointment, but a glance at the clock showed me that I was too late.

I was determined to wait up for his return, so I piled some coals upon the fire and took down a novel from the shelf. My thoughts proved more interesting than the book, however, and I threw it on one side. An indefinable feeling of anxiety and depression weighed upon me. Twelve o'clock came, and then half-past, without any sign of my friend. It was nearly one when I heard a step in the street outside, and then a knocking at the door. I was surprised, as I knew that my friend always carried a key—however, I hurried down and undid the latch. As the door flew open I knew in a moment that my worst apprehensions had been fulfilled. Barrington Cowles was leaning against the railings outside with his face sunk upon his breast, and his whole attitude expressive of the most intense despondency.

As he passed in he gave a stagger, and would have fallen had I not thrown my left arm around him. Supporting him with this, and holding the lamp in my other hand, I led him slowly upstairs into our sitting-room. He sank down upon the sofa without a word. Now that I could get a good view of him, I was horrified to see the change which had come over him. His face was deadly pale, and his very lips were bloodless. His cheeks and forehead were clammy, his eyes glazed, and his whole expression altered. He looked like a man who had gone through some terrible ordeal, and was thoroughly unnerved.

"My dear fellow, what is the matter?" I asked, breaking the silence. "Nothing amiss, I trust? Are you unwell?"

"Brandy!" he gasped. "Give me some brandy!"

I took out the decanter, and was about to help him, when he snatched it from me with a trembling hand, and poured out nearly half a tumbler of the spirit. He was usually a most abstemious man, but he took this off at a gulp without adding any water to it. It seemed to do him good, for the colour began to come back to his face, and he leaned upon his elbow.

"My engagement is off, Bob," he said, trying to speak calmly, but with a tremor in his voice which he could not conceal. "It is all over."

"Cheer up!" I answered, trying to encourage him. "Don't get down on your luck. How was it? What was it all about?"

"About?" he groaned, covering his face with his hands. "If I did tell you, Bob, you would not believe it. It is too dreadful—too horrible—unutterably awful and incredible! O Kate, Kate!" and he rocked himself to and fro in his grief; "I pictured you an angel and I find you a—"

"A what?" I asked, for he had paused.

He looked at me with a vacant stare, and then suddenly burst out, waving his arms: "A fiend!" he cried. "A ghoul from the pit! A vampire soul behind a lovely face! Now, God forgive me!" he went on in a lower tone, turning his face to the wall; "I have said more than I should. I have loved her too much to speak of her as she is. I love her too much now."

He lay still for some time, and I had hoped that the brandy had had the effect of sending him to sleep, when he suddenly turned his face towards me.

"Did you ever read of wehr-wolves?" he asked.

I answered that I had.

"There is a story," he said thoughtfully, "in one of Marryat's books, about a beautiful woman who took the form of a wolf at night and devoured her own children. I wonder what put that idea into Marryat's head?"

He pondered for some minutes, and then he cried out for some more brandy. There was a small bottle of laudanum upon the table, and I managed, by insisting upon helping him myself, to mix about half a drachm with the spirits. He drank it off, and sank his head once more upon the pillow. "Anything better than that," he groaned. "Death is better than that. Crime and cruelty; cruelty and crime. Anything is better than that," and so on, with the monotonous refrain, until at last the words became indistinct, his eyelids closed over his weary eyes, and he sank into a profound slumber. I carried him into his bedroom without arousing him; and making a couch for myself out of the chairs, I remained by his side all night.

In the morning Barrington Cowles was in a high fever. For weeks he lingered between life and death. The highest medical skill of Edinburgh was called in, and his vigorous constitution slowly got the better of his disease. I nursed him during this anxious time; but through all his wild delirium and ravings he never let a word escape him which explained the mystery connected with Miss Northcott. Sometimes he spoke of her in the tenderest words and most loving voice. At others he screamed out that she was a fiend, and stretched out his arms, as if to keep her off. Several times he cried that he would not sell his soul for a beautiful face, and then he would moan in a most piteous voice, "But I love her—I love her for all that; I shall never cease to love her."

When he came to himself he was an altered man. His severe illness had emaciated him greatly, but his dark eyes had lost none of their brightness. They shone out with startling brilliancy from under his dark, overhanging brows. His manner was eccentric and variable—sometimes irritable, sometimes recklessly mirthful, but never natural. He would glance about him in a strange, suspicious manner, like one who feared something, and yet hardly knew what it was he dreaded. He never mentioned Miss Northcott's name—never until that fatal evening of which I have now to speak.

In an endeavour to break the current of his thoughts by frequent change of scene, I travelled with him through the highlands of Scotland, and afterwards down the east coast. In one of these peregrinations of ours we visited the Isle of May, an island near the mouth of the Firth of Forth, which, except in the tourist season, is singularly barren and desolate. Beyond the keeper of the lighthouse there are only one or two families of poor fisher-folk, who sustain a precarious existence by their nets, and by the capture of cormorants and solan geese. This grim spot seemed to have such a fascination for Cowles that we engaged a room in one of the fishermen's huts, with the intention of passing a week or two there. I found it very dull, but the loneliness appeared to be a relief to my friend's mind. He lost the look of apprehension which had become habitual to him, and became something like his old self. He would wander round the island all day, looking down from the summit of the great cliffs which gird it round, and watching the long green waves as they came booming in and burst in a shower of spray over the rocks beneath.

One night—I think it was our third or fourth on the island—Barrington Cowles and I went outside the cottage before retiring to rest, to enjoy a little fresh air, for our room was small, and the rough lamp caused an unpleasant odour. How well I remember every little circumstance in connection with that night! It promised to be tempestuous, for the clouds were piling up in the north-west, and the dark wrack was drifting across the face of the moon, throwing alternate belts of light and shade upon the rugged surface of the island and the restless sea beyond.

We were standing talking close by the door of the cottage, and I was thinking to myself that my friend was more cheerful than he had been since his illness, when he gave a sudden, sharp cry, and looking round at him I saw, by the light of the moon, an expression of unutterable horror come over his features. His eyes became fixed and staring, as if riveted upon some approaching object, and he extended his long thin forefinger, which quivered as he pointed.

"Look there!" he cried. "It is she! It is she! You see her there coming down the side of the brae." He gripped me convulsively by the wrist as he spoke. "There she is, coming towards us!"

"Who?" I cried, straining my eyes into the darkness.

"She—Kate—Kate Northcott!" he screamed. "She has come for me. Hold me fast, old friend. Don't let me go!"

"Hold up, old man," I said, clapping him on the shoulder. "Pull yourself together; you are dreaming; there is nothing to fear."

"She is gone!" he cried, with a gasp of relief. "No, by heaven! there she is again, and nearer—coming nearer. She told me she would come for me, and she keeps her word."

"Come into the house," I said. His hand, as I grasped it, was as cold as ice.

"Ah, I knew it!" he shouted. "There she is, waving her arms. She is beckoning to me. It is the signal. I must go. I am coming, Kate; I am coming!"

I threw my arms around him, but he burst from me with superhuman strength, and dashed into the darkness of the night. I followed him, calling to him to stop, but he ran the more swiftly. When the moon shone out between the clouds I could catch a glimpse of his dark figure, running rapidly in a straight line, as if to reach some definite goal. It may have been imagination, but it seemed to me that in the flickering light I could distinguish a vague something in front of him— a shimmering form which eluded his grasp and led him onwards. I saw his outlines stand out hard against the sky behind him as he surmounted the brow of a little hill, then he disappeared, and that was the last ever seen by mortal eye of Barrington Cowles.

The fishermen and I walked round the island all that night with lanterns, and examined every nook and corner without seeing a trace of my poor lost friend. The direction in which he had been running terminated in a rugged line of jagged cliffs overhanging the sea. At one place here the edge was somewhat crumbled, and there appeared marks upon the turf which might have been left by human feet. We lay upon our faces at this spot, and peered with our lanterns over the edge, looking down on the boiling surge two hundred feet below. As we lay there, suddenly, above the beating of the waves and the howling of the wind, there rose a strange wild screech from the abyss below. The fishermen—a naturally superstitious race—averred that it was the sound of a woman's laughter, and I could hardly persuade them to continue the search. For my own part I think it may have been the cry of some sea-fowl startled from its nest by the flash of the lantern. However that may be, I never wish to hear such a sound again.

And now I have come to the end of the painful duty which I have undertaken. I have told as plainly and as accurately as I could the story of the death of John Barrington Cowles, and the train of events which preceded it. I am aware that to others the sad episode seemed commonplace enough. Here is the prosaic account which appeared in the Scotsman a couple of days afterwards:—

"*Sad Occurrence on the Isle of May.*—The Isle of May has been the scene of a sad disaster. Mr. John Barrington Cowles, a gentleman well known in University circles as a most distinguished student, and the present holder of the Neil Arnott prize for physics, has been recruiting his health in this quiet retreat. The night before last he suddenly left his friend, Mr. Robert Armitage, and he has not since been heard of. It is almost certain that he has met his death by falling over the cliffs which surround the island. Mr. Cowles' health has been failing for some time, partly from over study and partly from worry connected with family affairs. By his death the University loses one of her most promising alumni."

I have nothing more to add to my statement. I have unburdened my mind of all that I know. I can well conceive that many, after weighing all that I have said, will see no ground for an accusation against Miss Northcott. They will say that, because a man of a naturally excitable disposition says and does wild things, and even eventually commits self-murder after a sudden and heavy disappointment, there is no reason why vague charges should be advanced against a young lady. To this, I answer that they are welcome to their opinion. For my own part, I ascribe the death of William Prescott, of Archibald Reeves, and of John Barrington Cowles to this woman with as much confidence as if I had seen her drive a dagger into their hearts.

You ask me, no doubt, what my own theory is which will explain all these strange facts. I have none, or, at best, a dim and vague one. That Miss Northcott possessed extraordinary powers over the minds, and through the minds over the bodies, of others, I am convinced, as well as that her instincts were to use this power for base and cruel purposes. That some even more fiendish and terrible phase of character lay behind this—some horrible trait which it was necessary for her to reveal before marriage—is to be inferred from the experience of her three lovers, while the dreadful nature of the mystery thus revealed can only be surmised from the fact that the very mention of it drove from her those who had loved her so passionately. Their subsequent fate was, in my opinion, the result of her vindictive remembrance of their desertion of her, and that they were forewarned of it at the time was shown by the words of both Reeves and Cowles. Above this, I can say nothing. I lay the facts soberly before the public as they came under my notice. I have never seen Miss Northcott since, nor do I wish to do so. If by the words I have written I can save any one human being from the snare of those bright eyes and that beautiful face, then I can lay down my pen with the assurance that my poor friend has not died altogether in vain.

An Apt Pupil
A Short Story

When people heard the name of Professor Draycott they pictured to themselves a man past middle life, and they were surprised to find, on meeting the gentleman, that he was very little over thirty, and looked younger than that. He was indeed a young man to have attained such a position as that which he occupied, but that naturally was all the more to his credit.

Draycott had obtained during the past year or two a reputation for curing complaints and diseases by means of hypnotism. He was a firm believer in that science and occasionally delivered lectures on the subject. He had been invited to Whitelock, where mesmerism was having a vogue, to deliver a course of four lectures in the public hall, and he had managed to sandwich this course between two other courses which he was to deliver in different parts of the country. He was exceedingly pleased to have the opportunity of going to Whitelock, as that city was noted as a centre of intelligence, and he prophesied that hypnotism would make a great stride in public favor if he could succeed in making a hit there.

Three of the lectures had been given and he was now preparing to deliver the fourth. It was Saturday, and it would be necessary for him to leave Whitelock on Sunday afternoon in order to reach Malton, where he was to deliver another course, early on Monday.

In his concluding lecture, Professor Draycott always endeavored to impress upon his audience a fact concerning which he himself had not the slightest doubt: this was that everybody possessed the power of hypnotism to a greater or less extent.

He was always enthusiastic about his subject and spoke in a tone that in many cases carried conviction with it, but on this occasion, having due regard to the important city in which he was endeavoring to propagate the science, he was actually preparing a short speech on this particular point in order that every word should tell.

The hall was a large one, but it was simply crowded on that Saturday evening. The professor was delighted; it proved how great was the interest excited on the previous evenings, and augured well for the future of hypnotism.

Draycott warmed to his work as he had never done before; he explained the theory and he gave practical examples of his power on various members of the audience who honored him by stepping up to the platform. Then came the final remarks.

With an earnestness that abundantly demonstrated his convictions, Professor Draycott told the audience that every one of them had this strange power latent within his or her being; that if it were developed it would enable each one to do much for the alleviation of suffering and the cure of disease in his own circle; and that every one was under the moral obligation to cultivate the gift for the benefit of mankind. There were some, he told his hearers, who disputed his assertion, but it was perfectly true and they would find it so if they made up their minds to try.

It was late that night before the professor could woo sleep, his ears still rang with the plaudits of the audience at the conclusion of what had been a remarkable seance, and he was so elated with his success that it was a wonder he was able to sleep at all. But when unconsciousness did fall upon him, it lasted for many hours—for he was thoroughly exhausted with his efforts—and he slept until nine o'clock on the Sunday morning.

After breakfast he went for a long walk, returning to his hotel for luncheon at one o'clock. That repast finished, he set to work leisurely to pack his bag for his journey.

The course of lectures had been arranged on a somewhat peculiar basis so far as payment was concerned. He usually had his fee paid in advance, but as the proprietors of the hall at Whitelock had had some doubt as to the success of the venture the professor had agreed to accept a percentage of the money received for admission. This was paid to him at the close of the lecture on Saturday evening, and in cash.

The result had been far better than any one had anticipated, and he found himself with over a hundred pounds in notes and coin as his share of the proceeds. The notes he placed in his pocket book, while the gold and silver—being heavy—he stowed away in his bag.

He had finished packing his bag and was looking round to see if he had forgotten anything, when a porter knocked at the door and handed him a card. It bore the name of Miss Dora Callan.

"The lady says she would like to see you on a very urgent matter," said the porter, deferentially.

"But I do not know this lady," returned Draycott, surveying the card with a perplexed air. "Are you sure she mentioned my name?"

"Yes, sir, she said I was to give it to Professor Draycott, the hypnotist," replied the man.

"Very well, I will come down," said Draycott. And two minutes later he found himself bowing to a remarkably pretty young lady.

"You wish to see me on some urgent matter, I understand?" asked Draycott, when they were both seated. "We are, of course, strangers, and I am wondering—"

"Oh yes, I know you must be!" She spoke with some confusion, which seemed to add to her beauty. I know it must seem—very—rude of me to disturb you, but I thought you could help me to cure some one."

She was very timid, but the professor rather liked that; he had never given much thought to the opposite sex, except to think that some of its members were very bold and forward, and this pretty face rendered more bewitching by the shyness of its owner, was causing him to experience quite a new feeling.

"To cure somebody?" inquired Draycott overcoming the tendency to forget science. "I shall be glad to assist you if it lies in my power. Let me know exactly what you mean."

The young lady explained in a rather somewhat hesitating manner, as though she were still afraid that the great man might resent the intrusion, that her mother had been suffering for some time from ill-defined pains which it had been impossible up to the present to dissipate; that during the past week her sufferings had increased considerably, and the medical man who attended her had been unable to alleviate them. The young lady had been present at the lecture on the preceding evening, and had heard the professor's remarks about the power of hypnotism being latent in every one. This had suggested to her that she might be able to do something for her mother, if she could obtain information concerning the methods to be employed. How was she to go to work in order to exercise the power which, according to Draycott, she possessed. Once more, she reminded the hypnotist of his remarks on that point, and concluded with a timid observation that perhaps he was not quite sure that every one had the power.

Draycott felt just a little bit nettled at the idea of any doubt being cast upon his statement; he was also strangely stirred by the apparent timidity and the beauty of the young woman who sat facing him; and he was anxious both to prove that he was correct, and do something to relieve the mother from pain. By helping the mother he would be doing a service to the young lady also.

"I am quite sure," he observed, gently, yet firmly, "that you possess the power to a greater degree than many other persons. Your eyes shine with much brilliancy, and although you are somewhat timid at times, it is my belief that you are gifted with considerable will power."

Unconsciously, for the professor was not quite aware of what he was saying, he had spoken the truth; a close observation of the young woman's eyes revealed great strength of character. "This is how you proceed."

Draycott drew his chair a little nearer to hers, looked at her fixedly, and began to make passes with his hand.

"You fix your eyes full upon those of the person whom you intend to hypnotize," he continued. "Then you make a few movements with your hands, just as I am doing, in order to confuse them. It is strange how effective these few movements are upon the minds of the ordinary individual. And the combined action upon the mind of these movements and the glare of the eye is remarkable, even in the case of a person who may claim to be fairly strong-minded. Only when a person deliberately makes up his mind that he will not be mesmerised is the action of these two methods rendered null; on the other hand, if the patient is willing or unconscious of what is about to be done, the result is certain."

"Oh, thank you so much!" said Miss Callan, in a tone that was full of gratitude, "I feel sure that I shall be able to send my mother off. Your lucid explanation has quite cleared away the doubts I entertained. Now let me see. Had I not better go through the movements here, so that you can see whether I do them correctly? But perhaps I am taking up too much of your time. Oh, dear! I have been here quite a long time already, and I am afraid that I have been very rude in thus bothering you."

"Not at all!" Draycott hastened to assure her, and he did it with a warmth that would have surprised all his scientific friends. His face was animated, though there was a slight flush on his cheeks and in appearance he was very different from the cool, studious-looking man of science who posed as the apostle of hypnotism. "This has been a very pleasant experience for me—very pleasant indeed! And I am charmed to have the opportunity of propagating the science and conferring immediate benefit upon a human being at the same time. By all means make the experiment, and I will correct you if you are wrong."

Draycott shifted his chair still a little nearer to Miss Callan and lay back with an air of great contentment, as though he were a patient willing to be operated upon. This was decidedly a pleasant experience; he had never gone through anything like it before, and he caught himself wondering dreamily whether a bachelor's life was really the blessed condition which he had hitherto imagined it. Just imagine what it must be to have a partner for life similar to the girl who was now gazing at him with those glorious eyes. How pretty she looked! And how deftly she moved those dainty little hands in front of his face! He felt half tempted to grasp them and ask her to be his wife. That would have been rather sudden, but Draycott believed in quick decisions.

He tried to tell her that she was performing her task splendidly, but the words would not come; his eyes were kept fixed by the glare of hers—yes, it was really a glare. In a dazed manner he recognized that she was exercising the mesmeric influence over him, and he felt pleased; he would tell her afterwards how the gleam from her eyes had fascinated him, how the pretty face with its slightly flushed cheeks had enchanted him; how splendidly she had understood what he had explained to her about the movements, and all the rest of it.

"Now," said Miss Dora Callan, two minutes later, "I think we can proceed to business. How much money did you get out of your lectures?"

"Just over a hundred pounds," replied the hypnotized professor.

"Ah! I thought it would have been a little more than that," continued Miss Callan, "and where is that money?"

"The notes are in my pocket-book, but the gold and silver are in my bag," came from the lips of Draycott.

"It was a rather foolish arrangement about the matter of payment," resumed Miss Callan, pleasantly. "It got into the papers, you see, and it made some people say that if you were so devoted to science you ought not to have worried about such trifles as fees. Kindly give me your pocket-book."

Draycott did as he was bid, and Miss Callan quietly extracted the notes and handed the pocket-book back to its owner.

"Now I will trouble you to go upstairs and fetch your bag. It would not be quite the proper thing or I would prefer to accompany you or even to get the bag myself. But you had better bring it down into this cosy little reception room, which, fortunately, we have entirely to ourselves."

Professor Draycott left the room without the least show of resistance, and returned in due course with his bag. Miss Callan quietly locked the door on the inside and then requested the professor to find the money, and hand it to her. The hypnotized man did as he was told.

"Thank you," Miss Callan smiled pleasantly as she took five pounds from the bag containing the gold and let them fall among the professor's papers and clothing in his travelling bag.

"You will want some money for your journey. I understand that you leave by the 5:30 train this afternoon?"

Draycott nodded assent.

"Very well. I will write a short note which will explain to you what has happened, otherwise you may be inclined to blame the hotel authorities for the loss of your money when you wake up."

She took up a pen and wrote a few lines rapidly on one of the sheets of paper that lay on the table. When she had finished she sealed it in an envelope and addressed it to Professor Draycott.

"Take this and go back to your room, where you are to remain in this condition until five o'clock. You will just have time to catch your train and I shall be out of your reach."

With a smile of intense satisfaction and a pretty bow Miss Callan turned her back on Draycott, unlocked the door and walked out.

When Professor Draycott came to his senses at five o'clock, he gazed in bewilderment at the envelope which he still held. Rising from his chair, he looked about him in an endeavor to explain to himself how it was that he felt so confused.

"I must have been asleep." he murmured. "How did this letter come here and who brought it?"

The simplest way to solve the mystery was to open the letter, and, as a man of science, Draycott recognized the fact. He cut the envelope and began to read.

The note told him what had happened on that eventful afternoon, and it further explained that the writer, being sadly in want of money, had hit upon the bold idea of hypnotizing the professor himself and relieving him of the proceeds of his lectures.

Fortune and a pretty face had enabled her to carry out her plan successfully.

"You ought to be greatly pleased," the writer concluded, "at this proof of the accuracy of your views, and at having so apt a pupil. I do not know whether we shall ever meet again—probably not—but neither of us is likely to forget the experience of this afternoon. It was pleasant to me, and I am convinced that you found it equally agreeable—at least, at the beginning.

Draycott examined his pocket-book then his bag. It was perfectly true, he had been robbed by a pretty and daring female thief; he was too much of a scientist to spend useless time in giving vent to his vexation and indignation; he was convinced that he had been hypnotized by the young woman who had called upon him, and that the hotel people were not to blame for an act of dishonesty on the part of an employee. Then he suddenly remembered his train.

The thoughts of the learned man were not agreeable ones as he travelled toward the town where he was to stay that night, and from which he would take an early morning train to Malton, but it is impossible to conjecture what they would have been had he known that Miss Callan, much disguised, was a passenger in the train. When he alighted at his destination he lingered on the platform and watched the train as it left the station to continue its journey. He was just turning away as the last car passed him, when a woman's voice uttered the words: "Good-night, Professor Draycott."

He started and stared. The voice was familiar and the mocking tone was significant. Then it came to him—it was his afternoon visitor.

The train was gone. He might have made an attempt to catch her, but he really had very little positive proof to convince a judge and jury that she had taken the money, and just think of the ridicule that would be heaped upon him for having allowed himself to be caught in that way.

Professor Draycott's friends have remarked that he has ceased to allude in his lectures a fact which he formerly emphasized, namely, that every human being possesses the power of hypnotism.

Philip Darrell's Wife

By B.L. Farjeon

The unexpected news that my friend, Philip Darrell, was married gave me no pleasure. I regarded it, indeed, as a kind of treachery. We had agreed never to marry, and had planned our annual summer holiday in the Tyrol, which, of course, must now be abandoned. The secrecy of the proceedings annoyed me, and this secrecy was kept up even in the affectionate letter in which he announced the event. He married in Rouen, where he had not a friend. "I have the handsomest woman in Europe for a wife," he wrote. "I enclose her portrait. In a couple of months we shall be in London."

Mrs. Philip Darrell was a magnificent creature, if her portrait told a true tale. Dark, lustrous eyes, with noble eyebrows and eyelashes, large mouth and nose, rather sensuous and inviting lips, low forehead, and a wealth of black hair. Her age I judged to be about thirty-five, which would make her seven years older than Philip. A discomforting discrepancy.

The features in Mrs. Darrell's face which principally attracted me were her eyes. After the first examination of the portrait my eyes wandered involuntarily to hers, and a dreamy sensation stole over me to which I insensibly yielded. When I became conscious of this fascination, I wrested my attention from the picture, and presently I found myself wandering again to those compelling orbs, which seemed, as it were, to hold me charmed. I put the portrait hastily away in a drawer; it was not pleasant to feel that it exercised over me a mysterious power, for which I could find no intelligent reason. In the middle of the night I awoke and saw Mrs. Darrell's eyes shining upon me in the dark. Why should I light a candle, rise from my bed, take out the picture, and gaze upon it with a perturbed spirit, seeing only the lustrous eyes which followed every remonstrant movement of my head? My folly made me angry, and I thrust the portrait back in the drawer beneath a mass of papers. There it remained for a week, by which time I had recovered my composure, and felt once more master of myself.

At the end of this week there came to dine with me two gentlemen who were also on terms of friendly intimacy with Philip—Dr. Lessing, a celebrated specialist in mental diseases, and Mr. Storey, manager of an important life assurance company. The conversation turned upon Philip, and learning that they had not heard of his marriage I mentioned that I had a portrait of the bride, and produced it. Dr. Lessing was the first to examine it, and I observed that he devoted a considerable time to a study of the picture. He then passed it over to Mr. Storey, who gave utterance to a startled exclamation.

"If I am not mistaken," he said, "I know the lady."

"Ah," I exclaimed, with a feeling of satisfaction, "that is capital. You can tell us something about her. What is your opinion doctor?"

"Most men would consider her handsome," was the reply. "Such a face on the stage would be very attractive. I should like to see her play Lucretia Borgia. Observe the eyes of the portrait. It is not that they follow you whichever way you look—that is the case in many portraits—but that they exercise a fascination over you. There exists in them a haunting power."

"I have felt it," I said, greatly startled.

"And your mind has been disturbed—you have become gloomy, pessimistic. They haunt you, I repeat, and haunt you for evil."

"Wonderfully true."

"Nothing wonderful in it. I should advise you to avoid this woman."

"That I shall not do. When Darrell comes to London I shall court her society."

"Be on your guard. Unless my experiences and studies are at fault she possesses a strong mesmeric power, and as determined a will to give it effect. My judgement of Darrell leads me to the conclusion that he is not a strong-minded man; in which case his union with this woman can hardly be a happy one."

"You are condemning upon theoretical grounds," I said, and turned to Mr. Storey. "You, however, can give us facts."

"I side with Lessing," he said.

"Your facts, your facts!" I cried impatiently.

"They form a little story. Did Darrell tell you the name of the lady he has married?"

"No."

"Strange, is it not? The inference is that she pledged him to silence. I will supply the omission. Her name was Madame Van Loop."

"Madame! A widow?"

"Twice widowed. She is a Dutchwoman. Her first husband was a gentleman of the name of Kempden, and with him she lived four years. He died, and she afterwards married Mr. Van Loop."

"What did her first husband die of?" inquired Dr. Lessing.

"Of a rope. He hanged himself."

Dr. Lessing smiled gravely, and asked if Mr. Kempden was insured.

"There was an insurance on his life for £10,000, and there was a difficulty about it. Eventually the widow accepted a third of the sum. Mr. Kempden's fortune—not so large as she expected, I believe—was left unreservedly to her."

"A proof," I interposed, "that he loved her and had confidence in her."

"Shortly after her second marriage a proposal was made in our office for an insurance on the life of Henry Van Loop, for no less a sum than £20,000. It was a sound life; Mr. Van Loop had not an ailment. Nevertheless I declined it. Fortunately."

"How fortunately?"

"Her second husband died within two years of his marriage."

"What did Mr. Van Loop die of?" asked Dr. Lessing.

"Well, it was a curious coincidence. He, also, died of a rope. He hanged himself. He was rich, and she inherited everything; not a shilling was left to any of his blood relatives."

"You seem to be intimately acquainted with her history," I observed.

"When an important proposal is made to us and refused, our interest does not end there. We ascertain all possible particulars relating to the applicant."

"Were there any children?"

"None, by either marriage."

"Let us hope," said Dr. Lessing, "that Darrell's life is not insured."

"Is not this going too far," I remonstrated. "It is admitted that her two husbands committed suicide, and you are virtually proclaiming her a murderess."

"I made no accusations," said Dr. Lessing, "but you will admit that there is something peculiar in Mrs. Darrell's matrimonial career. In the course of my professional investigations I have met with many strange experiences, and I know for a certainty that crimes may be committed by suggestion, and that what looks like suicide may be actual murder."

"A startling theory."

"It is not theory; it is fact. Relatively, according to the strength of their will-power, human beings can influence one another for good or evil. Call it what you will, magnetism, mesmerism, hypnotism, we know that it exists, and it has to be reckoned with. An actor, by sheer force of earnestness and self-concentration, can move a multitude to tears or laughter. How much more potent is it when the full strength of the magnetic current is brought to bear upon a mind which has been prepared for the evil suggestion that leads him to commit murder or suicide? The guilt lies not at his door, but at the door of the person who exercised this influence over him. The law, however, as it stands, cannot touch the actual criminal" —I think it was my earnest gaze that caused him to break off suddenly and to say, "And now let us talk of something more agreeable."

We did so, but whatever we talked about my mind continued to dwell upon the subject we had dropped. I was glad when my guests took their leave, and I could give full play to my morbid imaginings. The portrait was on a side table, and a stronger power than my own compelled me to set it before me to gaze upon it, until my mind became enfeebled, and I was no longer master of myself. There are influences which, when a man yields to them, afford him pleasure, plunge him for a time into ecstatic delirium. The drunkard, the opium smoker, have periods of exultation; they are carried to the heights, they revel in delightful dreams, they are deliciously maddened by fancies and visions. But the effect produced upon me now was one of profound, hopeless depression. The salt was gone out of my days—there was nothing to live for. Light, beauty, the joy of living, were clothed in funeral garb. There was a grey, leaden sky, the wind sobbed, the trees swayed with mournful moans. Was there no escape from this universal misery? One, and only one—the grave!

At three o'clock in the morning I awoke, shivering. I had fallen asleep in my chair. Wine, spirits and fruit were on the table. The decanter nearest my hand contained brandy. Blindly, unthinkingly, I half filled a tumbler with liquor and drank it off. In a moment my depression took flight; courage, resolution, returned. I seized Mrs. Darrell's portrait, and tearing it to pieces flung it into the grate, in which the fire was still smouldering. Bending forward, I watched the strips of cardboard curl and twist like the writhings of serpents, until the picture was utterly destroyed. Even then my feverish fancy traced the fatal eyes in the white ashes. I drank more brandy, and went to bed.

Four months elapsed before Philip returned to London with his wife. In the meantime I had received three or four letters from him, written in high spirits; he was the happiest man in the world, his wife was an angel, and so on, and so on. His last letter, however, was written in a more despondent mood. He said his liver was out of order, in which respect I had a fellow feeling for him.

His arrival in London was announced by an invitation to dinner at the Langham, and to the Langham I went, tingling with curiosity. They gave me a cordial welcome. Mrs. Darrell was as beautiful as her portrait, and my conscience pricked me as I thought of the fate of the luckless picture. Her manners were gracious and pleasant, and when dinner was over, and we were at our claret, she referred quite openly to her being older than Philip.

"Confess now," she said, "that you were alarmed when you heard that Philip had married a woman older than himself."

"He did not tell me," I replied. "I was inclined to be angry with him for being so uncommunicative. Between such old friends as ourselves—"

She interrupted me. "There should be no secrets."

"I was about to say as much."

"O," she said vivaciously, "but everyone has secrets. Yourself, for instance. Have *you* not a skeleton in your cupboard? Dear me—those skeletons? Eh, Philip?" He nodded, gloomily it appeared to me. "Ah, well, don't let us talk of them. Shall I sing to you?"

She sang beautifully in French and Italian, and showed herself to be an accomplished woman.

"You remain in London, I hope," I said.

"Oh, yes; it is Philip's wish, and therefore mine. We shall take a furnished house for six months; that will give us time to look about us. We have packets of letters from house agents, and to-morrow we commence the hunt."

So we chatted on till it was time for me to leave. Philip walked part of the way home with me, and it was only when we were alone together that it struck me how small a part he had taken in the conversation. I asked him if he was not well.

"Not very bright," he said. "That fiend dyspepsia had tight hold of me. What do you think of my wife?"

"She is a beautiful and accomplished lady," I answered.

"Yes," he said, and seemed to be considering. "Let us meet often; you do me good."

He spoke of mutual friends, and inquired after Dr. Lessing and Mr. Storey.

"I intend to ask Storey to insure my life," he said.

I started. "Your own wish, Philip?"

"I suppose so. My wife and I were talking of such matters, and it came into my head."

"Now," thought I, "did she put it there?" But I said nothing of the conversation between our mutual friends and myself relating to the insurances on the lives of Mrs. Darrell's two former husbands. I wondered if he knew anything about them.

As I anticipated, the policy was not granted, and Philip expressed his surprise to me. I suggested that the doctor's report was unfavourable; I had to say something.

"That may be," Philip replied, "but this particular doctor is an ass. I have had myself examined by two physicians who are connected with life assurance companies, and they say there is nothing whatever the matter with me. True, I am suffering from an unaccountable depression, but it will wear off in time. The singular part of the affair is that I have been rejected by other offices on grounds not stated."

I could have enlightened him, but did not. There is a freemasonry among insurance companies, and Mr. Storey had struck the warning note.

Meanwhile, the furnished house had been taken, and I was invited to inspect it. It did not meet with my approval. The neighbourhood was gloomy, and the windows at the back faced a churchyard. Philip's low spirits would have been better served by a brighter outlook. The more I saw him the greater grew my anxiety concerning him. All my endeavors to dispel his melancholy were in vain. I remonstrated, I scolded, I preached—and I might as well have talked to a stone. I spoke also to Mrs. Darrell.

"Yes," she said, "it is a pity that Philip is inclined to mope."

"He never was," I remarked.

"Ah, but then, you see," she rejoined, in her brightest manner, "we all of us live two lives, an outer life and an inner life. And O! the care we take to keep the curtain down. Quite right, too. What should we see if it were raised? Dry bones, grinning skulls, withered hopes, miserable tragedies. We cannot escape from them; it is best they should be hidden."

She covered her eyes with her hand, as though suddenly overcome by sad thought, and only removed it to wipe away her tears. But I asked myself if she were acting.

One evening I dropped in upon Philip, unaware, and found him alone. His wife had gone to a theatre, and he was sitting with his elbow on the table, and his chin resting in his hand. Before him was a striking photograph of Mrs. Darrell, with her haunting eyes. I inquired why he had not accompanied her to the theatre, and he replied that she had said he would not like the piece that was being played. Now, it was a comedy, which I had seen, and laughed at rarely, and I told him so.

"Just the kind of thing you ought to see; it would wake you up."

"She knows best," he said. "You have no idea how considerate she is. I persuaded her to go."

"Then it was your idea in the first instance?"

"No, it was hers. She can't get much enjoyment out of my society."

He was utterly spiritless, and do what I might I could not rouse him out of the fatal lethargy which had fallen upon him.

"Look here, Philip," I said at last. "You should see a doctor."

"A doctor! What for? There is nothing the matter with me—nothing. I am as well as you are. It is only this horrible depression—"

"Which has been upon you too long. It ought to be attended to."

He gave the usual answer—

"O, it will wear off."

When we conversed he hardly looked at me. When his eyes were not fixed upon the portrait of his wife they were turned to the floor; we were sitting on opposite sides of the table, and thinking a glass of wine would do him good I asked him to join me. He pointed to the sideboard saying there were glasses and wine and spirits there, and rising to get them I saw at his feet a coil of rope.

"What is that rope there for?" I asked.

"Nothing. It is the rope my poor wife's last husband hanged himself with."

"For God's sake, Philip," I cried, and grasped his arm. He shook me off, and exclaimed—

"Are you crazy? There's no harm to it."

"Who gave it to you?"

"No one. My wife showed it to me."

"But why keep such a horrible memento?"

"Why not?" he retorted. "It is a link in her life—and mine. What do you keep gazing at it in that way for? Do you think it is alive, that it can speak, that it can move?" He pushed it under the table with his foot. "There, it is out of sight; don't let us talk about it any longer. By the bye, you haven't seen the upper part of the house. Everything is in apple pie order now, and I am sure my wife would not object."

Glad to get away from the symbol of a ghastly tragedy I followed him upstairs, and he took me through the rooms. We came to one on the top floor, used as a box room, and as he held up the candle I noticed a stout beam stretching from wall to wall, about three feet over our heads. Philip's eyes were fixed upon it with strange intentness. This beam, and the rope downstairs, sent a shiver through me, and I hurried him below as quickly as possible.

Now I must leave others to decide whether I was justified in carrying out an idea that occurred to me. I felt as if some desperate effort should be made to pluck Philip from his morbid state, to drive him as it were, out of himself, to make him forget. I had tried fair means and failed: I would try violent means. I determined to make him drunk.

I succeeded. Drinking moderately myself I plied him with liquor, and at eleven o'clock he sat before me in a helpless state of intoxication. My plan had served one good purpose; as he drank, his despondency abated, and for the first hour he was even cheerful. I then endeavoured to persuade him to get to bed, intending afterwards to take my departure; but I did not succeed, and I could obtain no assistance from the domestics. The only alternative was to wait for Mrs. Darrell's return from the theatre, and hand Philip over to her care.

It was past midnight before she came. She let herself in with her latch key, and her movements were singularly quiet. She stepped softly to the room in which we sat, and seemed to listen at the door before she opened it.

"You here!" she cried, and then, in a voice of alarm, "Has anything happened to Philip?"

"Only—you see," I answered, feeling rather awkward as I pointed to her husband, whose arms were stretched upon the table, and his face hidden on them.

She raised his head, and he looked at her with a foolish smile. Her eyes travelled to the glasses and bottles.

"Yes, I see," she said, and if looks could kill I should have fallen dead at her feet.

"Can I help you to get him to bed?" I asked.

She answered by throwing open the door. "Leave my house," she said, sternly.

"But Mrs. Darrell," I remonstrated, "I assure you—"

"I will call the servants to turn you out if you do not go instantly. I have suspected you all through. Now I know you."

I saw that there was no arguing with her, so with a bow, and a few stammering words that I would explain all to-morrow, I stepped towards the street door, she followed me with a candle. I was glad when I found myself outside, but it was with a disturbed mind that I walked home to my bed. On the following day I called at the house. Mrs. Darrell came to the street and forbade me to call again.

Thus was a long and tried friendship broken by a woman of whom I had a profound distrust, and from Philip I did not receive a line; nor did I hear anything of him for five or six weeks, and then the news was startling. It was conveyed to me by Dr. Lessing and Mr. Storey, who, late in the night, paid me an unexpected visit.

"Have you heard?" they asked simultaneously, as they entered the room.

"Heard what?"

They handed me the latest special edition of an evening paper, and pointed to an article, headed, "Melancholy suicide."

My friend, Philip Darrell, had hanged himself.

I was inexpressibly grieved, and yet, when I thought it over, it all seemed so natural. The rope, the beam, his wretched despondency, her haunting eyes—indeed, there had been moments when I had not dared to acknowledge to myself the fear of such a tragedy.

"Philip is the third," said Dr. Lessing. "She has committed three murders by suggestion, has inherited three fortunes (for you will see that the poor fellow has left her his sole heiress), and there is no law to touch her."

"Public opinion," I suggested.

"She will be pitied. Say that we had the courage, or rather the hardihood, to air our impressions—the effect her portrait and then her personality had upon you, and my theory, as you called it—we should be scouted as calumniators and defamers of an unfortunate lady. The law could reach us, but not her."

"There will be an inquest."

"Yes—nothing will come of it. He has been suffering some time from depression. She called in a doctor, I believe, and I will undertake to say that he was never allowed to see Philip unless she was present. She should have called in me."

"You were a true prophet," I remarked.

Dr. Lessing shrugged his shoulders. "It was not very wonderful. I have my eye on other cases quite as simple, which in the judgment of the public, will end in mystery. There is no mystery in them whatever. Cause and effect—nothing more. A certain influence, a certain result. Studies in psychology. We are speaking here in confidence, and I do not hesitate to pronounce this woman a murderess of a most dangerous type; but I would not dare to express myself in such a fashion outside this room. She is a murderess, and she knows she is safe."

"Is she human. Has she any feeling?" I cried in indignation.

"Yes, why not?" There is a wide range of human feeling. I could give you the names of a score of wholesale poisoners and murderers of both sexes, some of whom were exceedingly pious. History supplies examples."

"Philip hanged himself in a room at the top of the house."

"The room with the beam which he took you to see on the last evening you spent with him. I have little doubt that Mrs. Darrell selected the house with an eye to that beam. How often did poor Philip wake up in the night, and see in the darkness the beam and the rope, the spiritual ghost of himself gliding up the stairs to put them to their destined use?"

The image sent shudders through me. Dr. Lessing had a most distressing method of conviction in every word he uttered.

It all turned out as he predicted. There was an inquest with the usual verdict. Unsound mind, and an expression of commiseration with the widow, whose grief was publicly poignant. And she inherited the whole of Philip's fortune.

෨)ଔ

Twelve months afterwards, in Paris, I saw two persons issue from a jeweller's shop in the Rue de la Paix and step into a carriage that was waiting for them. One was a youngish man, fair, blue-eyed, with a weak face, the other a beautiful woman, who gave him a beaming smile as he took his seat by her side. The man I did not know. The woman was Madame Van Loop, as I prefer to call her.

Was the young man the fourth, and were there a beam and a rope waiting for him?

An Experiment in Conscience
By Montefiore Bienenstok

I.

The quiet harmony of this peaceful New England home completely fascinated him. To a man whose worldliness was the result of the severest friction with the grindstone of human experience, the society of this country girl came as a lull in the stormy turmoil of his life. They were as a mighty river and a stagnant pool. With mingled feeling of pleasure and pain he noticed the sad expression which crept into her face when he told her that he had gained his start in life by withholding the report of a gold mine which he, as a mining expert had been sent to investigate, until he had secretly bought up most of the stock at a very nominal figure. This man of the world, this cynic of religious tenets she was taught to respect, a man whose speculations on Wall Street had made the commercial welkin ring with his name, tried to explain the necessity for a certain amount of hypocrisy for success in business, in society, and in the world at large.

To Ellen Nash, descended from a long line of Puritan ancestors whose religious opinions had been the goad which drove them to the New World, Giles Van Cleave appeared as one of Chopin's nocturnes as played by an indifferent player who could not draw forth the soul, and who often struck some false notes. His sneers at the Bible, his jesting at goodness which he, like Napoleon, imagined might become a stumbling-block to greatness, she took only as discords that training and environment had wrought on him; nevertheless his views severely shocked her moral sensitiveness.

During the two weeks which he spent with them, she often wondered why he attracted her. He was wealthy, good-looking and refined; he had made good use of the advantages of a liberal education and of travel, but withal he was a man whose moral nature was totally warped by the battle for wealth. The two had little in common. He at the vortex of society's maelstrom, at home in the ball-room and at ease everywhere; she a country girl whose knowledge of the world was derived solely from reading, whose education had been received at a small female seminary some ten miles from the village in which she lived. Righteousness with her was life, with him a huge joke. Often she felt annoyed for admiring him, and vaguely wondered why her respect had not turned to bitter contempt at his raillery of the ideas which she held most sacred.

"No, I would not marry for love pure and simple," he said one afternoon as they were seated in the old-fashioned music room overlooking the lawn. "Of course I love Miss Van Sant, to whom I am engaged, but I am sure I would not marry her unless she had—well, a little money to make her somewhat more charming."

"But that is very wrong, is it not?" asked the girl, rather shocked.

"Wrong?" he replied. "Pshaw! What is wrong anyway? It is only a conventional term, and what is right to-day may be wrong to-morrow. As long as money enters into every question of my life I can't see why it should not enter this. Cupid can't pay rent, and while some men can afford to marry for what you call love, I am not one of them. I have an ambition to gratify and matrimony must not be a millstone around my neck, but rather an aerial machine which elevates me. Of course you may say that true love elevates a man, but love usually comes if a man's wife can gratify her every whim and indulge her expensive caprices."

"You would have me believe that you are worse than you really are," said Ellen archly, for the sentiment expressed hurt her more than she was willing to admit.

"I do not know why I talk to you in this way," he answered, picking up his hat from the chair. "Perhaps it's because I decided to throw off the conventional trammels of society and be thoroughly myself while enjoying your father's hospitality." He arose and looked at her. "Nonsense! You're not offended at the bosh I've been talking? I am sorry if I hurt your feelings. Come, suppose we take a ride before dinner."

She followed him slowly into the hallway, and soon the two were galloping down the road side by side.

II.

Living in the country where social duties did not occupy much of her attention, Ellen Nash had developed a love for the occult. Theosophy and esoterics became her favorite themes. She devoted all of her leisure to reading works on hypnotism and spiritualism, making all sorts of experiments and inquiries in her favorite subjects until she had become quite proficient in the mastery of many of their most intricate details. Her love for psychology and its phenomena had been encouraged by one of the instructresses of the seminary she had attended; but her father, a wealthy mill owner, considered her hypnotic attempts tinged with the witchcraft for which his ancestors had condemned women in the early colonial days. In spite of this parental opposition Ellen secretly practiced her hypnotic powers, and soon acquired a local reputation for possessing faculties for which the simple-minded country folk in no way envied her. As time went on she became an adept, subjecting people to her will, and many became mistrustful of this apparently simple country girl.

She surprised Giles Van Cleave, who soon noticed her knowledge on this subject, but not being fond of the introspective he preferred to talk with her of other things, and she with a woman's intuition realized this and humored him to the "top of his bent."

As they rode along on the outskirts of the village he made some flippant remarks about the monotony of a farmer's life. To all this persiflage she paid little attention. She was as one who reads a printed page without comprehending its meaning; what he said seemed blurred and indistinct. His running fire of sarcastic wit was answered in monosyllables. At last he felt that something was weighing upon her mind, and as the twilight began to deepen they silently turned homewards.

"Why not?" she had been thinking; "I have studied for the last six years, and now that an opportunity is within my grasp why should I waste it? To-night I will quietly get him under my influence and he shall go back to New York a changed man. I will be as the pianist who draws melody from the nocturne. I will infuse my ideas of morality into him and then he must drop his levity. As an eraser blots out the pencil marks on a paper so I will blot out his false ideas."

Thus Ellen mused, and it was this that gave her face the thoughtful expression—it was this that took her mind far away from his witticisms.

That evening the strains of Schumann's Slumber Song gently caressed his ear as he sat in the library glancing over some books Ellen was handing him, while her sister's music seemed to vibrate through his being; it sounded weird and uncanny, dreamy and distant.

"Take this book which has been in our family these many generations," said Ellen.

Her voice sounded hollow and commanding. He took the book and walked automatically. "I feel so very queer," said he with a forced laugh, sinking on the sofa. "I hope I am not going to be sick." Ellen glided toward him. As she approached he felt as if a luminous sun was being swept from his vision. He saw her gesticulating strangely, murmuring words that had no meaning. He tried to rise. She came nearer, mumbling more words he faintly heard, then all was darkness.

"There!" said Ellen, seating herself beside the young man seemingly asleep, "I will make a good man of you. You are an easier subject than I had imagined. Henceforth you shall have a conscience to assert itself whenever you will try to do wrong."

"Are you willing to undergo this change?" whispered the girl into his ear, and the lips of the young man faintly uttered, "Yes."

For almost an hour Ellen kept her eyes riveted upon the sleeper, from time to time touching his forehead and breast, and breathing words of admonition into his mouth.

The young man answered as if in a trance. Finally she shook him lightly and he awoke with a start.

"Well, I admit that my company isn't as interesting as some of your city acquaintances, but I hardly expected that you would fall asleep right before my eyes," said the girl, laughingly.

"I—I beg your pardon," he said stammering; "I suppose horseback riding was too much for me. I'm not much of an equestrian, you know. Permit me to wish you good-night."

He left the room still somewhat dazed, while she watched his retreating figure. Still pondering over her experiment a loud peal resounded through the house. Some one said: "A telegram for Mr. Van Cleave." Presently she heard his footsteps on the stairs and a moment after he entered the room.

"Important business necessitates my immediate presence in New York. I regret that I have to curtail such a pleasant visit," he said, "but business before pleasure, you know. I must leave on the first train in the morning."

III.

The business which had torn Giles so summarily from his much-needed rest was of a very complicated nature. By the advice and earnest solicitations of a friend and distant relative, his father had been inveigled into investing a large capital in an unfinished railroad which was to connect two western towns. In an amazingly short space of time the new road was completed and its bonds floated on the market. Among those in control was a friend of the family whose ruinous policy had made a failure of the undertaking. This road was about to go into the hands of a receiver. Mr. Van Cleave had long ago foreseen this result, and now realized that it could on these terms so compete with the large road as to force the greater corporation either to lose its trade or buy up the new concern at practically any price its stockholders might ask. At about this time disaster followed disaster in his speculations on change. He was greatly in debt, and in immediate need of a large sum, but hesitated to sell his railroad stock at its present low figure. At this juncture he telegraphed for Giles.

The sun shone brightly into the finely appointed office as if anxious to brighten the gloom imprinted on the faces of the two occupants. Van Cleave, the father, was aristocratic looking, of fine figure, regular features, and that polish which the social world bestows upon its favorites. Like his son he was a financier of the highest rank, and his opinions on monetary questions were often quoted. He was a speculator, a man of genius, one who understood the effects of congressional legislation upon the industries of the land; but practical man though he was he had a deep respect for the principles of political economy, and his most profound conclusions were often based on the theories of this science.

"Money is tight, we have reached the full extent of our credit; now, Giles, what would you suggest in the emergency?" he said, looking keenly at his son. "It is evident that we must have money. By selling our railroad stock we may keep on our feet, but it has depreciated so that it won't help us stand much strain; besides, I want to hold on to that as long as I can."

"I am sure I can see no other way," said Giles gloomily, moving his chair away from the desk toward the middle of the room as if for a long talk. "We have contracted certain debts which this stock will cover; to keep it would be dishonest."

"Dishonest!" ejaculated Mr. Van Cleave in amazement; "why, Giles, I don't understand you."

"Well, father, let us be candid with one another. When we went into that transaction we knew what the result would be. After the road fails its competitor will be forced to buy it owing to the low rates at which it can run, and naturally the terms of that sale will not be at all in accordance with the actual value of the road. To hold the stock in the face of such facts is an underhanded piece of business to which I can never be a party. No, I am too conscientious to see a road which has been running successfully and honestly duped by a few unscrupulous men who decided to squeeze and extort money from it in such a nefarious manner. It is manifestly unjust, and as I said before, I cannot be a party to it."

"Have you lost your senses?" and the scorn shook Mr. Van Cleave's voice and form. "What right have you—you who have acquired wealth by every known business trick—to preach to me about right and wrong. I do not wish to withdraw this stock, it will certainly make our fortune. We must meet our obligations in some other way."

The result of Ellen's experiment was beginning to show itself. Giles's resentment at what he believed was a wrong was apparent both in his words and his actions. "You may do as you please," he said angrily, "but my share of that stock must be sold at once. I am not a knave. I promised to meet certain debts on a certain day and God aiding me I shall do so even if I lose a fortune by it."

"Giles," said the old man solemnly, "you look at the question in a very unbusiness-like manner. But why not get the notes extended? I am sure a little tact will do the trick. The holders of this paper will grant us a little more time."

Giles flushed. It pained him to hear his father talk thus. A week ago there would have been no argument on such a subject, but now things were different. His moral horizon had grown broader, and right and wrong entered into all the affairs of his life. The current of his ideas conflicted, for even while he was talking he hated himself for this sudden change of view and wondered what it was that thus impelled him to oppose his own interests. His father was a man of judgment and resource, but to hold that stock was dishonest, to get an extension on notes when he could easily raise the money to pay them was a moral wrong, he would not sanction it. No, the stock must go.

"Since you are so obstinate and foolish," went on Mr. Van Cleave, "I can suggest but one last resource." He hesitated for a moment, then proceeded and talked as one who had deliberated for a long time before saying what was on his mind. "You are to be married in three months. Mr. Van Sant promised his daughter one hundred thousand dollars when she married you. We need the money, you must make an excuse to marry sooner.

"Every fiber in Giles's body tingled with shame and smothered anger. A moral wave swept over him. His conscience cried out in agony. He could not understand it; this revulsion which shook his nature from its very foundation. He seemed to be suffocating for want of air. Could this be his father, who proposed matrimony, holy matrimony, as a nefarious scheme to help his business interests? The office furniture began to whirl before him, he caught sight of his face in the glass on the desk. It was livid with passion.

"I must get out of this horrible temptation," he mumbled as if to himself. "Father, from the bottom of my heart I pity you, but I should never so far forget that I was a man of honor as to sully my name by the expedient you offer." He turned, left the room, rushed past the clerks in the outer office and slamming the door behind him he walked out into the fresh air, his honor a vampire sucking on his conscience.

"I hope Giles is not sick. I never saw him act so strangely before, but he will come around in time," mused Mr. Van Cleave, bending over the ledger.

IV.

The piano lamp with its gorgeously decorated paper shade of pink and blue cast its cheerful reflection over the exquisitely furnished parlors. Deep in the recesses of a richly upholstered chair a young lady with black hair and sparkling eyes was gazing dreamily at a photograph on an onyx table. Her gown harmonized with the surroundings, displaying all the perfections of her fine figure. She was as handsome a type of American womanhood as could well be conceived, this Kathleen Van Sant, the prospective bride of Giles Van Cleave.

"How handsome he is," she said, looking at the photograph. "What a lucky girl I am to be loved by such a man." Then she fell to musing and her thoughts reveled in the happiness of her coming marriage. They would have a little home of their own, she would share his joys and his sorrows, make all his burdens easier to bear, be the sunshine which illumined his existence. All her life she had admired him, for he was in nowise like the social gadflies who scorched their wings on her brilliant beauty. She was in the realms of heavenly delight when a sharp ring interrupted her ecstatic flights. She hastily arose. A few moments more, and the door opened admitting Giles Van Cleave, the subject of her meditations.

"I—I hardly expected you back from the country so soon," she blurted out radiantly happy.

He quietly divested himself of his overcoat and they entered the parlor. His face was set and stern, his eyes glinted with a hidden fire, his actions stiff and constrained; the kiss which she almost forced him to give her lacked warmth. After they were seated he asked her some very formal questions about her father. She tried to draw from him a few incidents of his recent vacation, and finally compelled by his unusually distant manner, she said:

"Giles, there is something the matter with you, won't you tell me?" She spoke so earnestly it startled him. A tragedy of the direst importance entangled him. He had a duty to perform, a most odious, contemptible duty. He felt like a soldier who faces a battery knowing it to be certain death, but who from sheer patriotism cannot run away. His conscience would not permit him to delay, he must be true to himself, true to his ideas of morality.

"Kathleen," he said after a long pause, "I am going to tell you something that will break your heart as God knows it does mine."

"Why not let such things be hidden as in the tomb of secrecy?" she answered. "Why should you tell that which will be, as you say, detrimental to both of us? If you have lost money, I have enough for both; if you have business trouble I will help you. Come! there is no earthly reason why you should be so sad."

"Great God! this is awful," murmured Giles; "Kathleen, you would not have me shirk my duty, you cannot ask me to subvert my manhood by doing that which my whole after life will cry out against as a sin to God, to you, and to myself? You must understand; you must be told before it is too late." He bowed his head in abject misery, his voice was choked, he could say no more.

During this speech Kathleen's face had become as white as the marble hearthstone; she was but the ghost of what she had been a few moments before. A dazed expression swept over her face. "You mean that—that you do not—love me?," she gasped.

He watched her steady herself to keep from falling, but a curious fatality impelled him to proceed. His duty was clear, he must be a man. "I have made you a promise of marriage," he said waveringly, "and it rests with you whether or not that promise be fulfilled, but before we go any further I have a confession which it is my duty as an honorable man to make to you."

"Would you rob me of all that makes life precious?" interrupted Kathleen. "Have you not repeated vows of eternal love which bound me to you more firmly than any knot human hands can tie? You are mine, I am yours. No matter what crime you have committed, no matter how degraded or debased the world may consider you, I love you."

Giles was suffering torments of the damned. This brief moment inflicted the greatest agony of his life. He must hesitate no longer. "I have been a hypocrite, a liar and a cheat," he said passionately. "I wooed and won you for your money alone. I wanted to join your wealth to mine. I never loved you as a man should love her who is to be the world to him." Then he paused. Her eyes were closed, she seemed asleep.

"Go on," she gently murmured, "turn the screws of the rack a little tighter; have no fear, I can bear it."

"But my conscience smites me with the enormity of my crime; the moral being, dormant in every individual, is awake and refuses to permit this outrage."

"But, Giles, does my love count for naught? You are my existence. Without you I am but a poor swimmer on a billowy sea. Could you not in time learn to love me as you feel that you should? I am willing to wait, it will all come," she murmured softly.

He knew not how to reply; for one brief moment he wavered in his resolution, then a terrible pang vibrated every chord of his being as an eruption shakes a volcano. He could not resist it. "I promised to marry you, and I will keep my word," cried he despairingly, "but I can never learn to love you, and our union will never be a happy one, as I shall always despise myself for being so despicably contemptible. Forgive me for inflicting a momentary pain instead of a lifelong one. I cannot do otherwise."

Kathleen arose and drew her magnificent figure up to its full height; her words were low and distinct, cutting and cold. "Despite the mischief you have done, even after you have shown what a villain you are, a villain with a conscience," and she laughed hysterically, "I still have some sparks of love for you which all your perfidy cannot quench." She moved majestically toward the hall, took his hat and coat from the rack, handed them to him while he stood automatically watching her. Then she quietly opened the door and said as gently as she had spoken before, "Go."

V.

The Promontory, a small hotel in the heart of the Adirondacks, had opened its doors for the entertainment of its summer guests. Situated on the highest point of the mountains, the bracing climate furnished a delightful change from the heat of New York. It was to this retired spot that Kathleen Van Sant, after several months of wrestling with a fever that threatened to consume body and soul, came to build up her wasted tissues, to forget, if possible, the past. But resolution could not shake off that horrible winding sheet of memory which she knew would pursue her to the grave. She wanted to be alone, her money availed not, the sympathy of her friends was only additional misery. In long walks, in wearisome mountain climbs, in summer novels she endeavored to drown her sorrow.

To this resort came another, but for a different reason. Mr. Nash, whose mind had done its duty as faithfully as the wheels in his mill, felt the need of a vacation. The seaside resorts were too fashionable for this puritanic New Englander, he wanted the peace and quiet of the country, combined with the intercourse of people from the city. Ellen naturally looked upon even this out-of-the-way place as a haven for new experiences. Since the advent of Giles into her life she had had a craving for travel, a longing to acquire more of the ways of the world. And thus these two young women, different in training, so diverse in their conceptions of the problems of life, were thrown together.

Their height was the same, but Kathleen, now slender, appeared head and shoulders taller than her newly made friend; for in spite of their difference of character a friendship for which neither could account sprang up between them. While Ellen's face possessed that dreamy, faraway look of one who had devoted much of her time to study and hard thinking, Kathleen's, even tragic and drawn as it now was, still wore that vivacious, merry light which indicated the high development of her sense of humor, her practical and energetic mind.

Ellen soon became deeply interested in her friend's personality. She insisted on accompanying her almost everywhere. Kathleen was food for her psychological reasonings. That something had gone wrong she immediately perceived, but just what it was she could not clearly fathom. She again and again rejected the idea of its being a love affair, as no man, she thought, would trifle with a girl so beautiful, charming and wealthy. To all allusions to her trouble Kathleen returned an evasive answer, thus to a greater extent piquing Ellen's curiosity and interest. She learned that Kathleen had been on the threshold of another world, but the cause of the sickness puzzled her. The more she saw of her friend the more she knew that she had heard her name somewhere before, but she was entirely at sea as to a time or a place.

Ellen found her sympathies go forth to this evidently heartbroken girl, the mystery surrounding her lending an additional charm.

As they stood one afternoon on a high ridge overlooking the valley and a small town with its factories, the smoke of commerce curling far away in the distance, Ellen said in musing tones: "I feel as if I were but a spectator and the busy world below but a performance, played for my especial benefit. I seem to have no share in it all."

"While I," replied Kathleen sadly, "am like this stone," and she tossed a large rock down the mountain side, "which rolls down a hill to be battered and bruised by the hard knocks of the world's sharp edges."

"Your sadness and strange apathy are unaccountable," said Ellen. "Why should you feel so pessimistic? What trouble has clouded your life?"

"Do not speak of that, let me efface it from my mind. Tell me more about your scientific pursuits. You are the only person that I have ever met who knew enough about such subjects to discuss them rationally. In your talk I sink the weight of my burden; tell me of your experiments."

"Whatever may trouble you I know of but one remedy," answered Ellen. "If you could devote your life to doing good, the satisfaction of knowing that you are some use in the world will heal your sufferings. In all my study the one good deed which I attempted to do has more than repaid me for all my labors."

"I should very much like to hear about it," said Kathleen absently.

"It came about in this way," said Ellen, seating herself on a ledge opposite to her companion. "A gentleman with whom my father did some business visited us not long ago. He was the most polished man I had ever met."

"And naturally you fell in love with him," put in Kathleen smilingly.

"Not at all, at least I would hardly call it that," said Ellen blushing. "But I had never met a man like him before. He was so refined, so courteous and so wicked. He did not believe in God, said the Bible was all rot and nonsense. He talked so shockingly about marriage, derided love as a factor to happiness, and scoffed at everything which I regarded as holy. You know my folks are Puritans and such talk annoyed me more than I cared to tell. He claimed that right was a purely conventional term; if success attended an action that was sufficient proof that the action was right."

"He is a good deal like thousands of men whom I have met," interrupted Kathleen. "I believe I understand just what sort of a man he was," and a mental photograph was distinctly outlined before her. "What did you do? That's the main point of the story, is it not?"

"His remarks made me angry, they were so cold and harsh, so I decided to change him," went on Ellen.

"To change him?" echoed Kathleen.

"Yes," answered Ellen, "to make a good man of him, to give him a conscience. It was not a difficult experiment, he was a very easy subject. No, I cannot tell you just how I did it," she said, noting the look of inquiry on Kathleen's face; "you would have to understand more about the science. If my experiment was successful, and I see no reason why it should not be, he went back to the world with the same ideas of what is right and wrong that I possess. I did the best deed of my life by creating a good man. You see hypnotism can be turned to good as well as bad uses."

All this was startlingly new to Kathleen. Even as she was a theme for reflection for Ellen, so was Ellen a curious species of humanity to her. After all, hypnotism might play a greater part for good in the world than she had ever dreamed. "And do you know the result of your experiment?" she asked interestedly.

"No," answered Ellen, "he went back to New York so suddenly that I could not watch the effect of the experiment upon him."

"Perhaps I could tell you. I know a good many men in New York such as you have described."

"If you do maybe you have noticed some change in him. He is a Mr. Van Cleave, Giles Van Cleave, a speculator on Wall Street."

Kathleen rose, her gaunt form towering above Ellen, still seated on the ledge. Her eyes gleamed with all their former brilliancy, a savage expression swept over her beautiful face. Like a tragedy queen she stood glaring at the girl at her feet. "Mischief-maker! Interferer in the divine workings of nature! I hate you!'" she hissed, turning from the surprised girl, and with rapid strides she passed down the mountain path, leaving Ellen much in doubt as to her sanity.

VI.

The trees were beginning to shed their garlands of leaves; and the earth was gradually assuming the frigid appearance which is hers after she has thrown off her garment of green. Desolation raised its head and hushed the gladsome songs of the birds. Like nature around him, Giles Van Cleave was desolate and gloomy. The tongue of social New York wagged merrily over his downfall, while many of the component parts of that tongue only saw in it another clever ruse, a spoke in the wheel whereby the great financiers, Jarvis Van Cleave and son rolled on to fortune. This very element imagined they saw the strivings of these two men to become America's greatest railroad magnates. Giles knew that he acted as an honest, upright man should act, but many of those who had not looked into the affair, and among them were some whom he had thought his friends, sneered, thought differently, and looked at him with suspicion.

The ugly rumors which reached him, about his jilting of Miss Van Sant, pained him as would red hot pincers applied to his flesh. He must leave New York; it were best that he and his father should separate. Mr. Van Cleave was too much a man of resource to be unable to recover in time from this blow, but with Giles it was different. He foolishly imagined that he was but the charred stump of the blooming tree he had once been, and that he must begin life anew on a new basis. He must seek a new soil on which to plant the seed of prosperity gathered from his former business experiences. And in this frame of mind he decided to go to India.

Before bidding adieu to his native land, perhaps forever, he made a trip down to the village in which Ellen lived, to settle up some business affairs which he had with her father, and was persuaded to spend a few days with the Nashes before embarking.

The scene on the mountain side was ever fresh in Ellen's memory and the moment she saw Giles enter the house she jumped to the conclusion that the mystery of her former friend's behavior was on the eve of a solution. She welcomed him with all the cordiality her dreamy, unenthusiastic nature possessed. He, in turn, was surprised to note how pleased he was to see her. A new sensation had stolen upon him, it was as unaccountable as it was queer.

After the evening meal when he sat opposite her in the library she sought to unravel the skein of gnarled thought which had puzzled her all the summer. "I met a Miss Van Sant this summer," she said slowly, gazing at him intently to note the effect of her words. "She—"

"And so it has reached even you," he interrupted her in despair. "When a man does his duty I cannot see why every one should make it so hard for him. I was engaged to her, but before our marriage I found out that it was all a mistake, that I did not love her as I should, and so—I broke off the match."

It was now Ellen's time to feel a peculiar sensation of horror creep over her. She had tried to make a good man of him. Alas! Too well she had succeeded. But three months ago he was a prosperous business man, to-day he was an adventurer seeking his fortune in distant lands. She suddenly conceived the idea that even this reverse of fortune might be turned to her account as an investigator.

For the next three days she watched him as a chemist watches an experiment in one of his test tubes. His levity was gone. He loved right and hated wrong. The farmer was no longer an object of ridicule, but a being in whose behalf Giles was strangely interested. He saw the farmer from an ethical standpoint and thought that by helping him he could elevate at least one portion of humanity. He eagerly consented to attend church with the Nashes Sunday morning, and was as devout a worshiper as could be found at this shrine of holiness. Ellen marveled much at this change. He was now attuned to her touch. The nocturne emitted sounds which she had desired. But were they pleasing to her? A hundred times, no. The very discordant notes which she had changed were the notes that had pleased her most though she knew it not. The sweet melodies of the nocturne she had always derived from the people about her, and his difference to them had been the charm which attracted her to him. She saw it all.

Vainly did she combat with her former ideal. She could not understand how right had so plainly been wrong. She liked him better as he had been. Why should this be? At last a logical explanation dawned upon her, and it came in the words of Miss Van Sant, "Interferer in the divine workings of nature." She had made a mistake. God had made this man, and her attempts to change him had worked his ruin. What a fool she had been to imagine that a Puritan girl's ideas of morality grafted into the mind of a man of the world could have anything but an evil influence over him. And yet had she not intended to do right? She had pitted morality against nature, but nature triumphed. She acknowledged her mistake and resolved to rectify it. But her attempts to again get him under her influence were futile. His conscience withstood the feeble blows of her hypnotic hammer, it was as the rock in the foundation of a building; she saw that its removal would cause destruction, and gloomily she accepted defeat.

VII.

It was the day of his departure. A terrible rainstorm beat its dreary tattoo against the window panes. Giles gazed out at the splashing drops, while Ellen, seated at his side, moodily watched his forlorn expression.

"You look as if you had lost your last friend on earth," she said. "Cheer up. India is not such a bad place; you can come back again very soon."

"It isn't that," answered Giles, huskily. "When I leave the United States the last tie that binds me to earth will be severed forever. I shall be a wanderer on the face of the earth."

She saw in this the result of her experiment, that horrible manipulation with that which should not have concerned her. She tried to cheer him, it was in vain.

"I should feel happier if I left some one behind who had some interest in my welfare," he said. "Some one to whom I could write; some one, whom some day my return might gladden. Ellen," he pursued earnestly, "you certainly understand what I mean. For you I have broken my engagement, for you I would face the dangers of the Indian jungle with hope in my heart, and courage to carry me onward. Ellen, it is you I love. I loved you from the moment I saw you. Won't you be the beacon light shining on me from my native land while struggling in far-off India? Give me some hope, and, if you will, I shall stay at home and be contented forever by your side."

The passionate words, the pleading face had a wonderful effect on Ellen. For a moment she longed to throw herself at his feet and beg his pardon for the great wrong she had done him. Then she only saw the transformed being, the man whose wife she could never be, for she knew she did not love him; and as an accompaniment to the splashing rain streaming its weird song on the window panes she gently told it to him and sent him away to India.

Madame Valprez: A Monte Carlo Romance

By Emeric Hulme-Beaman

ALFRED MOLYNEUX had lost heavily. He passed out of the play rooms, through the swing doors, into the marble colonnaded atrium of the Casino, and, walking across to the restaurant at the other end, ordered a whisky-and-soda and a cigar, for which he paid five francs. He was gloomily conscious the next moment that this was the last five-franc piece he had in his pocket, and the reflection caused him, for the fiftieth time that evening, to anathematise his luck.

Lighting his cigar, he sauntered back into the magnificent vestibule, where he presently flung himself down upon one of the sofas near the Salles de Jeu. A ceaseless stream of people passed backward and forward in front of him—some entering, some leaving the rooms; others idly promenading over the tessellated floor, smoking, chatting and laughing.

He had been three days at Monte Carlo, and had spent nearly a year's income. Why had he come? He could not say. The vaguest impulse had directed him to the Riviera, when he had set out with the half-formed intention of taking a month's holiday in Northern Italy. He found himself in Monte Carlo quite by accident, as it were, without any preconceived plan of journeying there. It was at best an unfortunate impulse, to whatever caprice attributable. He would wire to his bankers in London, and leave to-morrow afternoon for Florence. Arrived at this resolution, he flicked the ash off his cigar and happened to look up. He found his eyes resting on the eyes of a lady who was regarding him with an amused expression. Molyneux gave a little exclamation of surprise, and started to his feet.

"Why, Madame Valprez!" he said.

The lady smiled.

"So you recognise me, Mr. Molyneux?" she replied, a little humorously, as she took his hand.

"The occasion of our last meeting was not of a kind to permit me easily to forget you!" he said, smiling, too.

The lady addressed as Madame Valprez looked at him a moment without speaking.

"How long have you been here?" she asked, abruptly, turning away her eyes.

"I came on Wednesday."

"And this is Friday. I hear your new book is a great success, Mr. Molyneux? I congratulate you."

"Thanks. And what brings Madame Valprez to Monte Carlo?" enquired Molyneux, laughing.

"I may ask—what brings *you* to Monte Carlo, Mr. Molyneux?" retorted Madame Valprez.

Molyneux shrugged his shoulders.

"That is precisely the question that I have been asking myself for the last half hour," he replied, "and to which I can find no answer! An indolent caprice, I suppose."

"Ah—an indolent caprice," repeated the lady, with a slight drawl. "For myself, I frequently visit Monte Carlo in the early spring. You are going into the rooms?"

"I have just come out of them."

"A winner, I hope?"

"No, a loser."

Madame Valprez gave a sympathetic little laugh. She was a slight woman of medium height, and with nothing striking about her except her eyes and her voice; the former were deep, thoughtful and singularly luminous; the latter was low and musical, and could assume at times a tone of remarkable persuasiveness, even to the point of a vaguely suggested authority.

"I am sorry to hear it," she remarked. "Will you not come in and try your luck again?"

"I have already lost my last five-franc piece!" smiled Molyneux, ruefully. "I shall return to my hotel."

"So early? It is scarcely nine o'clock!"

"I have my arrangements to make. I intend to leave to-morrow."

Madame Valprez stood still a moment, as though irresolute whether to enter the rooms herself.

"At what hotel are you staying, Mr. Molyneux?" she asked.

"The 'Beau Rivage.' And you? The 'Paris,' I suppose?"

Madame Valprez nodded.

"I only arrived this morning—the 20th of February," she added, placing a careful and slow emphasis upon the words.

Molyneux started slightly.

"The 20th of February," he repeated. "So it is. The date seems to carry some transitory and elusive association to my mind that I cannot recall—ah! it is gone again!" he laughed.

Madame Valprez smiled curiously.

"Do you know," she said lightly, "I want particularly to see you!"

"I am quite at your service," said Molyneux, elevating his eyebrows.

"In that case," said she, "Perhaps you would not mind accompanying me for half-an-hour to the 'Paris'? A cup of coffee on the restaurant verandah would not be disagreeable."

"With all the pleasure in life, Madame Valprez!" agreed Molyneux, preparing to escort her to the *vestiaire*, where Madame's cloak and his own hat and stick were deposited.

"I have read your book," she said, as they passed out together into the gorgeous moonlight, "and of course it interested me greatly. On the whole you have cleverly avoided pitfalls in the treatment of your subject—but, Mr. Molyneux, you betray still the insufficient knowledge of the dilettante—not so much in what you omit as in what you imply. Your conclusions, pardon me, have something of the arrogance of the ill-informed!"

"You must remember that I had not then the advantage of Madame Valprez's instructions!" said Molyneux, smiling.

"No. When we first met, three months ago, your book was already finished."

"You are quite right. It was too late then to alter my written opinions on the subject. I took Charcot as my authority."

"Charcot!" repeated Madame Valprez, with the slightest inflection of contempt. "Well, Dr. Charcot is an able experimenter, I do not deny it. His theories are sound enough as far as they go, but—"

"But," interpolated Molyneux with a smile, "they do not go as far as yours, Madame Valprez!"

"I was not quite going to say that—ah, here we are at the 'Paris.' Let us find a table on the verandah, where it is not too crowded," and Madame Valprez, followed by Molyneux, threaded her way through the gay, noisy groups with which the fashionable restaurant was already thronged, till they reached a spot at the further end of the fairy-lit verandah, where, perceiving a vacant table in a secluded corner, they sat down.

"You spoke just now," said Madame Valprez presently, "of 'an indolent caprice.' What did you mean by that?"

"The result of some idle and irresponsible impulse," replied Molyneux vaguely.

"Ah, an idle impulse! Do you recollect our last meeting in London?"

"I have already said that it would be difficult to forget it!" replied Molyneux, with a little laugh, as his thoughts went back to an afternoon in November when he had been ushered into the small but luxuriously-furnished sitting-room in Bond Street, where for a few weeks the fashionable lady mesmerist had taken up her residence in town, and had there witnessed some desultory manifestations of the science which this lady professed. Molyneux had expressed a wish to submit himself to the test of Madame Valprez's power; the lady, after some slight hesitation, had yielded to his request. The gaze of her deep, soft eyes had produced an effect singularly soothing, and one of which the impression even yet lingered, like a pleasant after-taste, in Molyneux's memory. After the first lotus-like abandonment to the pleasing lethargy that ensued, Molyneux's mind became a blank, and he was conscious only of having fallen (gradually it seemed) into a dreamless sleep, from which he was awakened by the low tones of Madame Valprez's voice. The incident, however, had left a lasting impression on Molyneux's mind; he had, therefore, spoken the truth when, in reply to Madame Valprez's inquiry, he said that it would be difficult for him to forget the occasion of their last meeting.

"I suppose," smiled Madame Valprez, "that I must take that as a compliment?"

"The recollection is entirely a pleasing one," replied Molyneux, bowing.

"Well," remarked Madame Valprez, "it is of that recollection—or, rather, of the occasion to which it refers—that I want to speak, Mr. Molyneux. When you visited me in my rooms you were under mesmerism for a quarter of an hour. It was long enough to almost convince me that in you I had found an extraordinarily sympathetic subject. I wished, however, to verify that conviction by an experiment. The experiment," she added slowly, "has answered quite satisfactorily."

"The experiment!" said Molyneux. "What experiment?"

"You spoke just now," proceeded his companion, "of an impulse prompting you to come to Monte Carlo. That impulse was not a vague nor irresponsible one—but a genuine impulse, acting unconsciously, and supplied by me."

"What!" cried Molyneux, starting in surprise.

"Three months ago," said Madame Valprez, "while you were in a mesmeric sleep at my rooms in Bond Street I imposed upon you a strong 'suggestion.' I instructed you to meet me in the Casino at Monte Carlo on the 20th February. You have carried out my instructions to the letter, Mr. Molyneux" she concluded with a smile.

Molyneux made no immediate reply. He gazed upon Madame Valprez with an expression in which astonishment, incredulity and annoyance were equally blended. Then he gave a forced laugh.

"If that is true," said he, "I find myself in some measure the slave of a singularly distasteful bondage."

His companion laughed good-naturedly.

"Pray do not say that! It was a harmless enough experiment, and you, least of all, should object to the furtherance of this science by the test of actual proofs! But," she continued more seriously, "I must confess that I had an ulterior object, to attain which I should again require your help. The success of this experiment was but the first step towards testing a still more advanced theory that I hold."

"You interest me, Madame Valprez!" said Molyneux. "What, then, is your advanced theory?"

Madame Valprez leaned over and placed her hand lightly on his arm.

"My friend," said she, "you have lost money?"

Molyneux shrugged his shoulders.

"A considerable amount—worse luck!"

"Still it might cause you to entertain the less aversion to making some more?"

"Why, what do you mean?"

"I mean," said Madame Valprez, speaking slowly and impressively, "that I have formed a project by which I think it would be possible to win a large sum—possibly even a fortune—at the tables, Mr. Molyneux!"

"But what possible project could lead to so happy a result?" laughed Molyneux.

"A project evolved from the theory to which I have just referred. I have, as you are aware, for many years past given the most earnest study to the less explored and more intricate problems of mesmerism. I have pushed my researches far; and I believe that with a subject sympathetically endowed I can achieve a result hitherto unattempted. You seem to me, Mr. Molyneux, to present the temperamental qualifications for which I have been seeking—a singular and sensitive sensibility, combined with an earnest and impressionable mental equipment. We should work together to attain this result!"

"I confess that you excite my curiosity," replied Molyneux.

"My ulterior object was to discover to what degree you were liable to hypnotic suggestion. Your presence here is the strongest proof of your complete subjection to mesmeric impulse. I am convinced that I could do anything with you, Mr. Molyneux!"

Molyneux stirred uneasily, feeling her eyes upon him.

"No, no! I did not intend to wound your vanity! The strongest characters are often the best mesmeric subjects—it is merely the accident of temperament. Now for my theory. It is this—that, given favourable conditions and perfect accord between subject and operator, it would be possible, by projecting the thoughts of the 'subject' into the immediate future, to make him partially, if not wholly, for the time being, clairvoyant."

"And you imagine that I fulfil the requirements of such a subject?" asked Molyneux.

"I do," replied Madame Valprez calmly. "It remains only for you to say whether or not you agree to the actual test of an experiment."

"But the project—?" inquired Molyneux with increased curiosity.

"Depends upon the success of the experiment, and will equally benefit both you and me," she answered.

Molyneux nodded.

"Ah, I begin to see!" he said. "But is it not a little far-fetched?"

"No, I believe it to be practicable. At least, it is worth a trial—do you not think so?"

Molyneux was filled with a sudden consciousness of the possibilities latent in his companion's suggestion; he was sensible of a thrill of excitement in the contemplation of them, and his reply was not without a certain half-suppressed eagerness.

"Your confidence is contagious!" he said. "Yes, I think—perhaps—it is worth a trial. At worst, the experiment can but fail—"

"Whereas, if it succeeds," interrupted Madame Valprez.

"I shall, at least, have my revenge on the bank!" laughed Molyneux.

Half-an-hour later Molyneux—whether persuaded against his better judgment by the strange influence of his companion's personality, or really in agreement with his own voluntary inclinations, it would not have been easy for him to decide—found himself sitting in Madame Valprez's private room in the "Paris" Hotel, his hostess in an easy chair opposite him, and between them a small table with a roulette diagram upon it, and a score of roulette cards.

"Now, Mr. Molyneux," began Madame Valprez, "you must clearly understand that for the successful operation of any experiment—more especially such an experiment as this—it is quite necessary that you should completely and unreservedly resign your will to the control of mine."

"Yes," said Molyneux, "I understand that; and am willing to do it, as far as I am able. What next?"

"Next, try and concentrate your thoughts as much as you can upon the centre table of the second Roulette Room in the Casino. Imagine," she went on, speaking in slow, even and persuasive tones, "that you are seated at that table and are playing. It is to-morrow, and two o'clock. Perhaps you are not playing, but merely looking on, and noting very carefully, as they come up, the various numbers and colours—" She fixed her eyes full upon Molyneux. He leaned back in his chair and nodded.

"Yes—yes. I can fancy myself in the position you indicate—go on."

"The *séance*," she proceeded, "has not long commenced—for you must remember that it is only two o'clock, and perhaps the table is not very crowded—"

"Perhaps," repeated Molyneux mechanically, "the table is not very crowded—"

"And so," continued Madame Valprez, "it would be easy for you to keep your attention fixed on the board—you would possibly notice the croupiers—?" Molyneux's head had fallen back, and his eyes were wide and glassy—"The croupiers," repeated she, with sudden authority—"do you notice the croupiers?"

"Yes," came Molyneux's reply in an odd, impassive tone.

"Describe them."

"One to my right, controlling the roulette, dark, hook-nosed, a short, black moustache, pointed; opposite him—a short, fat-faced man—grey whiskers—"

Madame Valprez laughed.

"I recognise the persons you describe. Very well. Now, remember. *It is two o'clock to-morrow afternoon, and you have just sat down at the centre table in the second room.*"

"Yes," said Molyneux slowly.

Madame Valprez took up one of the loose cards that were lying on the table, and a pencil.

"Keep your attention on the board," she said in low, clear tones.

Molyneux remained in his position, rigid and impassive, his eyes wide open like those of a somnambulist.

"Is the ball rolling?"

"Yes."

"Has it stopped?"

"Yes."

"The game?"

"*Quatre noir, pair et manque,*" replied Molyneux in the passionless parrot voice of a croupier. Madame Valprez jotted the number down on the card. Again she repeated the same question and again came the response—

"*Vingt et un, rouge, impair et passe,*" from Molyneux.

And in a similar manner Molyneux quickly announced twenty numbers, which Madame Valprez carefully wrote down upon her card. Then she paused and looked at his unconscious figure with a strange smile, in which were at once satisfaction, triumph and doubt.

"Wake!" she said.

Into Molyneux's eyes came a sudden light of conscious recognition; he spoke as if there had been no interval between the present moment and his last remark, a quarter of an hour ago; but he was aware, at the same time, of the slightest sensation of lethargy, such as one feels on being roused from a deep sleep.

"Well," he remarked with a smile, "what next? The experiment—"

"Has been completed!" said Madame Valprez, and pointed to the roulette card on the table.

"What!" cried Molyneux. "You don't mean to say that—"

"Yes, my friend!" she interrupted him, "you have been clairvoyant for more than ten minutes past! Here is the result," and she handed him the card with the figures jotted down upon it.

"That is very remarkable," said he—"I remember nothing of all this, though, truly, I am conscious of a slight drowsiness! Then I have been in a mesmeric sleep?"

Madarie Valprez inclined her head.

"And predicted twenty numbers on the central roulette board of the second room," she answered, smiling—"There they are!"

"What!" again exclaimed Molyneux, casting his eye over the pencilled numerals. Then he looked at Madame Valprez inquiringly. She seemed to interpret his glance, for she replied—

"Yes, there is, of course, the possibility! We may be taking a will-o'-the-wisp for our guide—still, if on the other hand, the figures—the whole scene which you described in your sleep—were not merely subjective impressions, but actual previsioned facts, consider, Mr. Molyneux, what a marvellous field of untried metaphysical activities becomes opened up by our experiment! Consider, too," she added with a gleam of excitement, borrowed, it seemed, from that of her listener—"to what purely personal advancement of our interests—our worldly interests—we can apply the first and immediate consequence of this experiment!"

"If," replied Molyneux, rising and pacing the room, "it prove not to be a will-o'-the-wisp."

"The first five minutes at the roulette table will teach us that," said she. "You will not leave Monte Carlo after all?" she asked with an odd smile.

"No," said Molyneux. "I shall wait—at least—till to-morrow evening!"

"Then, my friend, remember to be at the Casino punctually at—nay, a little before, two o'clock. I will meet you there; and, as it is getting late—"

Molyneux bowed.

"I will say *au revoir*," he replied, "and good night."

In a state of hardly repressed excitement he walked over to the Casino the following afternoon, and was met at the entrance by Madame Valprez.

"Let us go at once to the table!" she said. "With regard to money—"

"I may say at once that I have none," broke in Molyneux. "I told you yesterday that I had lost my last piece, and of course I have not had time to receive a fresh supply from England yet."

"That is of no consequence," said she. "Our experiment is a joint one, and we will share whatever we may win."

"But if we lose—"

"I do not mind taking the risk—to the amount of £50. For the first five numbers we will stake low. If we find that they correspond with the predicted numbers which I have written down here, we will, of course, increase our stakes."

They passed into the Salles de Jeu and made their way to the centre table in the second room. Play had not long commenced—it was not yet two o'clock—and they found a couple of vacant chairs, which they occupied.

Madame Valprez took a rouleau of gold pieces from her chatelaine, and laid it on the table in front of her.

"The first number," she said in a low tone to Molyneux, "was *quatre*. We will wait till *quatre* turns up before commencing to stake. It is not due, remember, until two o'clock!"

So for several turns of the board they waited and watched the game. At five minutes to two there was a change of croupiers. Madame Valprez looked up with a slight appearance of anxiety, and then an expression of satisfaction, almost of relief, passed over her countenance. The new croupier to the right of Molyneux was a dark, hook-nosed man, with a sharp, alert face, and a short, pointed moustache. The croupier who took his place opposite him, almost immediately afterwards, was short, fat, and wore grey whiskers. Madame Valprez identified both men by sight. They were the two whom Molyneux had described in his mesmeric trance the evening before. The following turns of the board were watched by both Molyneux and his companion with growing interest. "*Rien ne va plus*" had been called for the third coup, and the next moment Molyneux gave a little gasp—for the number that turned up was four. He could not suppress an exclamation— and now for the first time he was oddly conscious of a feeling of retrospect with regard to what was about immediately to ensue.

"Wait!" said Madame Valprez, laying a cautious hand upon his sleeve.

"What—you will not stake on 21? I know it will come!" he answered quickly.

"You *know?*" she said, bending upon him a strange glance, half of inquiry.

"Yes—I—I seem to know!"

"Well, let us see!" she said.

The game was made, the ball spun round, and a few seconds later the croupier called—

"*Vingt et un, rouge, impair, et passe!*"

"There!" cried Molyneux, "I knew it!"

"We will begin," said Madame Valprez in a tone of decision. She looked at her card.

"A louis on *sixteen*" she said. "We will not risk too much at first."

"Sixteen,—yes," nodded Molyneux, "sixteen the next number!"

The louis was staked, and the number "*seize*" was called.

Madame Valprez said nothing, but her face took on a sudden look of concentration, as though her will were working strongly to a particular object. Molyneux, whose features were mobile, betrayed by his expression the excitement which he now began to feel in an extraordinary degree. His companion crossed out the number 16 on her card and named "*trois*," and as she uttered the number, Molyneux again felt that singular sensation of certainty—as if he were looking back upon the event from a point beyond and saw the fact declared. Still Madame Valprez would stake but the louis, and when the second time it won, Molyneux leant back and regarded her with something of reproach in his glance. Madame Valprez smiled.

"There is plenty of time," she said, answering his implied protest. "I shall not be satisfied till we have the corroboration of ten consecutive numbers. That would, to my mind, almost constitute proof, and we shall still have ten numbers left."

Following this resolve, Madame Valprez continued to stake—and with never varying success—single louis for eight coups more, checking each number on her card as in turn it appeared, as it were, with the unerring and inexorable certainty of some fatal compulsion. Molyneux's eyes glistened and he breathed hard. Excitement began to run high, and was electrically communicated from player to player. At the tenth coup the attention of the whole table was rivetted upon Madame Valprez and Molyneux. Madame Valprez made a rapid calculation of the winnings that lay in little gold piles and notes before herself and Molyneux.

"We have won something over five thousand francs," she remarked to him.

"And we ought to have broken the bank!" he exclaimed, pettishly.

"It is not too late!" she smiled again—and this time with peculiar confidence.

"The maximum—at last?" he inquired.

Madame Valprez nodded.

"Of course," she said.

Molyneux drummed on the table with that absent fixed look that implies the acme of restrained excitement.

"Put this on *sept*," Madame Valprez said to Molyneux, pushing towards him a roll of notes.

"This sort of thing can't last, you know!" observed an old gentleman to his neighbour, and he placed the maximum on the last dozen as he spoke, to emphasise his opinion. Others, too, fought shy of the early numbers, fancying such luck could not hold. One gentleman, only, staked a five-franc piece on *sept en plein*; the rest of the table smiled half expectantly. But when the ball stopped, the croupier to the right of Molyneux looked at him and shrugged his shoulders, elevating his eyebrows resignedly.

"*Sept, rouge, impair et manque!*" he cried out. "*Sept en plein le maxime,*" he added, "*et cinq francs en plein,*" and a bundle of notes was pushed across to Molyneux and his companion. Molyneux wiped his forehead with his pocket handkerchief.

"By Gad!" he muttered, "this, as the Yankees say, licks creation! How many more numbers are there?"

"Nine," replied Madame Valprez.

"Oh, plunge to the hilt!" entreated Molyneux. "Fifteen is the next; I know. *Carré, cheval,* the *colour, impair, manque,* the middle dozen, and *en plein*! We shall make a fortune!"

His enthusiasm was contagious; Madame Valprez's hand trembled as she passed him the pieces and notes to stake; her eyes shone strangely and her pulses quickened. A buzz of amazement had risen on all sides of them.

"Fifteen," however, turned up, and amidst a gasping clamour of excited comment, notes to the amount of nearly a thousand pounds were passed to Madame Valprez and Molyneux. The fever of anticipation was at its height. Oddly enough, the excitement of Madame Valprez and Molyneux, having reached a certain climax, now gave way to a calm and impassive tranquillity—for with them expectancy had become dulled by an unerring conviction of the result. They played like machines, heedless of the hundred eyes that were hanging upon their every movement, and of the ever-increasing pile of gold and notes that rose in front of them. At the eighteenth coup there was a slight pause and a quick, whispered consultation between the croupiers. Again Madame Valprez increased her winnings by another thousand pounds. "*Quelle diablesse de femme!*" the whisper went round, and the exclamations of amazement were redoubled, accompanied by shrugs, laughs and significant comments. Madame Valprez handed the notes in bundles to Molyneux, who carefully folded them and put them away in his pocket book. The twentieth number on Madame Valprez's card had arrived.

"*Trente trois*" she said in a low tone—and Molyneux placed the stakes upon every combination of the numeral, as before. There was a sudden and absolute stillness as the croupier gave the initial twist to the board and the ball spun round the disc. With its final click there came a simultaneous gasp of expectation; and a moment after the croupier's voice announced the number thirty-three. Then there arose almost an uproar—people laughed, applauded, and clapped their hands, some even shouted in the delirium of communicated enthusiasm—for never before in the whole annals of Monte Carlo had a player been known to name sixteen consecutive numbers without a single mistake. The croupier pushed a pyramid of notes and gold towards Molyneux; then at a signal from his confrères he rose from his seat. The others did the same.

"Messieurs," he said, "the bank is closed."

"Come," said Molyneux, in a whisper, "let us get out of this crowd as quickly as possible," and he and Madame Valprez left their chairs, after the lady had hastily thrust the remainder of her pile of notes and gold into her chatelaine. But with all the haste in the world they could by no means escape the distinction of sudden notoriety. Many followed to catch a further glimpse of the players who had broken the bank in half-an-hour; and a hundred comments were levelled at them as they wended their way through the crowd. Before they reached the doors a gentleman elbowed his way towards them.

"Monsieur," he said, abruptly, addressing Molyneux—"pardon me, but do you play on a system? If so, I will pay you £5,000 for your system!"

Molyneux bowed coldly.

"I don't play on a system," he said, and immediately turned his back upon the intruder. At length they reached the main entrance, and a minute later were standing once more in the glorious sunshine of the gardens.

"Shall we go across to the Café de Paris?" asked Molyneux.

"I think it would be wiser to go to the hotel," replied Madame Valprez.

"It is simply marvellous!" exclaimed Molyneux, drawing a deep breath.

"I wonder what Dr. Charcot would say to it!" observed she, with an odd smile.

"Ah, Dr. Charcot! Well, there is a greater than Dr. Charcot!" added Molyneux gallantly.

"My friend," said Madame Valprez, "we have won more than ten thousand pounds. But for the present—"

Molyneux nodded; her tone plainly enough indicated her meaning.

"Yes, yes. Perhaps six months hence will be soon enough—"

"To repeat the experiment? I think it would. Ten thousand a year should be a sufficient income. Meantime devote yourself to your writing."

"And you—?"

She smiled a little sadly.

"I have my aims," she said. "To make money is the least of them—ah, if I could only develop my theories to the benefit of mankind—but I have strange forebodings. These abnormal gifts, what are they given us for? I often feel oppressed by the sense of some weighty trust, one quite beyond my power to fulfil! Yet,—well, well!" she added lightly, and with a quick change of humour, "it is our duty to make the best of our opportunities and to enjoy the good things of life while we may, Mr. Molyneux! So—shall we say in six months' time?"

Molyneux laughed as he took her hand.

"Yes," he agreed, "in six months' time!"

But the experiment was destined never to be repeated. Before three months out of six were completed Madame Valprez, one of the greatest mesmerists of the age, had passed to the other side of the Valley.

The Parasite
By Arthur Conan Doyle
Part I.

March 24. The spring is fairly with us now. Outside my laboratory window the great chestnut-tree is all covered with the big, glutinous, gummy buds, some of which have already begun to break into little green shuttlecocks. As you walk down the lanes you are conscious of the rich, silent forces of nature working all around you. The wet earth smells fruitful and luscious. Green shoots are peeping out everywhere. The twigs are stiff with their sap; and the moist, heavy English air is laden with a faintly resinous perfume. Buds in the hedges, lambs beneath them — everywhere the work of reproduction going forward!

I can see it without, and I can feel it within. We also have our spring when the little arterioles dilate, the lymph flows in a brisker stream, the glands work harder, winnowing and straining. Every year nature readjusts the whole machine. I can feel the ferment in my blood at this very moment, and as the cool sunshine pours through my window I could dance about in it like a gnat. So I should, only that Charles Sadler would rush upstairs to know what was the matter. Besides, I must remember that I am Professor Gilroy. An old professor may afford to be natural, but when fortune has given one of the first chairs in the university to a man of four-and-thirty he must try and act the part consistently.

What a fellow Wilson is! If I could only throw the same enthusiasm into physiology that he does into psychology, I should become a Claude Bernard at the least. His whole life and soul and energy work to one end. He drops to sleep collating his results of the past day, and he wakes to plan his researches for the coming one. And yet, outside the narrow circle who follow his proceedings, he gets so little credit for it. Physiology is a recognized science. If I add even a brick to the edifice, every one sees and applauds it. But Wilson is trying to dig the foundations for a science of the future. His work is underground and does not show. Yet he goes on uncomplainingly, corresponding with a hundred semi-maniacs in the hope of finding one reliable witness, sifting a hundred lies on the chance of gaining one little speck of truth, collating old books, devouring new ones, experimenting, lecturing, trying to light up in others the fiery interest which is consuming him. I am filled with wonder and admiration when I think of him, and yet, when he asks me to associate myself with his researches, I am compelled to tell him that, in their present state, they offer little attraction to a man who is devoted to exact science. If he could show me something positive and objective, I might then be tempted to approach the question from its physiological side. So long as half his subjects are tainted with charlatanerie and the other half with hysteria we physiologists must content ourselves with the body and leave the mind to our descendants.

No doubt I am a materialist. Agatha says that I am a rank one. I tell her that is an excellent reason for shortening our engagement, since I am in such urgent need of her spirituality. And yet I may claim to be a curious example of the effect of education upon temperament, for by nature I am, unless I deceive myself, a highly psychic man. I was a nervous, sensitive boy, a dreamer, a somnambulist, full of impressions and intuitions. My black hair, my dark eyes, my thin, olive face, my tapering fingers, are all characteristic of my real temperament, and cause experts like Wilson to claim me as their own. But my brain is soaked with exact knowledge. I have trained myself to deal only with fact and with proof. Surmise and fancy have no place in my scheme of thought. Show me what I can see with my microscope, cut with my scalpel, weigh in my balance, and I will devote a lifetime to its investigation. But when you ask me to study feelings, impressions, suggestions, you ask me to do what is distasteful and even demoralizing. A departure from pure reason affects me like an evil smell or a musical discord.

Which is a very sufficient reason why I am a little loath to go to Professor Wilson's tonight. Still I feel that I could hardly get out of the invitation without positive rudeness; and, now that Mrs. Marden and Agatha are going, of course I would not if I could. But I had rather meet them anywhere else. I know that Wilson would draw me into this nebulous semi-science of his if he could. In his enthusiasm he is perfectly impervious to hints or remonstrances. Nothing short of a positive quarrel will make him realize my aversion to the whole business. I have no doubt that he has some new mesmerist or clairvoyant or medium or trickster of some sort whom he is going to exhibit to us, for even his entertainments bear upon his hobby. Well, it will be a treat for Agatha, at any rate. She is interested in it, as woman usually is in whatever is vague and mystical and indefinite.

10.50 P.M. This diary-keeping of mine is, I fancy, the outcome of that scientific habit of mind about which I wrote this morning. I like to register impressions while they are fresh. Once a day at least I endeavor to define my own mental position. It is a useful piece of self-analysis, and has, I fancy, a steadying effect upon the character. Frankly, I must confess that my own needs what stiffening I can give it. I fear that, after all, much of my neurotic temperament survives, and that I am far from that cool, calm precision which characterizes Murdoch or Pratt-Haldane. Otherwise, why should the tomfoolery which I have witnessed this evening have set my nerves thrilling so that even now I am all unstrung? My only comfort is that neither Wilson nor Miss Penclosa nor even Agatha could have possibly known my weakness.

And what in the world was there to excite me? Nothing, or so little that it will seem ludicrous when I set it down.

The Mardens got to Wilson's before me. In fact, I was one of the last to arrive and found the room crowded. I had hardly time to say a word to Mrs. Marden and to Agatha, who was looking charming in white and pink, with glittering wheat-ears in her hair, when Wilson came twitching at my sleeve.

"You want something positive, Gilroy," said he, drawing me apart into a corner. "My dear fellow, I have a phenomenon — a phenomenon!"

I should have been more impressed had I not heard the same before. His sanguine spirit turns every fire-fly into a star.

"No possible question about the bona fides this time," said he, in answer, perhaps, to some little gleam of amusement in my eyes. "My wife has known her for many years. They both come from Trinidad, you know. Miss Penclosa has only been in England a month or two, and knows no one outside the university circle, but I assure you that the things she has told us suffice in themselves to establish clairvoyance upon an absolutely scientific basis. There is nothing like her, amateur or professional. Come and be introduced!"

I like none of these mystery-mongers, but the amateur least of all. With the paid performer you may pounce upon him and expose him the instant that you have seen through his trick. He is there to deceive you, and you are there to find him out. But what are you to do with the friend of your host's wife? Are you to turn on a light suddenly and expose her slapping a surreptitious banjo? Or are you to hurl cochineal over her evening frock when she steals round with her phosphorus bottle and her supernatural platitude? There would be a scene, and you would be looked upon as a brute. So you have your choice of being that or a dupe. I was in no very good humor as I followed Wilson to the lady.

Any one less like my idea of a West Indian could not be imagined. She was a small, frail creature, well over forty, I should say, with a pale, peaky face, and hair of a very light shade of chestnut. Her presence was insignificant and her manner retiring. In any group of ten women she would have been the last whom one would have picked out. Her eyes were perhaps her most remarkable, and also, I am compelled to say, her least pleasant, feature. They were gray in color, — gray with a shade of green, — and their expression struck me as being decidedly furtive. I wonder if furtive is the word, or should I have said fierce? On second thoughts, feline would have expressed it better. A crutch leaning against the wall told me what was painfully evident when she rose: that one of her legs was crippled.

So I was introduced to Miss Penclosa, and it did not escape me that as my name was mentioned she glanced across at Agatha. Wilson had evidently been talking. And presently, no doubt, thought I, she will inform me by occult means that I am engaged to a young lady with wheat-ears in her hair. I wondered how much more Wilson had been telling her about me.

"Professor Gilroy is a terrible sceptic," said he; "I hope, Miss Penclosa, that you will be able to convert him."

She looked keenly up at me.

"Professor Gilroy is quite right to be sceptical if he has not seen any thing convincing," said she. "I should have thought," she added, "that you would yourself have been an excellent subject."

"For what, may I ask?" said I.

"Well, for mesmerism, for example."

"My experience has been that mesmerists go for their subjects to those who are mentally unsound. All their results are vitiated, as it seems to me, by the fact that they are dealing with abnormal organisms."

"Which of these ladies would you say possessed a normal organism?" she asked. "I should like you to select the one who seems to you to have the best balanced mind. Should we say the girl in pink and white? — Miss Agatha Marden, I think the name is."

"Yes, I should attach weight to any results from her."

"I have never tried how far she is impressionable. Of course some people respond much more rapidly than others. May I ask how far your scepticism extends? I suppose that you admit the mesmeric sleep and the power of suggestion."

"I admit nothing, Miss Penclosa."

"Dear me, I thought science had got further than that. Of course I know nothing about the scientific side of it. I only know what I can do. You see the girl in red, for example, over near the Japanese jar. I shall will that she come across to us."

She bent forward as she spoke and dropped her fan upon the floor. The girl whisked round and came straight toward us, with an enquiring look upon her face, as if some one had called her.

"What do you think of that, Gilroy?" cried Wilson, in a kind of ecstasy.

I did not dare to tell him what I thought of it. To me it was the most barefaced, shameless piece of imposture that I had ever witnessed. The collusion and the signal had really been too obvious.

"Professor Gilroy is not satisfied," said she, glancing up at me with her strange little eyes. "My poor fan is to get the credit of that experiment. Well, we must try something else. Miss Marden, would you have any objection to my putting you off?"

"Oh, I should love it!" cried Agatha.

By this time all the company had gathered round us in a circle, the shirt-fronted men, and the white-throated women, some awed, some critical, as though it were something between a religious ceremony and a conjurer's entertainment. A red velvet arm-chair had been pushed into the centre, and Agatha lay back in it, a little flushed and trembling slightly from excitement. I could see it from the vibration of the wheat-ears. Miss Penclosa rose from her seat and stood over her, leaning upon her crutch.

And there was a change in the woman. She no longer seemed small or insignificant. Twenty years were gone from her age. Her eyes were shining, a tinge of color had come into her sallow cheeks, her whole figure had expanded. So I have seen a dull-eyed, listless lad change in an instant into briskness and life when given a task of which he felt himself master. She looked down at Agatha with an expression which I resented from the bottom of my soul — the expression with which a Roman empress might have looked at her kneeling slave. Then with a quick, commanding gesture she tossed up her arms and swept them slowly down in front of her.

I was watching Agatha narrowly. During three passes she seemed to be simply amused. At the fourth I observed a slight glazing of her eyes, accompanied by some dilation of her pupils. At the sixth there was a momentary rigor. At the seventh her lids began to droop. At the tenth her eyes were closed, and her breathing was slower and fuller than usual. I tried as I watched to preserve my scientific calm, but a foolish, causeless agitation convulsed me. I trust that I hid it, but I felt as a child feels in the dark. I could not have believed that I was still open to such weakness.

"She is in the trance," said Miss Penclosa.

"She is sleeping!" I cried.

"Wake her, then!"

I pulled her by the arm and shouted in her ear. She might have been dead for all the impression that I could make. Her body was there on the velvet chair. Her organs were acting — her heart, her lungs. But her soul! It had slipped from beyond our ken. Whither had it gone? What power had dispossessed it? I was puzzled and disconcerted.

"So much for the mesmeric sleep," said Miss Penclosa. "As regards suggestion, whatever I may suggest Miss Marden will infallibly do, whether it be now or after she has awakened from her trance. Do you demand proof of it?"

"Certainly," said I.

"You shall have it." I saw a smile pass over her face, as though an amusing thought had struck her. She stooped and whispered earnestly into her subject's ear. Agatha, who had been so deaf to me, nodded her head as she listened.

"Awake!" cried Miss Penclosa, with a sharp tap of her crutch upon the floor. The eyes opened, the glazing cleared slowly away, and the soul looked out once more after its strange eclipse.

We went away early. Agatha was none the worse for her strange excursion, but I was nervous and unstrung, unable to listen to or answer the stream of comments which Wilson was pouring out for my benefit. As I bade her good-night Miss Penclosa slipped a piece of paper into my hand.

"Pray forgive me," said she, "if I take means to overcome your scepticism. Open this note at ten o'clock to-morrow morning. It is a little private test."

I can't imagine what she means, but there is the note, and it shall be opened as she directs. My head is aching, and I have written enough for to-night. To-morrow I dare say that what seems so inexplicable will take quite another complexion. I shall not surrender my convictions without a struggle.

March 25. I am amazed, confounded. It is clear that I must reconsider my opinion upon this matter. But first let me place on record what has occurred.

I had finished breakfast, and was looking over some diagrams with which my lecture is to be illustrated, when my housekeeper entered to tell me that Agatha was in my study and wished to see me immediately. I glanced at the clock and saw with sun rise that it was only half-past nine.

When I entered the room, she was standing on the hearth-rug facing me. Something in her pose chilled me and checked the words which were rising to my lips. Her veil was half down, but I could see that she was pale and that her expression was constrained.

"Austin," she said, "I have come to tell you that our engagement is at an end."

I staggered. I believe that I literally did stagger. I know that I found myself leaning against the bookcase for support.

"But—but—" I stammered. "This is very sudden, Agatha."

"Yes, Austin, I have come here to tell you that our engagement is at an end."

"But surely," I cried, "you will give me some reason! This is unlike you, Agatha. Tell me how I have been unfortunate enough to offend you."

"It is all over, Austin."

"But why? You must be under some delusion, Agatha. Perhaps you have been told some falsehood about me. Or you may have misunderstood something that I have said to you. Only let me know what it is, and a word may set it all right."

"We must consider it all at an end."

"But you left me last night without a hint at any disagreement. What could have occurred in the interval to change you so? It must have been something that happened last night. You have been thinking it over and you have disapproved of my conduct. Was it the mesmerism? Did you blame me for letting that woman exercise her power over you? You know that at the least sign I should have interfered."

"It is useless, Austin. All is over."

Her voice was cold and measured; her manner strangely formal and hard. It seemed to me that she was absolutely resolved not to be drawn into any argument or explanation. As for me, I was shaking with agitation, and I turned my face aside, so ashamed was I that she should see my want of control.

"You must know what this means to me!" I cried. "It is the blasting of all my hopes and the ruin of my life! You surely will not inflict such a punishment upon me unheard. You will let me know what is the matter. Consider how impossible it would be for me, under any circumstances, to treat you so. For God's sake, Agatha, let me know what I have done!"

She walked past me without a word and opened the door.

"It is quite useless, Austin," said she. "You must consider our engagement at an end." An instant later she was gone, and, before I could recover myself sufficiently to follow her, I heard the hall-door close behind her.

I rushed into my room to change my coat, with the idea of hurrying round to Mrs. Marden's to learn from her what the cause of my misfortune might be. So shaken was I that I could hardly lace my boots. Never shall I forget those horrible ten minutes. I had just pulled on my overcoat when the clock upon the mantel-piece struck ten.

Ten! I associated the idea with Miss Penclosa's note. It was lying before me on the table, and I tore it open. It was scribbled in pencil in a peculiarly angular handwriting.

"MY DEAR PROFESSOR GILROY [it said]: Pray excuse the personal nature of the test which I am giving you. Professor Wilson happened to mention the relations between you and my subject of this evening, and it struck me that nothing could be more convincing to you than if I were to suggest to Miss Marden that she should call upon you at half-past nine to-morrow morning and suspend your engagement for half an hour or so. Science is so exacting that it is difficult to give a satisfying test, but I am convinced that this at least will be an action which she would be most unlikely to do of her own free will. Forget any thing that she may have said, as she has really nothing whatever to do with it, and will certainly not recollect any thing about it. I write this note to shorten your anxiety, and to beg you to forgive me for the momentary unhappiness which my suggestion must have caused you. Yours faithfully; HELEN PENCLOSA."

Really, when I had read the note, I was too relieved to be angry. It was a liberty. Certainly it was a very great liberty indeed on the part of a lady whom I had only met once. But, after all, I had challenged her by my scepticism. It may have been, as she said, a little difficult to devise a test which would satisfy me.

And she had done that. There could be no question at all upon the point. For me hypnotic suggestion was finally established. It took its place from now onward as one of the facts of life. That Agatha, who of all women of my acquaintance has the best balanced mind, had been reduced to a condition of automatism appeared to be certain. A person at a distance had worked her as an engineer on the shore might guide a Brennan torpedo. A second soul had stepped in, as it were, had pushed her own aside, and had seized her nervous mechanism, saying: "I will work this for half an hour." And Agatha must have been unconscious as she came and as she returned. Could she make her way in safety through the streets in such a state? I put on my hat and hurried round to see if all was well with her.

Yes. She was at home. I was shown into the drawing-room and found her sitting with a book upon her lap.

"You are an early visitor, Austin," said she, smiling.

"And you have been an even earlier one," I answered.

She looked puzzled. "What do you mean?" she asked.

"You have not been out to-day?"

"No, certainly not."

"Agatha," said I seriously, "would you mind telling me exactly what you have done this morning?"

She laughed at my earnestness.

"You've got on your professional look, Austin. See what comes of being engaged to a man of science. However, I will tell you, though I can't imagine what you want to know for. I got up at eight. I breakfasted at half-past. I came into this room at ten minutes past nine and began to read the 'Memoirs of Mme. de Remusat.' In a few minutes I did the French lady the bad compliment of dropping to sleep over her pages, and I did you, sir, the very flattering one of dreaming about you. It is only a few minutes since I woke up."

"And found yourself where you had been before?"

"Why, where else should I find myself?"

"Would you mind telling me, Agatha, what it was that you dreamed about me? It really is not mere curiosity on my part."

"I merely had a vague impression that you came into it. I cannot recall any thing definite."

"If you have not been out to-day, Agatha, how is it that your shoes are dusty?"

A pained look came over her face.

"Really, Austin, I do not know what is the matter with you this morning. One would almost think that you doubted my word. If my boots are dusty, it must be, of course, that I have put on a pair which the maid had not cleaned."

It was perfectly evident that she knew nothing whatever about the matter, and I reflected that, after all, perhaps it was better that I should not enlighten her. It might frighten her, and could serve no good purpose that I could see. I said no more about it, therefore, and left shortly afterward to give my lecture.

But I am immensely impressed. My horizon of scientific possibilities has suddenly been enormously extended. I no longer wonder at Wilson's demonic energy and enthusiasm. Who would not work hard who had a vast virgin field ready to his hand? Why, I have known the novel shape of a nucleolus, or a trifling peculiarity of striped muscular fibre seen under a 300-diameter lens, fill me with exultation. How petty do such researches seem when compared with this one which strikes at the very roots of life and the nature of the soul! I had always looked upon spirit as a product of matter. The brain, I thought, secreted the mind, as the liver does the bile. But how can this be when I see mind working from a distance and playing upon matter as a musician might upon a violin? The body does not give rise to the soul, then, but is rather the rough instrument by which the spirit manifests itself. The windmill does not give rise to the wind, but only indicates it. It was opposed to my whole habit of thought, and yet it was undeniably possible and worthy of investigation.

And why should I not investigate it? I see that under yesterday's date I said: "If I could see something positive and objective, I might be tempted to approach it from the physiological aspect." Well, I have got my test. I shall be as good as my word. The investigation would, I am sure, be of immense interest. Some of my colleagues might look askance at it, for science is full of unreasoning prejudices, but if Wilson has the courage of his convictions, I can afford to have it also. I shall go to him to-morrow morning — to him and to Miss Penclosa. If she can show us so much, it is probable that she can show us more.

Part II.

March 26. Wilson was, as I had anticipated, very exultant over my conversion, and Miss Penclosa was also demurely pleased at the result of her experiment. Strange what a silent, colorless creature she is save only when she exercises her power! Even talking about it gives her color and life. She seems to take a singular interest in me. I cannot help observing how her eyes follow me about the room.

We had the most interesting conversation about her own powers. It is just as well to put her views on record, though they cannot, of course, claim any scientific weight.

"You are on the very fringe of the subject," said she, when I had expressed wonder at the remarkable instance of suggestion which she had shown me. "I had no direct influence upon Miss Marden when she came round to you. I was not even thinking of her that morning. What I did was to set her mind as I might set the alarum of a clock so that at the hour named it would go off of its own accord. If six months instead of twelve hours had been suggested, it would have been the same."

"And if the suggestion had been to assassinate me?"

"She would most inevitably have done so."

"But this is a terrible power!" I cried.

"It is, as you say, a terrible power," she answered gravely, "and the more you know of it the more terrible will it seem to you."

"May I ask," said I, "what you meant when you said that this matter of suggestion is only at the fringe of it? What do you consider the essential?"

"I had rather not tell you."

I was surprised at the decision of her answer.

"You understand," said I, "that it is not out of curiosity I ask, but in the hope that I may find some scientific explanation for the facts with which you furnish me."

"Frankly, Professor Gilroy," said she, "I am not at all interested in science, nor do I care whether it can or cannot classify these powers."

"But I was hoping—"

"Ah, that is quite another thing. If you make it a personal matter," said she, with the pleasantest of smiles, "I shall be only too happy to tell you any thing you wish to know. Let me see; what was it you asked me? Oh, about the further powers. Professor Wilson won't believe in them, but they are quite true all the same. For example, it is possible for an operator to gain complete command over his subject — presuming that the latter is a good one. Without any previous suggestion he may make him do whatever he likes."

"Without the subject's knowledge?"

"That depends. If the force were strongly exerted, he would know no more about it than Miss Marden did when she came round and frightened you so. Or, if the influence was less powerful, he might be conscious of what he was doing, but be quite unable to prevent himself from doing it."

"Would he have lost his own will power, then?"

"It would be over-ridden by another stronger one."

"Have you ever exercised this power yourself?"

"Several times."

"Is your own will so strong, then?"

"Well, it does not entirely depend upon that. Many have strong wills which are not detachable from themselves. The thing is to have the gift of projecting it into another person and superseding his own. I find that the power varies with my own strength and health."

"Practically, you send your soul into another person's body."

"Well, you might put it that way."

"And what does your own body do?"

"It merely feels lethargic."

"Well, but is there no danger to your own health?" I asked.

"There might be a little. You have to be careful never to let your own consciousness absolutely go; otherwise, you might experience some difficulty in finding your way back again. You must always preserve the connection, as it were. I am afraid I express myself very badly, Professor Gilroy, but of course I don't know how to put these things in a scientific way. I am just giving you my own experiences and my own explanations."

Well, I read this over now at my leisure, and I marvel at myself! Is this Austin Gilroy, the man who has won his way to the front by his hard reasoning power and by his devotion to fact? Here I am gravely retailing the gossip of a woman who tells me how her soul may be projected from her body, and how, while she lies in a lethargy, she can control the actions of people at a distance. Do I accept it? Certainly not. She must prove and re-prove before I yield a point. But if I am still a sceptic, I have at least ceased to be a scoffer. We are to have a sitting this evening, and she is to try if she can produce any mesmeric effect upon me. If she can, it will make an excellent starting-point for our investigation. No one can accuse me, at any rate, of complicity. If she cannot, we must try and find some subject who will be like Caesar's wife. Wilson is perfectly impervious.

10 P.M. I believe that I am on the threshold of an epoch-making investigation. To have the power of examining these phenomena from inside — to have an organism which will respond, and at the same time a brain which will appreciate and criticise — that is surely a unique advantage. I am quite sure that Wilson would give five years of his life to be as susceptible as I have proved myself to be.

There was no one present except Wilson and his wife. I was seated with my head leaning back, and Miss Penclosa, standing in front and a little to the left, used the same long, sweeping strokes as with Agatha. At each of them a warm current of air seemed to strike me, and to suffuse a thrill and glow all through me from head to foot. My eyes were fixed upon Miss Penclosa's face, but as I gazed the features seemed to blur and to fade away. I was conscious only of her own eyes looking down at me, gray, deep, inscrutable. Larger they grew and larger, until they changed suddenly into two mountain lakes toward which I seemed to be falling with horrible rapidity. I shuddered, and as I did so some deeper stratum of thought told me that the shudder represented the rigor which I had observed in Agatha. An instant later I struck the surface of the lakes, now joined into one, and down I went beneath the water with a fulness in my head and a buzzing in my ears. Down I went, down, down, and then with a swoop up again until I could see the light streaming brightly through the green water. I was almost at the surface when the word "Awake!" rang through my head, and, with a start, I found myself back in the arm-chair, with Miss Penclosa leaning on her crutch, and Wilson, his note book in his hand, peeping over her shoulder. No heaviness or weariness was left behind. On the contrary, though it is only an hour or so since the experiment, I feel so wakeful that I am more inclined for my study than my bedroom. I see quite a vista of interesting experiments extending before us, and am all impatience to begin upon them.

March 27. A blank day, as Miss Penclosa goes with Wilson and his wife to the Suttons'. Have begun Binet and Ferre's "Animal Magnetism." What strange, deep waters these are! Results, results, results — and the cause an absolute mystery. It is stimulating to the imagination, but I must be on my guard against that. Let us have no inferences nor deductions, and nothing but solid facts. I *know* that the mesmeric trance is true; I *know* that mesmeric suggestion is true; I *know* that I am myself sensitive to this force. That is my present position. I have a large new note-book which shall be devoted entirely to scientific detail.

Long talk with Agatha and Mrs. Marden in the evening about our marriage. We think that the summer vac. (the beginning of it) would be the best time for the wedding. Why should we delay? I grudge even those few months. Still, as Mrs. Marden says, there are a good many things to be arranged.

March 28. Mesmerized again by Miss Penclosa. Experience much the same as before, save that insensibility came on more quickly. See Note-book A for temperature of room, barometric pressure, pulse, and respiration as taken by Professor Wilson.

March 29. Mesmerized again. Details in Note-book A.

March 30. Sunday, and a blank day. I grudge any interruption of our experiments. At present they merely embrace the physical signs which go with slight, with complete, and with extreme insensibility. Afterward we hope to pass on to the phenomena of suggestion and of lucidity. Professors have demonstrated these things upon women at Nancy and at the Salpetriere. It will be more convincing when a woman demonstrates it upon a professor, with a second professor as a witness. And that I should be the subject — I, the sceptic, the materialist! At least, I have shown that my devotion to science is greater than to my own personal consistency. The eating of our own words is the greatest sacrifice which truth ever requires of us.

My neighbor, Charles Sadler, the handsome young demonstrator of anatomy, came in this evening to return a volume of Virchow's "Archives" which I had lent him. I call him young, but, as a matter of fact, he is a year older than I am.

"I understand, Gilroy," said he, "that you are being experimented upon by Miss Penclosa."

"Well," he went on, when I had acknowledged it, "if I were you, I should not let it go any further. You will think me very impertinent, no doubt, but, none the less, I feel it to be my duty to advise you to have no more to do with her."

Of course I asked him why.

"I am so placed that I cannot enter into particulars as freely as I could wish," said he. "Miss Penclosa is the friend of my friend, and my position is a delicate one. I can only say this: that I have myself been the subject of some of the woman's experiments, and that they have left a most unpleasant impression upon my mind."

He could hardly expect me to be satisfied with that, and I tried hard to get something more definite out of him, but without success. Is it conceivable that he could be jealous at my having superseded him? Or is he one of those men of science who feel personally injured when facts run counter to their preconceived opinions? He cannot seriously suppose that because he has some vague grievance I am, therefore, to abandon a series of experiments which promise to be so fruitful of results. He appeared to be annoyed at the light way in which I treated his shadowy warnings, and we parted with some little coldness on both sides.

March 31. Mesmerized by Miss P.

April 1. Mesmerized by Miss P. (Note-book A.)

April 2. Mesmerized by Miss P. (Sphygmographic chart taken by Professor Wilson.)

April 3. It is possible that this course of mesmerism may be a little trying to the general constitution. Agatha says that I am thinner and darker under the eyes. I am conscious of a nervous irritability which I had not observed in myself before. The least noise, for example, makes me start, and the stupidity of a student causes me exasperation instead of amusement. Agatha wishes me to stop, but I tell her that every course of study is trying, and that one can never attain a result with out paying some price for it. When she sees the sensation which my forthcoming paper on "The Relation between Mind and Matter" may make, she will understand that it is worth a little nervous wear and tear. I should not be surprised if I got my F. R. S. over it.

Mesmerized again in the evening. The effect is produced more rapidly now, and the subjective visions are less marked. I keep full notes of each sitting. Wilson is leaving for town for a week or ten days, but we shall not interrupt the experiments, which depend for their value as much upon my sensations as on his observations.

April 4. I must be carefully on my guard. A complication has crept into our experiments which I had not reckoned upon. In my eagerness for scientific facts I have been foolishly blind to the human relations between Miss Penclosa and myself. I can write here what I would not breathe to a living soul. The unhappy woman appears to have formed an attachment for me.

I should not say such a thing, even in the privacy of my own intimate journal, if it had not come to such a pass that it is impossible to ignore it. For some time, — that is, for the last week, — there have been signs which I have brushed aside and refused to think of. Her brightness when I come, her dejection when I go, her eagerness that I should come often, the expression of her eyes, the tone of her voice — I tried to think that they meant nothing, and were, perhaps, only her ardent West Indian manner. But last night, as I awoke from the mesmeric sleep, I put out my hand, unconsciously, involuntarily, and clasped hers. When I came fully to myself, we were sitting with them locked, she looking up at me with an expectant smile. And the horrible thing was that I felt impelled to say what she expected me to say. What a false wretch I should have been! How I should have loathed myself to-day had I yielded to the temptation of that moment! But, thank God, I was strong enough to spring up and hurry from the room. I was rude, I fear, but I could not, no, I *could* not, trust myself another moment. I, a gentleman, a man of honor, engaged to one of the sweetest girls in England — and yet in a moment of reasonless passion I nearly professed love for this woman whom I hardly know. She is far older than myself and a cripple. It is monstrous, odious; and yet the impulse was so strong that, had I stayed another minute in her presence, I should have committed myself. What was it? I have to teach others the workings of our organism, and what do I know of it myself? Was it the sudden upcropping of some lower stratum in my nature — a brutal primitive instinct suddenly asserting itself? I could almost believe the tales of obsession by evil spirits, so overmastering was the feeling.

Well, the incident places me in a most unfortunate position. On the one hand, I am very loath to abandon a series of experiments which have already gone so far, and which promise such brilliant results. On the other, if this unhappy woman has conceived a passion for me — But surely even now I must have made some hideous mistake. She, with her age and her deformity! It is impossible. And then she knew about Agatha. She understood how I was placed. She only smiled out of amusement, perhaps, when in my dazed state I seized her hand. It was my half-mesmerized brain which gave it a meaning, and sprang with such bestial swiftness to meet it. I wish I could persuade myself that it was indeed so. On the whole, perhaps, my wisest plan would be to postpone our other experiments until Wilson's return. I have written a note to Miss Penclosa, therefore, making no allusion to last night, but saying that a press of work would cause me to interrupt our sittings for a few days. She has answered, formally enough, to say that if I should change my mind I should find her at home at the usual hour.

10 P.M. Well, well, what a thing of straw I am! I am coming to know myself better of late, and the more I know the lower I fall in my own estimation. Surely I was not always so weak as this. At four o'clock I should have smiled had any one told me that I should go to Miss Penclosa's to-night, and yet, at eight, I was at Wilson's door as usual. I don't know how it occurred. The influence of habit, I suppose. Perhaps there is a mesmeric craze as there is an opium craze, and I am a victim to it. I only know that as I worked in my study I became more and more uneasy. I fidgeted. I worried. I could not concentrate my mind upon the papers in front of me. And then, at last, almost before I knew what I was doing, I seized my hat and hurried round to keep my usual appointment.

We had an interesting evening. Mrs. Wilson was present during most of the time, which prevented the embarrassment which one at least of us must have felt. Miss Penclosa's manner was quite the same as usual, and she expressed no surprise at my having come in spite of my note. There was nothing in her bearing to show that yesterday's incident had made any impression upon her, and so I am inclined to hope that I overrated it.

April 6 (evening). No, no, no, I did not overrate it. I can no longer attempt to conceal from myself that this woman has conceived a passion for me. It is monstrous, but it is true. Again, tonight, I awoke from the mesmeric trance to find my hand in hers, and to suffer that odious feeling which urges me to throw away my honor, my career, everything, for the sake of this creature who, as I can plainly see when I am away from her influence, possesses no single charm upon earth. But when I am near her, I do not feel this. She rouses something in me, something evil, something I had rather not think of. She paralyzes my better nature, too, at the moment when she stimulates my worse. Decidedly it is not good for me to be near her.

Last night was worse than before. Instead of flying I actually sat for some time with my hand in hers talking over the most intimate subjects with her. We spoke of Agatha, among other things. What could I have been dreaming of? Miss Penclosa said that she was conventional, and I agreed with her. She spoke once or twice in a disparaging way of her, and I did not protest. What a creature I have been!

Weak as I have proved myself to be, I am still strong enough to bring this sort of thing to an end. It shall not happen again. I have sense enough to fly when I cannot fight. From this Sunday night onward I shall never sit with Miss Penclosa again. Never! Let the experiments go, let the research come to an end; any thing is better than facing this monstrous temptation which drags me so low. I have said nothing to Miss Penclosa, but I shall simply stay away. She can tell the reason without any words of mine.

April 7. Have stayed away as I said. It is a pity to ruin such an interesting investigation, but it would be a greater pity still to ruin my life, and I *know* that I cannot trust myself with that woman.

11 P.M. God help me! What is the matter with me? Am I going mad? Let me try and be calm and reason with myself. First of all I shall set down exactly what occurred.

It was nearly eight when I wrote the lines with which this day begins. Feeling strangely restless and uneasy, I left my rooms and walked round to spend the evening with Agatha and her mother. They both remarked that I was pale and haggard. About nine Professor Pratt-Haldane came in, and we played a game of whist. I tried hard to concentrate my attention upon the cards, but the feeling of restlessness grew and grew until I found it impossible to struggle against it. I simply *could* not sit still at the table. At last, in the very middle of a hand, I threw my cards down and, with some sort of an incoherent apology about having an appointment, I rushed from the room. As if in a dream I have a vague recollection of tearing through the hall, snatching my hat from the stand, and slamming the door behind me. As in a dream, too, I have the impression of the double line of gas-lamps, and my bespattered boots tell me that I must have run down the middle of the road. It was all misty and strange and unnatural. I came to Wilson's house; I saw Mrs. Wilson and I saw Miss Penclosa. I hardly recall what we talked about, but I do remember that Miss P. shook the head of her crutch at me in a playful way, and accused me of being late and of losing interest in our experiments. There was no mesmerism, but I stayed some time and have only just returned.

My brain is quite clear again now, and I can think over what has occurred. It is absurd to suppose that it is merely weakness and force of habit. I tried to explain it in that way the other night, but it will no longer suffice. It is something much deeper and more terrible than that. Why, when I was at the Mardens' whist-table, I was dragged away as if the noose of a rope had been cast round me. I can no longer disguise it from myself. The woman has her grip upon me. I am in her clutch. But I must keep my head and reason it out and see what is best to be done.

But what a blind fool I have been! In my enthusiasm over my research I have walked straight into the pit, although it lay gaping before me. Did she not herself warn me? Did she not tell me, as I can read in my own journal, that when she has acquired power over a subject she can make him do her will? And she has acquired that power over me. I am for the moment at the beck and call of this creature with the crutch. I must come when she wills it. I must do as she wills. Worst of all, I must feel as she wills. I loathe her and fear her, yet, while I am under the spell, she can doubtless make me love her.

There is some consolation in the thought, then, that those odious impulses for which I have blamed myself do not really come from me at all. They are all transferred from her, little as I could have guessed it at the time. I feel cleaner and lighter for the thought.

April 8. Yes, now, in broad daylight, writing coolly and with time for reflection, I am compelled to confirm everything which I wrote in my journal last night. I am in a horrible position, but, above all, I must not lose my head. I must pit my intellect against her powers. After all, I am no silly puppet, to dance at the end of a string. I have energy, brains, courage. For all her devil's tricks I may beat her yet. May! I MUST, or what is to become of me?

Let me try to reason it out! This woman, by her own explanation, can dominate my nervous organism. She can project herself into my body and take command of it. She has a parasite soul; yes, she is a parasite, a monstrous parasite. She creeps into my frame as the hermit crab does into the whelk's shell. I am powerless. What can I do? I am dealing with forces of which I know nothing. And I can tell no one of my trouble. They would set me down as a madman. Certainly, if it got noised abroad, the university would say that they had no need of a devil-ridden professor. And Agatha! No, no, I must face it alone.

Part III.

I read over my notes of what the woman said when she spoke about her powers. There is one point which fills me with dismay. She implies that when the influence is slight the subject knows what he is doing, but cannot control himself, whereas when it is strongly exerted he is absolutely unconscious. Now, I have always known what I did, though less so last night than on the previous occasions. That seems to mean that she has never yet exerted her full powers upon me. Was ever a man so placed before?

Yes, perhaps there was, and very near me, too. Charles Sadler must know something of this! His vague words of warning take a meaning now. Oh, if I had only listened to him then, before I helped by these repeated sittings to forge the links of the chain which binds me! But I will see him to-day. I will apologize to him for having treated his warning so lightly. I will see if he can advise me.

4 P.M. No, he cannot. I have talked with him, and he showed such surprise at the first words in which I tried to express my unspeakable secret that I went no further. As far as I can gather (by hints and inferences rather than by any statement), his own experience was limited to some words or looks such as I have myself endured. His abandonment of Miss Penclosa is in itself a sign that he was never really in her toils. Oh, if he only knew his escape! He has to thank his phlegmatic Saxon temperament for it. I am black and Celtic, and this hag's clutch is deep in my nerves. Shall I ever get it out? Shall I ever be the same man that I was just one short fortnight ago?

Let me consider what I had better do. I cannot leave the university in the middle of the term. If I were free, my course would be obvious. I should start at once and travel in Persia. But would she allow me to start? And could her influence not reach me in Persia, and bring me back to within touch of her crutch? I can only find out the limits of this hellish power by my own bitter experience. I will fight and fight and fight — and what can I do more?

I know very well that about eight o'clock to-night that craving for her society, that irresistible restlessness, will come upon me. How shall I overcome it? What shall I do? I must make it impossible for me to leave the room. I shall lock the door and throw the key out of the window. But, then, what am I to do in the morning? Never mind about the morning. I must at all costs break this chain which holds me.

April 9. Victory! I have done splendidly! At seven o'clock last night I took a hasty dinner, and then locked myself up in my bedroom and dropped the key into the garden. I chose a cheery novel, and lay in bed for three hours trying to read it, but really in a horrible state of trepidation, expecting every instant that I should become conscious of the impulse. Nothing of the sort occurred, however, and I awoke this morning with the feeling that a black nightmare had been lifted off me. Perhaps the creature realized what I had done, and understood that it was useless to try to influence me. At any rate, I have beaten her once, and if I can do it once, I can do it again.

It was most awkward about the key in the morning. Luckily, there was an under-gardener below, and I asked him to throw it up. No doubt he thought I had just dropped it. I will have doors and windows screwed up and six stout men to hold me down in my bed before I will surrender myself to be hag-ridden in this way.

I had a note from Mrs. Marden this afternoon asking me to go round and see her. I intended to do so in any case, but had not excepted to find bad news waiting for me. It seems that the Armstrongs, from whom Agatha has expectations, are due home from Adelaide in the Aurora, and that they have written to Mrs. Marden and her to meet them in town. They will probably be away for a month or six weeks, and, as the Aurora is due on Wednesday, they must go at once — to-morrow, if they are ready in time. My consolation is that when we meet again there will be no more parting between Agatha and me.

"I want you to do one thing, Agatha," said I, when we were alone together. "If you should happen to meet Miss Penclosa, either in town or here, you must promise me never again to allow her to mesmerize you."

Agatha opened her eyes.

"Why, it was only the other day that you were saying how interesting it all was, and how determined you were to finish your experiments."

"I know, but I have changed my mind since then."

"And you won't have it any more?"

"No."

"I am so glad, Austin. You can't think how pale and worn you have been lately. It was really our principal objection to going to London now that we did not wish to leave you when you were so pulled down. And your manner has been so strange occasionally — especially that night when you left poor Professor Pratt-Haldane to play dummy. I am convinced that these experiments are very bad for your nerves."

"I think so, too, dear."

"And for Miss Penclosa's nerves as well. You have heard that she is ill?"

"No."

"Mrs. Wilson told us so last night. She described it as a nervous fever. Professor Wilson is coming back this week, and of course Mrs. Wilson is very anxious that Miss Penclosa should be well again then, for he has quite a programme of experiments which he is anxious to carry out."

I was glad to have Agatha's promise, for it was enough that this woman should have one of us in her clutch. On the other hand, I was disturbed to hear about Miss Penclosa's illness. It rather discounts the victory which I appeared to win last night. I remember that she said that loss of health interfered with her power. That may be why I was able to hold my own so easily. Well, well, I must take the same precautions to-night and see what comes of it. I am childishly frightened when I think of her.

April 10. All went very well last night. I was amused at the gardener's face when I had again to hail him this morning and to ask him to throw up my key. I shall get a name among the servants if this sort of thing goes on. But the great point is that I stayed in my room without the slightest inclination to leave it. I do believe that I am shaking myself clear of this incredible bond — or is it only that the woman's power is in abeyance until she recovers her strength? I can but pray for the best.

The Mardens left this morning, and the brightness seems to have gone out of the spring sunshine. And yet it is very beautiful also as it gleams on the green chestnuts opposite my windows, and gives a touch of gayety to the heavy, lichen-mottled walls of the old colleges. How sweet and gentle and soothing is Nature! Who would think that there lurked in her also such vile forces, such odious possibilities! For of course I understand that this dreadful thing which has sprung out at me is neither supernatural nor even preternatural. No, it is a natural force which this woman can use and society is ignorant of. The mere fact that it ebbs with her strength shows how entirely it is subject to physical laws. If I had time, I might probe it to the bottom and lay my hands upon its antidote. But you cannot tame the tiger when you are beneath his claws. You can but try to writhe away from him. Ah, when I look in the glass and see my own dark eyes and clear-cut Spanish face, I long for a vitriol splash or a bout of the small-pox. One or the other might have saved me from this calamity.

I am inclined to think that I may have trouble to-night. There are two things which make me fear so. One is that I met Mrs. Wilson in the street, and that she tells me that Miss Penclosa is better, though still weak. I find myself wishing in my heart that the illness had been her last. The other is that Professor Wilson comes back in a day or two, and his presence would act as a constraint upon her. I should not fear our interviews if a third person were present. For both these reasons I have a presentiment of trouble to-night, and I shall take the same precautions as before.

April 10. No, thank God, all went well last night. I really could not face the gardener again. I locked my door and thrust the key underneath it, so that I had to ask the maid to let me out in the morning. But the precaution was really not needed, for I never had any inclination to go out at all. Three evenings in succession at home! I am surely near the end of my troubles, for Wilson will be home again either today or tomorrow. Shall I tell him of what I have gone through or not? I am convinced that I should not have the slightest sympathy from him. He would look upon me as an interesting case, and read a paper about me at the next meeting of the Psychical Society, in which he would gravely discuss the possibility of my being a deliberate liar, and weigh it against the chances of my being in an early stage of lunacy. No, I shall get no comfort out of Wilson.

I am feeling wonderfully fit and well. I don't think I ever lectured with greater spirit. Oh, if I could only get this shadow off my life, how happy I should be! Young, fairly wealthy, in the front rank of my profession, engaged to a beautiful and charming girl — have I not everything which a man could ask for? Only one thing to trouble me, but what a thing it is!

Midnight. I shall go mad. Yes, that will be the end of it. I shall go mad. I am not far from it now. My head throbs as I rest it on my hot hand. I am quivering all over like a scared horse. Oh, what a night I have had! And yet I have some cause to be satisfied also.

At the risk of becoming the laughing-stock of my own servant, I again slipped my key under the door, imprisoning myself for the night. Then, finding it too early to go to bed, I lay down with my clothes on and began to read one of Dumas's novels. Suddenly I was gripped — gripped and dragged from the couch. It is only thus that I can describe the overpowering nature of the force which pounced upon me. I clawed at the coverlet. I clung to the wood-work. I believe that I screamed out in my frenzy. It was all useless, hopeless. I MUST go. There was no way out of it. It was only at the outset that I resisted. The force soon became too overmastering for that. I thank goodness that there were no watchers there to interfere with me. I could not have answered for myself if there had been. And, besides the determination to get out, there came to me, also, the keenest and coolest judgment in choosing my means. I lit a candle and endeavored, kneeling in front of the door, to pull the key through with the feather-end of a quill pen. It was just too short and pushed it further away. Then with quiet persistence I got a paper-knife out of one of the drawers, and with that I managed to draw the key back. I opened the door, stepped into my study, took a photograph of myself from the bureau, wrote something across it, placed it in the inside pocket of my coat, and then started off for Wilson's.

It was all wonderfully clear, and yet disassociated from the rest of my life, as the incidents of even the most vivid dream might be. A peculiar double consciousness possessed me. There was the predominant alien will, which was bent upon drawing me to the side of its owner, and there was the feebler protesting personality, which I recognized as being myself, tugging feebly at the overmastering impulse as a led terrier might at its chain. I can remember recognizing these two conflicting forces, but I recall nothing of my walk, nor of how I was admitted to the house.

Very vivid, however, is my recollection of how I met Miss Penclosa. She was reclining on the sofa in the little boudoir in which our experiments had usually been carried out. Her head was rested on her hand, and a tiger-skin rug had been partly drawn over her. She looked up expectantly as I entered, and, as the lamp-light fell upon her face, I could see that she was very pale and thin, with dark hollows under her eyes. She smiled at me, and pointed to a stool beside her. It was with her left hand that she pointed, and I, running eagerly forward, seized it, — I loathe myself as I think of it, — and pressed it passionately to my lips. Then, seating myself upon the stool, and still retaining her hand, I gave her the photograph which I had brought with me, and talked and talked and talked — of my love for her, of my grief over her illness, of my joy at her recovery, of the misery it was to me to be absent a single evening from her side. She lay quietly looking down at me with imperious eyes and her provocative smile. Once I remember that she passed her hand over my hair as one caresses a dog; and it gave me pleasure — the caress. I thrilled under it. I was her slave, body and soul, and for the moment I rejoiced in my slavery.

And then came the blessed change. Never tell me that there is not a Providence! I was on the brink of perdition. My feet were on the edge. Was it a coincidence that at that very instant help should come? No, no, no; there is a Providence, and its hand has drawn me back. There is something in the universe stronger than this devil woman with her tricks. Ah, what a balm to my heart it is to think so!

As I looked up at her I was conscious of a change in her. Her face, which had been pale before, was now ghastly. Her eyes were dull, and the lids drooped heavily over them. Above all, the look of serene confidence had gone from her features. Her mouth had weakened. Her forehead had puckered. She was frightened and undecided. And as I watched the change my own spirit fluttered and struggled, trying hard to tear itself from the grip which held it — a grip which, from moment to moment, grew less secure.

"Austin," she whispered, "I have tried to do too much. I was not strong enough. I have not recovered yet from my illness. But I could not live longer without seeing you. You won't leave me, Austin? This is only a passing weakness. If you will only give me five minutes, I shall be myself again. Give me the small decanter from the table in the window."

But I had regained my soul. With her waning strength the influence had cleared away from me and left me free. And I was aggressive — bitterly, fiercely aggressive. For once at least I could make this woman understand what my real feelings toward her were. My soul was filled with a hatred as bestial as the love against which it was a reaction. It was the savage, murderous passion of the revolted serf. I could have taken the crutch from her side and beaten her face in with it. She threw her hands up, as if to avoid a blow, and cowered away from me into the corner of the settee.

"The brandy!" she gasped. "The brandy!"

I took the decanter and poured it over the roots of a palm in the window. Then I snatched the photograph from her hand and tore it into a hundred pieces.

"You vile woman," I said, "if I did my duty to society, you would never leave this room alive!"

"I love you, Austin; I love you!" she wailed.

"Yes," I cried, "and Charles Sadler before. And how many others before that?"

"Charles Sadler!" she gasped. "He has spoken to you? So, Charles Sadler, Charles Sadler!" Her voice came through her white lips like a snake's hiss.

"Yes, I know you, and others shall know you, too. You shameless creature! You knew how I stood. And yet you used your vile power to bring me to your side. You may, perhaps, do so again, but at least you will remember that you have heard me say that I love Miss Marden from the bottom of my soul, and that I loathe you, abhor you!

"The very sight of you and the sound of your voice fill me with horror and disgust. The thought of you is repulsive. That is how I feel toward you, and if it pleases you by your tricks to draw me again to your side as you have done to-night, you will at least, I should think, have little satisfaction in trying to make a lover out of a man who has told you his real opinion of you. You may put what words you will into my mouth, but you cannot help remembering—"

I stopped, for the woman's head had fallen back, and she had fainted. She could not bear to hear what I had to say to her! What a glow of satisfaction it gives me to think that, come what may, in the future she can never misunderstand my true feelings toward her. But what will occur in the future? What will she do next? I dare not think of it. Oh, if only I could hope that she will leave me alone! But when I think of what I said to her — Never mind; I have been stronger than she for once.

April 11. I hardly slept last night, and found myself in the morning so unstrung and feverish that I was compelled to ask Pratt-Haldane to do my lecture for me. It is the first that I have ever missed. I rose at mid-day, but my head is aching, my hands quivering, and my nerves in a pitiable state.

Who should come round this evening but Wilson. He has just come back from London, where he has lectured, read papers, convened meetings, exposed a medium, conducted a series of experiments on thought transference, entertained Professor Richet of Paris, spent hours gazing into a crystal, and obtained some evidence as to the passage of matter through matter. All this he poured into my ears in a single gust.

"But you!" he cried at last. "You are not looking well. And Miss Penclosa is quite prostrated to-day. How about the experiments?"

"I have abandoned them."

"Tut, tut! Why?"

"The subject seems to me to be a dangerous one."

Out came his big brown note-book.

"This is of great interest," said he. "What are your grounds for saying that it is a dangerous one? Please give your facts in chronological order, with approximate dates and names of reliable witnesses with their permanent addresses."

"First of all," I asked, "would you tell me whether you have collected any cases where the mesmerist has gained a command over the subject and has used it for evil purposes?"

"Dozens!" he cried exultantly. "Crime by suggestion—"

"I don't mean suggestion. I mean where a sudden impulse comes from a person at a distance — an uncontrollable impulse."

"Obsession!" he shrieked, in an ecstasy of delight. "It is the rarest condition. We have eight cases, five well attested. You don't mean to say—" His exultation made him hardly articulate.

"No, I don't," said I. "Good-evening! You will excuse me, but I am not very well to-night." And so at last I got rid of him, still brandishing his pencil and his note-book. My troubles may be bad to hear, but at least it is better to hug them to myself than to have myself exhibited by Wilson, like a freak at a fair. He has lost sight of human beings. Everything to him is a case and a phenomenon. I will die before I speak to him again upon the matter.

April 12. Yesterday was a blessed day of quiet, and I enjoyed an uneventful night. Wilson's presence is a great consolation. What can the woman do now? Surely, when she has heard me say what I have said, she will conceive the same disgust for me which I have for her. She could not, no, she *could* not, desire to have a lover who had insulted her so. No, I believe I am free from her love — but how about her hate? Might she not use these powers of hers for revenge? Tut! why should I frighten myself over shadows? She will forget about me, and I shall forget about her, and all will be well.

April 13. My nerves have quite recovered their tone. I really believe that I have conquered the creature. But I must confess to living in some suspense. She is well again, for I hear that she was driving with Mrs. Wilson in the High Street in the afternoon.

April 14. I do wish I could get away from the place altogether. I shall fly to Agatha's side the very day that the term closes. I suppose it is pitiably weak of me, but this woman gets upon my nerves most terribly. I have seen her again, and I have spoken with her.

It was just after lunch, and I was smoking a cigarette in my study, when I heard the step of my servant Murray in the passage. I was languidly conscious that a second step was audible behind, and had hardly troubled myself to speculate who it might be, when suddenly a slight noise brought me out of my chair with my skin creeping with apprehension. I had never particularly observed before what sort of sound the tapping of a crutch was, but my quivering nerves told me that I heard it now in the sharp wooden clack which alternated with the muffled thud of the foot fall. Another instant and my servant had shown her in.

I did not attempt the usual conventions of society, nor did she. I simply stood with the smouldering cigarette in my hand, and gazed at her. She in her turn looked silently at me, and at her look I remembered how in these very pages I had tried to define the expression of her eyes, whether they were furtive or fierce. To-day they were fierce — coldly and inexorably so.

"Well," said she at last, "are you still of the same mind as when I saw you last?"

"I have always been of the same mind."

"Let us understand each other, Professor Gilroy," said she slowly. "I am not a very safe person to trifle with, as you should realize by now. It was you who asked me to enter into a series of experiments with you, it was you who won my affections, it was you who professed your love for me, it was you who brought me your own photograph with words of affection upon it, and, finally, it was you who on the very same evening thought fit to insult me most outrageously, addressing me as no man has ever dared to speak to me yet. Tell me that those words came from you in a moment of passion and I am prepared to forget and to forgive them. You did not mean what you said, Austin? You do not really hate me?"

I might have pitied this deformed woman — such a longing for love broke suddenly through the menace of her eyes. But then I thought of what I had gone through, and my heart set like flint.

"If ever you heard me speak of love," said I, "you know very well that it was your voice which spoke, and not mine. The only words of truth which I have ever been able to say to you are those which you heard when last we met."

"I know. Some one has set you against me. It was he!" She tapped with her crutch upon the floor. "Well, you know very well that I could bring you this instant crouching like a spaniel to my feet. You will not find me again in my hour of weakness, when you can insult me with impunity. Have a care what you are doing, Professor Gilroy. You stand in a terrible position. You have not yet realized the hold which I have upon you."

I shrugged my shoulders and turned away.

"Well," said she, after a pause, "if you despise my love, I must see what can be done with fear. You smile, but the day will come when you will come screaming to me for pardon. Yes, you will grovel on the ground before me, proud as you are, and you will curse the day that ever you turned me from your best friend into your most bitter enemy. Have a care, Professor Gilroy!" I saw a white hand shaking in the air, and a face which was scarcely human, so convulsed was it with passion. An instant later she was gone, and I heard the quick hobble and tap receding down the passage.

But she has left a weight upon my heart. Vague presentiments of coming misfortune lie heavy upon me. I try in vain to persuade myself that these are only words of empty anger. I can remember those relentless eyes too clearly to think so. What shall I do — ah, what shall I do? I am no longer master of my own soul. At any moment this loathsome parasite may creep into me, and then — I must tell some one my hideous secret — I must tell it or go mad. If I had some one to sympathize and advise! Wilson is out of the question. Charles Sadler would understand me only so far as his own experience carries him. Pratt-Haldane! He is a well-balanced man, a man of great common-sense and resource. I will go to him. I will tell him everything. God grant that he may be able to advise me!

Part IV.

6.45 P.M. No, it is useless. There is no human help for me; I must fight this out single-handed. Two courses lie before me. I might become this woman's lover. Or I must endure such persecutions as she can inflict upon me. Even if none come, I shall live in a hell of apprehension. But she may torture me, she may drive me mad, she may kill me: I will never, never, never give in. What can she inflict which would be worse than the loss of Agatha, and the knowledge that I am a perjured liar, and have forfeited the name of gentleman?

Pratt-Haldane was most amiable, and listened with all politeness to my story. But when I looked at his heavy set features, his slow eyes, and the ponderous study furniture which surrounded him, I could hardly tell him what I had come to say. It was all so substantial, so material. And, besides, what would I myself have said a short month ago if one of my colleagues had come to me with a story of demonic possession? Perhaps. I should have been less patient than he was. As it was, he took notes of my statement, asked me how much tea I drank, how many hours I slept, whether I had been overworking much, had I had sudden pains in the head, evil dreams, singing in the ears, flashes before the eyes — all questions which pointed to his belief that brain congestion was at the bottom of my trouble. Finally he dismissed me with a great many platitudes about open-air exercise, and avoidance of nervous excitement. His prescription, which was for chloral and bromide, I rolled up and threw into the gutter.

No, I can look for no help from any human being. If I consult any more, they may put their heads together and I may find myself in an asylum. I can but grip my courage with both hands, and pray that an honest man may not be abandoned.

April 15. It is the sweetest spring within the memory of man. So green, so mild, so beautiful! Ah, what a contrast between nature without and my own soul so torn with doubt and terror! It has been an uneventful day, but I know that I am on the edge of an abyss. I know it, and yet I go on with the routine of my life. The one bright spot is that Agatha is happy and well and out of all danger. If this creature had a hand on each of us, what might she not do?

April 16. The woman is ingenious in her torments. She knows how fond I am of my work, and how highly my lectures are thought of. So it is from that point that she now attacks me. It will end, I can see, in my losing my professorship, but I will fight to the finish. She shall not drive me out of it without a struggle.

I was not conscious of any change during my lecture this morning save that for a minute or two I had a dizziness and swimminess which rapidly passed away. On the contrary, I congratulated myself upon having made my subject (the functions of the red corpuscles) both interesting and clear. I was surprised, therefore, when a student came into my laboratory immediately after the lecture, and complained of being puzzled by the discrepancy between my statements and those in the text books. He showed me his note-book, in which I was reported as having in one portion of the lecture championed the most outrageous and unscientific heresies. Of course I denied it, and declared that he had misunderstood me, but on comparing his notes with those of his companions, it became clear that he was right, and that I really had made some most preposterous statements. Of course I shall explain it away as being the result of a moment of aberration, but I feel only too sure that it will be the first of a series. It is but a month now to the end of the session, and I pray that I may be able to hold out until then.

April 26. Ten days have elapsed since I have had the heart to make any entry in my journal. Why should I record my own humiliation and degradation? I had vowed never to open it again. And yet the force of habit is strong, and here I find myself taking up once more the record of my own dreadful experiences — in much the same spirit in which a suicide has been known to take notes of the effects of the poison which killed him.

Well, the crash which I had foreseen has come — and that no further back than yesterday. The university authorities have taken my lectureship from me. It has been done in the most delicate way, purporting to be a temporary measure to relieve me from the effects of overwork, and to give me the opportunity of recovering my health. None the less, it has been done, and I am no longer Professor Gilroy. The laboratory is still in my charge, but I have little doubt that that also will soon go.

The fact is that my lectures had become the laughing-stock of the university. My class was crowded with students who came to see and hear what the eccentric professor would do or say next. I cannot go into the detail of my humiliation. Oh, that devilish woman! There is no depth of buffoonery and imbecility to which she has not forced me. I would begin my lecture clearly and well, but always with the sense of a coming eclipse. Then as I felt the influence I would struggle against it, striving with clenched hands and beads of sweat upon my brow to get the better of it, while the students, hearing my incoherent words and watching my contortions, would roar with laughter at the antics of their professor. And then, when she had once fairly mastered me, out would come the most outrageous things — silly jokes, sentiments as though I were proposing a toast, snatches of ballads, personal abuse even against some member of my class. And then in a moment my brain would clear again, and my lecture would proceed decorously to the end. No wonder that my conduct has been the talk of the colleges. No wonder that the University Senate has been compelled to take official notice of such a scandal. Oh, that devilish woman!

And the most dreadful part of it all is my own loneliness. Here I sit in a commonplace English bow-window, looking out upon a commonplace English street with its garish buses and its lounging policeman, and behind me there hangs a shadow which is out of all keeping with the age and place. In the home of knowledge I am weighed down and tortured by a power of which science knows nothing. No magistrate would listen to me. No paper would discuss my case. No doctor would believe my symptoms. My own most intimate friends would only look upon it as a sign of brain derangement. I am out of all touch with my kind. Oh, that devilish woman! Let her have a care! She may push me too far. When the law cannot help a man, he may make a law for himself.

She met me in the High Street yesterday evening and spoke to me. It was as well for her, perhaps, that it was not between the hedges of a lonely country road. She asked me with her cold smile whether I had been chastened yet. I did not deign to answer her. "We must try another turn of the screw," said she. Have a care, my lady, have a care! I had her at my mercy once. Perhaps another chance may come.

April 28. The suspension of my lectureship has had the effect also of taking away her means of annoying me, and so I have enjoyed two blessed days of peace. After all, there is no reason to despair. Sympathy pours in to me from all sides, and every one agrees that it is my devotion to science and the arduous nature of my researches which have shaken my nervous system. I have had the kindest message from the council advising me to travel abroad, and expressing the confident hope that I may be able to resume all my duties by the beginning of the summer term. Nothing could be more flattering than their allusions to my career and to my services to the university. It is only in misfortune that one can test one's own popularity.

This creature may weary of tormenting me, and then all may yet be well. May God grant it!

April 29. Our sleepy little town has had a small sensation. The only knowledge of crime which we ever have is when a rowdy undergraduate breaks a few lamps or comes to blows with a policeman. Last night, however, there was an attempt made to break-into the branch of the Bank of England, and we are all in a flutter in consequence.

Parkenson, the manager, is an intimate friend of mine, and I found him very much excited when I walked round there after breakfast. Had the thieves broken into the counting-house, they would still have had the safes to reckon with, so that the defence was considerably stronger than the attack. Indeed, the latter does not appear to have ever been very formidable. Two of the lower windows have marks as if a chisel or some such instrument had been pushed under them to force them open. The police should have a good clue, for the wood-work had been done with green paint only the day before, and from the smears it is evident that some of it has found its way on to the criminal's hands or clothes.

4.30 P.M. Ah, that accursed woman! That thrice accursed woman! Never mind! She shall not beat me! No, she shall not! But, oh, the she-devil! She has taken my professorship. Now she would take my honor. Is there nothing I can do against her, nothing save — Ah, but, hard pushed as I am, I cannot bring myself to think of that!

It was about an hour ago that I went into my bedroom, and was brushing my hair before the glass, when suddenly my eyes lit upon something which left me so sick and cold that I sat down upon the edge of the bed and began to cry. It is many a long year since I shed tears, but all my nerve was gone, and I could but sob and sob in impotent grief and anger. There was my house jacket, the coat I usually wear after dinner, hanging on its peg by the wardrobe, with the right sleeve thickly crusted from wrist to elbow with daubs of green paint.

So this was what she meant by another turn of the screw! She had made a public imbecile of me. Now she would brand me as a criminal. This time she has failed. But how about the next? I dare not think of it — and of Agatha and my poor old mother! I wish that I were dead!

Yes, this is the other turn of the screw. And this is also what she meant, no doubt, when she said that I had not realized yet the power she has over me. I look back at my account of my conversation with her, and I see how she declared that with a slight exertion of her will her subject would be conscious, and with a stronger one unconscious. Last night I was unconscious. I could have sworn that I slept soundly in my bed without so much as a dream. And yet those stains tell me that I dressed, made my way out, attempted to open the bank windows, and returned. Was I observed? Is it possible that some one saw me do it and followed me home? Ah, what a hell my life has become! I have no peace, no rest. But my patience is nearing its end.

10 P.M. I have cleaned my coat with turpentine. I do not think that any one could have seen me. It was with my screw-driver that I made the marks. I found it all crusted with paint, and I have cleaned it. My head aches as if it would burst, and I have taken five grains of antipyrine. If it were not for Agatha, I should have taken fifty and had an end of it.

May 3. Three quiet days. This hell fiend is like a cat with a mouse. She lets me loose only to pounce upon me again. I am never so frightened as when everything is still. My physical state is deplorable — perpetual hiccough and ptosis of the left eyelid.

I have heard from the Mardens that they will be back the day after to-morrow. I do not know whether I am glad or sorry. They were safe in London. Once here they may be drawn into the miserable network in which I am myself struggling. And I must tell them of it. I cannot marry Agatha so long as I know that I am not responsible for my own actions. Yes, I must tell them, even if it brings everything to an end between us.

To-night is the university ball, and I must go. God knows I never felt less in the humor for festivity, but I must not have it said that I am unfit to appear in public. If I am seen there, and have speech with some of the elders of the university it will go a long way toward showing them that it would be unjust to take my chair away from me.

10 P.M. I have been to the ball. Charles Sadler and I went together, but I have come away before him. I shall wait up for him, however, for, indeed, I fear to go to sleep these nights. He is a cheery, practical fellow, and a chat with him will steady my nerves. On the whole, the evening was a great success. I talked to every one who has influence, and I think that I made them realize that my chair is not vacant quite yet. The creature was at the ball — unable to dance, of course, but sitting with Mrs. Wilson. Again and again her eyes rested upon me. They were almost the last things I saw before I left the room. Once, as I sat sideways to her, I watched her, and saw

that her gaze was following some one else. It was Sadler, who was dancing at the time with the second Miss Thurston. To judge by her expression, it is well for him that he is not in her grip as I am. He does not know the escape he has had. I think I hear his step in the street now, and I will go down and let him in. If he will—

May 4. Why did I break off in this way last night? I never went down stairs, after all — at least, I have no recollection of doing so. But, on the other hand, I cannot remember going to bed. One of my hands is greatly swollen this morning, and yet I have no remembrance of injuring it yesterday. Otherwise, I am feeling all the better for last night's festivity. But I cannot understand how it is that I did not meet Charles Sadler when I so fully intended to do so. Is it possible — My God, it is only too probable! Has she been leading me some devil's dance again? I will go down to Sadler and ask him.

Mid-day. The thing has come to a crisis. My life is not worth living. But, if I am to die, then she shall come also. I will not leave her behind, to drive some other man mad as she has me. No, I have come to the limit of my endurance. She has made me as desperate and dangerous a man as walks the earth. God knows I have never had the heart to hurt a fly, and yet, if I had my hands now upon that woman, she should never leave this room alive. I shall see her this very day, and she shall learn what she has to expect from me.

I went to Sadler and found him, to my surprise, in bed. As I entered he sat up and turned a face toward me which sickened me as I looked at it.

"Why, Sadler, what has happened?" I cried, but my heart turned cold as I said it.

"Gilroy," he answered, mumbling with his swollen lips, "I have for some weeks been under the impression that you are a madman. Now I know it, and that you are a dangerous one as well. If it were not that I am unwilling to make a scandal in the college, you would now be in the hands of the police."

"Do you mean—" I cried.

"I mean that as I opened the door last night you rushed out upon me, struck me with both your fists in the face, knocked me down, kicked me furiously in the side, and left me lying almost unconscious in the street. Look at your own hand bearing witness against you."

Yes, there it was, puffed up, with sponge-like knuckles, as after some terrific blow. What could I do? Though he put me down as a madman, I must tell him all. I sat by his bed and went over all my troubles from the beginning. I poured them out with quivering hands and burning words which might have carried conviction to the most sceptical. "She hates you and she hates me!" I cried. "She revenged herself last night on both of us at once. She saw me leave the ball, and she must have seen you also. She knew how long it would take you to reach home. Then she had but to use her wicked will. Ah, your bruised face is a small thing beside my bruised soul!"

He was struck by my story. That was evident. "Yes, yes, she watched me out of the room," he muttered. "She is capable of it. But is it possible that she has really reduced you to this? What do you intend to do?"

"To stop it!" I cried. "I am perfectly desperate; I shall give her fair warning to-day, and the next time will be the last."

"Do nothing rash," said he.

"Rash!" I cried. "The only rash thing is that I should postpone it another hour." With that I rushed to my room, and here I am on the eve of what may be the great crisis of my life. I shall start at once. I have gained one thing to-day, for I have made one man, at least, realize the truth of this monstrous experience of mine. And, if the worst should happen, this diary remains as a proof of the goad that has driven me.

Evening. When I came to Wilson's, I was shown up, and found that he was sitting with Miss Penclosa. For half an hour I had to endure his fussy talk about his recent research into the exact nature of the spiritualistic rap, while the creature and I sat in silence looking across the room at each other. I read a sinister amusement in her eyes, and she must have seen hatred and menace in mine. I had almost despaired of having speech with her when he was called from the room, and we were left for a few moments together.

"Well, Professor Gilroy — or is it Mr. Gilroy?" said she, with that bitter smile of hers. "How is your friend Mr. Charles Sadler after the ball?"

"You fiend!" I cried. "You have come to the end of your tricks now. I will have no more of them. Listen to what I say." I strode across and shook her roughly by the shoulder. "As sure as there is a God in heaven, I swear that if you try another of your deviltries upon me I will have your life for it. Come what may, I will have your life. I have come to the end of what a man can endure."

"Accounts are not quite settled between us," said she, with a passion that equalled my own. "I can love, and I can hate. You had your choice. You chose to spurn the first; now you must test the other. It will take a little more to break your spirit, I see, but broken it shall be. Miss Marden comes back to-morrow, as I understand."

"What has that to do with you?" I cried. "It is a pollution that you should dare even to think of her. If I thought that you would harm her—"

She was frightened, I could see, though she tried to brazen it out. She read the black thought in my mind, and cowered away from me.

"She is fortunate in having such a champion," said she. "He actually dares to threaten a lonely woman. I must really congratulate Miss Marden upon her protector."

The words were bitter, but the voice and manner were more acid still.

"There is no use talking," said I. "I only came here to tell you, — and to tell you most solemnly, — that your next outrage upon me will be your last." With that, as I heard Wilson's step upon the stair, I walked from the room. Ay, she may look venomous and deadly, but, for all that, she is beginning to see now that she has as much to fear from me as I can have from her. Murder! It has an ugly sound. But you don't talk of murdering a snake or of murdering a tiger. Let her have a care now.

May 5. I met Agatha and her mother at the station at eleven o'clock. She is looking so bright, so happy, so beautiful. And she was so overjoyed to see me. What have I done to deserve such love? I went back home with them, and we lunched together. All the troubles seem in a moment to have been shredded back from my life. She tells me that I am looking pale and worried and ill. The dear child puts it down to my loneliness and the perfunctory attentions of a housekeeper. I pray that she may never know the truth! May the shadow, if shadow there must be, lie ever black across my life and leave hers in the sunshine. I have just come back from them, feeling a new man. With her by my side I think that I could show a bold face to any thing which life might send.

5 P.M. Now, let me try to be accurate. Let me try to say exactly how it occurred. It is fresh in my mind, and I can set it down correctly, though it is not likely that the time will ever come when I shall forget the doings of to-day.

I had returned from the Mardens' after lunch, and was cutting some microscopic sections in my freezing microtome, when in an instant I lost consciousness in the sudden hateful fashion which has become only too familiar to me of late.

When my senses came back to me I was sitting in a small chamber, very different from the one in which I had been working. It was cosey and bright, with chintz-covered settees, colored hangings, and a thousand pretty little trifles upon the wall. A small ornamental clock ticked in front of me, and the hands pointed to half-past three. It was all quite familiar to me, and yet I stared about for a moment in a half-dazed way until my eyes fell upon a cabinet photograph of myself upon the top of the piano. On the other side stood one of Mrs. Marden. Then, of course, I remembered where I was. It was Agatha's boudoir.

But how came I there, and what did I want? A horrible sinking came to my heart. Had I been sent here on some devilish errand? Had that errand already been done? Surely it must; otherwise, why should I be allowed to come back to consciousness? Oh, the agony of that moment! What had I done? I sprang to my feet in my despair, and as I did so a small glass bottle fell from my knees on to the carpet.

It was unbroken, and I picked it up. Outside was written "Sulphuric Acid. Fort." When I drew the round glass stopper, a thick fume rose slowly up, and a pungent, choking smell pervaded the room. I recognized it as one which I kept for chemical testing in my chambers. But why had I brought a bottle of vitriol into Agatha's chamber? Was it not this thick, reeking liquid with which jealous women had been known to mar the beauty of their rivals? My heart stood still as I held the bottle to the light. Thank God, it was full! No mischief had been done as yet. But had Agatha come in a minute sooner, was it not certain that the hellish parasite within me would have dashed the stuff into her — Ah, it will not bear to be thought of! But it must have been for that. Why else should I have brought it? At the thought of what I might have done my worn nerves broke down, and I sat shivering and twitching, the pitiable wreck of a man.

It was the sound of Agatha's voice and the rustle of her dress which restored me. I looked up, and saw her blue eyes, so full of tenderness and pity, gazing down at me.

"We must take you away to the country, Austin," she said. "You want rest and quiet. You look wretchedly ill."

"Oh, it is nothing!" said I, trying to smile. "It was only a momentary weakness. I am all right again now."

"I am so sorry to keep you waiting. Poor boy, you must have been here quite half an hour! The vicar was in the drawing-room, and, as I knew that you did not care for him, I thought it better that Jane should show you up here. I thought the man would never go!"

"Thank God he stayed! Thank God he stayed!" I cried hysterically.

"Why, what is the matter with you, Austin?" she asked, holding my arm as I staggered up from the chair. "Why are you glad that the vicar stayed? And what is this little bottle in your hand?"

"Nothing," I cried, thrusting it into my pocket. "But I must go. I have something important to do."

"How stern you look, Austin! I have never seen your face like that. You are angry?"

"Yes, I am angry."

"But not with me?"

"No, no, my darling! You would not understand."

"But you have not told me why you came."

"I came to ask you whether you would always love me — no matter what I did, or what shadow might fall on my name. Would you believe in me and trust me however black appearances might be against me?"

"You know that I would, Austin."

"Yes, I know that you would. What I do I shall do for you. I am driven to it. There is no other way out, my darling!" I kissed her and rushed from the room.

The time for indecision was at an end. As long as the creature threatened my own prospects and my honor there might be a question as to what I should do. But now, when Agatha — my innocent Agatha — was endangered, my duty lay before me like a turnpike road. I had no weapon, but I never paused for that. What weapon should I need, when I felt every muscle quivering with the strength of a frenzied man? I ran through the streets, so set upon what I had to do that I was only dimly conscious of the faces of friends whom I met — dimly conscious also that Professor

Wilson met me, running with equal precipitance in the opposite direction. Breathless but resolute I reached the house and rang the bell. A white cheeked maid opened the door, and turned whiter yet when she saw the face that looked in at her.

"Show me up at once to Miss Penclosa," I demanded.

"Sir," she gasped, "Miss Penclosa died this afternoon at half-past three."

The Woman with the 'Oily Eyes'
The Story as told by Dr. Peter Haslar, F.R.C.S. Lond.
by Dick Donovan

Although often urged to put into print the remarkable story which follows I have always strenuously refused to do so, partly on account of personal reasons and partly out of respect for the feelings of the relatives of those concerned. But after much consideration I have come to the conclusion that my original objections can no longer be urged. The principal actors are dead. I myself am well stricken in years, and before very long must pay the debt of nature which is exacted from everything that lives.

Although so long a time has elapsed since the grim tragedy I am about to record, I cannot think of it even now without a shudder. The story of the life of every man and woman is probably more or less a tragedy, but nothing I have ever heard of can compare in ghastly, weird horror with all the peculiar circumstances of the case in point. Most certainly I would never have put pen to paper to record it had it not been from a sense of duty. Long years ago certain garbled versions crept into the public journals, and though at the time I did not consider it desirable to contradict them, I do think now that the moment has come when I, the only living being fully acquainted with the facts, should make them known, otherwise lies will become history, and posterity will accept it as truth. But there is still another reason I may venture to advance for breaking the silence of years. I think in the interest of science the case should be recorded. I have not always held this view, but when a man bends under the weight of years, and he sniffs the mould of his grave, his ideas undergo a complete change, and the opinions of his youth are not the opinions of his old age. There may be exceptions to this, but I fancy they must be very few. With these preliminary remarks I will plunge at once into my story.

It was the end of August 1857 that I acted as best man at the wedding of my friend Jack Redcar, C.E. It was a memorable year, for our hold on our magnificent Indian Empire had nearly been shaken loose by a mutiny which had threatened to spread throughout the whole of India. At the beginning of 1856 I had returned home from India after a three years' spell. I had gone out as a young medico in the service of the H.E.I.C., but my health broke down and I was compelled to resign my appointment. A year later my friend Redcar, who had also been in the Company's service as a civil engineer, came back to England, as his father had recently died and left him a modest fortune. Jack was not only my senior in years, but I had always considered him my superior in every respect. We were at a public school together, and both went up to Oxford, though not together, for he was finishing his final year when I was a freshman.

Although erratic and a bit wild he was a brilliant fellow; and while I was considered dull and plodding, and found some difficulty in mastering my subjects, there was nothing he tackled that he failed to succeed in, and come out with flying colours. In the early stage of our acquaintance he made me his fag, and patronised me, but that did not last long. A friendship sprang up. He took a great liking to me, why I know not; but it was reciprocated, and when he got his Indian appointment I resolved to follow, and by dint of hard work, and having a friend at court, I succeeded in obtaining my commission in John Company's service. Jack married Maude Vane Tremlett, as sweet a woman as ever drew God's breath of life. If I attempted to describe her in detail I am afraid it might be considered that I was exaggerating, but briefly I may say she was the perfection of physical beauty. Jack himself was an exceptionally fine fellow. A brawny giant with a singularly handsome face. At the time of his wedding he was thirty or thereabouts, while Maude was in her twenty-fifth year. There was a universal opinion that a better matched couple had never been brought together. He had a masterful nature; nevertheless was kind, gentle, and manly to a degree.

It may be thought that I speak with some bias and prejudice in Jack's favour, but I can honestly say that at the time I refer to he was as fine a fellow as ever figured as hero in song or story. He was the pink of honour, and few who really knew him but would have trusted him with their honour, their fortunes, their lives. This may be strong, but I declare it's true, and I am the more anxious to emphasise it because his after life was in such marked contrast, and he presents a study in psychology that is not only deeply interesting, but extraordinary.

The wedding was a really brilliant affair, for Jack had troops of friends, who vied with each other in marking the event in a becoming manner, while his bride was idolized by a doting household. Father and mother, sisters and brothers, worshipped her. She was exceedingly well connected. Her father held an important Government appointment, and her mother came from the somewhat celebrated Yorkshire family of the Kingscotes. Students of history will remember that a Colonel Kingscote figured prominently and honourably as a royalist during the reign of the unfortunate Charles I.

No one who was present on that brilliant August morning of 1857, when Jack Redcar was united in the bonds of wedlock to beautiful Maude Tremlett, would have believed it possible that such grim and tragic events would so speedily follow. The newly-married pair left in the course of the day for the Continent, and during their honeymoon I received several charming letters from Jack, who was not only a diligent correspondent, but he possessed a power of description and a literary style that made his letters delightful reading. Another thing that marked this particular correspondence was the unstinted—I may almost say florid—praise he bestowed upon his wife. To illustrate what I mean, here is a passage from one of his letters:

'I wish I had command of language sufficiently eloquent to speak of my darling Maude as she should be spoken of. She has a perfectly angelic nature; and though it may be true that never a human being was yet born without faults, for the life of me I can find none in my sweet wife. Of course you will say, old chap, that this is honeymoon gush, but, upon my soul, it isn't. I am only doing scant justice to the dear woman who has linked her fate with mine. I have sometimes wondered what I have done that the gods should have blest me in such a manner. For my own part, I don't think I was deserving of so much happiness, and I assure you I am happy—perfectly, deliciously happy. Will it last? Yes, I am sure it will. Maude will always be to me what she is now, a flawless woman; a woman with all the virtues that turn women into angels, and without one of the weaknesses or one of the vices which too often mar an otherwise perfect feminine character. I hope, old boy, that if ever you marry, the woman you choose will be only half as good as mine.'

Had such language been used by anyone else I might have been disposed to add a good deal more than the proverbial pinch of salt before swallowing it. But, as a matter of fact, Jack was not a mere gusher. He had a thoroughly practical, as distinguished from a sentimental, mind, and he was endowed with exceptionally keen powers of observation. And so, making all the allowances for the honeymoon romance, I was prepared to accept my friend's statement as to the merits of his wife without a quibble. Indeed, I knew her to be a most charming lady, endowed with many of the qualities which give the feminine nature its charm. But I would even go a step farther than that, and declare that Mrs. Redcar was a woman in ten thousand. At that time I hadn't a doubt that the young couple were splendidly matched, and it seemed to me probable that the future that stretched before them was not likely to be disturbed by any of the commonplace incidents which seem inseparable from most lives. I regarded Jack as a man of such high moral worth that his wife's happiness was safe in his keeping. I pictured them leading an ideal, poetical life—a life freed from all the vulgar details which blight the careers of so many people—a life which would prove a blessing to themselves as well as a joy to all with whom they had to deal.

When they started on their tour Mr. and Mrs. Redcar anticipated being absent from England for five or six weeks only, but for several reasons they were induced to prolong their travels, and thus it chanced I was away when they returned shortly before Christmas of the year of their marriage. My own private affairs took me to America. As a matter of fact a relative had died leaving me a small property in that country, which required my personal attention; the consequence was I remained out of England for nearly three years.

For the first year or so Jack Redcar wrote to me with commendable regularity. I was duly apprised of the birth of a son and heir. This event seemed to put the crown upon their happiness; but three months later came the first note of sorrow. The baby died, and the doting parents were distracted. Jack wrote:

'My poor little woman is absolutely prostrated, but I tell her we were getting too happy, and this blow has been dealt to remind us that human existence must be chequered in order that we may appreciate more fully the supreme joy of that after-life which we are told we may gain for the striving. This, of course, is a pretty sentiment, but the loss of the baby mite has hit me hard. Still, Maude is left to me, and she is such a splendid woman, that I ought to feel I am more than blest.'

This was the last letter I ever received from Jack, but his wife wrote at odd times. Hers were merely gossipy little chronicles of passing events, and singularly enough she never alluded to her husband, although she wrote in a light, happy vein. This set me wondering, and when I answered her

I never failed to inquire about her husband. I continued to receive letters from her, though at long intervals, down to the month of my departure from America, two years later.

I arrived in London in the winter, and an awful winter it was. London was indeed a city of dreadful night. Gloom and fog were everywhere. Everybody one met looked miserable and despondent. Into the public houses and gin palaces such of the poor as could scratch a few pence together crowded for the sake of the warmth and light. But in the streets sights were to be seen which made one doubt if civilisation is the blessing we are asked to believe it. Starving men, women and children, soaked and sodden with the soot-laden fog, prowled about in the vain hope of finding food and shelter. But the well-to-do passed them with indifference, too intent on their own affairs, and too wrapped in self-interests to bestow thought upon the great city's pariahs.

Immediately after my arrival I penned a brief note to Jack Redcar, giving him my address, and saying I would take an early opportunity of calling, as I was longing to feel once more the hearty, honest grip of his handshake. A week later a note was put into my hand as I was in the very act of going out to keep an appointment in the city. Recognising Mrs. Redcar's handwriting I tore open the envelope, and read, with what feelings may be best imagined, the following lines:

'For God's sake come and see me at once. I am heartbroken and am going mad. You are the only friend in the world to whom I feel I can appeal. Come to me, in the name of pity.

'MAUDE REDCAR.'

I absolutely staggered as I read these brief lines, which were so pregnant with mystery, sorrow, and hopelessness. What did it all mean? To me it was like a burst of thunder from a cloudless summer sky. Something was wrong, that was certain; what that something was I could only vaguely guess at. But I resolved not to remain long in suspense. I put off my engagement, important as it was, and hailing a hansom directed the driver to go to Hampstead, where the Redcars had their residence.

The house was detached and stood in about two acres of ground, and I could imagine it being a little Paradise in brilliant summer weather; but it seemed now in the winter murk, as if a heavy pall of sorrow and anguish enveloped it.

I was shown into an exquisitely furnished drawing-room by an old and ill-favoured woman, who answered my knock at the door. She gave me the impression that she was a sullen, deceptive creature, and I was at a loss to understand how such a woman could have found service with my friends— the bright and happy friends of three years ago. When I handed her my card to convey to Mrs. Redcar she impertinently turned it over, and scrutinized it, and fixed her cold bleared grey eyes on me, so that I was induced to say peremptorily, 'Will you be good enough to go to your mistress at once and announce my arrival?'

'I ain't got no mistress,' she growled. 'I've got a master;' and with this cryptic utterance she left the room.

I waited a quarter of an hour, then the door was abruptly opened, and there stood before me Mrs. Redcar, but not the bright, sweet, radiant little woman of old. A look of premature age was in her face. Her eyes were red with weeping, and had a frightened, hunted expression. I was so astounded that I stood for a moment like one dumbfounded; but as Mrs. Redcar seized my hand and shook it, she gasped in a nervous, spasmodic way:

'Thank God, you have come! My last hope is in you.'

Then, completely overcome by emotion, she burst into hysterical sobbing, and covered her face with her handkerchief.

My astonishment was still so great, the unexpected had so completely paralysed me for the moment, that I seemed incapable of action. But of course this spell quickly passed, and I regained my self-possession.

'How is it I find this change?' I asked. It was a natural question, and the first my brain shaped.

'It's the work of a malignant fiend,' she sobbed.

This answer only deepened the mystery, and I began to think that perhaps she was literally mad. Then suddenly, as if she divined my thoughts, she drew her handkerchief from her face, motioned me to be seated, and literally flung herself on to a couch.

'It's an awful story,' she said, in a hoarse, hollow voice, 'and I look to you, and appeal to you, and pray to you to help me.'

'You can rely upon my doing anything that lies in my power,' I answered. 'But tell me your trouble. How is Jack? Where is he?'

'In her arms, probably,' she exclaimed between her teeth; and she twisted her handkerchief up rope-wise and dragged it backward and forward through her hand with an excess of desperate, nervous energy. Her answer gave me a keynote. She had become a jealous and embittered woman. Jack had swerved from the path of honour, and allowed himself to be charmed by other eyes to the neglect of this woman whom he had described to me as being angelic. Although her beauty was now a little marred by tears and sorrow, she was still very beautiful and attractive, and had she been so disposed she might have taken an army of men captive. She saw by the expression on my face that her remark was not an enigma to me, and she added quickly: 'Oh, yes, it's true, and I look to you, doctor, to help me. It is an awful, dreadful story, but, mind you, I don't blame Jack so much; he is not master of himself. This diabolical creature has enslaved him. She is like the creatures of old that one reads about. She is in possession of some devilish power which enables her to destroy men body and soul.'

'Good God! this is awful,' I involuntarily ejaculated; for I was aghast and horror-stricken at the revelation. Could it be possible that my brilliant friend, who had won golden opinions from all sorts and conditions of men, had fallen from his pedestal to wallow in the mire of sinfulness and deception.

'It is awful,' answered Mrs. Redcar. 'I tell you, doctor, there is something uncanny about the whole business. The woman is an unnatural woman. She is a she-devil. And from my heart I pity and sorrow for my poor boy.'

'Where is he now?' I asked.

'In Paris with her.'

'How long has this been going on?'

'Since a few weeks after our marriage.'

'Good heavens, you don't say so!'

'You may well look surprised, but it's true. Three weeks after our marriage Jack and I were at Wiesbaden. As we were going downstairs to dinner one evening, we met this woman coming up. A shudder of horror came over me as I looked at her, for she had the most extraordinary eyes I have ever seen. I clung to my husband in sheer fright, and I noted that he turned and looked at her, and she also turned and looked at him.

"'What a remarkable woman," he muttered strangely, so strangely that it was as if some other voice was using his lips. Then he broke into a laugh, and, passing his arm round my waist, said: "Why, my dear little woman, I believe you are frightened."

"'I am," I said; "that dreadful creature has startled me more than an Indian cobra would have done."

"'Well, upon my word," said Jack, "I must confess she is a strange-looking being. Did ever you see such eyes? Why, they make one think of the fairy-books and the mythical beings who flit through their pages."

'During the whole of the dinner-time that woman's face haunted me. It was a strong, hard-featured, almost masculine face, every line of which indicated a nature that was base, cruel, and treacherous. The thin lips, the drawn nostrils, the retreating chin, could never be associated with anything that was soft, gentle, or womanly. But it was the eyes that were the wonderful feature—they absolutely seemed to exercise some magic influence; they were oily eyes that gleamed and glistened, and they seemed to have in them that sinister light which is peculiar to the cobra, and other poisonous snakes. You may imagine the spell and influence they exerted over me when, on the following day, I urged my husband to leave Wiesbaden at once, notwithstanding that the place was glorious in its early autumn dress, and was filled with a fashionable and light-hearted crowd. But my lightest wish then was law to Jack, so that very afternoon we were on our way to Homburg, and it was only when Wiesbaden was miles behind me that I began to breathe freely again.

'We had been in Homburg a fortnight, and the incident of Wiesbaden had passed from my mind, when one morning, as Jack and I were on our way from the Springs, we came face to face with the woman with the oily eyes. I nearly fainted, but she smiled a hideous, cunning, cruel smile, inclined her head slightly in token of recognition, and passed on. I looked at my husband. It seemed to me that he was unusually pale, and I was surprised to see him turn and gaze after her, and she had also turned and was gazing at us. Not a word was uttered by either of us, but I pressed my husband's arm and we walked rapidly away to our apartments.

"'It's strange," I remarked to Jack as we sat at breakfast, "that we should meet that awful woman again."

"'Oh, not at all," he laughed. "You know at this time of the year people move about from place to place, and it's wonderful how you keep rubbing shoulders with the same set."

'It was quite true what Jack said, nevertheless, I could not help the feeling that the woman with the oily eyes had followed us to Homburg. If I had mentioned this then it would have been considered ridiculous, for we had only met her once, and had never spoken a word to her. What earthly interest, therefore, could she possibly take in us who were utter strangers to her. But, looked at by the light of after events, my surmise was true. The creature had marked Jack for her victim from the moment we unhappily met on the stairs at Wiesbaden. I tell you, doctor, that that woman is a human ghoul, a vampire, who lives not only by sucking the blood of men, but by destroying their souls.'

Mrs. Redcar broke down again at this stage of her narrative, and I endeavoured to comfort her; but she quickly mastered her feelings sufficiently to continue her remarkable story.

'Some days later my husband and I moved along with the throng that drifted up and down the promenade listening to the band, when we met a lady whom I had known as a neighbour when I was at home with my parents. We stopped and chatted with her for some time, until Jack asked us to excuse him while he went to purchase some matches at a kiosk; he said he would be by the fountain in ten minutes, and I was to wait for him.

'My lady friend and I moved along and chatted as women will, and then she bade me good-night as she had to rejoin her friends. I at once hurried to the rendezvous at the fountain, but Jack wasn't there. I waited some time, but still he came not. I walked about impatiently and half frightened, and when nearly three-quarters of an hour had passed I felt sure Jack had gone home, so with all haste I went to our apartments close by, but he was not in, and had not been in. Half distracted, I flew back to the promenade. It was nearly deserted, for the band had gone. As I hurried along, not knowing where to go to, and scarcely knowing what I was doing, I was attracted by a laugh—a laugh I knew. It was Jack's, and proceeding a few yards further I found him sitting on a seat under a linden tree with the woman with the oily eyes.

"'Why, my dear Maude," he exclaimed, "wherever have you been to? I've hunted everywhere for you."

'A great lump came in my throat, for I felt that Jack was lying to me. I really don't know what I said or what I did, but I am conscious in a vague way that he introduced me to the woman, but the only name I caught was that of Annette. It burnt itself into my brain; it has haunted me ever since.

'Annette put out her white hand veiled by a silk net glove through which diamond rings sparkled. I believe I did touch the proffered fingers, and I shuddered, and I heard her say in a silvery voice that was quite out of keeping with her appearance:

"'If I were your husband I should take you to task. Beauty like yours, you know, ought not to go unattended in a place like this.'

'Perhaps she thought this was funny, for she laughed, and then patted me on the shoulder with her fan. But I hated her from that moment—hated her with a hatred I did not deem myself capable of.

'We continued to sit there, how long I don't know. It seemed to me a very long time, but perhaps it wasn't long. When we rose to go the promenade was nearly deserted, only two or three couples remained. The moon was shining brilliantly; the night wind sighed pleasantly in the trees; but the beauty of the night was lost upon me. I felt ill at ease, and, for the first time in my life, unhappy. Annette walked with us nearly to our door. When the moment for parting came she again offered me the tips of her fingers, but I merely bowed frigidly, and shrank from her as I saw her oily eyes fixed upon me.

"'Ta, ta!' she said in her fatal silvery voice; "keep a watchful guard over your husband, my dear; and you, sir, don't let your beautiful little lady stray from you again, or there will be grief between you.'

'Those wicked words, every one of which was meant to have its effect, was like the poison of asps to me; you may imagine how they stung me when I tell you I was seized with an almost irresistible desire to hurl the full weight of my body at her, and, having thrown her down, trample upon her. She had aroused in me such a feeling of horror that very little more would have begotten in me the desperation of madness, and I might have committed some act which I should have regretted all my life. But bestowing another glance of her basilisk eyes upon me she moved off, and I felt relieved; though, when I reached my room, I burst into hysterical weeping. Jack took me in his arms, and kissed and comforted me, and all my love for him was strong again; as I lay with my head pillowed on his breast I felt once more supremely happy.

'The next day, on thinking the matter over, I came to the conclusion that my suspicions were unjust, my fears groundless, my jealousy stupid, and that my conduct had been rude in the extreme. I resolved, therefore, to be more amiable and polite to Annette when I again met her. But, strangely enough, though we remained in Homburg a fortnight longer we did not meet; but I know now my husband saw her several times.

'Of course, if it had not been for subsequent events, it would have been said that I was a victim of strong hysteria on that memorable night. Men are so ready to accuse women of hysteria because they are more sensitive, and see deeper than men do themselves. But my aversion to Annette from the instant I set eyes upon her, and the inferences I drew, were not due to hysteria, but to that eighth sense possessed by women, which has no name, and of which men know nothing. At least, I mean to say that they cannot understand it.'

Again Mrs. Redcar broke off in her narrative, for emotion had got the better of her. I deemed it advisable to wait. Her remarkable story had aroused all my interest, and I was anxious not to lose any connecting link of it, for from the psychological point of view it was a study.

'Of course, as I have begun the story I must finish it to its bitter end,' she went on. 'As I have told you, I did not see Annette again in Homburg, and when we left all my confidence in Jack was restored, and my love for him was stronger than ever if that were possible. Happiness came back to me. Oh! I was so happy, and thinking I had done a cruel, bitter wrong to Jack in even supposing for a moment that he would be unfaithful to me. I tried by every little artifice a woman is capable of to prove my devotion to him.

'Well, to make a long story short, we continued to travel about for some time, and finally returned home, and my baby was born. It seemed to me then as if God was really too good to me. I had everything in the world that a human being can reasonably want. An angel baby, a brave, handsome husband, ample means, hosts of friends. I was supremely happy. I thanked my Maker for it all every hour of my life. But suddenly amongst the roses the hiss of the serpent sounded. One day a carriage drove up to our door. It brought a lady visitor. She was shown into our drawing-room, and when asked for her name made some excuse to the servant. Of course, I hurried down to see who my caller was, and imagine my horror when on entering the room I beheld Annette.

"'My dear Mrs. Redcar," she gushingly exclaimed, emphasising every word, "I am so delighted to see you again. Being in London, I could not resist the temptation to call and renew acquaintances."

The voice was as silvery as ever, and her awful eyes seemed more oily. In my confusion and astonishment I did not inquire how she had got our address; but I know that I refused her proffered hand, and by my manner gave her unmistakably to understand that I did not regard her as a welcome visitor. But she seemed perfectly indifferent. She talked gaily, flippantly. She threw her fatal spell about me. She fascinated me, so that when she asked to see my baby I mechanically rang the bell, and as mechanically told the servant to send the nurse and baby in. When she came, the damnable woman took the child from the nurse and danced him, but he suddenly broke into a scream of terror, so that I rushed forward; but the silvery voice said:

"'Oh, you silly little mother. The baby is all right. Look how quiet he is now."

'She was holding him at arm's length, and gazing at him with her basilisk eyes, and he was silent. Then she hugged him, and fondled him, and kissed him, and all the while I felt as if my brain was on fire, but I could neither speak nor move a hand to save my precious little baby.

'At last she returned him to his nurse, who at once left the room by my orders, and then Annette kept up a cackle of conversation. Although it did not strike me then as peculiar, for I was too confused to have any clear thought about anything—it did afterwards—she never once inquired about Jack. It happened that he was out. He had gone away early that morning to the city on some important business in which he was engaged.

'At last Annette took herself off, to my intense relief. She said nothing about calling again; she gave no address, and made no request for me to call on her. Even had she done so I should not have called. I was only too thankful she had gone, and I fervently hoped I should never see her again.

'As soon as she had departed I rushed upstairs, for baby was screaming violently. I found him in the nurse's arms, and she was doing her utmost to comfort him. But he refused to be comforted, and I took him and put him to my breast, but he still fought, and struggled, and screamed, and his baby eyes seemed to me to be bulging with horror. From that moment the darling little creature began to sicken. He gradually pined and wasted, and in a few weeks was lying like a beautiful waxen doll in a bed of flowers. He was stiff, and cold, and dead.

'When Jack came home in the evening of the day of Annette's call, and I told him she had been, he did not seem in the least surprised, but merely remarked:

'"I hope you were hospitable to her."

'I did not answer him, for I had been anything but hospitable. I had not even invited her to partake of the conventional cup of tea.

'As our baby boy faded day by day, Jack seemed to change, and the child's death overwhelmed him. He was never absolutely unkind to me at that period, but he seemed to have entirely altered. He became sullen, silent, even morose, and he spent the whole of his days away from me. When I gently chided him, he replied that his work absorbed all his attention. And so things went on until another thunderbolt fell at my feet.

'One afternoon Jack returned home and brought Annette. He told me that he had invited her to spend a few days with us. When I urged an objection he was angry with me for the first time in our married life. I was at once silenced, for his influence over me was still great, and I thought I would try and overcome my prejudice for Annette. At any rate, as Jack's wife I resolved to be hospitable, and play the hostess with grace. But I soon found that I was regarded as of very little consequence. Annette ruled Jack, she ruled me, she ruled the household.

'You will perhaps ask why I did not rise up in wrath, and, asserting my position and dignity, drive the wicked creature out of my home. But I tell you, doctor, I was utterly powerless. She worked some devil's spell upon me, and I was entirely under the influence of her will.

'Her visit stretched into weeks. Our well-tried and faithful servants left. Others came, but their stay was brief; and at last the old woman who opened the door to you was installed. She is a creature of Annette's, and is a spy upon my movements.

'All this time Jack was under the spell of the charmer, as I was. Over and over again I resolved to go to my friends, appeal to them, tell them everything, and ask them to protect me; but my will failed, and I bore and suffered in silence. And my husband neglected me; he seemed to find pleasure only in Annette's company. Oh, how I fretted and gnawed my heart, and yet I could not break away from the awful life. I tell you, doctor, that that woman possessed some strange, devilish, supernatural power over me and Jack. When she looked at me I shrivelled up. When she spoke, her silvery voice seemed to sting every nerve and fibre in my body, and he was like wax in her hands. To me he became positively brutal, and he told me over and over again that I was spoiling his life. But, though she was a repulsive, mysterious, crafty, cruel woman, he seemed to find his happiness in her company.

'One morning, after a restless, horrible, feverish night, I arose, feeling strangely ill, and as if I were going mad. I worked myself up almost to a pitch of frenzy, and, spurred by desperation, I rushed into the drawing-room, where my husband and Annette were together, and exclaimed to her:

'"Woman, do you not see that you are killing me? Why have you come here? Why do you persecute me with your devilish wiles? You must know you are not welcome. You must feel you are an intruder."

'Overcome by the effort this had cost me, I sank down on the floor on my knees, and wept passionately. Then I heard the silvery voice say, in tones of surprise and injured innocence:

'"Well, upon my word, Mrs. Redcar, this is an extraordinary way to treat your husband's guest. I really thought I was a welcome visitor instead of an intruder; but, since I am mistaken, I will go at once."

'I looked at her through a blinding mist of tears. I met the gaze of her oily eyes, but only for a moment, as I cowered before her, shrank within myself, and felt powerless again. I glanced at my husband. He was standing with his head bowed, and, as it seemed to me, in a pose of shame and humiliation. But suddenly he darted at me, and I heard him say: "What do you mean by creating such a scene as this? You must understand I am master here." Then he struck me a violent blow on the head, and there was a long blank.

'When I came to my senses I was in bed, and the hideous old hag who opened the door to you was bending over me. It was some little time before I could realise what had occurred. When I did, I asked the woman where Mr. Redcar was, and she answered sullenly:

'"Gone."

'"And the—Annette; where is she?" I asked.

'"Gone, too," was the answer.

'Another blank ensued. I fell very ill, and when my brain was capable of coherent thought again I learnt that I had passed through a crisis, and my life had been in jeopardy. A doctor had been attending me, and there was a professional nurse in the house; but she was a hard, dry, unsympathetic woman, and I came to the conclusion—wrongly so, probably—she, too, was one of Annette's creatures.

'I was naturally puzzled to understand why none of my relatives and friends had been to see me, but I was to learn later that many had called, but had been informed I was abroad with my husband, who had been summoned away suddenly in connection with some professional matters. And I also know now that all letters coming for me were at once forwarded to him, and that any requiring answers he answered.

'As I grew stronger I made up my mind to keep my own counsel, and not let any of my friends know of what I had gone through and suffered; for I still loved my husband, and looked upon him as a victim to be pitied and rescued from the infernal wiles of the she-demon. When I heard of your arrival in England, I felt you were the one person in the wide world I could appeal to with safety, for you can understand how anxious I am to avoid a scandal. Will you help me? Will you save your old friend Jack? Restore him to sanity, doctor, and bring him back to my arms again, which will be wide open to receive him.'

I listened to poor Mrs. Redcar's story patiently, and at first was disposed to look upon it as a too common tale of human weakness. Jack Redcar had fallen into the power of an adventuress, and had been unable to resist her influence. Such things had happened before, such things will happen again, I argued with myself. There are certain women who seem capable of making men mad for a brief space; but under proper treatment they come to their senses quickly, and blush with shame as they think of their foolishness. At any rate, for the sake of my old friend, and for the sake of his poor suffering little wife, I was prepared to do anything in reason to bring back the erring husband to his right senses.

I told Mrs. Redcar this. I told her I would redress her wrongs if I could, and fight her battle to the death. She almost threw herself at my feet in her gratitude. But when I suggested that I should acquaint her family with the facts, she begged of me passionately not to do so. Her one great anxiety was to screen her husband. One thing, however, I insisted upon. That was, the old woman should be sent away, the house shut up, and that Mrs. Redcar should take apartments in an hotel, so that I might be in touch with her. She demurred to this at first, but ultimately yielded to my persuasion.

Next I went to the old woman. She was a German Suisse—her name was Grebert. I told her to pack up her things and clear out at once. She laughed in my face, and impertinently told me to mind my own business. I took out my watch and said, 'I give you half an hour. If you are not off the premises then, I will call in the police and have you turned out. Any claim you have on Mrs. Redcar, who is the mistress here—shall be settled at once.'

She replied that she did not recognise my authority, that she had been placed there by Mr. Redcar, who was her master, and unless he told her to go she should remain. I made it plain to her that I was determined and would stand no nonsense. Mr. Redcar had taken himself off, I said; Mrs. Redcar was his lawful wife, and I was acting for her and on her behalf.

My arguments prevailed, and after some wrangling the hag came to the conclusion that discretion was the better part of valour, and consented to go providing we paid her twenty pounds. This we decided to do rather than have a scene, but three hours passed before we saw the last of the creature. Mrs. Redcar had already packed up such things as she required, and when I had seen the house securely fastened up I procured a cab, and conveyed the poor little lady to a quiet West-end hotel, close to my own residence, so that I could keep a watchful eye upon her.

Of course, this was only the beginning of the task I had set myself, which was to woo back the erring husband, if possible, to his wife's side, and to restore him to the position of happiness, honour, and dignity from which he had fallen. I thought this might be comparatively easy, and little dreamed of the grim events that were to follow my interference.

Three weeks later I was in Paris, and proceeded to the Hotel de l'Univers, where Mrs. Redcar had ascertained through his bankers where her husband was staying. But to my chagrin, I found he had departed with his companion, and the address he had given for his letters at the post-office was Potes, in Spain. As I had taken up the running I had no alternative but to face the long, dreary journey in pursuit of the fugitives, or confess defeat at the start.

It is not necessary for me to dwell upon that awful journey in the winter time. Suffice to say I reached my destination in due course.

Potes, it is necessary to explain, is a small town magnificently situated in the Liebana Valley, in the Asturian Pyrenees, under the shadow of Pico de Europa. Now, what struck me as peculiar was the fugitives coming to such a place at that time of the year. Snow lay heavily everywhere. The cold was intense. For what reason had such a spot been chosen? It was a mystery I could not hope to solve just then. There was only one small hotel in the village, and there Annette and Redcar were staying. My first impulse was not to let them know of my presence, but to keep them under observation for a time. I dismissed that thought as soon as formed, for I was not a detective, and did not like the idea of playing the spy. But even had I been so disposed, there would have been a difficulty about finding accommodation. Moreover, it was a small place, and the presence of a foreigner at that time of year must necessarily have caused a good deal of gossip. The result was I went boldly to the hotel, engaged a room, and then inquired for Redcar. I was directed to a private room, where I found him alone. My unexpected appearance startled him, and when he realised who I was, he swore at me, and demanded to know my business.

He had altered so much that in a crowd I really might have had some difficulty in recognising him. His face wore a drawn, anxious, nervous look, and his eyes had acquired a restless, shifty motion, while his hair was already streaked with grey.

I began to reason with him. I reminded him of our old friendship, and I drew a harrowing picture of the sufferings of his dear, devoted, beautiful little wife.

At first he seemed callous; but presently he grew interested, and when I referred to his wife he burst into tears. Then suddenly he grasped my wrist with a powerful grip, and said:

'Hush! Annette mustn't know this—mustn't hear. I tell you, Peter, she is a ghoul. She sucks my blood. She has woven a mighty spell about me, and I am powerless. Take me away; take me to dear little Maude.'

I looked at him for some moments with a keen professional scrutiny, for his manner and strange words were not those of sanity. I determined to take him at his word, and, if possible, remove him from the influence of the wicked syren who had so fatally lured him.

'Yes,' I said, 'we will go without a moment's unnecessary delay. I will see if a carriage and post-horses are to be had, so that we can drive to the nearest railway station.'

He assented languidly to this, and I rose with the intention of making inquiries of the hotel people; but simultaneously with my action the door opened and Annette appeared. Up to that moment I thought that Mrs. Redcar had exaggerated in describing her, therefore I was hardly prepared to find that so far from the description being an exaggeration, it had fallen short of the fact.

Annette was slightly above the medium height, with a well-developed figure, but a face that to me was absolutely repellent. There was not a single line of beauty nor a trace of womanliness in it. It was hard, coarse, cruel, with thin lips drawn tightly over even white teeth. And the eyes were the most wonderful eyes I have ever seen in a human being. Maude was right when she spoke of them as 'oily eyes.' They literally shone with a strange, greasy lustre, and were capable of such a marvellous expression that I felt myself falling under their peculiar fascination. I am honest and frank enough to say that, had it been her pleasure, I believe she could have lured me to destruction as she had lured my poor friend. But I was forearmed, because forewarned. Moreover, I fancy I had a much stronger will than Redcar. Any way, I braced myself up to conquer and crush this human serpent, for such I felt her to be.

Before I could speak, her melodious voice rang out with the query, addressed to Jack:

'Who is this gentleman? Is he a friend of yours?'

'Yes, yes,' gasped Jack, like one who spoke under the influence of a nightmare.

She bowed and smiled, revealing all her white teeth, and she held forth her hand to me, a delicately shaped hand, with clear, transparent skin, and her long lithe fingers were bejewelled with diamonds.

I drew myself up, as one does when a desperate effort is needed, and, refusing the proffered hand, I said:

'Madame, hypocrisy and deceit are useless. I am a medical man, my name is Peter Haslar, and Mr. Redcar and I have been friends from youth. I've come here to separate him from your baneful influence and carry him back to his broken-hearted wife. That is my mission. I hope I have made it clear to you?'

She showed not the slightest sign of being disturbed, but smiled on me again, and bowed gracefully and with the most perfect self-possession. And speaking in a soft gentle manner, which was in such startling contrast to the woman's appearance, she said:

'Oh, yes; thank you. But, like the majority of your countrymen, you display a tendency to arrogate too much to yourself. I am a Spaniard myself, by birth, but cosmopolitan by inclination, and, believe me, I do not speak with any prejudice against your nationality, but I have yet to learn, sir, that you have any right to constitute yourself Mr. Redcar's keeper.'

Her English was perfect, though she pronounced it with just a slight foreign accent. There was no anger in her tones, no defiance. She spoke softly, silvery, persuasively.

'I do not pretend to be his keeper, madame; I am his sincere friend,' I answered. 'And surely I need not remind you that he owes a duty to his lawful wife.'

During this short conversation Jack had sat motionless on the edge of a couch, his chin resting on his hands, and apparently absorbed with some conflicting thoughts. But Annette turned to him, and, still smiling, said:

'I think Mr. Redcar is quite capable of answering for himself. Stand up, Jack, and speak your thoughts like a man.'

Although she spoke in her oily, insidious way, her request was a peremptory command. I realised that at once, and I saw as Jack rose he gazed at her, and her lustrous eyes fixed him. Then he turned upon me with a furious gesture and exclaimed, with a violence of expression that startled me:

'Yes, Annette is right. I am my own master. What the devil do you mean by following me, like the sneak and cur that you are? Go back to Maude, and tell her that I loathe her. Go; relieve me of your presence, or I may forget myself and injure you.'

Annette, still smiling and still perfectly self-possessed, said:

'You hear what your friend says, doctor. Need I say that if you are a gentleman you will respect his wishes?'

I could no longer control myself. Her calm, defiant, icy manner maddened me, and her silvery voice seemed to cut down on to my most sensitive nerves, for it was so suggestive of the devilish nature of the creature. It was so incongruous when contrasted with her harsh, horribly cruel face. I placed myself between Jack and her, and meeting her weird gaze, I said, hotly:

'Leave this room. You are an outrage on your sex; a shame and a disgrace to the very name of woman. Go, and leave me with my friend, whose reason you have stolen away.'

She still smiled and was still unmoved, and suddenly I felt myself gripped in a grip of iron, and with terrific force I was hurled into a corner of the room, where, huddled up in a heap, I lay stunned for some moments. But as my senses returned I saw the awful woman smiling still, and she was waving her long white bejewelled hand before the infuriated Jack, as if she were mesmerising him; and I saw him sink on to the sofa subdued and calmed. Then addressing me she said:

'That is a curious way for your friend to display his friendship. I may be wrong, but perhaps as a medical man you will recognise that your presence has an irritating effect on Mr. Redcar, and if I may suggest it, I think it desirable that you should depart at once and see him no more.'

'Devil!' I shouted at her. 'You have bewitched him, and made him forgetful of his honour and of what he owes to those who are dear to him. But I will defeat you yet.'

She merely bowed and smiled, but deigned no reply; and holding her arm to Jack, he took it, and they passed out of the room. She was elegantly attired. Her raven hair was fascinatingly dressed in wavy bands. There was something regal in her carriage, and gracefulness in her every movement; and yet she filled me with a sense of indefinable horror; a dread to which I should have been ashamed to own to a little while ago.

I tried to spring up and go after them, but my body seemed a mass of pain, and my left arm hung limp and powerless. It was fractured below the elbow. There was no bell in the room, and I limped out in search of assistance. I made my way painfully along a gloomy corridor, and hearing a male voice speaking Spanish, I knocked at a door, which was opened by the landlord. I addressed him, but he shook his head and gave me to understand that he spoke no English. Unhappily I spoke no Spanish. Then he smiled as some idea flitted through his mind, and bowing me into the room he motioned me to be seated, and hurried away. He returned in about five minutes accompanied by Annette, whom he had brought to act as interpreter. I was almost tempted to fly at her and strangle her where she stood. She was undisturbed, calm, and still smiled. She spoke to the man in Spanish, then she explained to me that she had told him I had slipped on the polished floor, and falling over a chair had injured myself, and she had requested him to summon the village surgeon if need be.

Without waiting for me to reply she swept gracefully out of the room. Indeed, I could not reply, for I felt as if I were choking with suppressed rage. The landlord rendered me physical assistance and took me to my bedroom, where I lay down on the bed, feeling mortified, ill, and crushed. Half an hour later a queer-looking old man, with long hair twisted into ringlets, was ushered into my room, and I soon gathered that he was the village surgeon. He spoke no English, but I explained my injury by signs, and he went away, returning in a little while with the necessary bandages and splints, and he proceeded rather clumsily to bandage my broken arm. I passed a cruel and wretched night. My physical pain was great, but my mental pain was greater. The thought forced itself upon me that I had been defeated, and that the fiendish, cunning woman was too much for me. I felt no resentment against Jack. His act of violence was the act of a madman, and I pitied him. For hours I lay revolving all sorts of schemes to try and get him away from the diabolical influence of Annette. But though I could hit upon nothing, I firmly resolved that while my life lasted I would make every effort to save my old friend, and if possible restore him to the bosom of his distracted wife.

The case altogether was a very remarkable one, and the question naturally arose, why did a man so highly gifted and so intelligent as Jack Redcar desert his charming, devoted, and beautiful wife, to follow an adventuress who entirely lacked physical beauty. Theories without number might have been suggested to account for the phenomenon, but not one would have been correct. The true answer is, Annette was not a natural being. In the ordinary way she might be described as a woman of perverted moral character, or as a physiological freak, but that would have been rather a misleading way of putting it. She was, in short, a human monstrosity. By that I do not mean to say her body was contorted, twisted, or deformed. But into her human composition had entered a strain of the fiend; and I might go even further than this and say she was more animal than human. Though in whatever way she may be described, it is certain she was an anomaly—a human riddle.

The morning following the outrage upon me found me prostrated and ill. A night of racking pain and mental distress had told even upon my good constitution. The situation in which I found myself was a singularly unfortunate one. I was a foreigner in an out-of-the-way place, and my want of knowledge of Spanish, of course, placed me at a tremendous disadvantage.

The landlord came to me and brought his wife, and between them they attended to my wants, and did what they could for my comfort. But they were ignorant, uncultivated people, only one remove from the peasant class, and I realised that they could be of little use to me. Now the nearest important town to this Alpine village was Santander, but that was nearly a hundred miles away. As everyone knows who has been in Spain, a hundred miles, even on a railway, is a considerable journey; but there was no railway between Santander and Potes. An old ramshackle vehicle, called a diligence, ran between the two places every day in the summer and twice a week in the winter, and it took fourteen hours to do the journey. Even a well-appointed carriage and pair could not cover the distance under eight hours, as the road was infamous, and in parts was little better than a mule track. I knew that there was a British consul in Santander, and I was hopeful that if I could communicate with him he might be able to render me some assistance. In the meantime I had to devise some scheme for holding Annette in check and saving my friend. But in my crippled and prostrate condition I could not do much. While lying in my bed, and thus revolving all these things in my mind, the door gently opened and Annette glided in—'glided' best expresses her movement, for she seemed to put forth no effort. She sat down beside the bed and laid her hand on mine.

'You are ill this morning,' she said softly. 'This is regrettable, but you have only yourself to blame. It is dangerous to interfere in matters in which you have no concern. My business is mine, Mr. Redcar's is his, and yours is your own, but the three won't amalgamate. Jack and I came here for the sake of the peace and quietness of these solitudes; unhappily you intrude yourself and disaster follows.'

Her voice was as silvery as ever. The same calm self-possessed air characterised her; but in her oily eyes was a peculiar light, and I had to turn away, for they exerted a sort of mesmeric influence over me, and I am convinced that had I not exerted all my will power I should have thrown myself into the creature's arms. This is a fact which I have no hesitation in stating, as it serves better than any other illustration to show what a wonderful power of fascination the remarkable woman possessed. Naturally I felt disgusted and enraged, but I fully recognised that I could not fight the woman openly; I must to some extent meet her with her own weapons. She was cunning, artful, insidious, pitiless, and the basilisk-like power she possessed not only gave her a great advantage but made her a very dangerous opponent. At any rate, having regard to all the circumstances and my crippled condition, I saw that my only chance was in temporising with her. So I tried to reason with her, and I pointed out that Redcar had been guilty of baseness in leaving his wife, who was devoted to him.

At this point of my argument Annette interrupted me, and for the first time she displayed something like passion, and her voice became hard and raucous.

'His wife,' she said with a sneer of supreme contempt. 'A poor fool, a fleshly doll. At the precise instant I set my eyes upon her for the first time I felt that I should like to destroy her, because she is a type of woman who make the world common-place and reduce all men to a common level. She hated me from the first and I hated her. She would have crushed me if she could, but she was too insignificant a worm to do that, and I crushed her.'

This cold, brutal callousness enraged me; I turned fiercely upon her and exclaimed:

'Leave me, you are a more infamous and heartless wretch than I believed you to be. You are absolutely unworthy the name of woman, and if you irritate me much more I may even forget that you have a woman's shape.'

She spoke again. All trace of passion had disappeared. She smiled the wicked insidious smile which made her so dangerous, and her voice resumed its liquid, silvery tones:

'You are very violent,' she said gently, 'and it will do you harm in your condition. But you see violence can be met with violence. The gentleman you are pleased to call your friend afforded you painful evidence last night that he knows how to resent unjustifiable interference, and to take care of himself. I am under his protection, and there is no doubt he will protect me.'

'For God's sake, leave me!' I cried, tortured beyond endurance by her hypocrisy and wickedness.

'Oh, certainly, if you desire it,' she answered, as she rose from her seat. 'But I thought I might be of use. It is useless your trying to influence Mr. Redcar—absolutely useless. His destiny is linked with mine, and the human being doesn't exist who can sunder us. With this knowledge, you will do well to retrace your steps; and, if you like, I will arrange to have you comfortably conveyed to Santander, where you can get a vessel. Anyway, you will waste your time and retard your recovery by remaining here.'

'I intend to remain here, nevertheless,' I said, with set teeth. 'And, what is more, madame, when I go my friend Redcar will accompany me.'

She laughed. She patted my head as a mother might pat the head of her child. She spoke in her most insidious, silvery tones.

'We shall see, mon cher—we shall see. You will be better to-morrow. Adieu!'

That was all she said, and she was gone. She glided out of the room as she had glided in.

I felt irritated almost into madness for some little time; but as I reflected, it was forced upon me that I had to deal with a monster of iniquity, who had so subdued the will of her victim, Redcar, that he was a mere wooden puppet in her hand. Force in such a case was worse than useless. What I had to do was to try and circumvent her, and I tried to think out some plan of action.

All that day I was compelled to keep my bed, and, owing to the clumsy way in which my arm had been bandaged, I suffered intolerable pain, and had to send for the old surgeon again to come and help me to reset the fracture. I got some ease after that, and a dose of chloral sent me to sleep, which continued for many hours. When I awoke I managed to summon the landlord, and he brought me food, and a lantern containing a candle so that I might have light. And, in compliance with my request, he made me a large jug of lemonade, in order that I could have a drink in the night, for I was feverish, and my throat was parched. He had no sooner left the room than Annette entered to inquire if she could do anything for me. I told her that I had made the landlord understand all that I desired, and he would look after me, so she wished me good-night and left. Knowing as I did that sleep was very essential in my case, I swallowed another, though smaller, dose of chloral, and then there was a blank.

How long I slept I really don't know; but suddenly, in a dazed sort of way, I saw a strange sight. The room I occupied was a long, somewhat meagrely furnished, one. The entrance door was at the extreme end, opposite the bed. Over the doorway hung a faded curtain of green velvet. By the feeble light of the candle lantern I saw this curtain slowly pulled on one side by a white hand; then a face peered in; next Annette entered. Her long hair was hanging down her back, and she wore a nightdress of soft, clinging substance, which outlined her figure. With never a sound she moved lightly towards the bed, and waved her hand two or three times over my face. I tried to move, to utter a sound, but couldn't; and yet what I am describing was no dream, but a reality. Slightly bending over me, she poured from a tiny phial she carried in the palm of her hand a few drops of a slightly acrid, burning liquid right into my mouth, and at that instant, as I believe, it seemed to me as if a thick, heavy pall fell over my eyes, for all was darkness.

I awoke hours later. The winter sun was shining brightly into my room. I felt strangely languid, and had a hot, stinging sensation in my throat. I felt my pulse, and found it was only beating at the rate of fifty-eight beats in the minute. Then I recalled the extraordinary incident of the previous night, which, had it not been for my sensations, I might have regarded as a bad dream, the outcome of a disturbed state of the brain. But as it was, I hadn't a doubt that Annette had administered some subtle and slow poison to me. My medical knowledge enabled me to diagnose my own case so far, that I was convinced I was suffering from the effects of a potent poisonous drug, the action of which was to lower the action of the vital forces and weaken the heart. Being probably cumulative, a few doses more or less, according to the strength of the subject, and the action of the heart would be so impeded that the organ would cease to beat. Although all this passed through my brain, I felt so weak and languid that I had neither energy nor strength to arouse myself, and when the landlord brought me in some food I took no notice of him. I knew that this symptom of languor and indifference was very characteristic of certain vegetable poisons, though what it was Annette had administered to me I could not determine.

Throughout that day I lay in a drowsy, dreamy state. At times my brain was clear enough, and I was able to think and reason; but there were blanks, marked, no doubt, by periods of sleep.

When night came I felt a little better, and I found that the heart's action had improved. It was steadier, firmer, and the pulse indicated sixty-two beats. Now I had no doubt that if it was Annette's intention to bring about my death slowly she would come again that night, and arousing myself as well as I could, and summoning all my will power, I resolved to be on the watch. During the afternoon I had drunk milk freely, regarding it as an antidote, and when the landlord visited me for the last time that evening I made him understand that I wanted a large jug of milk fresh from the cow, if he could get it. He kept cows of his own; they were confined in a chalet on the mountain side, not far from his house, so that he was able to comply with my request. I took a long draught of this hot milk, which revived my energies wonderfully, and then I waited for developments. I had allowed my watch to run down, consequently I had no means of knowing the time. It was a weary vigil, lying there lonely and ill, and struggling against the desire for sleep.

By-and-by I saw the white hand lift the curtain again, and Annette entered, clad as she was on the previous night. When she came within reach of me I sprang up in the bed and seized her wrist.

'What do you want here?' I demanded angrily. 'Do you mean to murder me?'

Her imperturbability was exasperating. She neither winced nor cried out, nor displayed the slightest sign of surprise. She merely remarked in her soft cooing voice, her white teeth showing as her thin lips parted in a smile:

'You are evidently restless and excited to-night, and it is hardly generous of you to treat my kindly interest in such a way.'

'Kindly interest!' I echoed with a sneer, as, releasing her wrist, I fell back on the bed.

'Yes; you haven't treated me well, and you are an intruder here. Nevertheless, as you are a stranger amongst strangers, and cannot speak the language of the country, I would be of service to you if I could. I have come to see if you have everything you require for the night.'

'And you did the same last night,' I cried in hot anger, for, knowing her infamy and wickedness, I could not keep my temper.

'Certainly,' she answered coolly; 'and I found you calmly dozing, so left you.'

'Yes—after you had poured poison down my throat,' I replied.

She broke into a laugh—a rippling laugh, with the tinkle of silver in it—and she seemed hugely amused.

'Well, well,' she said; 'it is obvious, sir, you are not in a fit state to be left alone. Your nerves are evidently unstrung, and you are either the victim of a bad dream or some strange delusion. But there, there; I will pardon you. You are not responsible just at present for your language.'

As she spoke she passed her soft white hand over my forehead. There was magic in her touch, and it seemed as if all my will had left me, and there stole over me a delightful sense of dreamy languor. I looked at her, and I saw her strange eyes change colour. They became illumined, as it were, by a violet light that fascinated me so that I could not turn from her. Indeed, I was absolutely subdued to her will now. Everything in the room faded, and I saw nothing but those marvellous eyes glowing with violet light which seemed to fill me with a feeling of ecstacy. I have a vague idea that she kept passing her hand over my face and forehead; that she breathed upon my face; then that she pressed her face to mine, and I felt her hot breath in my neck.

Perhaps it will be said that I dreamed all this. I don't believe it was a dream. I firmly and honestly believe that every word I have written is true.

Hours afterwards my dulled brain began to awake to things mundane. The morning sun was flooding the room, and I was conscious that somebody stood over me, and soon I recognised the old surgeon, who had come to see that the splints and bandages had not shifted. I felt extraordinarily weak, and I found that my pulse was beating very slowly and feebly. Again I had the burning feeling in the throat and a strange and absolutely indescribable sensation at the side of the neck. The old doctor must have recognised that I was unusually feeble, for he went to the landlord, and returned presently with some cognac which he made me swallow, and it picked me up considerably.

After his departure I lay for some time, and tried to give definite shape to vague and dreadful thoughts that haunted me, and filled me with a shrinking horror. That Annette was a monster in human form I hadn't a doubt, and I felt equally certain that she had designs upon my life. That she had now administered poison to me on two occasions seemed to me beyond question, but I hesitated to believe that she was guilty of the unspeakable crime which my sensations suggested.

At last, unable longer to endure the tumult in my brain, I sprang out of bed, rushed to the looking-glass, and examined my neck. I literally staggered back, and fell prostrate on the bed, overcome by the hideous discovery I had made. It had the effect, however, of calling me back to life and energy, and I made a mental resolution that I would, at all hazards, save my friend, though I clearly recognised how powerless I was to cope with the awful creature single-handed.

I managed to dress myself, not without some difficulty; then I summoned the landlord, and made him understand that I must go immediately to Santander at any cost. My intention was to invoke the aid of the consul there. But the more I insisted, the more the old landlord shook his head. At length, in desperation, I rushed from the house, hoping to find somebody who understood French or English. As I almost ran up the village street I came face to face with a priest. I asked him in English if he spoke my language, but he shook his head. Then I tried him with French, and to my joy he answered me that he understood a little French. I told him of my desire to start for Santander that very day, but he said that it was impossible, as, owing to the unusual hot sun in the daytime there had been a great melting of snow, with the result that a flooded river had destroyed a portion of the road; and though a gang of men had been set to repair it, it would be two or three days before it was passable.

'But is there no other way of going?' I asked.

'Only by a very hazardous route over the mountains,' he answered. And he added that the risk was so great it was doubtful if anyone could be found who would act as guide. 'Besides,' he went on, you seem very ill and weak. Even a strong man might fail, but you would be certain to perish from exhaustion and exposure.'

I was bound to recognise the force of his argument. It was a maddening disappointment, but there was no help for it. Then it occurred to me to take the old priest into my confidence and invoke his aid. Though, on second thoughts, I hesitated, for was it not possible—nay, highly probable—that if I told the horrible story he and others would think I was mad. Annette was a Spanish woman, and it was feasible to suppose she would secure the ear of those ignorant villagers sooner than I should. No, I would keep the ghastly business to myself for the present at any rate, and wait with such patience as I could command until I could make the journey to Santander. The priest promised me that on the morrow he would let me know if the road was passable, and, if so, he would procure me a carriage and make all the preparations for the journey. So, thanking him for his kindly services, I turned towards the hotel again. As I neared the house I observed two persons on the mountain path that went up among the pine trees. The sun was shining brilliantly; the sky was cloudless, the air crisp and keen. The two persons were Annette and Redcar. I watched them for some minutes until they were lost to sight amongst the trees.

Suddenly an irresistible impulse to follow them seized me. Why I know not. Indeed, had I paused to reason with myself it would have seemed to me then a mad act, and that I was risking my life to no purpose. But I did not reason. I yielded to the impulse, though first of all I went to my room, put on a thicker pair of boots, and armed myself with a revolver which I had brought with me. During my extensive travelling about America a revolver was a necessity, and by force of habit I put it up with my clothes when packing my things in London for my Continental journey.

Holding the weapon between my knees, I put a cartridge in each barrel, and, providing myself with a stick in addition, I went forth again and began to climb the mountain path. I was by no means a sanguinary man; even my pugnacity could only be aroused after much irritation. Nevertheless, I knew how to defend myself, and in this instance, knowing that I had to deal with a woman who was capable of any crime, and who, I felt sure, would not hesitate to take my life if she got the chance, I deemed it advisable to be on my guard against any emergency that might arise. As regards Redcar, he had already given me forcible and painful evidence that he could be dangerous; but I did not hold him responsible for his actions. I regarded him as being temporarily insane owing to the infernal influence the awful woman exercised over him. Therefore it would only have been in the very last extremity that I should have resorted to lethal weapons as a defence against him. My one sole aim, hope, desire, prayer, was to rescue him from the spell that held him in thrall and restore him to his wife, his honour, his sanity. With respect to Annette, it was different. She was a blot on nature, a disgrace to humankind, and, rather than let her gain complete ascendency over me and my friend, I would have shot her if I had reason to believe she contemplated taking my life. It might have involved me in serious trouble with the authorities at first, for in Spain the foreigner can hope but for little justice. I was convinced, however, that ultimately I should be exonerated.

Such were the thoughts that filled my mind as I painfully made my way up the steep mountain side. My fractured arm was exceedingly painful. Every limb in my body ached, and I was so languid, so weak that it was with difficulty I dragged myself along. But worse than all this was an all but irresistible desire to sleep, the result, I was certain, of the poison that had been administered to me. But it would have been fatal to have slept. I knew that, and so I fought against the inclination with all my might and main, and allowed my thoughts to dwell on poor little Maude Redcar, waiting desolate and heartbroken in London for news. This supplied me with the necessary spur and kept me going.

The trees were nearly all entirely bare of snow. It had, I was informed, been an unusually mild season, and at that time the sun's rays were very powerful. The path I was pursuing was nothing more than a rough track worn by the peasants passing between the valley and their hay chalets dotted about the mountain. Snow lay on the path where it was screened from the sun by the trees. I heard no sound, saw no sign of those I was seeking save here and there footprints in the snow. I frequently paused and listened, but the stillness was unbroken save for the subdued murmur of falling water afar off.

In my weakened condition the exertion I had endured had greatly distressed me; my heart beat tumultuously, my pulses throbbed violently, and my breathing was stertorous. I was compelled at last to sit down and rest. I was far above the valley now, and the pine trees were straggling and sparse. The track had become very indistinct, but I still detected the footsteps of the people I was following. Above the trees I could discern the snow-capped Pico de Europa glittering in the brilliant sun. It was a perfect Alpine scene, which, under other circumstances, I might have revelled in. But I felt strangely ill, weak, and miserable, and drowsiness began to steal upon me, so that I made a sudden effort of will and sprang up again, and resumed the ascent.

In a little time the forest ended, and before me stretched a sloping plateau which, owing to its being exposed to the full glare of the sun, as well as to all the winds that blew, was bare of snow. The plateau sloped down for probably four hundred feet, then ended abruptly at the edge of a precipice. How far the precipice descended I could not tell from where I was, but far far below I could see a stream meandering through a thickly wooded gorge. I took the details of the scene in with a sudden glance of the eye, for another sight attracted and riveted my attention, and froze me with horror to the spot. Beneath a huge boulder which had fallen from the mountain above, and lodged on the slope, were Annette and Redcar. He was lying on his back, she was stretched out beside him, and her face was buried in his neck. Even from where I stood I could see that he was ghastly pale, his features drawn and pinched, his eyes closed. Incredible as it may seem, horrible as it sounds, it is nevertheless true that that hellish woman was sucking away his life blood. She was a human vampire, and my worst fears were confirmed.

I am aware that an astounding statement of this kind should not be made lightly by a man in my position. But I take all the responsibility of it, and I declare solemnly that it is true. Moreover, the sequel which I am able to give to this story more than corroborates me, and proves Annette to have been one of those human problems which, happily for the world, are very rare, but of which there are several well authenticated cases.

As soon as I fully realised what was happening I drew my revolver from the side pocket of my jacket and fired, not at Annette, but in the air; my object being to startle her so that she would release her victim. It had the desired effect. She sprang up, livid with rage. Blood—his blood—was oozing from the sides of her mouth. Her extraordinary eyes had assumed that strange violet appearance which I had seen once before. Her whole aspect was repulsive, revolting, horrible beyond words. Rooted to the spot I stood and gazed at her, fascinated by the weird, ghastly sight. In my hand I still held the smoking revolver, levelled at her now, and resolved if she rushed towards me to shoot her, for I felt that the world would be well rid of such a hideous monster. But suddenly she stooped, seized her unfortunate victim in her arms, and tore down the slope, and when the edge of the precipice was reached they both disappeared into space.

The whole of this remarkable scene was enacted in the course of a few seconds. It was to me a maddening nightmare. I fell where I stood, and remembered no more until, hours afterwards, I found myself lying in bed at the hotel, and the old surgeon and the priest sitting beside me. Gradually I learnt that the sound of the shot from the revolver, echoing and re-echoing in that Alpine region, had been heard in the village, and some peasants had set off for the mountain to ascertain the cause of the firing. They found me lying on the ground still grasping the weapon, and thinking I had shot myself they carried me down to the hotel.

Naturally I was asked for explanations when I was able to talk, and I recounted the whole of the ghastly story. At first my listeners, the priest and the doctor, seemed to think I was raving in delirium, as well they might, but I persisted in my statements, and I urged the sending out of a party to search for the bodies. If they were found my story would be corroborated.

In a short time a party of peasants started for the gorge, which was a wild, almost inaccessible, ravine through which flowed a mountain torrent amongst the débris and boulders that from time to time had fallen from the rocky heights. After some hours of searching the party discovered the crushed remains of Jack Redcar. His head had been battered to pieces against the rocks as he fell, and every bone in his body was broken. The precipice over which he had fallen was a jagged, scarred, and irregular wall of rock at least four thousand feet in height. The search for Annette's body was continued until darkness compelled the searchers to return to the village, which they did bringing with them my poor friend's remains. Next day the search was resumed, and the day after, and for many days, but with no result. The woman's corpse was never found. The theory was that somewhere on that frightful rock face she had been caught by a projecting pinnacle, or had got jammed in a crevice, where her unhallowed remains would moulder into dust. It was a fitting end for so frightful a life.

Of course an official inquiry was held—and officialism in Spain is appalling. It was weeks and weeks before the inevitable conclusion of the tribunal was arrived at, and I was exonerated from all blame. In the meantime Redcar's remains were committed to their eternal rest in the picturesque little Alpine village churchyard, and for all time Potes will be associated with that grim and awful tragedy. Why Annette took her victim to that out of the way spot can only be guessed at. She knew that the death of her victim was only a question of weeks, and in that primitive and secluded hamlet it would arouse no suspicion, she being a native of Spain. It would be easy for her to say that she had taken her invalid husband there for the benefit of his health, but unhappily the splendid and bracing air had failed to save his life. In this instance, as in many others, her fiendish cunning would have enabled her to score another triumph had not destiny made me its instrument to encompass her destruction.

For long after my return to England I was very ill. The fearful ordeal I had gone through, coupled with the poison which Annette had administered to me, shattered my health; but the unremitting care and attention bestowed upon me by my old friend's widow pulled me through. And when at last I was restored to strength and vigour, beautiful Maude Redcar became my wife.

NOTE BY THE AUTHOR.—The foregoing story was suggested by a tradition current in the Pyrenees, where a belief in ghouls and vampires is still common. The same belief is no less common throughout Styria, in some parts of Turkey, in Russia, and in India. Sir Richard Burton deals with the subject in his 'Vikram and the Vampire.' Years ago, when the author was in India, a poor woman was beaten to death one night in the village by a number of young men armed with cudgels. Their excuse for the crime was that the woman was a vampire, and had sucked the blood of many of their companions, whom she had first lured to her by depriving them of their will power by mesmeric influence.

Sequel to the Woman with the 'Oily Eyes'
The Story of Annette
From Official Records

At the time the inquiry was held into the circumstances of Jack Redcar's death, the authorities deemed it their duty to find out something of Annette's past history. In this they were aided by certain documents discovered amongst her belongings, and, by dint of astute and patient investigation, they elicited the following remarkable facts. Her real name was Isabella Ribera, and she was born in a little village in the Sierra Nevada, of Andalusia. Her mother was a highly respectable peasantwoman, of a peculiarly romantic disposition, and fond of listening to and reading weird and supernatural stories. Her father was also a peasant, but intellectual beyond his class. By dint of hard work, he acquired a considerable amount of land and large numbers of cattle, and ultimately became the mayor of his village.

There were two peculiarities noticed about Isabella Ribera when she was born. She had an extraordinary amount of back hair, and the lids of her eyes remained fast sealed until she was a year old. An operation was at first talked about, but the child was examined by a doctor of some repute in the nearest town, and he advised against the operation, saying that it was better to let nature take her course. When the girl was in her thirteenth month she one day suddenly opened her eyes, and those who saw them were frightened. Some people said that they were seal's eyes, others that they were the eyes of a snake, and others, again, that 'the devil looked through them.' The superstitious people in the village urged the parents to consult the priest, and this was done, with the result that the infant was subjected to a religious ceremony, with a view to exorcising the demon which was supposed to have taken possession of her.

As the girl grew she displayed amazing precocity. When she was only four she was more like a grown woman in her acts and ways than a child, and the intuitive knowledge she exhibited only served to increase the superstitious dread with which she inspired people. One day, when she was nearly five, her father had a pig killed. The girl witnessed the operation, and seemed to go almost mad with delight. And suddenly, to the horror and consternation of those looking on, she threw herself on the dying animal and began to drink the blood that flowed from the cut throat. Somebody snatched her up and ran screaming with her to her mother, who was distracted when she heard the story.

The incident, of course, soon became known all over the village, and indeed far beyond it, and a fierce hatred of the child seized upon the people. The consequence was, the parents had to keep a very watchful eye over her. They were seriously advised to have the girl strangled, and her body burnt to ashes with wood that had been blessed and consecrated by the priests. Fearing that an attempt would be made upon her life by the villagers, Isabella's parents secretly conveyed her away and took her to Cordova, where she was placed in the care of the mother superior of a convent.

At this place she was carefully trained and taught, but was regarded as an unnatural child. She seemed to be without heart, feeling, or sentiment. Her aptitude for learning was looked upon as miraculous, and a tale of horror or bloodshed afforded her an infinite amount of enjoyment.

When she was a little more than twelve she escaped from her guardians and disappeared.

For a long time no trace of her was forthcoming, then it became known that she had joined a band of gipsies, and gained such a dominating influence and power over them, that she was made a queen and married a young man of the tribe. A month afterwards he was found dead one morning in his tent. The cause of his death remained a mystery, but it was noticed that there was a peculiar blue mark at the side of his neck, from which a drop or two of blood still oozed.

A few weeks after her husband's death, Isabella, queen of the gipsies, announced to her tribe that she was going to sever herself from them for a time and travel all over Europe. Where she went to during the succeeding two years will never be known; but she was next heard of in Paris, where she was put upon her trial, charged with having caused the death of a man whom she alleged was her husband. She was then known as Madame Ducoudert. The husband had died in a very mysterious manner. He seemed to grow bloodless, and gradually faded away. And after his death certain signs suggested poison. An autopsy, however, failed to reveal any indications of recognised poisons. Nevertheless madame was tried, but no evidence was forthcoming to convict her, and she was acquitted.

Almost immediately afterwards she quitted Paris with plenty of money, her husband, who was well off, having left her all his property. The Paris police, through their agents and spies, ascertained that she proceeded direct to Bordeaux, where, in a very short time, she united herself to a handsome young man, the only son of an exceedingly wealthy Bordeaux wine merchant. She had changed her name at this stage to Marie Tailleux. She had a well-developed figure, an enormous quantity of jet black hair, and perfect teeth. In other respects she was considered to be ugly, by some even repulsive. And yet she exercised a fatal fascination over men, though women feared and hated her.

She went from Bordeaux to London with the wine merchant's son, and six months later the English people were treated to a sensation. 'Madame and Monsieur Tailleux' travelled extensively about England and Scotland. Monsieur fell ill, soon after arriving, of some nameless disease. His illness was characterised by prostration, languor, bloodlessness. He consulted several doctors, who prescribed for him without effect.

The pair at last took up their residence at a very well-known metropolitan hotel, where they lived in great style, spent money lavishly, and were supposed to be people of note. But one morning monsieur was found dead in bed, and as no doctor had been treating him for some time, and the cause of death could not be certified, an inquest was ordered and a post-mortem became necessary. Those who made the examination had their suspicions aroused. They believed there had been foul play—at any rate, the man had died of poison. The police were communicated with: result, the arrest of madame, and columns and columns of sensational reports in the papers.

Amongst madame's belongings was found a little carved ebony box containing twelve receptacles for twelve tiny phials. Some of these phials were empty, others full of liquid that varied in colour; that is, in one phial it was yellow, in another red, in another green, in another blue, and yet another held what seemed to be clear water.

The chemical analysis of the contents of the stomach quite failed to justify the suspicions of poison. But the blood had a peculiar, watery appearance; the heart was flabby and weak. Madame accounted for possession of the phials by saying they contained gipsy medicine of great efficacy in certain diseases. There was such a small quantity in each phial as to make analysis practically impossible; certain animals, however, were treated with some of the contents, and seemed actually to improve under the treatment. Under the circumstances, of course, there was nothing for it but to release madame, as the magistrate said there was no case to go before a jury.

It is worthwhile to quote the following description of the woman at this time. It appeared in a report in the *Times*.

'The prisoner is a most extraordinary looking woman, and appears to be possessed of some wonderful magnetic power, which half fascinates one. It is difficult to say wherein this power lies, unless it be in her eyes. They are certainly remarkable eyes, that have a peculiar, glistening appearance like oil. Then her voice is a revelation. Until she speaks one would be disposed to say the voice of such a harsh-featured woman would be hard, raucous, and raspy. But its tones are those of a silver bell, or a sweet-toned flute. Her self-possession is also marvellous, and she smiles sweetly and fascinatingly. Somehow or another she gives one the impression that she has some of the attributes of the sirens of old, who were said to lure men to their destruction. Possibly this is doing the woman an injustice; but it is difficult to resist the idea. Her hands, too, are in striking contrast to her general physique. They are long, thin, lithe, and white. Taken altogether, she cannot certainly be described as an ordinary type of woman, and we should be disposed to say that, allied to great intelligence, was a subtle cunning and a cruelty of disposition that might make her dangerous.'

This description was written during the time the woman was a prisoner. The writer showed that he had a keen insight, and had he but known some of her past history he would probably have written in a much more pronounced way.

'Madame Tailleux' was discharged for the want of legal evidence, and Madame Tailleux soon afterwards left England and went to America, where she became 'Miss Anna Clarkson'; and though nobody knew anything at all about her, she had no difficulty in making her way into so-called Society; but not as an associate and companion of women, who shunned and hated her as she hated them; but men followed her, as men are alleged to have followed Circe. Indeed, in some respects, the classical description of Circe with her magic and potions might apply to Isabella Ribera, with the many aliases.

In a very little while Phineas Miller fell a victim to her potent spells. Phineas was a young man, a stockbroker, and rich. The twain journeyed to Florida, from whence Phineas wrote to an intimate friend that he was strangely ill, and he believed the climate was affecting him. He looked like a corpse, he said. He was languid. He took no interest in anything. He suffered from a peculiar prostration, and found a difficulty in moving about. Yet he experienced no pain, and at times sank into a dreamy state that was pleasant. He thought, however, as soon as he left that part of the country he would be all right.

He was doomed, however, never to leave that part of the country. He went out one day with Miss Anna Clarkson, and an old negro, to shoot in the swamps. They had a boat which was in charge of the negro. That evening, Miss Clarkson returned alone. She was drenched and covered with slime and mud. There had been an accident. The boat had capsized by striking against a sunken tree. They were all thrown into the water. She managed to cling to the boat, and ultimately to right it, but her companions disappeared. The negro, she thought, was taken by a crocodile.

A search-party went out to try and recover the bodies. The negro was never found, Miller was. He presented an extraordinary appearance, and those who examined him said he had not died by drowning. This theory, however, found no favour. Men were often drowned in the swamps, which swarmed with alligators and crocodiles, huge snakes, and other repulsive things. When a man once got into the water he had no chance. It was a perfect miracle how Miss Clarkson escaped. 'Poor thing, she must have had an awful time of it.'

It is true that crocodiles, alligators, and snakes did swarm in the swamps, and the remarkable thing was that Miller's body was recovered. Much sympathy was shown for Miss Clarkson; Miller was duly buried and forgotten in a week.

Amongst the lady's most pronounced sympathisers was a Mr. Lambert Lennox, an Englishman engaged in fruit-farming. He was about forty-five, a widower with two daughters and a son. It was generally agreed that he was one of the finest men in Florida. He was an athlete. He stood six feet two in his stockings. His health was perfect. It was his boast that he had never been laid up a day with illness.

Mr. Lennox had some business to transact in Jamaica, West Indies, and sailed for that island in one of the trading vessels. In the same vessel went 'poor' Miss Clarkson. A month or two later Mr. Lennox, Jun., received from Mr. Lennox, Sen., a letter dated from Jamaica, in the West Indies. Amongst much other news the writer told his son that he had not been well. He had a strange *ænemic* appearance, felt weak and languid, had no energy, suffered from unquenchable thirst, and was constantly falling asleep suddenly, often at the most inopportune moments. He had consulted a doctor, who was of opinion that the climate of Jamaica didn't suit him, and he advised him to get away as soon as possible. 'I shall therefore be home in about six weeks,' Mr. Lennox added. But in the meantime he departed for his long home. Mr. Lambert Lennox died somewhat suddenly one morning, and was buried in the evening. The doctor who had been attending him certified that he had succumbed to low fever. The next mail that went out bore the sad intelligence to his family, and people marvelled much when they heard that handsome Lambert Lennox, the man with the iron constitution, had slipped away so quickly, more particularly as long residence in Florida had inured him to a hot climate and miasma.

It was found difficult to trace Miss Clarkson's movements during the next two or three years, but there were grounds for believing that she travelled extensively, and amongst other places visited India, and in this connection there was a somewhat vague and legendary story told. At a hill station a strange and mysterious woman put in an appearance. She was thought to be either a Spaniard or a Portuguese. She was known as Mademoiselle Sassetti, though why 'Mademoiselle,' if Spanish or Portuguese, was not explained. But that is a detail.

This mysterious lady claimed to have occult powers. She could read anyone's future. She could perform miracles. The women kept away from her because they were afraid of her, though there was no definite statement as to how this fear arose. But the men showed no fear, as became them, and amongst others who consulted her was a handsome, much beloved young military officer. His frequent visits to the sorceress caused a good deal of talk, as it was bound to do in an Indian hill station. Grey-bearded men shook their heads sadly, and wise and virtuous women turned up their noses and muttered mysterious interjections such as 'Ah!' 'Oh !' 'Umph.'

One day the station was startled by a report that the young officer had been found dead in a jungle in one of the valleys. He had been bitten by a cobra, so the report said, for there was a peculiar little blue mark at the side of his neck.

If the virtuous ones didn't actually say it served him right, they thought it; and the grey beards looked more knowing than ever, and mumbled that the young officer had been dining somewhere not wisely but too well, and had mistaken the jungle for his bedroom, and gone to sleep, otherwise how did the cobra manage to bite him in the neck.

It seemed a plausible theory. Anyway it got over a difficulty, and it brought an unpleasant little scandal to a tragic and abrupt end. So the virtuous ones went about their many occupations again, and the atmosphere was purer when it was known that the sorceress had disappeared as mysteriously as she had come.

The next direct evidence we got was that under the name of Isabella Rodino the adventuress turned up in Rome, where she rented a small but expensive villa in the fashionable Via Porta Pia. Everyone who knows Rome knows how exclusive society is, but while Isabella Rodino made no attempt to be received by Roman society she attracted to her villa some of the male representatives of the best families in the city. Amongst these gentlemen was the scion of one of the oldest Roman houses.

Now it may be said boldly here, and that without any reflections, that the young gentlemen of Rome, as of most other continental cities, are allowed a good deal more latitude than would be accorded to the same class in, say, cold-blooded, unromantic, prosaic, and commonplace London, whose soot and grime, somehow, seem to grind their way into people's brains and hearts. Anyway the young gentleman referred to, whose baptismal name was Basta, did not at first provoke any very severe criticism, but he was destined ultimately to give the Romans a sensation to talk about for the proverbial nine days, for one Sunday morning a humble fisherman, having some business on the Tiber, fished out of that classic river the stark body of the scion. Over Rome flew the news, and those who loved him, and looked to him to uphold the honour and dignity of his family, were horror stricken.

Now, it's a very curious thing that his distracted relatives firmly believed that the young prodigal had in a moment of remorse, after a night's debauch, flung himself into eternity via the Tiber, and so mighty was their pride that they used their wealth, their influence, and their power to stifle inquiry, and caused a report to be circulated that Basta had met his end through accident. It is no less curious that the family doctor who examined the body was of opinion that there was something mysterious about the lad's death, for he certainly had not died by drowning, and on one side of the neck was a peculiar little bluish puncture. But as the family persisted in *their* view, the doctor, not wishing to lose their influential patronage, observed a discreet silence.

A week later, however, an agent of the police called on Isabella Rodino, and did something more than hint that it was desirable that within twenty-four hours she should leave Rome as quietly and unobtrusively as possible. The result of this functionary's call was that Isabella Rodino journeyed to Florence by that night's mail train. It was known that she only sojourned two days in the fair city on the Arno.

After that there is another hiatus of something like two years in her known career, and it is not easy to fill it up. And this brings us to that fatal night at Wiesbaden, when ill-starred Jack Redcar met the enchantress on the hotel stairs. From that point to the moment when, her role being finished, she disappeared forever from the ken of men, the reader of the story can fill in for himself. She played out her last act under the name of Annette. In selecting her many names she seemed actuated by a fine sense of poetic euphony, and in selecting her victims she was guided by a 'damnable' discrimination.

'Annette,' as we will now call her, was a human riddle, and she illustrates for the millionth time the trite adage that 'Truth is stranger than Fiction,' besides which she presents the world with an object lesson in the study of the occult.

The Female Hypnotist in Fiction, 1840–1910

The following is an extensive annotated bibliography of 19th and early 20th century novels, dime novels, and short stories having female hypnotists/mesmerists as characters. The majority of the works listed are available online through one or more of the following websites:

- Digital Commons @ University of South Florida
  https://digitalcommons.usf.edu/dime

- Gale's American Fiction, 1774-1920
  https://www.gale.com/c/american-fiction-1774-1920

- Google Books - https://books.google.com

- HathiTrust - https://www.hathitrust.org

- Illinois Digital Newspaper Collections
  https://idnc.library.illinois.edu

- Internet Archive - https://archive.org/details/texts

- Nineteenth Century UK Periodicals (Gale)
  https://www.gale.com/intl/primary-sources/19th-century-uk-periodicals

- Northern Illinois University Libraries
  https://dimenovels.lib.niu.edu

- Papers Past - https://paperspast.natlib.govt.nz/

- Project Gutenberg - https://www.gutenberg.org

- Proquest British Periodicals
  https://about.proquest.com/en/products-services/british_periodicals

- Trove Digitized Newspapers - https://trove.nla.gov.au

- Villanova Digital Library
  https://digital.library.villanova.edu/Item/vudl:24093

Note: Italicized annotations are excerpts taken from book reviews and plain text annotations are the work of the editor.

Anonymous. "An African Star: A Theatrical Story" *London Journal* 9 (May 1910): 81-82. Available online via Proquest British Periodicals: http://www.proquest.com/products-services/british_periodicals.html.

Princess Malaeska, an African woman working for a traveling theater group as a snake charmer is infatuated with Leonard Linwood, the lead performer of the stage show, but Linwood is engaged to Maggie St. Clair. Malaeska, in a fit of jealousy, hypnotizes Maggie with the hope that one of her snakes will kill her while she is in her hypnotic trance; Malaeska's evil venture fails, and she leaves the traveling show and returns to Africa.

_____. "An Apt Pupil: A Short Story" *Ovens and Murray Advertiser* (Aug. 1905): 7. Available online via Trove Digitized Newspapers: http://trove.nla.gov.au/newspaper/article/200140876.

Professor Draycott, a hypnotist and lecturer, always made it a point in his lectures to stress that almost every person has the latent power to be a good hypnotist; and his point is proven when a young woman that attended one of his performances, hypnotizes him in to giving her all the money he had received from the proceeds of his lecture.

_____. "Between Two Worlds" *Argosy* 43 (Feb. 1887): 99-111. Available online via HathiTrust and Google Books: https://babel.hathitrust.org/cgi/pt?id=mdp.39015065716337&view=1up&seq=111.

A woman uses her mesmeric powers to enable a young woman to communicate with the spirit of her dead lover in Heaven; but she ceases the mesmeric sessions because she feels that there is a danger in continuing to indulge the couple in the practice of such celestial meetings.

_____. "Countess Clara" *Argosy* 52 (July 1891): 29-47. Available online via HathiTrust and Google Books: https://babel.hathitrust.org/cgi/pt?id=osu.32435051195931&view=1up&seq=39.

Countess Clara uses her hypnotic powers over a young woman to help her romantic interest, Sir Ralph Beauvoir, regain ownership of his family estate, but when Clara is informed that Sir Ralph is secretly engaged to an American heiress, Clara ceases her hypnotic control over the woman, and works in concert with the woman's physician to put an end to Sir Ralph's gold digging efforts to marry the American heiress.

_____. "An Experiment in Mesmerism." *Temple Bar* 60 (Nov. 1880): 338-47. Available online via HathiTrust: http://babel.hathitrust.org/cgi/pt?id=mdp.39 015065359138;view=1up;seq=346.

A young woman unintentionally mesmerizes a man she detests into falling in love with her; he somehow talks her into marrying him but he ends up dying the night of their wedding day. (Note: also published under the title "A Mesmeric Experiment" in the *London Reader,* January 29, 1881, pp.332-334)

_____. "The Influence of Josephine Carr." *Our Paper* 19 (Aug. 1903): 530-531. Available online via Google Books and HathiTrust: https://babel.hathitrust.org/ cgi/pt?id=nyp.33433003028184&view=1up&seq=540.

Fred Armitage's wife Dorothy was prone to follow fads (the most recent being spiritualism and hypnotism); Fred breaks her of it when he pretends to have fallen under the hypnotic influence of Dorothy's friend Josephine.

_____. "My Wife's Hypnotic Experiences." *Oakleigh Leader* (Feb. 1894): 6. Available online via Trove Digitized Newspapers: http://trove.nla.gov.au/ newspaper/article/66215326.

A story of hypnotic blackmail, where a female hypnotist, feigning to be a French maid, hypnotizes the wife of a wealthy man, and states that she will restore the man's wife back to her normal faculties for 5000 francs.

_____. "The New Hypnotism." *Judy: The London Serio-Comic Journal* (June 1897): 302. Available online via Proquest British Periodicals: http://www.proquest. com/products-services/british_periodicals.html.

A man is placed into a hypnotic trance by looking too long at a moving bicycle wheel; his wife takes advantage of his hypnotized state, and has him write her a check for 20 pounds so she can purchase the new bonnet he had long been denying her.

_____. "Suggestion." *Romance* 3 (Sept. 1891): 186-91. Available online via HathiTrust: http://babel.hathitrust.org/cgi/pt?id=umn.31951002796908k;vie w=1up;seq=192.

A woman with a suicide wish hypnotizes a man to behead her.

_____. "The Toad's Curse." *Fraser's Magazine* 48 (Sept. 1853): 286-99. Available online via HathiTrust and Google Books: https://babel.hathitrust.org/cgi/pt?id =umn.319510007429458&seq=290.

Horace Sommerling is tormented by the memory of killing a preternatural toad when he was a young boy. When Sommerling is an adult, he saves a beautiful woman named Isola from a life of slavery; Isola's beauty and mesmeric charms holds Sommerling in a state of ardent thraldom for many months, but when Sommerling punches Isola in a fit of temper and nearly kills her, she seeks her revenge, in part, by resurrecting Sommerling's guilty memory of his killing of the supernatural toad (Isola has clairvoyant powers, as well as mesmeric ones, which allows her to know about Horace's guilty toad memory). Note: the toad in the story appears to have some sort of mesmeric powers as well.

_____."Under the Influence" *Cape Illustrated Magazine* (Sept. 1891): 18. Available online via 19th Century UK Periodicals (Gale Cengage): http://gale.cengage.co.uk/ product-highlights/history/19th-century-uk-periodicals-parts-1-and-2.aspx.

A woman hypnotizes her fiancé to steal money from his employer.

A'Beckett, Arthur William. "Killed By the Dead" *The Australasian* (Apr. 1870): 519. Available online via Trove Digitized Newspapers: https://trove.nla.gov.au/ newspaper/article/138064336.

Reginald Raynor is on death row in Newgate prison, but he claims to be innocent of the crime of murder; he tells one of his jailers that a woman had placed him into a mesmeric trance and forced him to kill her with a knife (the woman was seeking revenge against Raynor for causing the death of her sister, so she sacrificed her life with the hopes that Raynor would hang for the crime). Raynor escapes from prison by mesmerizing the guard in charge of watching him, but the story ends with Raynor dying in an asylum, the victim of an apoplectic fit. [Note: this story originally appeared in the February, 1870 issue of the *Britannia*]

Alcott, Louisa May. "Behind a Mask; or, A Woman's Power" *Flag of Our Union* 21 (Oct. 1866): 649-52. Available online via the Internet Archive, Project Gutenberg and Proquest's American Periodicals Series: http://www.archive.org/stream/behinda maskorawo08677gut/8bhmk10.txt.

Theresa Strouth Gaul, in her abstract to her article "Trance-Formations: Mesmerism and 'A Woman's Power' in Louisa May Alcott's Behind a Mask" (**Women's Studies**, Vol. 32, October-November, 2003, pp.835-851), states: *In her pseudonymous thriller,* **Behind a Mask; or, A Woman's Power,** *Louisa May Alcott invests her central character, Jean Muir, with mysterious powers to influence those around her. While Jean is never identified as a mesmerist, nor is mesmerism ever explicitly mentioned, Alcott grants her heroine the traits indelibly associated with mesmerism in the nineteenth century: a piercing gaze, the ability to provoke physical sensations, and a mysterious power to conform others' wills to her own.* Muir wields her power to get a wealthy gentleman to marry her, and several other men to fall in love with her. [Note: this novelette was written under the pseudonym, A. M. Barnard, and first appeared serially in the **Flag of Our Union**, v.21, n.41, Oct. 13,

1866, p.649-652; v.21, n.42, Oct. 20, 1866, p.665-668; v.21, n.43, Oct. 27, 1866, p.681-683; v.21, n.44, Nov. 3, 1866, p.697-698]

_____. "A Pair of Eyes; or, Modern Magic" *Frank Leslie's Illustrated Newspaper* 17:421 (Oct. 1863): 69-71.

A wealthy heiress, Agatha Eure, hypnotizes the artist Max Erdmann while he is incorporating the likeness of her eyes into a portrait of Lady Macbeth. Agatha and Max marry; Agatha begins to cast a spell over Max which compels him to return to her every time he leaves the house. A contest of their wills ensues, and Max flees to a house in a remote village to escape Agatha, but she comes to him through a terrible rainstorm. Soon after her arrival, she drops dead, but her spirit and voice continue to haunt Max the rest of his life. [Note: "A Pair of Eyes" was published anonymously in two parts in *Frank Leslie's Illustrated Newspaper* (Oct. 24, 1863 on pp.69-71 and Oct. 31, 1863 on pp.85-87)].

Arthur, T.S. (Timothy Shay). *The Angel and the Demon*. Philadelphia: J.W. Bradley, 1858. Online via Internet Archive and Hathi Trust:

http://archive.org/details/angelanddemontal00arthrich
http://catalog.hathitrust.org/api/volumes/oclc/9247093.html.

A thrilling work, in which Mrs. Dainty procures an angel, in the person of the accomplished Florence Harper, as governess, whose influence upon the children is productive of the best results. In her fondness for and abuse of authority she makes the position of Florence a very trying one, until, finally, she hurriedly discharges her. She then engages a demon, in the person of Mrs. Jeckyl, as governess, who becomes repulsive to every one, and employs mesmeric means and familiar spirits among the children until she is sent away. Afterwards one of the children is stolen, when Uncle John, the angel and the demon, all figure prominently.—(From an advertisement that appears in the book: **Woman to the Rescue: A Story of a New Crusade** (1874))

Bartlett, M. De L. "The Triumph of Madame Marsky" *Duluth Herald* (Nov. 1910): 75. Colonel Graham embarrasses the hypnotist Madame Marsky at a private party when he calls her a cheat and a vulgar charlatan, but the Madame gets her revenge when she hypnotizes the Colonel at a public performance and has him apologize to her in front of the audience. [Note: this story was reprinted in the *Urbana Courier Herald*, July 22, 1913 http://idnc.library.illinois.edu/cgi-bin/illinois?a=d&d=TUC19130722.2.55#]

Bates, Arlo. "Miss Gaylord and Jenny" *Atlantic Monthly* 94 (Dec. 1904): 835-44. Available online via Google Books and HathiTrust: http://babel.hathitrust.org/cgi/pt?id=uc1.32106009128247;view=1up;seq=845.

Alice Gaylord is a decorous and rather colorless Boston girl, who is betrothed to a Dr. Carroll. She undergoes the strain of a long experience of filial nursing, and is finally released a nervous patient of the man who has hoped to marry her. She becomes a victim of self-hypnotism; and in the hypnotic state another personality gets the ascendency, a vivacious and vulgar and charming personality which calls itself Jenny, and sets itself to win away the doctor from his decorous Alice. He feels her charm, and is finally driven in self-defence to threaten her with a red-hot poker. She casts herself at his feet. "The wail of her pleading almost unmanned him ... The thought surged into his mind that perhaps she has as much claim to consciousness as Alice; he seemed to be murdering this strange creature kneeling to him with streaming eyes and quivering mouth." However, he stands firm to his guns, and in spite of the wiles of Jenny succeeds in marrying his proper Alice; after which it conveniently happens that Jenny is heard of no more, though in Alice's daughter she is destined to gain a sort of foothold in the flesh. To make such a story credible, as it is here made, is certainly more than a bit of literary sleight-of-hand.— **The Nation,** Vol. 87 (July 23, 1908): p.75 [Note: this story is reprinted in Bates's book **The Intoxicated Ghost and Other Stories** (1908)].

Becke, Louis. *The Strange Adventures of James Shervinton, and Other Stories.* London: T. Fisher Unwin, 1902. Available online via HathiTrust, Google Books, and Project Gutenberg: http://catalog.hathitrust.org/Record/002602038.

The female character, Niabon, in the title story, possesses mesmeric powers.

Bienenstok, Montefiore. "An Experiment in Conscience" *American Jewess* 2 (Jan. 1896): 202-8. University of Michigan Library Digital Collections: http://quod.lib.umich.edu/a/amjewess/taj1895.0002.004/32:17 http://quod.lib.umich.edu/a/amjewess/taj1895.0002.005/39:17.

A woman with hypnotic powers uses them to change an irreligious and money-driven man-of-the-world into an honest, spiritual and thoughtful man; the man's hypnotically-made moral transformation leads to many unintended negative consequences. [Note: part 2 of this short story published in *American Jewess* Vol. 2, February, 1896, pp. 261-265]

Bryce, Lloyd. *Romance of an Alter Ego.* New York: Brentano's, 1889. Available online through the Internet Archive and Google Books: https://archive.org/details/cihm_00309.

A novel of mistaken identity and mesmerism. A wealthy cattle rancher from the West (Aaron Simoni) comes to New York City for a visit, and is barely in town for a few hours before he meets a woman (Edna Dalzelle) who claims he is her husband who had deserted her shortly after their marriage four years earlier. A lawsuit is filed and a court ruling sustains Edna's suit. Edna is under the hypnotic influences of a mesmeric medium named Rebecca Seaton and a half-mad scientist named

Dr. James Henry. Aaron Simoni finds himself in several complicated situations— assassination attempts on his life by a gang of Anarchists, false murder charges, the knowledge that he is married to the same woman as his long-thought-dead twin brother, etc.. The novel closes with a hypnotic experiment performed on Edna by Rebecca Seaton and Dr. Henry (they have Edna attempt to kill Aaron Simoni at a labor rally, with the thought that they can stop her at the last second). [Note: This novel was also published under the title: *An Extraordinary Experience*].

Buchanan, Williams and Charles Gibbon. "The Barrister's Story: Recalled to Life" In: Williams Buchanan and Charles Gibbon. *Storm-Beaten; or Christmas Eve at the "Old Anchor" Inn*. p.18-42). London: Ward and Lock, 1862. Available online via Google Books: http://access.bl.uk/item/viewer/ark:/81055/vdc_100023600784.0x000001 https://books.google.com/books?id=YEpWAAAAcAAJ&pg=PA18.

*The Barrister's story, **Recalled to Life**, which stands first in the collection, is a strange tale of Mesmerism, the Mesmerist being a young French lady, who, being deeply in love with the barrister himself, attempts to make away with his wife during his absence, by putting her into a mesmeric sleep, and leaving her to die under its influence; but, fortunately, the husband discovers her condition ere it is too late, and makes the Mesmerist, Miss Dupesne, awaken her.—The Era*, January 26, 11862, p.5 [Note: the barrister has strong mesmeric powers of his own, and he uses them to force Dupesne to awaken his wife]

Buell, Mary E. *The Sixth Sense; or, Electricity: A Story for the Masses* . Boston: Colby & Rich, 1891. Available online via HathiTrust and Google Books: https://catalog. hathitrust.org/Record/100586746.

The novel mixes Christianity, occultism, and science; and a portion of the story deals with using mesmerism/magnetism to heal the sick.

Burgess, Gelett. *Lady Mechante; or, Life As It Should Be: Being Divers Precious Episodes in the Life of a Naughty Nonpareille: A Farce in Filigree*. New York: Frederick A. Stokes Company, 1909. Available online via HathiTrust and the Internet Archive: http://catalog.hathitrust.org/Record/001020891.

A satirical novel dealing with the life an adventurous woman in London, Boston, San Francisco, and New York. While in San Francisco, she gathers the elect members of that city's society into a "hypnotic club."

Butler, Rayne (Renée Butler-Wilkins). *In the Power of Two*. London: Simpkin, Marshall, Hamilton, Kent & Co., 1896. Available online via the British Library: http:// access.bl.uk/item/pdf/lsidyv3a84445c.

Mr. Rayne Butler has attempted to deal with a power of which he but faintly understands the real nature and possibilities, and in consequence we get a story of considerable promise *marred in the performance. "In the Power of Two" is a story of hypnotic influence exercised on a young heiress by two people, one of whom is her scheming cold-blooded guardian who, needless to state, is in pursuit of her fortune. The other is a maiden lady who has taken a great interest in the girl, and having paid considerable attention to the exercise of hypnotic power pits her knowledge and strength against the evil influence that is wrecking her young friend's life. The hypnotism here dealt with is the hypnotism of the charlatan and the country fair, and has no counterpart in actual fact. Apart from this, the story is unusually well written and is of a very entertaining nature, containing more than the usual allotment of incident and a sympathetic delineation of some pleasing traits in character and disposition, particularly that of the old maiden lady, Euphemia Wade, who is one of the two in whose power the fate of Violet Layton rests. There is something, too, to be said for the ingenuity of the plot which gives the motive for so much original, if rather impractical, scheming.—**Literary World**, Vol. 54 (August 21, 1896): p.143 [Note: this story was first published serially under the title "The Spider and the Fly"].*

C.B.M. "An Experience" *Sydney Mail* (Nov. 1866): 8. Available online via Trove Digitized Newspapers: http://trove.nla.gov.au/ndp/del/article/166661207 http://nla.gov.au/nla.news-article166660634.

A scheming female mesmerist fails in her attempt to get a wealthy young man to marry her (the mesmerist doesn't use her power to get the man to marry her directly, but insteads attempts to fend off a female competitor). [Note: 2nd part of story continued in the *Sydney Mail*, November 17, 1866, p.8]

Campbell, Gilbert Sir. *A Wave of Brain Power*. London: Ward, Lock and Co., 1889. Published serially in the *Launceston Examiner* (Australia) under the title "The Great Grill Street Conspiracy"; several chapters are available online via Australia's Trove website: http://trove.nla.gov.au/.

"A Wave of Brain Power" is an extraordinary story of the influence which one mind may exert over another. Keenly thrilling and entrancing as the narrative is, the reader revolts against such absurdities as are continually presented. A young man, a literary hack, becomes acquainted with a fellow lodger, and old and striking gentleman greatly given to studying the occult sciences. The latter exercises his remarkable will power over David Acland, the youth referred to, and makes him his unwitting tool in a great Clan-na-Gael conspiracy to burn London. Repeatedly Acland is thrown into mesmeric trances by his dread companion, and while unconscious is made to carry out his revolutionary behests. Acland, however, had a sweetheart, the niece of a General. This young lady, grieving over her lover's absent-mindedness and growing despondency, discovers that she also has a wonderful gift of brain power, and this power she exercises over her lover. Thus the unfortunate youth is the prey of rival mesmerists, if we may call them such. The General is called in to assist in worsting the old sorcerer, who is a sort of

"No. 1" among the Fenians. We leave the reader to find how all in the end comes right, not, however, before Acland is arrested and makes a confession of the strange influence which haunts and moves him. The sorcerer-in-chief, it should be mentioned, is finally mistaken for "Jack the Ripper," and trampled to death by a London mob. Truly, such stories as "A Wave of Brain Power" speak not highly either for the brains of those who write or those who read them.—**Dundee Courier**, November 22, 1889, p.6 [Note: this story was latter published under the title "The Great Grill Street Conspiracy"]

Campbell, Helen. "In the Meshes of a Terrible Spell" *Arena* 5 (Dec. 1891): 102-24. Online via Google Books and HathiTrust: http://babel.hathitrust.org/cgi/pt?id =uc1.$b200177;view=1up;seq=120.

Margaret, after spending a lengthy time away overseas, returns home to her father and stepmother. She soon realizes that her father is under the hypnotic control of her stepmother Ruth; Margaret now finds herself in a hypnotic battle of wills with Ruth. Knowing that Ruth has the upper-hand in the battle, Margaret calls on Mr. Edgarton, a hypnotist, for assistance. Edgarton places Ruth into a trance to find out why she is trying to control both her husband and Margaret. Ruth fears hereditary insanity is upon her, and feels that by starting a new life (by putting an end to both her husband and Margaret) she can put off the madness for a while. In the end Edgarton marries Margaret and cures Ruth of her mental illness.

Carling, John R. *The Viking's Skull*. Boston: Little, Brown, and Company, 1904. Available online via HathiTrust, Google Books, and the Internet Archive: https://archive. org/details/vikingsskull00carlgoog.

Story of a man who recovers treasure hidden by one of his Viking ancestors, and how the same man clears the memory of his father who had been wrongfully convicted of murder. The novel has a female hypnotist who uses her mesmeric powers to obtain information and to get a confession out of a man about a crime he had committed.

Carter, Allen. "Confessions of a Hypnotist: Trapped" *Evening News (Sydney)* (Apr. 1892): 3. Available online via Trove Digitized Newspapers: http://trove.nla.gov. au/ndp/del/article/112942345.

Mrs. Rowland is under the hypnotic control of her personal assistant Elise Lorette; Mr. Rowland is concerned for his wife's welfare and calls upon the hypnotist John Van Helden to help. Van Helden gains hypnotic control over Elise Lorette and forces her to free Mrs. Rowland from her trance state; Lorette does as she is bidden to do, but with the assistance of another male hypnotist she in turn has Van Helden hypnotized and framed for a crime which puts him in prison for two months.

Carter, Nicholas. *Nick Carter's Three Perils; or, A Story of Hypnotic Power*. New York: Street & Smith, 1903. Available online via Northern Illinois University Libraries: http://dimenovels.lib.niu.edu/islandora/object/dimenovels%3A50611.

The hypnotic power in this dime novel is wielded by a female hypnotist and a male hypnotist and they use their mesmeric influence to cause others to rob and attempt murder, and only Nick Carter , the famous detective is able to stop them. [No. 365 in the *Nick Carter Weekly* series]

Coen, W. "Stronger Than Death" *Telegraph* (*Brisbane, Australia*) (Nov. 1896): 6. Available online via Trove Digitized Newspapers: http://trove.nla.gov.au/newspaper/article/172138502.

A couple, Alice Winn and Alfred Aldis, make a hypnotic pact to never be separated by "time or circumstance, waking or sleeping, in life or death", and that they will come to each other whenever summoned. The life and death portion of their pact gets tested when Alfred becomes ill and dies while travelling overseas on business; Alice, sensing that something has happened to Alfred, hypnotically summons Alfred to return home—and sure enough, he shows up at the next meeting of their hypnotism club. [Note: both Alice and Alfred are hypnotists since they hypnotize each other to complete their pact]

Crawford, F. Marion (Francis Marion). *The Witch of Prague: A Fantastic Tale*. New York: Collier, 1890. Available online via HathiTrust, Project Gutenberg, Google Books, and the Internet Archive: https://archive.org/details/witchofpraguefan00crawuoft.

In this story F. Marion Crawford has substituted hypnotism for the occultism which lent mystery to some of his previous novels. The result is a tale which is strange and interesting, but not at all mysterious in the light of modern science and the experiments of the physicians of the Paris Salpetriere. The scene is laid in Prague, apparently more for atmospheric effect than anything else, and perhaps also because it is comparatively new ground for the average novel reader. A nameless "Wanderer," who has been roaming the world in search of a lost love, meets in the old Bohemian Capital "Unorna," a lonely, wealthy and beautiful young woman with wonderful hypnotic or mesmeric power. He also meets there and old acquaintance, "Keyork Arabian, "a sort of scientific madman, who is using "Unorna's" hypnotic power to assist in an experiment in indefinitely prolonging the life of an aged scholar. A young Jew of the higher class, "Israel Kafka," is madly in love with "Unorna," but she has no eyes for him after seeing the "Wanderer." Failing in attracting the "Wanderer" by ordinary means, she endeavors to hypnotize him into love for her. "Kafka" is a hidden witness of her attempt. On discovering this "Unorna" punishes his indiscretion in one of the most dramatic incidents of the story. Bringing him under her hypnotic influence she causes him to live in mind through *the experience of a Jewish boy who, centuries before, was tortured to death in Prague by his people, for recreancy to his faith. Upon discovering the trick which has been played upon him "Kafka," beside himself with jealousy and rage, intensified by strong religious prejudice, goes to "Unorna's" house to kill her. The "Wanderer" warns her and she takes refuge in a convent. There she meets "Beatrice" whom the "Wanderer" has so long sought, and who has sought temporary seclusion there. "Unorna" discovers this fact, and in her jealous madness determines to kill "Beatrice" hypnotically. Her passion, however, is not satisfied by the idea of simply taking her life; she proposes that she shall die in deadly sin by influencing her to commit sacrilege in the chapel of the convent. This gives the author another opportunity for a highly dramatic scene, which he fully improves. "Unorna's" attempt is frustrated by the casual entrance of one of the nuns, and she flees to her own house, where "Kafka," after his attempt to murder her, is lying prostrated by nervous exhaustion, watched by the "Wanderer." A curious scene is now enacted, in which the "Wanderer" is hypnotized into believing that "Unorna" is "Beatrice." The awakening of her own conscience checks "Unorna" in this deception, and she seeks the advice of the aged scholar who has been so long lying in hypnotic slumber in her house. Under his influence she rights the wrong she has done, brings the "Wanderer" and "Beatrice" together and expires from the violence of her own emotions in receiving their forgiveness. Of course this weird story is not without its lesson, which is the danger of fooling with hypnotism. Recent examples in real life have shown that plainly so far as those acted upon and society at large are concerned, but this tale also shows the demoralizing effect upon the hypnotizer of exercising this irresponsible power over the minds and actions of others. Of course Mr. Crawford has told his story in his usual masterly manner, but he makes the frequent mistake of reeling off consecutive pages of didactic philosophy, and on the whole the novel is inferior, as a work of art to many of his previous works.—**Daily Evening Bulletin** (San Francisco), Issue 153 October 3, 1891, Col. C*

Creelman, James. *Eagle Blood*. Boston: Lothrop Publishing Company, 1902. Available online via HathiTrust, Google Books, and the Internet Archive: http://www. archive.org/details/eagleblood00creeiala.

Mr. Creelman once proved himself an agreeable writer of reminiscences; he now augments his reputation by showing an ability to produce a pleasing novel. Mr. Creelman has observed his fellow-man. Furthermore he possesses a gift for putting these observations to the most advantageous use. He takes a young English lord and after bankrupting him, despatches him to America. There he conducts him, under an assumed name, through the course of some rather unique experiences, of which not the least is a forced marriage, while under the influence of hypnotic suggestion. The trouble brought about by this marriage is really the main portion of the story and includes the life of the hero in the Philippines during the recent war there up to the time when all the complications being untangled, the proper finale is effected.—**Book News**, Vol. 21 November, 1902, p.151 [Note: Miss Grush, the female hypnotist in the story, uses her powers to get the main character to marry her]

Dahlgren, Madeleine Vinton. *The Secret Directory: A Romance of Hidden History*. Philadelphia: H. L. Kilner & Co., 1896. Available online via HathiTrust: http://catalog.hathitrust.org/Record/007655285.

Freemasonry and its formularies have furnished the motive of many romances, but none so wonderful as Mrs. Dahlgren's new one entitled **The Secret Directory**. *Chief figures in the drama are Mazzini, Garibaldi, and others of the Carbonari chiefs, besides an American admiral, who is inveigled into participation in some of the blood-curdling and blasphemous rites which accompany the orgies of the secret crew. It is a wild kind of story and contains enough tragedy to satisfy the most morbid craving. Its style is vigorous and picturesque, but at times it assumes the appearance of sensational journalistic statement more than the artistic work of the weaver of historical romance. Much of it savors strongly of the discussion over Diana Vaughan and the Luciferian worship, of which the reading world is growing somewhat bored.*

The mysterious power called hypnotism is introduced unreservedly, for the purpose of giving us a glimpse of the Masonic ritual, by means of a confession drawn from one of the fraternity while under the influence of one of the female characters. The case with which the victim gives up his secrets under this compulsion demands a credulity on the part of the reader hardly justified by any pseudo-scientific hypothesis.—**Catholic World**, Vol. 64, February 1897, p.698

Dale, Alan (Real name Alfred J. Cohen). *An Old Maid Kindled*. New York: G. W. Dillingham, 1890. Available online via Gale's *American Fiction, 1774-1920*: http://www.gale.com/american-fiction-1774-1920/.

Madam Catski, a fortune-teller with strong hypnotic powers, hypnotizes Mabel Vocifrington (the "old maid" from the title of the novel) to fall in love with a young man. The young man, Bertie Silverstoke, is Madam Catski's illegitimate son who has been separated from Catski for years, and Mabel is just a pawn in Catski's attempt to be reunited with her long lost child. The story is further complicated because Mabel was jilted decades earlier by a man name Reginald Morton, and Morton, it turns out was Catski's lover and the father of Bertie Silverstoke. Bertie breaks off his relationship with Mabel and marries a plain, but wealthy girl named Bryronia Ansonby. The closing scene of the novel takes place in a hotel room, on the night of Bertie and Byronia's wedding, where Bertie discovers the dead body of Mabel, dressed in an ancient, yellow wedding dress—the dress she was to wear for her marriage to Reginald Morton. [Madam Catski exits the novel when she hypnotizes a man to steal diamonds for her, and she is forced to flee from the police.]

Davis, Kate Buffington. "A Daughter of Lilith and a Daughter of Eve" *The Arena* 3:14 (Jan. 1891): 212-25. Available online via HathiTrust and Google Books: https://babel.hathitrust.org/cgi/pt?id=wu.89063082051&seq=236.

A beautiful and forceful woman uses her hynotic powers to get a man to marry her, but even though the man is legally and hypnotically tied to his controlling wife, his love lies with another.

De Havilland, Saumarez. *The Mystic Serpent.* London: Iliffe & Son, 1891.

*In his unbridled quest for something startling in the way of horrors, Mr. Saumarez De Havilland has hit upon a peculiarly ghastly find. Vivisection as practised on the lower animals has hitherto figured in the eyes of the public as the high water-mark of brutality and callousness to suffering. But the author of "The Mystic Serpent" caps the recognised climax of cruelty by suggesting a new development of surgical atrocities in which a human creature is tortured alive for the good of science. Vivisection, however, is only a side dish in Mr. de Havilland's menu of horrors. Hypnotism, as practiced by a fiendish personage of extraordinary powers, is the great stand-by. This Professor Sergius has carried the development of will power to unprecedented lengths. Every member of the club over which he presides is absolutely enslaved by his influence. At his "hypnotic suggestion" one man goes off and commits a murder. Another kills himself. Finally a check is exerted on the magician's omnipotence from a very unexpected source. A woman pits her personal magnetism against his, and a struggle ensues, whose issue we shall not anticipate. There is feverish excitement pervading the recital of this gruesome romance which will serve to attract a certain class of readers as strongly as it will repel those possessed of a healthier taste and a truer sense of proportion.—**Literary World**,* Vol. 44 (October 23, 1891): p.334

*The keynote of this story is hypnotism, foreshadowing its power and showing the good and bad uses it may be put to. The principal characters are Professor Sergius, a past master in the occult sciences, and who in his desire to increase his knowledge and power cares not what ill is wrought, and Maria Balehatchet, Arch-Priestess of the Gnostic Sisterhood, whose aim is to do good by means of the same knowledge and power possessed by the Professor. Subordinated and intermingled is a love interest, in the characters of Lilian Biford and Bertram Conyers, which gives an added interest. We doubt not that the book will prove interesting and entertaining on the whole, although the story would have gained by the omission of gruesome details of the dissecting-room.—**Hearth and Home**,* Issue 38 (February 4, 1892): p.360

De Morgan, John. *Robert Brendan, Bellboy; or, Under the Hypnotic Spell*. New York: Street & Smith, 1903. Available online via the University of South Florida Libraries Digital Collections: https://digitalcommons.usf.edu/brave_and_bold/23/.

A wealthy baroness is hypnotized by both a female hypnotist and a Mexican brigand to steal jewelry from her upper class acquaintances; but things are finally put right when the young Robert Brendan enters the picture. [Part of the series *Brave & Bold*, No. 29]

Dearmer, Mabel. *The Sisters*. New York: McClure Company, 1908. Available online via Google Books and HathiTrust: http://catalog.hathitrust.org/Record/008667978.

The story deals with the lives of the legitimate and illegitimate daughters of an English baronet. The mother of Rose de Winton, the abandoned child, is a wholly depraved and sordid individual without even the feeblest flutterings of mother love to protect her child from the furies of her insane rages. The mother of Ruth Templeton, the acknowledged daughter of Lord Templeton, is a saint, who forgives a faithless husband and simplifies the plot by dying and placing the burden of righting her husband's wrong on her daughter. How this young girl rescues the erring half sister from a life of shame is a melodramatic picture and gives a flavor of the old type of Sunday school literature to a book that otherwise is quite far removed from that class.—**Duluth News Tribune**, March 22, 1908, p.10 [Note: hypnotism plays only a minor part in the story. Ann Hand, a clairvoyant, makes predictions when placed in an hypnotic trance (first by a female Cornish "witch", and a second time by a Dr. Trelling). This novel was also published under the title "The Alien Sisters".]

Dering, Ross George pseud. (Real name Frederic Henry Balfour). *Dr. Mirabel's Theory*. New York: Harper & Brothers, 1893. Avaiblabe online through Hathi Trust and Google Books: http://catalog.hathitrust.org/Record/008666558.

In "Dr. Mirabel's Theory" Ross George Dering has written a story based on the evil possibilities of hypnotism, which appears in the Franklin Square Library. A beautiful woman contrives by secret agencies of mind-influence to do her husband to death, incited thereto by her love for her husband's physician. By slow degrees all is discovered and her suicide follows. The story ought to have an underplot, both to relieve the somberness of the situations and to give purpose to the other characters introduced.—**Literary World**, Vol. 24 (November 4, 1893): p.370

Dickens, Mary Angela. *On the Edge of a Precipice*. London: Hutchinson, 1899. Papers Past:

    https://paperspast.natlib.govt.nz/periodicals/NZGRAP18990909.2.5

    https://paperspast.natlib.govt.nz/periodicals/NZGRAP18990916.2.4

    https://paperspast.natlib.govt.nz/periodicals/NZGRAP18990923.2.5

    https://paperspast.natlib.govt.nz/periodicals/NZGRAP18990930.2.4

    https://paperspast.natlib.govt.nz/periodicals/NZGRAP18991007.2.4

    https://paperspast.natlib.govt.nz/periodicals/NZGRAP18991014.2.5

    https://paperspast.natlib.govt.nz/periodicals/NZGRAP18991021.2.5

    https://paperspast.natlib.govt.nz/periodicals/NZGRAP18991028.2.5

    https://paperspast.natlib.govt.nz/periodicals/NZGRAP18991104.2.7

    https://paperspast.natlib.govt.nz/periodicals/NZGRAP18991111.2.7

    https://paperspast.natlib.govt.nz/periodicals/NZGRAP18991118.2.5

    https://paperspast.natlib.govt.nz/periodicals/NZGRAP18991125.2.5.

"On the Edge of a Precipice" is a story of the well-known Svengali-Trilby kind, except that the role of Svengali is here taken by a woman, Miss Rachel Cochrane, and that the duty of Trilby is here not to sing like a prima-donna, but to act with wonderful dramatic power and feeling. Trilby—we mean Miss Violet Drummond—is apparently all the more amenable to hypnotic influence because of having just lost her memory from a blow on the head in a bicycle accident. We do not know how this theory would work out in practice, but it answers very respectably in a novel. Rachel Cochrane and her brother, Cecil, are hardly an attractive couple; having failed to obtain money from a rich uncle, they work their wicked will on his helpless daughter, who accidentally falls insensible into their harpy clutches. The brother and sister are hangers-on of the stage; Rachel is ugly, but has great histrionic gifts; and she conceives the very original idea of transferring these, by sheer effort of will, to the rather insipid, though beautiful, Violet. Consequently, Violet's rendering of the "star" part of "Virginia" takes the town, and, strange to say in her red wig, and under the assumed name of Miss Sylvia Maynard, she is not recognised, though apparently her bereaved father and lover have been scouring the country for weeks past in search of her. Now, though Cecil and Rachel are both undesirable as friends, Cecil is by far the greater devil of the two, and he resolves to marry Violet, seeing her a prospective gold mine. The brother and sister, like the two murderers of the babes in the wood, fall out, or, at least, Rachel repents, and in her repentance a chance of escape for Violet—the victim—presents itself. How Violet regains her memory, and escapes just in time from the edge of the precipice (i.e. marriage with Cecil), we must leave to the reader to discover. The story, though wildly invraisemblable and farfetched, is dramatically and vividly told, and we confess to feeling quite sorry that Violet, after reigning a queen of the stage, and being extolled everywhere for her beauty and ability, should eventually become, under stress (we suppose) of domestic life, merely "a kindly and rather stupid woman." It only shows

what latent possibilities may lie dormant in those of us who have never either suffered concussion of the brain from a bicycle accident, or found a convenient enemy to act as mesmerist.—**Daily News** (London), April 28, 1899 [Note: the author of this book is the granddaugher of the British writer Charles Dickens].

Don Jon. *Miss Incognita; or, An Experiment in Love*. Rome, Georgia: The Psychic Publishing Co., 1904. Available online via HathiTrust, Google Books, and the Internet Archive: http://catalog.hathitrust.org/Record/007655736.

Eidola Mandeville, a young Southern belle, is romantically pursued by two men: Dr. Dumas (whose real name is Eroslove) and Dr. Lindsey. Doctor Dumas wins the girl unfairly through hypnotism and the use of equipment called "vibratoners". Dr. Dumas seeks to take advantage of Eidola by way of a mock marriage, but is forced by Dr. Lindsey to make the marriage legal. After a short time, Dr. Dumas wants out of the marriage, so through fraudulent documents and a corrupt doctor, has Eidola placed in an insane asylum. Several years pass, and Dr. Dumas believes Eidola to be dead, but she is very much alive, and under the assumed name of "Miss Incognita" is seeking her revenge against Dumas. Miss Incognita's plot for redress is complicated, but among her tools of revenge are: incest (or the threat of), vibratoners, and her own use of hypnotism .

Donovan, Dick (Real name James Edward Preston Muddock). "The Woman With the "Oily Eyes"" In: Dick Real name James Edward Preston Muddock Donovan. *Tales of Terror*. p. 1-50). London: Chatto & Windus, 1899. Available online via HathiTrust and Google Books: https://babel.hathitrust.org/cgi/pt?id=osu.324 35051181022;view=1up;seq=13.

A female vampire wields her mesmeric power over a newlywed couple; she entices the husband to leave his wife and go with her to Spain where she drains him of his vitality and feasts on his blood.

Doughty, Francis Worcester (A New-York Detective pseud.) *The Bradys and the Chinese "Come-Ons"; or, Dark Doings in Doyers Street*. New York: Frank Tousey, 1906. Available online via Stanford's Dime Novel and Story Paper Collection and Google Books: https://purl.stanford.edu/wf967mh6423.

A male Chinese hypnotist, working for a criminal gang in New York City, uses hypnotism to wrest money out of two brothers. Hypnotism is also used to locate a grave containing diamonds, as well as to ship a young woman in a trance-state across the country via Wells Fargo (this same woman was hypnotized to be a fortune teller, she is eventually freed from her hypnotic bondage by the Brady detectives, and placed in the care of a benevolent female hypnotist). [Note: part of *Secret Service, Old and Young King Brady, Detectives*, no. 369, February 16, 1906]

Doyle, Arthur Conan. "John Barrington Cowles" In: Arthur Conan Doyle. *The Captain of the Polestar, and Other Tales.* p. 230-266). London: Longmans, Green, and Co., 1890. Available online via HathiTrust, Google Books, and the Internet Archive: https://babel.hathitrust.org/cgi/pt?id=hvd.32044086822772.

Kate Northcott casts an evil mesmeric power over her prospective husbands, a power which leads to their deaths; one of the unlucky fiancés to Miss Northcott is John Barrington Cowles. [Note: this story was originally published in 1884 in the April 12th and April 19th issues of the *Cassell's Saturday Journal*]

_____. *The Parasite.* Westminister: A. Constable and Co., 1894. Available online via HathiTrust, Google Books, Internet Archive, and Project Gutenberg: http://catalog.hathitrust.org/Record/006057850.

It is a somewhat creepy story that Mr. Conan Doyle tells in "The Parasite." The hero is a young Professor of physiology, who is induced to become the subject in some experiments in mesmerism. He is at first extremely sceptical, but soon has painful experience of the power of the mesmeric influence. The medium, who is a most unattractive cripple old woman, acquires a strong influence over him, and in spite of his repugnance uses it to make him fall in love with her. He fights against her influence, and in order to bring him properly into subjection she plays all sorts of tricks upon him. In the end, however, he gets the better of her. The story takes the form of a series of extracts from the Professor's diary. It is well told, and has a considerable air of reality.—**The Scotsman**, December 10, 1894, p.4

Dunn, Ella H. *The Castle of Many Mirrors, and Their Sequel.* Chicago: M.A. Donohue & Company, 1906. Available online via HathiTrust and Google Books: https://catalog.hathitrust.org/Record/100593360.

A beautiful female hypnotist uses her powers to weaken the mind of her wealthy benefactress, and then, when her benefactress goes "missing", she uses her hypnotic powers to get the benefactress's husband to fall in love with her, but all turns out right in the end because of the faith and tenacity of a loving daughter.

Egan, Mary Clint. "Hypnotized Love" *Daily Standard Union* (Jan. 1896): 6. Available online via Fulton History: http://fultonhistory.com/Fulton.html.

An elderly woman claims to have hypnotized a young couple to fall in love.

Eliot, George (Real name Mary Ann Evans). "The Lifted Veil" *Blackwood's Edinburgh Magazine* 86 (July 1859): 24-48. Available online via HathiTrust: https://babel.hathitrust.org/cgi/pt?id=uc1.31210001790938;view=1up;seq=32.

This novelette was first published anonymously in **Blackwood's** in 1859. The narrator of the story, Latimer, is a clairvoyant. Latimer is bewitched by Bertha, the fiancée of Latimer's brother Alfred, who Latimer marries after Alfred's death from a hunting accident. While there is no overt appearance of mesmerism in the story, a few scholars have argued that either Bertha subtly mesmerizes Latimer or it's a case of mesmeric trance without the machinations of a mesmerist (see Malcolm Bull's "Mastery and Slavery in *The Lifted Veil*" **Essays in Criticism**, Vol. 48 (July 1998): pp.244-261, and Martin Willis's "George Eliot's *The Lifted Veil* and the Cultural Politics of Clairvoyance" in **Victorian Literary Mesmerism** (New York: Rodopi, 2006): pp.145-161). The story also contain a dramatic scene involving the resuscitation of a woman via blood transfusion.

Erckmann, Emile and Alexandre Chatrian. "Suggested Suicide" *Romance* 2:3 (July 1891): 332-46. Available online via HathiTrust and Google Books: https://babel. hathitrust.org/cgi/pt?id=hvd.32044092784826;view=1up;seq=338.

An artist, living in a garret apartment in Nuremberg, witnesses an old woman who users her hypnotic powers to induce patrons of an inn to hang themselves. [Note: this story is also published under the title "The Invisible Eye"].

Everett, Ruth. "The Hypnotism of Bella B." *National Harness Review* 57:3 (June 1907): 46-48. Available online via Google Books and HathiTrust: https://babel. hathitrust.org/cgi/pt?id=nyp.33433069089773&view=1up&seq=592.

Isabel Prentice, through the use of faked hypnotism on a thoroughbred racehorse, gets her father to finally agree to let her marry the man she loves.

Fane, Violet pseud. (Real name Mary Montgomery Lamb Singleton Currie). *The Story of Helen Davenant*. London: Chapman and Hall, 1889. Online via HathiTrust, the Internet Archive, and Google Books: http://catalog.hathitrust.org/Record/005273213 http://archive.org/details/storyofhelendave01fane http://books.google.com/books?id=kksmAAAAMAAJ&pg=PP1#v=onepage& q&f=false.

*The villain is a woman, a Polish princess, who constrains her brother by mesmeric power to murder her inconvenient husband. The murder, principally through the means of marvellous dreams, is eventually discovered and the poor heroine who had incautiously married the murderer is naturally placed in a very embarrassing situation.—***Boston Daily Advertiser** October 8, 1889, p.5

Farjeon, B.L. (Benjamin Leopold). "Philip Darrell's Wife" *Weekly Irish Times* (Aug. 1903): 4. Papers Past: https://paperspast.natlib.govt.nz/periodicals/ NZGRAP19030711.2.9.

A female hypnotist marries, and then hypnotically wills her husbands to commit suicide by hanging themselves (she thus gains their estates and in some cases, insurance money); Philip Darrell is the third husband of the evil hypnotist to meet his demise at the end of a rope.

Fenwicke-Allan, Ellam (Mrs. Charlton Anne). *A Woman of Moods: A Social Cinematographe*. London: Burns & Oates, Limited, 1897.

> *Valeria Di Salustri is a young lady of remarkable beauty and commanding presence. Her father was an Italian nobleman, who died while she was yet very young; her mother an English woman, who remained in Italy after the death of her husband, while Valeria was sent at the age of six to an English nunnery to be educated. Soon after the story opens we find Valeria engaged, under ominous circumstances, to a young English squire; and it is while describing her supremely happy married life that the writer presents the best of her clever sketches of conventional English society. By and by, Valeria's mother appears in England, and soon the young wife, now a mother, learns the terrible secret of her father's death. He had died mad. And the events which follow are conceived to point the lesson which Valeria's daughter in after years teaches to the Order of which she is the head, that no woman should marry who knows that there is any hereditary taint in her blood, as of lunacy, scrofula, or inebriety. Among the other principals brought upon the stage is an eminent artist, connected with whom are related incidents that constitute a novel of themselves, bearing upon the desertion of him by his wife, the reappearance of her and of her lovely daughter under the most remarkable of circumstances, a pretty love match, and much else to attract and interest. Feats in hypnotism, and appearances of the White Lady as the ghost of the heroine, are worked in with considerable effect.*—*The Scotsman*, September 9, 1897, p.7 (Note: Valeria hypnotizes a friend, urging him to leave his wife on a fixed date. For a lengthy review of this novel see, *The Academy*, Vol. 52 (September 4, 1897): p.61)

Fraser, W.A."The Medicine-Making of Naskiwis" *Red Book* 1 (May 1903): 13-20. Google Books: https://www.google.com/books/edition/The_Canadian_Magazine_of_ Politics_Scienc/kqZOAQAAIAAJ?hl=en&gbpv=1&dq=%22The+Medicine- Making+of+Naskiwis%22&pg=PA19.

> Jan Olsen is controlled by Naskiwis, a beautiful Indian princess he once loved but has now fled in fear from. Naskiwis power over Olsen appears to be either a case of witchcraft or long distance hypnotism. [Note: The *Canadian Magazine* printing of the story available online via Google Books]

G.F.G. "One Woman's Will" *Every Week* (Aug. 1891): 189-91. Available online via Proquest British Periodicals: http://www.proquest.com/products-services/ british_periodicals.html.

> An engaged man, recuperating from an illness, is entrance by a woman with strong hypnotic powers, and when the woman goes to force this man to propose marriage to her, she is killed accidently by a stray bullet—her death saves the man from being unfaithful to his fiancée.

Garland, Hamlin. *The Tyranny of the Dark*. New York: Harper & Brothers, 1905. Available online via Hathi Trust and Google Books: http://catalog.hathitrust. org/Record/000433591.

*The heroine of the tale is a Western girl, beautiful and blooming, but strangely obsessed or endowed with uncanny "psychic" powers, and the action hinges on a struggle between excellent old-fashioned human love and mysterious hypnotic influences. Each influence of course, is represented by a man—the first by a young chemist and biologist, the second by a clergyman. It is the "psychic" or clerical influence which the author (who has a taste for occult studies) calls the "tyranny of the dark."—***New York Times*** April 29, 1905, p.287* [Viola Lambert, the heroine, appears to suffer from a strong case of auto-hypnosis].

Gerrare, Wirt pseud. (Real name William Oliver Greener). *Rufin's Legacy: A Theosophical Romance*. London: Hutchinson & Co., 1891. Available online via the British Library: http://access.bl.uk/item/pdf/lsidyv3aee1525.

Rufin's Legacy, *by W. Gerrare, is called a "theosophical romance," which is not much in its favour. It deals with a morbid theme, in which Nihilism and mesmerism are curiously mixed up. The author has evidently studied in the school of Dostoieffsky—- without much profit.—***The Argus*** (Melbourne, Australia), January 7, 1891, p.6*

*Nihilism and secret societies combine with strange supernatural powers in "Rufin's Legacy", where a murderous lady spirits away girls by mesmeric attraction, annihilates their will-power, and transfers her own being to their bodies that she may never grow old. Certainly W. Gerrare produces an ingenous catalogue of horrors warranted to confuse any ordinary reader's brains.—***The Graphic*** (London), Issue 1104, January 24, 1891*

[Note: A lengthy plot summary can be found in the *Fantastic Victoriana*: https:// web.archive.org/web/20160312171458/http://www.reocities.com/jessnevins/ vicf.html] .

Grant, Ethel Watts-Mumford. "The Tangled Web" *New Broadway Magazine* 20 (June 1908): 275-84. Google Books: https://books.google.com/books?id=np5EAQA AMAAJ&pg=PA275&lpg=PA275.

Story has both a female and a male hypnotist. Nellie Gaynor, an attractive young widow, uses her hypnotic powers to steal expensive jewels; Dr. Boyd Wendham uses his hypnotic powers to discover that Gaynor is the person behind the theft of the jewels. [This story ran in series in the ***New Broadway Magazine***, it is continued in Issues 1-4 (July-October) of Vol. 21].

Griffith, George Chetwynd. *The White Witch of Mayfair*. London: F. V. White & Co., 1902.

The heroine is one Lena Castello, daughter of a "Spanish hidalgo" married to an Englishwoman. He is a titled adventurer, and his wife and daughter are adventuresses more accomplished than he. Lena, in her twenty-first year, has mastered every European tongue, is exceptionally expert in chiromancy, thought-reading, crystal-gazing, hypnotism, toxicology, the use of fire-arms and weapons of steel—in fact, has already slain her woman in a duel with rapiers. She is the most angelic-featured and fascinating woman in London society, to the highest circles of which, as the daughter of a nobleman, she has access. In her long list of accomplishments forgery is included, and one Falconer, a "private detective," holds evidence of the fact. His one unsatisfied ambition is to penetrate into "society." He soliloquises: "I have power ... I could get quite a number of highly-respected M.P.'s into such trouble that they would either have to resign their seats or lose them through criminal process. I could keep the Divorce Court busy for ten years to come, and the Old Bailey for about five." It occurs to him that a matrimonial alliance with an attractive and titled lady whose acquaintance with the secret peccadilloes of aristocratic womankind is only paralleled by his own peculiar stores of compromising facts would make a strong combination. But the ambitions of the White Witch lie in another direction, and relations between the two are strained. ... A somewhat stupid lieutenant who has won the V.C. in South Africa, and who possesses some, though not all, of the instincts of a gentleman with the further advantages of a great estate and a fortune of many millions sterling, is beguiled from his allegiance to his sweetheart, Lady Madge (whose beauty is unparalleled and who has in a single season "refused two coronets and three big fortunes"), and marries the Witch. Nearly a year of idyllic conjugal bliss follows, the wicked and designing young woman suddenly developing a capacity for the purest and most unselfish affection. There is, however, a dead fly in the bride's ointment, for the scoundrel Falconer blackmails her unsparingly. "Hypnotism"—the modern novelist's equivalent for a "deus ex machina"—is now greatly in evidence. By its mean the aforetime "ass" Lieut. Grayson, scarce knowing what he is doing, wins a fiercely-contested election, making brilliant speeches, paralysing opponents and electrifying his intimate friends by his minute and profound knowledge of finance and statecraft generally. In fact, the Ministry he supports are disquieted, preferring followers of less transcendent genius. But the brains, the mastery of recondite information, and the burning eloquence, are all supplied by occult means by the beautiful girl-wife of twenty-one. One marvels why this gifted and unscrupulous female does not put some of her "juju" on the obnoxious Falconer, who, threatening her with the alternative of disgraceful exposure, is persistently urging her to murder her husband and marry himself; but the idea of using her powers for her own emancipation does not occur to her. And she, moreover, has it in her power to consign her persecutor to the gallows. To do so, however, would cut the story short in an undeveloped condition. When the inevitable clearing-off takes place it does not lack in thoroughness—the objectionable characters, eight in all, murder each other in divers ways "in one act." The reader is in no wise shocked at the tragic end of creatures who have no blood to shed, only sawdust and bran. After this, the conclusion is tame. Grayson, happily released from the spell, regains all his native stupidity, but has sufficient sense to propose to Madge.—Evening Post (Wellington, New Zealand), Vol. 64 (November 1, 1902): p.3 (Lena, the White Witch, uses her hypnotic powers to make Lieut. Grayson fall in love with her, and to improve Grayson's public speaking skills).

Grimwood, Ethel St. Clair (Mrs. Frank St. Clair Grimwood). *The Power of an Eye: A Novel.* London: F. V. White & Co., 1892. Library of Congress: https://www.loc.gov/item/07000289/.

The scene of this story is laid for the better and most exciting part in India. Here we are concerned in the rebellion of the Maharajah at Ajpur and his attack upon the British residents, the most important of whom he takes prisoners. They are rescued from their captivity, however, by a girl who possesses the power of mesmerism—hence the title of the story. Attired in the garb of a native, she penetrates to the presence of the Maharajah, and there wills that he shall sign an order for the release of his captives. Unfortunately, in making her escape with the rest of the party, she is shot in the shoulder, and her heroism is the cause of her death.—Publishers' Circular, Vol. 57 (July 23, 1892): p.83

Hall, Violette. "The Professor's Human Battery" In: *The American Authors of the West.* p. 401-411). Chicago: Belford Publishing Company, 1893. Available online via Google Books and HathiTrust: http://babel.hathitrust.org/cgi/pt?id=umn.319 510016279242;view=1up;seq=407.

Professor Kleinhymer gets his family members to channel their collective thoughts into hypnotic energy; the results of their use of this hypnotic power leads to surprising, and not entirely pleasant happenings (e.g. the Professor finds himself in an apron cooking lunch instead of his paid cook; his daughter gets two men to propose marriage to her; and his son brings a complete Wild West Show to their backyard).

Harley, Cecil. *The Shadow of a Song.* London: Cassell & Company, 1893. Google Books: https://www.google.com/books/edition/The_Shadow_of_a_Song/kv3ff0J5JzkC.

A fascinating story of hypnotism, and quite unique in its way as "Undine," which, more in point of contrast than of resemblance, it recalls at times. It is a young maiden who brings about the chief witchery of the plot, and the lover whom she victimises carries out, in trance-state, the behests of the girl's brother, who contrives to forge a cheque for a thousand pounds and leads the lover to present it at the bank. There is a fine vein of sentiment in the novel, and the characters are admirably individualised.—**Liverpool Mercury** Issue 14119, April 5, 1893 [the female hypnotist gets a man to commit a crime, though he is totally unconscous of the act]

Hawthorne, Julian. "Mr. Dunton's Invention" In: Julian Hawthorne. *Six Cent Sam's*. p. 9-26). St. Paul: Price-McGill Company, 1893. Available online via HathiTrust, Google Books, and the Internet Archive: http://babel.hathitrust.org/cgi/pt?id=uc2.ark:/13960/t00000234;view=1up;seq=15.

Mr. Dunton, inventor, is being treated with hypnotism for a nervous condition; two hypnotists are working on him, a doctor and the doctor's daughter. While Dunton is in a hypnotic trance, the hypnotists steal an idea for an invention of his, which they in turn go and file a patent for.

Hayward, C.F.R. *The Mentons: Was It a Crime?* Chicago: Donohue, Henneberry & Co., 1887. Available online via HathiTrust, Google Books, and the Internet Archive: http://catalog.hathitrust.org/Record/003799203.

Miss Menton, the heroine, is a woman reared by a scientific father, her mother having died when she was a child. She never knew what home life was. She had traveled over the world, met savants and brilliant men in every clime. She was beautiful, accomplished, learned. She met a German count in Paris and fell in love with him. They were to have been married, but the villain in the story, an American rogue, kills him in a duel. Several years after Miss Menton is living in New York and among the visitors at her house is an American artist, an impressionable fellow, who falls madly in love with her. He unconsciously introduces the villain to Miss Menton's home. Remembering her lover she determines to be revenged, and uses the artist to that end. Finding that he was susceptible to the hypnotic influence, she hypnotizes him and causes him to kill the slayer of her lover. The artist is tried for the offense, Miss Menton opportunely dies, leaving a written confession, which, with expert testimony, clears the artist, who, nevertheless, held the murdered man had committed suicide.—**Rocky Mountain News**, October 25, 1887, p.2

Holmes, Oliver Wendell. *Elsie Venner: A Romance of Destiny*. Boston: Ticknor and Fields, 1861. Available online via HathiTrust, Google Books, and Project Gutenberg: http://catalog.hathitrust.org/Record/001692752.

Elsie Venner's mother died in childbirth from the effects of a rattlesnake bite. The fatal poison which infected her mother runs in Elsie's veins and has given her a serpentine nature which leaves her cold and aloof in manner. Elsie possesses hypnotic powers which she uses to great effect on her school teacher, Helen Darley. Elsie also has the power to calm snakes by merely looking at them.

Hopkins, Annie G. "Lady Brockden's Niece" *Belgravia* 92 (Jan. 1897): 97-112. Available online via Google Books and HathiTrust: http://babel.hathitrust.org/cgi/pt?id= njp.32101080220922;view=1up;seq=107.

Sybil (Lady Brockden's niece) attempts to use hypnotism to steal Jennie Holker's fiancé, George Powell; Sybil comes close in tricking George into loving her, but ultimately she fails, and a final act of jealousy leads to her own death.

Hopkins, Tighe. *Lady Bonnie's Experiment.* New York: Henry Holt & Co., 1895. Available online via the Internet Archive: http://archive.org/details/ ladybonniesexpe00hopkgoog.

It relates the chance meeting of the hero with a very pretty woman in a ride from Dover to London. He entertains his fair companion with an audacious tale and she revenges herself by hypnotizing him. Other chance meetings occur between the two and finally they become friends. This leads to an acquaintance between the hero and a young lady who is the heir to an estate which has been devised to the hero. They fall in love with each other, and any possible litigation over the property is settled by their marriage.— **Utica Weekly Herald**, October 29, 1895, p.9

Hulme-Beaman, Emeric. "Madame Valprez: A Monte Carlo Romance" *Harmsworth Magazine* 6 (Feb. 1901-July 1901): 449-58. Available online via HathiTrust and Google Books: https://babel.hathitrust.org/cgi/pt?id=nyp.33433081672200&v iew=1up&seq=463.

The hypnotist, Madame Valprez, uses her powers to guide a clairvoyant man to predict the winning numbers at a Monte Carlo roulette table, resulting in tremendous wealth for the pair.

Hume, Fergus. *For the Defense.* Chicago: Rand, McNally & Company, 1898. Available online via HathiTrust, Google Books, and the Internet Archive: http://catalog. hathitrust.org/Record/007662828.

Hypnotic suggestion is a powerful influence in a novel which deals also with Voodooism, and the devil's stick, an instrument of Ashantee sorcery that is brought into peculiar play. The scene is in Surrey, England. Maurice Aylmer incurs the displeasure of Dr. Etwald, a hypnotist, by falling in love with a beautiful West Indian, whom the doctor also loves. Dr. Etwald thereupon conspires with a negress and priestess of Obi, and the singular incidents recorded come to pass.— **The Annual American Catalogue**, 1898, p.94 [The female character Dido has strong hypnotic powers, and a jewel, the "Voodoo stone" also has the power to place people into a trance . Hypnotism is used in the story to gather information, to cause one person to steal, and another to commit murder (or what is thought to be a murder)].

_____. *The Mother of Emeralds.* London: Hurst and Blackett, 1901. Available online via HathiTrust, and the Internet Archive: http://catalog.hathitrust.org/Record/100763165.

Story deals with a lost race of Incas living in a hidden city in Peru. The female leader of this lost race hypnotizes and drugs a man in an attempt to make him become her consort.

Hussey, Eyre. *Dulcinea.* London: Edward Arnold, 1902.

"Dulcinea," by Eyre Hussey is mainly the history of a mare, who gives her name to the story, of a benevolent bookmaker and of Kitty Henderson. The bookmaker has founded and supports on the profits of his business and association which he calls the Fighters' Aid Society. The business of this society is to give assistance by way of loan to hard workers who have been unfortunate. Amongst the persons thus benefited is Kitty Henderson, a young lady who to much personal charm adds the power of mesmerising people and animals. Thus she is able to mesmerise a blind, half-demented girl back to sight and sanity, and it only needs a few passes with the hand to make a stubborn horse take his fences like one of the best. By means of Dulcinea Frank Donaldson, her owner and Kitty's lover, makes enough money to save himself from an awkward position.— **Sydney Morning Herald,** (December 6, 1902): p.4

Ino. "Purely in the Interest of Science" *Vogue* 6:22 (Nov. 1895): 354, 356. Available online via Proquest Vogue Archive: https://www.proquest.com/products-services/vogue_archive.html.

A practical, but plain looking, woman discovers that she possesses hypnotic powers which can be used to bend men romantically to her will.

Isaacs, George. "Not for Sale: A Tale of Mystery and Mesmerism" In: George Isaacs. *Not for Sale: A Selection of Imaginative Pieces.* Adelaide: Sims & Elliott, 1869. Available online via the University at Buffalo Institutional Repository: https://ubir.buffalo.edu/xmlui/handle/10477/75672.

A woman mesmerizes a potential suitor, resulting in some ill effects for him, and marriage to another man for her.

J.P.H. "How I Was Mesmerised Into Matrimony" *London Journal* 64 (July 1876): 36-37. Available online via Proquest British Periodicals: https://about.proquest.com/en/products-services/british_periodicals/.

A man falls in love with a woman, partially due to being attracted to her because of her glass eye.

Jenks, George C. *Wild Pete, the Broncho-Buster Detective; or, Corralling the Ranch Counterfeiters: The Story of the Death-in-Life Band's Last Stand.* New York: Beadle & Adams, 1893. Available online via Northern Illinois University Libraries: https://dimenovels.lib.niu.edu/islandora/object/dimenovels%3A174102#page/1/mode/1up.

The detective, Wild Pete, is called upon to catch a gang of counterfeiters, and in the process he also assists a young woman who is under the influence of an evil hag that possesses mesmeric powers over her. [Note: *Beadle's New York Dime Library;* Vol. 59, no. 755]

Jocelyn, Robert Mrs. (Ada Maria). *A Distracting Guest: A Novel.* London: F. V. White, 1889.

*The heroines of "A Distracting Guest" are two cousins, who have grey and green eyes respectively; and though, according to the French rhyme, these features should doom one of the ladies au paradis and the other aux enfers, there is not much to choose between them in the way of fitness for either of those destinations. Lady Joan—an earl's daughter, who narrates the story—is brought into contact with her handsome cousin Gladys, a young woman with a white face, green eyes, and a cynical smile. One is led to expect that Gladys will be the villain of the piece, but she never does anything worse than fall into trances, walk about the house in a mesmeric sleep (into which Joan unexpectedly finds that she has the power of throwing her), see ghosts, and flirt with every man she meets in her uncle's house. She certainly causes Joan a good deal of trouble by seeming to rob her of her sweetheart; but she has other views in the matter of sweethearts, and all comes out well in the end. There is plenty of mesmerism, ghostly mystification, and "those sort of things," as Mrs. Jocelyn would put it; and if the story is carelessly written, with occasional misquotations and other slips, it is unquestionably amusing.—*The Athenaeum,* No. 3206 (April 6, 1889): p.437*

_____. *Run to Ground: A Sporting Novel.* London: Hutchinson, 1894.

Hunting and hypnotism form the double theme of Mrs. Robert Jocelyn's "Run to Ground". As to the latter element, we are afraid that the authoress has failed to show her usual constructive ingenuity. The situation is this—-Captain Alexander, who had been cheating at cards, conspires with an accomplice, for their common self-protection, to bring home the offence to an innocent brother officer, Lord George Goring. They succeed so well that the charge is fully brought home to their victim, who dies uncleared. He has his believers, however; notably a Princess Dagmar Saravoski, who six years later sees her way to righting the wrong done to the man she loved by means of hypnotism. So she gives a dinner party to the persons concerned, including Captain Alexander, and throws into a trance a young girl whom she has brought under her influence. In this condition the girl becomes clairvoyante, and tells the whole story of the conspiracy just *as it actually happened. But as all this was already in the mind of the Princess (who had no proof of her suspicion) the girl's revelation would, according to hypnotic theories, be but a reflection of the operator's belief, and therefore prove nothing. One is left, logically, with the impression that Captain Alexander, and not Lord George, against whom all the real evidence had been overwhelming, was the victim of injustice. Of course there is no fault to found with the hunting business, which is sufficiently spirited. It is in refreshing contrast with the staginess of the rest of the story—-which, however, is interesting, even when it is least "convincing."*—**The Graphic** (London), July 6, 1895*

Kappey, Sophie (Mrs. Alfred Hart). "A Society Sphinx." *The Ludgate Illustrated Magazine* 6 (Jan. 1894): 261-72. Available online via HathiTrust and Google Books: https://babel.hathitrust.org/cgi/pt?id=uc1.a0004085742&view=1up&seq=273.

A female hypnotist uses her powers to get another woman to steal expensive jewels for her, but she is forced by a more powerful male hypnotist to confess to her crime while in a hypnotic trance. [Note: part 2 of this story appears in Vol. 6 *Ludgate Illustrated Magazine* (February, 1894): pp.385-392]

Kempster, Aquila. *The Mark.* New York: Doubleday, Page & Co., 1903. Available online via the Internet Archive: http://archive.org/details/cu31924022497071.

Allan Meredith, an English doctor attached to a Bombay hospital, is discovered, by the sign of a curious birthmark on his chest, to have in his veins the blood of a long dead Rajput prince, whose reincarnation, as a great leader, a sort of warrior messiah, had long been promised by the priests and soothsayers, to his own particular people. Yah Mahommed, the man of mystery, and Loda, a woman soothsayer and hypnotist of the bazaars, discover this matter of the birthmark and set about making use of their knowledge for their own advantage. They entangled Meredith, and under Loda's hypnotic spells the prosaic doctor drops his own personality for that Prince Lalkura, the long expected avatar. Latter these two plotters, Mahommed and Loda, find themselves losing power over their Frankenstein; he takes the centre of the stage as the true prince, dominates them both, shows Loda that she is not Loda at all, but Soodal, his queen, loved and lost ages since, and that Yah Mahommed is their hereditary foe. So the three are swept into the maelstrom and take up again the struggle for love and power where they had dropped it two centuries before, and fight it out to the bitter end.— **Jersey Journal** (Jersey City, NJ), November 12, 1903, p.13

Kernahan, Coulson Mrs. (Mary Jean Gwynne Bettany). *Devastation.* London: John Long, 1904.

Sir Percival Wentworth pushes his wife into a lake, and leaves her under the impression that she is drowned. As it turns out, Lady Wentworth is very much alive, and through the use of her hypnotic powers (and the assistance of an old school friend who has developed occult gifts) she seeks revenge against her husband.

Knox, Jackson. *Falconbridge the Sphynx Detective; or, The Siren of the Baleful Eye.* New York: Beadle & Adams, 1889. Available online via Northern Illinois University Libraries: https://dimenovels.lib.niu.edu/islandora/object/dimenovels:168354#page/1/mode/1up.

Madelaine Valdemar, an evil woman with strong hypnotic powers, is the governess for Garda Bardine. Valdemar is in love with Garda's wealthy father, Walsingham Bardine; Madelaine longs to become Walsingham's wife, but first she must "remove" Bardine's current wife, Agathe. Madelaine achieves her objective by hypnotizing Garda to poison Agathe. A detective is hired by Mr. Bardine to investigate Agathe's death, and the detective, as well as Agathe's physician, becomes suspicious of Madelaine and her hypnotic powers. Madelaine hypnotically controls Garda and one of Bardine's servants, and has them attempt to murder the detective and the physician—the attempts fail and Madelaine escapes, leaving the detective with a diary containing a history of her hypnotic exploits. [Note: *Beadle's New York Dime Library*; Vol. 43, no. 548]

Krikorian, Jessie. *A Daughter of Mystery.* London: Griffith, Farran, 1892.

> The "Daughter of Mystery" is the offspring of a reputed witch. She is dirty and ragged, ill kept to a degree, but possesses "large dark eyes, like the eyes of a forest stag, soft and timid," and a face which, when clean, reveals promise of great beauty. Being rescued from her degradation by kind Lady Byng, who takes the girl into her service, the little wretch promptly evinces her gratitude by falling in love with that lady's husband, and eventually uses her unnatural powers to force her patroness into an act of suicide. This she accomplishes in rather a curious way, namely, by willing that the unfortunate lady shall wander forth from her house in a state of mesmeric trance, and place herself on the railway lines in front of an approaching train. Afterwards remorse—considerably accelerated in its coarse, be it said, by the discovery that Sir Talbot Byng does not care for her—takes hold of the child of mystery, and she expiates her crime by perishing in precisely the same fashion as her mistress.—**Publishers' Circular**, Vol. 57 (July 30, 1892): pp.105-106

L'Epine, Charles. *The Lady of the Leopard.* London: Greening & Co., 1899.

> Karen Herries, the young woman in question, is a study in impossible womanhood. The child of an Englishman and a Spanish-Cuban woman, she is endowed with extraordinary mesmeric gifts. She can control and mesmerise snakes and leopards, and, of course, in her hands men's hearts are as the clay of the potter. She has been inspired by her father with the belief that the estate of St. Angela belongs by right to him, and therefore to her, and a good deal of the story turns upon her visit to England, and her attempt, which for a time is successful, to get the property from its owner. Some idea of the absurdity of the story may be gathered by the fact that the lady at certain times seems

*to take the form of a leopard, and on one occasion when Sir David becomes too uxorious, she claws him pretty nearly to death. The characters are all unlikely and unloveable, and it is impossible to say anything good for the story.—**The Scotsman**, May 15, 1899, p.3*

Lee, Eldon. *The Burden of 1909: A Prophecy*. London: Stanley Paul & Co., 1909.

*This rather startling booklet is in the nature of a prophecy. A neurotic boy is hypnotised by his sister, and is asked what is "to happen in the year so soon to dawn." The reply is disconnected and spasmodic, but the reader gathers that for a time the forces of evil are to prevail, that women are to endure much suffering, and that new power will be given "to the methods of blood and pain." Well, we shall see.—**Publishers' Circular**, Vol. 90, June 5, 1909, p.878*

Lee, Mary Holland. *Margaret Salisbury*. Boston: Arena Publishing Co., 1894. Available online via HathiTrust and Google Books: http://catalog.hathitrust.org/Record/006775701.

*Margaret Salisbury, an orphan, and the ward of a wealthy southerner, only awakens to the consciousness of the psychic power she possesses when she decides to visit a friend in New England. While staying in the vicinity of Rockport, a Miss Appleton from Boston, seeing that she can make Margaret subservient to her by exercising hypnotic influence, brings her power to bear on the girl. The results of her machinations are seen not only in the life of Margaret but in the life of the hero.—**Publishers' Weekly**, March 31, 1894, p.481*

*The villain is a woman. Her weapon is the hypnotic power. Miss Appleton (the villain) and Margaret Salisbury (the heroine) love the same man. Miss Appleton so gains control over her rival that she compels her to accept the proffered love of another. Margaret is all unaware of what she has done, or of the malicious power that is being exercised over her. She escapes, however, from this net that is spread for her, only to be caught again later on, and while under the spell is married to General Curtis, an honorable man. After the ceremony Margaret becomes aware of the step she has taken, but is unable to comprehend why she should have married this man, whom she accepts but does not love. Her husband realizes her situation and is delicate enough to give her back her freedom.—**The Herald** (Los Angeles), May 6, 1894, p.9*

Lockett, Jeannie. "The Garston House Tragedy" *Australian Town and Country Journal* (Dec. 1888): 14. Available online via Australia's Trove website: https://readallaboutit.com.au/#/title/51434.

Story contains both a female and a male hypnotist. The female hypnotist, Madeline Garston, is the murderer of Robert Garston (her uncle); Madeline uses her mesmeric powers in an attempt to get another woman, Hester Wrayburn, to believe that she had committed the murder. The male hypnotist, George Felton, uses his powers to get Madeline to confess to the murder while in a hypnotic trance; thus freeing Hester from blame for the crime. [Note: story ran serially in the *Australian Town and Country Journal* from December 1, 1889 through May 25, 1889]

Ludlum, Jean Kate. *Lida Campbell, or, Drama of a Life*. New York: Robert Bonner's Sons, 1892. Available online via HathiTrust and the Internet Archive: http://catalog.hathitrust.org/Record/007666157.

A woman with strong hypnotic and spiritual powers uses them to get her estranged husband (a well-known author) to write a novel with a purpose for her; she also uses her hypnotic power in an attempt to poison her brother to death.

M.A.B. "The Fair Mesmerist" *Green Mountain Gem* 7 (Jan. 1849): 201-6. Available online via Google Books and HathiTrust: https://babel.hathitrust.org/cgi/pt?id =umn.31951000731487n&view=1up&seq=294.

Constance Wilton is engaged to her cousin Eustace Montgomery; even though neither one loves the other they stay together because it was their grandmother's wish for them to be married. Constance is an amateur mesmerist and she places Eustace into trances to alleviate his headaches. A kindly neighbor with hypnotic powers, Englehart, is in love with Constance and ends up wooing her away from Eustace. [Note: this story was also published in 1873 under the title "Love and Mesmerism" in **Bow Bells** Vol. 19, pp.282-283].

Maartens, Maarten. *The Healers*. New York: D. Appleton & Company, 1906. Available online via Hathi Trust and Google Books: http://catalog.hathitrust.org/Record/001199387.

The central figure of the story is an idiot youth of title, whom his uncle guardian and heir has brought to the great brain specialist Charcot. The latter entrusts the case to a young Dutch pupil, who has studied all the latest developments of hypnotism, suggestion, double personality, and so forth. He and his wife, a Sumatran half-caste, are the "healers" of the title (for the wife is a skilled hypnotist and a clairvoyante to boot), and they are more successful with the congenital idiot than with his uncle, who imagines himself tainted with hereditary insanity. The book has thus two aspects. To some it will appeal as a study in "psychiatry" and mental derangement; to others the character of the old Dutch bacteriologist, will seem by far the most successful in the book, which cannot fail to be interesting to any reader.—The Guardian, February 21, 1906, p.5

Madison, Marie. "A Scientific Revenge" *New York Clipper* (Oct. 1895): 499-500. Available online via Illinois Digital Newspaper Collections and Trove Digitized Newspapers: http://trove.nla.gov.au/ndp/del/article/108866650.

Helen Halliday is a young woman who possesses both strong mesmeric powers and the ability to read people's thoughts. During a hypnotic demonstration given by a friend of the family she learns that her cousin Bruce Halliday had murdered her father. Helen now seeks revenge and she uses her hypnotic influence to torture Bruce with the memory of his crime, and then she puts the idea in his mind to commit suicide, which he does.

Maher, Zena A. *The Witch Hypnotizer.* San Francisco: The Bancroft Company, 1892. Available online via HathiTrust: https://catalog.hathitrust.org/Record/006518016.

The "witch hypnotizer" is a religious woman whose influence bends others to her will, though for benevolent reasons (e.g. she gets a drunkard to stop drinking; helps a man marry a woman he has wronged; helps a woman forge a stronger relationship with God; helps a prostitute find respectable employment, etc.). A large part of the book is made up of texts and stories from Scripture.

Marble, C.C. "Told at the Club: A Story of Two Continents" *London Journal*:171 (Feb. 1893): 11-12. Available online via Proquest British Periodicals: https://about.proquest.com/en/products-services/british_periodicals/.

A woman named Mara exerts a strong hypnotic influence over Sir Edward Faircourt, Sir Edward's wife, and even Sir Edward's physician.

Marsh, Richard pseud. (Real name Richard Bernard Heldmann). *The Beetle.* London: Skeffington & Son, 1897. Available online via Google Books, Project Gutenberg and the Internet Archive: https://archive.org/details/beetle00mars/mode/2up.

*A weird story of a man who, while in Egypt, is decoyed into what he calls "a den of demons." He remains here for some months, the helpless victim to the mesmeric power of the goddess of the den. He witnesses horrible sights, and one day attempts to strangle the woman who has charge of him, and she changes into a beetle. After many frightful adventures the man returns to London, but is haunted by this beetle, who has hypnotic powers. The narrative is taken up in turn by different people, every effort being made to make the flesh creep through descriptions of loathsome episodes.—**Annual American Catalogue**, 1898, p.126*

[Note: First published serially in the periodical **Answers**, under the title: **The Peril of Paul Lessingham: The Story of a Haunted Man.** For a detailed look at *The Beetle* see Minna Vuohelainen's "Richard Marsh's *The Beetle* (1897): a late Victorian popular novel" **Working With English**, Vol 2, pp.89-100 (https://web.archive.org/web/20240303111512/https://www.nottingham.ac.uk/english/documents/working-with-english/volume-2-1/vuohelainen-richard-marsh's-the-beetle-1897-a-late-victorian-popular-novel.pdf)].

Marsh, Richard pseud. (Real name Richard Bernard Heldmann). "The Burglar's Blunder" *Gentleman's Magazine* 268 (May 1890): 433-48. Available online via Google Books and HathiTrust: https://babel.hathitrust.org/cgi/pt?id=mdp.39 015012849264&view=1up&seq=449.

A cunning burglar is completely outwitted by a beautiful young woman who possesses great hypnotic powers.

Marsh, Richard pseud. (Real name Richard Bernard Heldmann). "Magical Music" *Gentleman's Magazine* 270 (May 1891): 433-51. Available online via HathiTrust and Google Books: http://babel.hathitrust.org/cgi/pt?id=njp.32101077263166 ;view=1up;seq=443.

The Reverend Alan Macleod is tricked into getting married by his conniving aunt and her conspirator Miss Vesey—a woman that can hypnotize people through the music she plays on her piano.

Mathers, Helen (also known as Mrs. Reeves). *The Sin of Hagar*. London: Hutchinson, 1896. Available online via Google Books: https://books.google.com/books?id=-SJAAAAAYAAJ.

So far as there is a plot it is the familiar one of two suitors for one lady—Nadége, the daughter of a Lord. Sir William Cassilis is the favoured one, and the father, unable to alter the course of Nadége's affections, consents to the engagement, but, having regard to her youth, prohibits matrimony. Nadége is sent to a boarding school, where she has Miss Hagar Gregorias as companion. Hagar, also an admirer of Cassilis, is aware of the passionate regard for Nadége entertained by Blake Trelawney, a titled gentleman, who had made various dire threats against Cassilis. Hagar is a hypnotist, and by dint of this power endeavours to mould matters to her own liking. For a time her evil machinations are useless. Sir William Cassilis and Nadége are secretly married, but Hagar pursues her purpose with unrelenting determination. Nadége is ultimately hypnotised, and endeavours while in this state to poison her husband. Hagar acts the part of rescue, a separation ensues, and Nadége, in accordance with her scheme, flees to Trelawney. The black art is detected by Cassilis, who never once doubted his wife, and Trelawney is proved the honourable gentleman. Nadége, freed from the slavery to which she had been subject, appears in her true character, and Hagar commits suicide.— **Dundee Courier & Argus**, *May 20, 1896, p.6*

Maude, F.W. *Victims*. London: Bliss, Sands and Foster, 1894.

There is a good deal of ability in this hopeless novel, where wayward loves, and hypnotism, and hereditary alcoholism run riot. The marital relations of the different personages are a trifle perplexing. Nina M'Mahon apparently had intimate relations of a kind with both

*John Musgrave, the "hero," and David Morton, the "villain," before the period at which the story commences. Then John Musgrave becomes co-respondent in a divorce case as to a Lady Southcourt just as he is about to propose to Gladys Gainsford. Perhaps he was innocent, but Gladys out of her purity refuses him and marries Morton, the prophet of an American Socialistic community, who is temporarily invalided at Pau. Upon his marriage Morton becomes a raging dipsomaniac, and most of the book is a study of his mania. Nina M'Mahon is brought in to cure him, hypnotises him, and casts Gladys into somnambulistic trances, in one of which she enters Musgrave's bed-room. Another divorce case follows—Morton v. Morton—in which the hero is once more an innocent co-respondent. Then he departs for America to ferret out damaging facts as to Nina's past career; he succeeds, but is almost killed in an accident, so Gladys is telegraphed for, and crosses the Atlantic to nurse him. He recovers under her care, and shows her the documents which are to cause the Queen's Proctor to intervene. Her answer is to burn them, and to declare she is content to live with him. Marry him she will not, because, although a Protestant, she holds the Catholic doctrine that marriage is a sacrament and cannot be dissolved; to live in adultery, however, seems to have no practical objections. Meantime David has married Nina. Then Nina dies; David dies; and Gladys dies— and curtain! We do not generally tell a novelist's story, but in this case one scarce knows what criticism is to say. Gladys has an exceedingly bitter life, and there is pathos in the lives of all such women; but we cannot see what Mr. Maude's object in concocting such a very unsavoury salad as is "Victims."—**Glasgow Herald**, February 1, 1894*

McClintock, Letitia. "Caterina: A Story of Mesmerism" *Argosy* 49 (Mar. 1890): 202-23. Available online via Google Books and HathiTrust: http://babel.hathitrust.org/cgi/pt?id=mdp.39015065716212;view=1up;seq=218.

Setting is Amsterdam in the year 1598. Caterina is an artist with strong mesmeric powers, which she uses on the young clairvoyant Teresa. Caterina and Teresa's husbands are on a polar expedition in the Arctic, and their ship, the "Orange" is months past its expectant arrival date; Caterina puts Teresa in a trance so she can describe the status of their husbands' expedition; Caterina captures these descriptions in her detailed paintings. A servant in Caterina's household has witnessed Caterina's and Teresa's clairvoyant sessions and viewed the resulting paintings; with this knowledge she lets her neighbors know that Caterina and Teresa are practicing witchcraft. Some town folk start a fire to the house with Caterina and Teresa inside, but they are saved in the nick of time by the returning Polar explorers.

Meade, L.T. (Elizabeth Thomasina Meade). *The Blue Diamond*. London: Chatto & Windus, 1901. Available online via Google Books: https://www.google.com/books/edition/The_Blue_Diamond/_-ZMAQAAMAAJ.

The history of the Blue Diamond is hardly worth retailing. It has come down as an heirloom in a family, but has eventually been handed over to the Roman Church. According to a stipulation made by the donor it is for one year in the possession of a young wife who lives in perpetual terror of its loss. Her attendant, a Russian of the name of Nadine, steals the diamond, but mesmerises a young girl visiting in the family into the belief that she is the criminal. This unfortunate girl undergoes all the horror of believing herself a thief until the true story is divulged.—**Literary World**, Vol. 63 (March 15, 1901): p.246 [Note: also published serially under the title: "Nadine, The Russian: A Thrilling Tale of the Great Blue Diamond" in the *Examiner* (Launceston, Tasmania), available online via Australia's *Trove* website.]

_____. *On the Brink of a Chasm: A Record of Plot and Passion*. London: Chatto & Windus, 1898. Available online via the Library of Congress and Project Gutenberg: https://www.gutenberg.org/ebooks/64534.

Hypnotism is an inviting topic for a sensational novel, and Mrs. Meade has not been able to resist the temptation. She founds her story apparently on a remarkable case of mesmeric trance in Paris (declared to be a fact) in which several of the most distinguished doctors of the day were convinced that death had actually taken place. In the present case the medium is a baronet only seven years of age, round whose supposed death the novelist writes her "record or plot and passion," to quote the secondary title she has given the book. We have the conventional villain who, failing to win the hand of the heroine, lives only for revenge. His rival happens to be next heir to the young baronet's title and estates, and it is the easiest thing in the world to have the child murdered and the guilt laid at the hero's door; for the child is delicate and the nurse is a passionate woman whose blind love for the villain will lead her to do anything for him. So, on condition that he marries her, she promises to poison the medicine which the hero is to give the invalid boy. In due course the child is supposed to die and to be buried; but as a matter of fact, the nurse who is possessed of wonderful powers of mesmerism, has only placed him in a trance, and afterwards packed him off alive and well without anyone being the wiser. The villain bides his time; not until the hero and heroine have been married six months does he deal his blow. Then he trumps up his murder charge, and, with circumstantial evidence which the hero is rather clumsily made to exaggerate, the arrest takes place. Needless to say, it all comes right in the end; the nurse confesses, the real baronet turns up again, and the villain has to quit the country at once. "The Brink of a Chasm", we fear, is not a story which will add greatly to Mrs. Meade's reputation.— **Publishers' Circular**, Vol. 69 (October 15, 1898): p.456

_____. *The Sorceress of the Strand*. London: Ward, Lock & Co., 1903. Available online via A Celebration of Women Writers: http://digital.library.upenn.edu/women/meade/sorceress/sorceress.html.

Series of linked stories featuring the beautiful and cunning, criminal mastermind— Madame Sara. Madame Sara has lots of tools in her evil arsenal, one of them being her hypnotic powers. [Note: orginally published in *The Strand Magazine*, October 1902-March 1903; *The Strand Magaine* is available online via Google Books]

Meade, L.T. (Elizabeth Thomasina Meade) and Clifford Halifax. "The Adventures of a Man of Science: VI: The Panelled Bedroom" *Strand Magazine* 12 (Dec. 1896): 664-77. Available online via Google Books and HathiTrust: http://babel. hathitrust.org/cgi/pt?id=njp.32101045356415;view=1up;seq=672.

Mr. Gilchrist is a guest at a friend's mansion during the Christmas holidays, and is staying in a paneled bedroom which contains several hidden doorways and rooms. A fellow guest, Louisa Enderby, is an amazing mesmerist who is using Constance Perowne (Gilchrist's host granddaughter) as a subject in her hypnotic experiments; Gilchrist (himself a powerful hypnotist) disapproves of Enderby's experiments with Constance and informs Enderby of his opinion. Enderby warns Gilchrist to stay out of her way, and if he doesn't she will seek vengeance. Also, while in a semi-hypnotic trance, Enderby has informed Gilchrist that she killed Constance's father (everyone thought he had drown) and is intent on controlling Constance, with the hope of obtaining Constance's inherited wealth and property. Enderby hypnotizes Constance to lead Gilchrist into one of the mansion's hidden chambers, she locks him in, entombing him, and leading him to certain death due to lack of oxygen. Gilchrist finds a way out of the chamber, and when Enderby sees him, she thinks she is seeing a ghost; the stress from this ghostly visitation leads to Enderby dying a week later.

Mensiaux, Marie De. "A Latent Power" *The Theatre* 22 (Feb. 1889): 85-92. Available online via HathiTrust: http://babel.hathitrust.org/cgi/pt?id=mdp.3901509110 9838;view=1up;seq=103.

Alma Power has latent hypnotic powers which she unintentionally wields over a hypnotic charlatan which nearly leads to a drowning.

Mitchell, Edward Page. "The Facts in the Ratcliff Case" *Evening Star* (Nov. 1879): 6. Available online via Chronicling America and as part of Project Gutenberg Australia: http://chroniclingamerica.loc.gov/lccn/sn83045462/1879-11-22/ed-1/seq-6/ http://gutenberg.net.au/ebooks06/0606901.txt.

A woman with strong hypnotic power uses it to murder her husband. [Note: story first published in the **New York Sun**, March 7, 1879].

Moberly, L.G. (Lucy Gertrude). *A Waif of Destiny*. London: Ward, Lock & Co., 1910.

Story deals with a league of anarchists, led by a female hypnotist, who wields her hypnotic powers to get Englishmen to sell their country out to foreign powers (in this case, Germany). Roma Carstairs, the "waif of destiny," finds herself caught up in the doings of the league, and under the control of Madame von Hagen, the hypnotist in the novel.

Moodie, Mrs. (Susanna). "Mildred Rosier: A Tale of the Ruined City" *Literary Garland* 2 (Jan. 1844): 63-68. Available online via HathiTrust and Google Books: http:// babel.hathitrust.org/cgi/pt?id=mdp.39015068413460;view=1up;seq=77.

A handsome smuggler uses mesmerism to inveigle Mildred Rosier (a young, beautiful, and free-spirited girl) to fall in love with him. The story also contains an elderly woman with mesmeric powers. [Note: this novel was published serially on the following pages of Vol. 2 of the *Literary Garland*: pp.63-68, 111-119, 157-163, 215-223, 241-246, 299-305, 401-405, 433-445, 481-490, 529-548]

Morris, Clara. "In Paris Suddenly" In: Clara Morris. *A Silent Singer*. p. 161-170). New York: Brentano's, 1899. Available online via Google Books and HathiTrust: http:// babel.hathitrust.org/cgi/pt?id=uc2.ark:/13960/t3pv6c93r;view=1up;seq=177.

A beautiful and stately woman with a mesmeric and murderous past, casts a hypnotic spell over an actress during the performance of a play.

Old Ironnerve, Jr. *Back From the Dead; or, The Old Hypnotist's Crime*. New York: Munro's Publishing Hourse, 1895. Available online via Villanova University Digital Library: http://digital.library.villanova.edu/Item/vudl:289634.

Hypnotism is used for robbery, insurance fraud, and attempted murder in the story, and the hypnotic power is apparently (it's unclear which folks actually have powers) wielded by several people: an old male mesmerist, a bookkeeper, and a widow of a murdered banker. A gem in the beginning of the story appears to have hypnotic powers, but this is never fully explained. [Note: part of *Old Cap. Collier Library* , No. 590, April, 1895]

Oliphant, Philip Laurence. *The Little Red Fish*. London: Edward Arnold, 1903.

*Mesmerism, to be effective, requires, at this time of day, to be done well. Mr. Oliphant's heroine, whom we first meet at a country house in Scotland, was, by right of her great grandmother, the Ranee of Moralsarpur. The Government of India had set a usurper on the throne of her ancestors. It was her ambition, by means of the Little Red Fish, and its hypnotic power, to regain her birth-right.—***The Academy and Literature** (Feburary 28, 1903): p.204

The Little Red Fish, which is made of stained ivory, and whose eye is an opal with a ruby set in the middle of it, is the "luck" of the State of Moralsarpar. It has never been seen by more than two living persons at the same time, and when this story opens it has come into the hands of Kara Millman. Now, Kara is a beautiful woman, with a dash of Indian blood in her veins; she is also by descent the Ranee of Moralsarpar; and with the Little Red Fish, and her trick of mesmerism to aid her, she hopes to oust the English from her State and mount the throne.—**Daily Mail** (London), March 3, 1903, p.2 [Note: Kara drives a man to insanity and suicide through the use of her hypnotic powers. For a lengthy review of "The Little Red Fish" see a review in **The Tablet**, August 1, 1903, pp.168-169. https://babel.hathitrust.org/cgi/pt?id=uc1. e0000264739&seq=178].

Phillips, J.A. *The Ghost of a Dog.* Ottawa: A. S. Woodburn, Printer, 1885. Available online via HathiTrust: https://babel.hathitrust.org/cgi/pt?id=aeu.ark:/13960/ t8hd8871r;view=1up;seq=147.

Contains a chapter "How I Was Mesmerised" which deals with a man feigning to be hypnotized by a woman he loves, thus enabling him to win her hand in marriage.

Phillips, L.M. (Ludern Merriss). *The Mind Reader.* New York: F. Tennyson Neely, 1898. Available online via HathiTrust and Google Books: http://catalog.hathitrust. org/Record/100587341.

Seymour Joselyn is an evil man who attempts to hypnotize a young college graduate, Frank Gilbert, into playing a part in his shady business transactions. Joselyn sends the naive Gilbert to Nevada to oversee the operations of a gold mine there; while in Nevada Gilbert meets with many dangers but is protected from harm by the mystical interventions of two good-hearted hypnotists/clairvoyants: Interice Goodwin—a skilled hypnotist who possesses great astral and spiritual powers, and Miss Hendee Vallee—a beautiful clairvoyant with strong hypnotic powers.

_____. *Miskel: A Novel.* Franklin, Ohio: Editor Publishing Co., 1895. Available online via HathiTrust and Google Books: http://catalog.hathitrust.org/ Record/100586496.

Readers who are fond of mystery and occultism will find "Miskel" a novel to their taste. It abounds in hypnotism, clairvoyance, mind reading, Hindoo jugglery and Hindoo thuggism. Miskel is an Anglo-Indian girl, stolen from her parents and brought to America, where she passes as the adopted daughter of Mrs. Orson, who is the real heroine of the story. This woman is a beautiful, fascinating, dangerous, serpent-like creature, who is an adept in hypnotism and is aided by two familiar spirits in the shape of two tongueless Hindoo servants, who do her will and at the same time dominate her by means of their occult powers. She gets a wealthy and respected banker into her hypnotic tolls and brings him to the verge of suicide. Miskel's father, an English officer in India, is abducted at the same time that his child is stolen, and for twelve long years *is kept a prisoner in a wild and almost inaccessible valley. The narrative of his discovery and rescue is the most interesting and romantic part of the story. At the end the wicked are punished or brought in repentance and the good are rewarded according to their wishes in the proper, old-fashioned way. While the author appears to accept as genuine the hypnotic and other occult manifestations he depicts, he evidently regards them as productive of evil rather than good. His novel is by no means a fruitless production, but it has the one merit without which all others are wasted—it is interesting.—***Syracuse Evening Herald***, September 25, 1895, p.9 [Note: the main hypnotist in the story is Mrs. Annie Orson, but her two Indian servants, Satika and Oudh, also possess hypnotic powers].

Pierson, Helen W. "The Ruby Necklace" *National Magazine* 5 (Mar. 1897): 571-74. Available online via Google Books and HathiTrust: https://babel.hathitrust.org/cgi/pt?id=mdp.39015074652390&view=1up&seq=583.

A young detective hired to guard valuable gifts at a wedding reception is hypnotized by the household's governess into stealing an expensive ruby necklace.

Quick, Herbert. *Double Trouble; or, Every Hero His Own Villain.* Indianapolis: Bobbs-Merrill Company, 1906. Available online via HathiTrust, Google Books and Project Gutenberg: https://catalog.hathitrust.org/Record/000243665.

*Florian Amidon, a banker of Hazelhurst, Wisconsin, starts on a journey. He has not got very far when he suddenly and mysteriously becomes somebody else. In his new character, it seems, he is Eugene Brassfield, and with that name he wanders to Bellevale, Pennsylvania, settles down, lives for several years, and becomes a leading citizen. One night, while on his way to New York, he falls out of his berth in the sleeper, and the shock awakens him as Amidon, his existence as Brassfield becoming a complete blank. But his clothes, the papers found in his pockets, and the reception he meets when he reaches New York, all afford convincing evidence that he is Brassfield. One letter, in particular, shows him that he is engaged to marry a girl of Bellevale, who has the most unbounded affection for him. In his perplexity, he consults a pair of hypnotists—a German professor with a lovely daughter—who find that the Brassfield personality emerges when he is put to sleep under their influence. By taking notes of what he says during a succession of these trances, they construct for him an outline of his Brassfield life and character, and impart the facts to him after he is awakened. Armed with this material, he repairs to Bellevale, accompanied by his friends the hypnotists, and with the help of the notes supplied him, tries to fit himself into the existence concerning which his memory has nothing to tell him. The resulting complications are extremely amusing, and keep the reader's interest alert to the end.—***The Dial***, Vol 40 (April 16, 1906): p.263*

Randolph, Edmund. *One of Us*. London: Sampson Low, Marston, Searle & Rivington, 1882. Available online via The Internet Archive and Google Books: https://archive.org/details/oneusanovel02randgoog.

An American adventuress, married to an English peer, casts a mesmeric spell over two persons—the hero, who tells the story, and the British Premier. She throws the latter into a trance in order to extort political secrets.— **The Globe**, August 11, 1882, p.6

Rebak, Henry. *Bound by a Spell*. London: John Dicks, office of Bow Bells, 1872. Available online via Google Books: https://books.google.com/books?vid=BL:A0021866202.

A boy, supposedly an orphan, left for years in a boys' boarding school, knows of no relatives. The schoolmaster wishes to make him marry his daughter who had been seduced by another man. The daughter hypnotizes him, "binds him by a spell," and marries him. After a month he runs away to London, meets some old acquaintances, has good and bad fortune, is saved at last and finds his father. [Source: *The House of Beadle and Adams*, by Albert Johannsen, Vol. I, page 193, Item #122; note: also published as #122 of Beadle and Adams *Fireside Library*; the story is sometimes wrongly attributed to Hugh Conway].

Reynolds, Gertrude Minnie (Mrs. Baillie Reynolds). *Nigel Ferrard*. London: Hurst and Blackett, 1899.

To the lovers of sensational fiction this last novel of G. M. Robins will appeal forcibly. Commencing with the tragic murder of a man by his rival in love, whilst undergoing an operation which was witnessed by a girl who had in her sleep walked to a skylight through which all was seen, the fate of the child who falls through the skylight on to the dead body of the victim in a swoon from which she recovers with the loss of her memory will be followed with interest. "Oh, what a tangled web we weave, when first we practice to deceive," is well illustrated by subsequent events, although we do not accuse the authoress of attempting a moral. Unaware of the true cause of his cousin's death, Nigel Ferrard, hardly out of his student days, who has assisted the murderer Marchmont, is overwhelmed at the supposed result of the operation, the more so when Marchmont reminds him that he is next of kin to the dead man. He decides to adopt the girl Gwennie, trusting to her loss of memory continuing to silence her, the only witness. Meanwhile Marchmont marries the woman for whom he has committed the crime. Gifted with the power of hypnotism, and a thirst for revenge, his fascinating wife worms the half-suspected secret out of the unfortunate Gwennie, who, having married Ferrard, remembers all, and is filled with horror as the belief that she is the wife of a murderer, dawns up her. It is a thrilling story with a clever plot, well told from first to last.— **The Country Gentleman**, Issue 1911, December 24, 1898 [Note: hypnotism is only presented towards the end of the novel and it plays a minor role in the story, all-in-all].

Richardson, Warren. *Dr. Zell and the Princess Charlotte: An Autobiographical Relation of Adventures in the Life of a Distinguished Modern Necromancer, Seer and Theosophist.* New York: L. Kabis and Co., 1892. Available online via Internet Archive and Google Books: http://archive.org/details/drzellandprince00richgoog.

> *The story of Dr. Zell is a narrative of theosophical and occult interest and will especially commend itself to the class of readers inclined to such studies, though containing sufficient plot and incident to make it readable to the less thoughtful. Dr. Zell's life is given from boyhood. When a mere boy, impelled by hereditary impulses, he wandered at will through a library unusually rich in mystic lore. In after life he became such an adept that he was able to compel another person to exchange bodies with him, but not being influenced by entirely pure motives in this act of soul-transference, he paid the penalty in the loss of adept power and remorse that embittered his life. From his views given on several life topics, it does not appear that a knowledge of the occult world would afford much aid in solving questions of vital importance to the interests of the present.*—**Rocky Mountain News**, (January 18, 1892): p.8 [Note: both Dr. Zell and a character named Madam Aurelian possess strong hypnotic powers].

Rita, pseud. (Real name Eliza Margaret Jane Humphreys). *The Doctor's Secret: A Novel.* London: F. V. White & Co., 1890.

> *It has been foretold only too truly that recent discussions on hypnotism must inevitably provoke a harvest of hypnotic stories. "The Doctor's Secret," by Rita, is amongst the primeurs of the crop. The hero, a youthful and, of course, intensely sceptical doctor, is mesmerized, or subjugated, or bedevilled, or whatever the correct phrase may be, by his next-door neighbour, the young and beautiful wife of an old, ugly, and drivelling student. She has a lover whom she finds it desirable to poison, and she compels the unfortunate doctor to give her his morphia needle for the purpose. The doctor is arrested. The lady visits him and makes him promise to keep her secret. Then she forces the murdered man's valet to confess himself guilty, and the doctor is let out. Like a bold man, he makes love to the murderess's sister—or rather surrenders to that forward young person's advances. Strolling about one evening they come upon a mouldy summer-house, and the doctor pokes about with his stick. He sees an odd light round the place at night, and returns to investigate. He finds a dead baby, and is nearly throttled by its mamma—the mystic murderess. But she had ceased to be mystic, so far as the doctor was concerned, when he unearthed the baby. Fear of this discovery had made her "a terrified heap of shuddering womanhood" on a former occasion. This time she poisoned herself. The doctor seems to have persevered in his desperate purpose of marrying the sister. But what became of the valet? He is left in gaol a confessed murderer, and the only witness who could disprove his confession is killed off.*—**The Times** (London), September 15, 1890, p.4

_____. *The Ladye Nancye*. London: Ward and Downey, 1887. Available online via HathiTrust, Google Books, and the Internet Archive: https://catalog.hathitrust.org/Record/011698203.

The novel is set in the Channel Islands where a woman with mesmeric powers obtains mastery over Nancette, the heroine of the story.

Robertson, Keith. *A Knave of Diamonds*. Edinburgh: William Paterson, 1885.

*Mr. Silas Wadd, a knave of diamonds, spends his life in effecting robberies of precious stones on a scale which would have placed him at the head of the list of millionaires in a very few weeks had he only the discrimination to stop. Mr. Wadd is aided in his favourite pursuit by the remarkable power he possesses, from spiritual, magnetic, or other unexplained agencies, of making people to exactly as he chooses, rob for him, murder for him, travel about for him like so many miserable unpaid bagmen. And yet, in spite of these unexampled facilities, Mr. Wadd not only fails to make himself happy, but he gets shot on the steps of a Paris café, just as any ordinary malefactor might. Can the spiritual powers really do no more for us than this?—**Daily News** (London, England), December 22, 1885; Issue 12386 [Note: the story also contain a female hypnotist, Madame Menier, who hypnotizes a woman, and this woman, while in her magnetic trance shoots the hypnotist Wadd]*

Rowe, Henrietta G. *Queenshithe*. Buffalo: Charles Wells Moulton, 1895. Available online via HathiTrust and Google Books: http://catalog.hathitrust.org/Record/007092346.

The heroine Roxy Rae, is a brave, true hearted Maine girl, who struggles hard to provide for her younger brother and sister, who have been left to her care. She braids straw hats and she invents a new braid, which has a great success. An envious relative steals the secret from her by a bit of hypnotism. The relative has a bound girl who hates her, but loves Roxy. She is very keen and smart and she sees Roxy working on the new braid and learns the secret. Then her mistress wrings the device from her in her sleep for Peg, the bound girl is a somnambulist. When Peg finds out what she has done she disappears and the neighbors believe her mistress has murdered her. Roxy is in danger of losing all the benefits of her invention, but she goes to Washington and President Jefferson becomes interested in her and sees to it that this Yankee queen shall be placed in a position by the patent office where she shall have the toll that her ingenuity entitles her to. Peg is discovered, the wicked relative rescued from jail and makes restitution.— **Brooklyn Daily Eagle**, September 1, 1895, p.20

Scott, G. Firth. *The Last Lemurian: A Westralian Romance*. London: James Bowden, 1898. Available online through the National Library of Australia and Project Gutenberg Australia: http://nla.gov.au/nla.gen-vn5038460.

It deals with the real and the impossible, the ethereal and the theoretical, and has a strong touch of hypnotism. It is a bushman's story. The scenes are principally located in South Australia and London. The object is the search for wealth, and gold is secured which would far outvie the recently discovered Klondyke. It is almost impossible to summarize a story full of so many astounding episodes. Two bushmen, after fighting their way through bush and desert, arrive at a range of mountains inhabited by the last Lemurian (or yellow woman), with her hordes of shrivelled-up mummies and "Bunyip." The latter is half-fashioned like a man and half like a lizard. The last Lemurian is a woman of large stature—20 ft. high—and with supernatural or hypnotic power, luminous with greenish phosphorescence. Her imps have been ordinary mortals who have gone to the mountain range in search of gold and, having fallen a victim to her overpowering will, have become her slaves. Upon them—or their blood—she has lived, thus reducing ordinary men to pigmies. To obtain some mastery over her, the bushmen had to murder the "Bunyip"; and this being done, one of them—known as The Hatter—first assuming that he was the King of Night, ordered her, if she wished to ace her lover, to cover the Bunyip's body with bricks of gold. This was done, and the two men returned to the bush with their spoil. But "The Hatter" had fallen a victim to the hypnotic gaze of the Yellow Woman, and subsequently both adventurers were compelled, by an uncontrollable force, to return to the land of the last Lemurian. Their experiences subsequently are intensely thrilling. Rocks fade away amidst volcanoes, the hordes vanish in the rush of water, the last Lemurian meets her fate. The Hatter, too, falls a victim, but not before the hero of the story—Halwood—discovers in the home of the Lemurian a girl for whom his spirit has yearned. She has been in a cataleptic trance for centuries, and shortly after being awakened her spirit leaves her, but not before Halwood has perceived that she still lives in the flesh if he can only trace her.—**Reynold's Newspaper**, Issue 2494, May 29, 1898

Sheldon-Williams, Miles. *The Power of Ula*. London: Ward Lock & Co., 1906.

Two young giants, doubtless intended by Nature to be heroes, but who have not been successful in passing some of the learned tests imposed on candidates for a commission in His Majesty's forces, meet in London Miss Ula Valdien, who by hypnotic influence is able to make these young gentlemen do pretty much as she pleases. This Ula of the Valdi has claims on the throne of that country—run apparently on Amazonian lines—and takes out a supply of up-to-date firearms and other fighting material, including the two young giants aforesaid, in order to force her claims. On their arrival these same gentlemen find it more congenial to fight on behalf of the rightful wearer of the Crown of the Valdi, and so upset the plans of Ula. This is not accomplished without many stirring events that are skilfully drawn.—**Dundee Courier**, April 28, 1906, p.6 [Note: Ula also places gold rings on the men's hands which appear to have hypnotic powers over them as well.]

Sheppard, Elizabeth Sara. *Almost a Heroine*. London: Hurst and Blackett, 1859. Available online via HathiTrust, Google Books and the Internet Archive: https:// catalog.hathitrust.org/Record/007683021.

The novel doesn't contain much in the way of mesmerism, but the character Erselie uses her formidable magnetic influence to keep a sick man from dying.

Sidgwick, M.C. "The Power of a Will" *Belgravia* 98 (Feb. 1899): 132-61. Available online via HathiTrust and Google Books: https://babel.hathitrust.org/cgi/pt?id =coo.31924065956892&view=1up&seq=142.

Apparently, through the power of hypnotism, a woman projects an image of her worse self into the thoughts of the man she has recently married; but once she becomes aware of what she has done, she is able to salvage her marriage.

Sims, A.K. (Real name John H. Whitson). *The Texan Detective; or, The Stranger Sport From Spokane*. New York: Beadle & Adams, 1895. Available online via Northern Illinois University Libraries: https://dimenovels.lib.niu.edu/islandora/object/ dimenovels%3A176979#page/1/mode/1up.

Mesquite Mat and his gang of crooks are close to having total control of the town of Maverick City, only Judge Gilbert Gale stands in their way. Judge Gale has hired two detectives, Caleb Strong ("The Sport from Spokane") and Hy Hiram ("The Texan Detective") to assist him in dealing with Mesquite Mat and his band of desperadoes. Nancy Stackpole is in love with Mesquite Mat and will do anything to win his approval—Nancy has hypnotic powers and she uses them to control Judge Gilbert's daughter, Gladys. Nancy puts Gladys in a trance and has her: 1) drug Caleb Strong's coffee, so Mat's gang can kidnap him, 2) poison her father to death (he lives, thanks to an antidote given by a physician), and 3) attempt to burn incriminating government records dealing with Mesquite Mat's phony business schemes. All ends well, thanks to the intervention of detectives Strong and Hiram. [Note: story is no.887 in the *Beadle's New York Dime Library*, Vol. 69]

Sinclair. "Valeria" *Ballou's Monthly Magazine* 56 (Sept. 1882): 244-52. Available online via HathiTrust and Google Books: http://babel.hathitrust.org/cgi/pt?id=nyp.3 3433081756219;view=1up;seq=242.

An evil man with assistance from his beautiful mesmerist stepdaughter Valeria, attempt to rob and murder a wealthy young man. [Note: Valeria's mesmeric powers are not used directly to commit a crime]

Somerville, E. "A Night in the Suburbs" *Argosy* 43 (Summer 1887): 66-75. Available online via HathiTrust: https://babel.hathitrust.org/cgi/pt?id=uiug.3011208149 0366&view=1up&seq=322.

A young child, feigning to be lost, tricks a man into taking her to her house, which is located in a very isolated neighborhood. Her parents, a pair of murderous robbers, invite the man into their home and attempt to get him to spend the night there, and when he declines their offer, the girl's mother uses her mesmeric powers to get him to change his mind. The man finds a dead body in the room he is slated to spend the night in, so at an opportune time, he escapes from the house and goes to the police to report the incident.

Southworth, Emma Dorothy Eliza Nevitte. *The Trail of the Serpent; or, The Homicide at Hawke Hall*. New York: A.L. Burt Company, 1907. Available online via The Women's Genre Fiction Project and Google Books:

https://web.archive.org/web/20160201141622

http://womenwriters.library.emory.edu/genrefiction/toc.php?id=estrail

https://web.archive.org/web/20160201141620

http://womenwriters.library.emory.edu/genrefiction/toc.php?id=esheart

https://web.archive.org/web/20160201141620/http://womenwriters.library.emory.edu/genrefiction/toc.php?id=estest.

Story of a British aristocrat, the Earl of Hawkewood, who is wrongly believed to have been murdered, and of his lover who has been sent to a penal colony in Australia for a crime she did not commit. The story contains a female mesmerist named Old Nan Crook, who uses her mesmeric powers to send a clairvoyant in the quest of the mortal remains of the Earl, for there is a monetary award promised for the discovery of the remains. [Note: *The Trail of the Serpent* was initially published serially in *The Ledger*; published in book form as a trilogy in 1907, part 2 was titled *A Tortured Heart*, part 3 published under the title *The Test of Love*]

St. Luz, Berthe (pseud.) *Tamar Curze*. New York: R. F. Fenno & Company, 1908. Available online via HathiTrust, and Google Books: http://catalog.hathitrust.org/Record/000325077.

Tamar Curze, in whom the chief interest of the story centres, is a young woman who comes from India to live with relatives in England. While she has the appearance of a woman, it is discovered that at times, in the night, she becomes a leopardess, prowling about the grounds and giving vent to the animal instinct and thirst for blood. As a woman she possesses a strong hypnotic power, but her influence is an evil one. Prof. D'Herbelot is the first to discover the secret of Tamar Curze, and in a letter which he writes just before his death tries to open the eyes of a colleague to the mystery surrounding the young woman and her Hindu nurse, Ayah, whom he designates as a pair of theurgists.—**The Bookman** Vol. 28 (October, 1908): p.184

Standish, Burt L. (Real name William G. Patten). *Clear-Grit Cal, The Never-Say-Die Detective; or, The Strange Case of Captain Scudd.* New York: Beadle & Adams, 1892. Available online via Northern Illinois University Libraries: https://dimenovels. lib.niu.edu/islandora/object/dimenovels%3A141187#page/1/mode/1up.

A detective investigating a murder case believes that the main suspect may have committed the crime while under hypnotic control by another; that turns out not to be the case, but the suspect when put into a hypnotic trance reveals who did commit the murder. [*Beadle's Half Dime Library*, No. 774]

Standish, Hal (Real name Harvey K. Shackleford). *Fred Fearnot and the Snake-Charmer; or, Out With the Circus Fakirs.* New York: F. Tousey, 1906. Available online via Bowling Green State University's Digital Gallery: https://digitalgallery. bgsu.edu/collections/item/13364.

Mademoiselle Florizell is a snake charmer for a travelling circus, who possesses hypnotic powers which she uses to control her snakes, as well as to direct a man to kill another man she hates. Florizell has a romantic crush on the story's protagonist, Fred Fearnot, and her jealousy leads her to wield her powers over Fearnot's fiancée, Millie Olcott. However, all comes right at the end, and Florizell, Fearnot, and Millie are all chums by the story's conclusion. [No. 383 in the *Work and Win* series]

Stephens, Riccardo. *The Cruciform Mark:The Strange Story of Richard Tregenna, Bachelor of Medicine (Univ. Edin.).* London: Chatto & Windus, 1896.

*The incidents of the life of a medical student and matters of medical interest cannot easily be successfully treated in a novel. A romance which begins and ends with a post-mortem examination, and which contains no fewer than two death-bed scenes, two murders, two suicides, and one death from apoplexy, can hardly fail to be gruesome and unattractive to the general public. At the same time the theories put forward and the incidents described are so fanciful and unscientific that the medical mind is repelled. A lady, who flits through the story like a banshee, is proved at the end to be at the bottom of all unaccountable murders and suicides, for she exercises a strange fascination over her victims, and by "suggestion" causes a small cruciform mark to appear on their necks. When this comes out they lose self-control, and are bound to commit the murder or suicide to which she has doomed them. She is, however, unaware of the crimes committed under her influence, for she leads a double existence, passing from the normal state of a beautiful young lady courted in society to that of a designing and relentless murderess.—***British Medical Journal***, September 18, 1897, p.709*

Stoker, Bram. *The Jewel of Seven Stars.* London: Heinemann, 1903. Available online via Project Gutenberg, the Internet Archive, and Google Books: https://archive.org/ details/BramStoker-TheJewelOfSevenStars.

A mummified queen (Tera) is removed from her Egyptian tomb and taken back to England by Abel Trelawny, an Egyptologist and adventurer. A jewel containing seven stars is found in her tomb and contains the key to the queen's reanimation. The mummified Tera appears to exert some type of hypnotic influence over Trelawny.

Sturgis, Julian. *Thraldom.* New York: D. Appleton & Co., 1887. Available online via Hathi Trust and Google Books: http://catalog.hathitrust.org/Record/000122200.

> *Mesmerism plays a large part in the story, the heroine being under the complete control of her companion, an unscrupulous woman, through this power. She almost succeeds in making her marry her son, but the girl's love for some one else, and the son's conscience help frustrate her evil designs.*—**Annual American Catalogue** 1887, p.166

Sullivan, J.F. (James Frank). "The Queer Side of Things: The End of War" *Strand Magazine* 3 (June 1892): 644-49. Available online via HathiTrust and Google Books: https://babel.hathitrust.org/cgi/pt?id=mdp.39015056049268&view=1up&seq=650.

Two spirits converse about mankind and his penchant for making war; one of the spirits foresees the day when war will be made through the use of hypnotism; where soldiers will force their enemy into sleepy submission or death via hypnotic trance.

Sweetapple, Anna Mapleson. "Strong Delusion" *Chronicle (Adelaide, Australia)* (Dec. 1901): 18-19. Available online via Trove Digitized Newspapers: https://trove.nla.gov.au/newspaper/article/87813446.

Madge Tereston and her cousin, Harry Brindlake fall under the hypnotic influence of the Watsons, an unscrupulous spiritualist couple; Mrs. Watson hypnotizes Madge to tell falsehoods and forge checks; but eventually the cousins break free from their hypnotic captivity.

The Yarnspinner. "Dorrick's Widow" In: Captain Alfred Thompson. *The Skirts of Chance.* p. 237-240). New York: Town Topics Publishing Company, 1893. Available online via HathiTrust and Google Books: https://babel.hathitrust.org/cgi/pt?id=osu.32435073953267&seq=239.

A woman marries for money and social position, but soon she begins to feel her degradation for having done so. She regains her sense of self-worth by gaining control over her husband through her hypnotic powers, and she eventually uses her power to purposefully cause his death. [Note: this volume is Number 9 (September, 1893) of the quarterly *Tales from Town Topics*]

Tytler, Sarah pseud. (Real name Henrietta Keddie). *The Witch-Wife.* London: Chatto & Windus, 1897. Available online via HathiTrust and Google Books: https://babel.hathitrust.org/cgi/pt?id=uiug.30112047688228.

The burning of poor Sonsy Sibbie, we are told, is modelled on the burning of the last witch so punished in Scotland. Sibbie was a harmless sorceress, indeed, kind and comely, and with no familiars beyond the poor and the maimed among beasts and birds, all of which she mothers out of sheer large-heartedness. She keeps one beautiful dog, whose blackness, together with his faithfulness to his mistress, is reckoned suspicious. Unfortunately for herself, Sibbie was well in advance of her time and class. In a primitive but still practical manner, she could juggle with hypnotism, administer laudanum, and even, apparently, inject morphia or some equally powerful equivalent. In days so bigoted, it availed her nothing that her arts were never used except in kindness. She was tried for her life, condemned on the feeblest evidence, and burnt on the summit of the Knock, a hill consecrated to the hanging and burning of witches. The reader grows fond of Sibbie in the course of her story, and is distinctly relieved to find her able to wield her poor "black art" with sufficient force to kill herself painlessly before the flame has touched her.—St. **James Gazette** (London), December 9, 1897, p.16

*Miss Tytler introduces a witch-burning, but the martyr, if we understand what is meant, escaped torture by using morphia, or some such drug, hypodermically. Sibbie was too much in advance of her age. She was an accomplished hypnotist, rather too accomplished. We conceive that a hypnotized patient, in his trance, will not, probably cannot, reveal secrets known to him in his primary personality, and more than, after waking, he can remember what occurred in his trance. Sibbie, however, worms military information out of a hypnotized soldier, and then uses it to prevent a Covenanting rising in which her foster child is engaged.—**The Times** (London), February 3, 1898, p.11*

Victor, Mrs. M. V. "Under a Shadow; or, How Dark Eyes Didn't Win" *Beadle's Monthly* 1 (May 1866): 463-69. Available online via HathiTrust and Google Books: https://babel.hathitrust.org/cgi/pt?id=mdp.39015063756814;view=1up;seq=467.

Annie Kirkland uses mesmerism to cure her cousin Helen Marshall of headaches, but when Helen becomes engaged to the handsome Mr. Thornton, Annie's jealousy causes her to use her mesmeric powers to embarrass Helen at a social gathering with the hopes of stopping her cousin's engagement. Mr. Thornton eventually figures out the truth, and the story ends with the couple reunited.

Walls, C.V. "Ingenious Bank Robberies: A Detective's Story" *Union County Courier* (Aug. 1886): 4. Available online via Chronicling America and Newspapers.com and The Westminster Detective Library:

https://chroniclingamerica.loc.gov/lccn/sn84022137/1886-08-11/ed-1/seq-4

https://web.archive.org/web/20240417200449

https://wdl.mcdaniel.edu/node/910.

A female hypnotist uses her powers to rob several banks, but is brought to justice when her fiancé (a detective assigned to the robberies) discovers that she is the thief.

Walsh, George Ethelbert. "An Experiment in Hypnotism" *Home and Country* 9 (June 1894): 2500-2503. Available online via HathiTrust and Google Books: https:// babel.hathitrust.org/cgi/pt?id=nyp.33433104905314&seq=374.

A man is in love with a woman that likes to dabble in occult topics, but when she takes up the study of hypnotism it leads to a hypnotic duel between their will powers, but the story ends with the couple professing their love to each other.

Webber, Charles W. *Spiritual Vampirism: The History of Etherial Softdown, and Her Friends of the "New Light"*. Philadelphia: Lippincott, Grambo & Co., 1853. Available online via HathiTrust, Project Gutenberg, and Google Books: https:// catalog.hathitrust.org/Record/100687565.

The book starts out with an introductory essay concerning mesmerism and its influence over Odic or life forces on the human body. The novel itself follows the doings of Etherial Softdown, a medium, mesmerist, and gold digger who has her sights on a man named Stewart Manton. Mesmerism, clairvoyance, abolition, and women's rights all find their way into the story. [Note: this novel was also published under the title *Yieger's Cabinet*]

Wilson, William R.A.*A Knot of Blue*. Boston: Little, Brown & Co., 1905. Online via the Internet Archive and Google Books: http://www.archive.org/details/ aknotblue00cogoog.

A story of love and villainy in old Quebec. The she-villain uses the weapons of poison and hypnotism to draw the hero away from his allegiance to the maiden with the knot of blue. The tale moves heavily and scarcely rises above the level of the commonplace.— **The Congregationalist and Christian World,** July 15, 1905, p.91

Wood, Henry Mrs. (Real name Ellen Wood). "A Mesmerist of the Years Gone By" *Argosy* 36 (Dec. 1883): 519-34. Available online via HathiTrust: http://babel. hathitrust.org/cgi/pt?id=uc1.b3035496;view=1up;seq=543.

A female mesmerist/clairvoyant is called upon to inform a woman of the status of her lover who is fighting in a war; the mesmerist "sees" that the woman's lover is numbered among the dead and a few days later her mesmeric vision is confirmed.

Wood, Joanna E. *A Daughter of Witches*. Toronto: W. J. Gage & Company, 1900. Available online through Early Canadiana Online; also available through the Internet Archive: http://eco.canadiana.ca/view/oocihm.09291/5?r=0&s=1 https://archive.org/details/daughterofwitche00wooduoft.

The heroine is a handsome, strong-willed, passionate damsel called Vashti, descended from a French woman who had been burnt as a witch. She herself is suspected by her *neighbours of what the author calls "witchery," and has, besides, a turn for hypnotising people; so that if she is fascinating, she is also a little uncanny. Hypnotism, by the way, is rather popular in American fiction of the moment, and very tiresome it is. Vashti is in love with her cousin, physically in love with him only, for he is by no means her equal in other respects; good-hearted enough, but with very moderate wits, a weakness for drink, and a desire to marry another cousin. Vashti is angry at this, and turns to a young man of higher culture and pantheistic leanings. With a touch of her hypnotic power she persuades him not only that she is the loveliest creature on earth (of which he is convinced), but that he himself has a talent for pulpit preaching. The results are divers, and shall be left to the reader's discovering. The book is not badly written, and the minor characters are good, the study of Temperance Tribbey, the New England servant, being almost excellent.—***The Standard*** (London), Issue 23814 October 23, 1900, p.4 [Note: Vashti uses hypnotism to cure her husband of headaches; she also uses her hypnotic powers to control the content of his sermons].

Woods, Margaret L. *The Invader*. London: William Heinemann, 1907. Available online via Hathi Trust and Google Books: http://catalog.hathitrust.org/Record/000326375.

*It is a tale in which the heroine leads a "Dr. Jekyl and Mr. Hyde" existence. As no one has before ascribed a dual life to the fair sex, it is therefore unique, and although the authoress has failed in skilful handling of her subject, she has nevertheless produced a very readable story. The heroine, Milly, a good, meek, and rather dull young woman, suddenly, after being hypnotized by a girl friend develops two distinct personalities. As Milly, she is sweet, stupid, devoted and conventional. As Mildred she is brilliant, seductive and diabolical. It is a noteworthy fact, that while Milly's goodness is admired, Mildred's seductive brilliancy wins the love, not only of her husband, but also of their little child, friends and servants thus not exactly verifying the well worn adage, "Be good and you will be happy." The ending is tragic, but the authoress could not do otherwise than end the story tragically with so complicated a tangle.—***The Christian Work and the Evangelist***, Vol. 82, May 25, 1907, p.684*

The following are all available from
Amazon and Barnes & Noble
in print and on Kindle

Also Available...

Death by Suggestion gathers together *twenty-two stories from the 19th and early 20th century where hypnotism is used to cause death—either intentionally or by accident. Revenge is a motive for many of the stories, but this anthology also contains tales where characters die because they have a suicide wish, or they need to kill an abusive or unwanted spouse, or they just really enjoy inflicting pain on others. This volume also includes an introduction which provides* a brief history of hypnotism as well as a listing of real-life cases where the use of hypnotism led to (or allegedly led to) death.— Back cover

"*Donald K. Hartman's DEATH BY SUGGESTION, is a melange of crime fiction featuring stabbings, clifftop suicides, hangings and the odd strangulation. Hartman offers an admirable introduction, exploring the history of hypnotism and defining the terms 'mesmerism' and 'hypnotism.' He discusses the positive and negative applications of hypnotism today before looking at modern criminal cases as well as those well-reported cases relating to his selection of stories.*"

—*TIMES LITERARY SUPPLEMENT*, January 15, 2019, p.30

nd...

The Hypno-Ripper. This is the second volume in the *Hypnotism in Victorian and Edwardian Era Fiction* series, published by Themes & Settings in Fiction Press. The two stories collected here were published during the time of the Jack the Ripper killings, and they are among the earliest fictional accounts dealing with the Whitechapel murders. Both of these stories have Jack the Ripper being an American, who travelled from New York City to London to commit the murders, and the Ripper commits his crimes while under the  influence of hypnotism. The first story, "The Whitechapel Mystery; A Psychological Problem ("Jack the Ripper")," is a novel authored by N. T. Oliver, and originally published in 1889 by the Eagle Publishing Company. The second story, "The Whitechapel Horrors," is a short tale, published anonymously in two American newspapers, shortly after the murder of Mary Jane Kelly in November 1888. Also included is a lengthy biographical profile on Edward Oliver Tilburn. "N. T. Oliver" was a pseudonym for the highly interesting Edward Oliver Tilburn. Besides being an author, Tilburn was a minister, actor, lecturer, secretary for several cities' Chambers of Commerce, snake-oil salesman, Christian psychologist, as well as an accused embezzler, shady real estate broker, and a self-proclaimed medical doctor.

nd...

The Hypnotic Tales of Rafael Sabatini is the third volume in the *Hypnotism in Victorian and Edwardian Era Fiction series*, containing several stories by a popular twenteeth century writer.

Today, few people would recognize the name "Rafael Sabatini," but in the 1920s and 1930s he was one of the world's most popular authors. Called "the Alexandre Dumas of Modern Fiction" and "the Prince of Storytellers," he almost single-handedly resurrected the genre of the swashbuckler in both literature and film. Historical romances and adventure stories were Sabatini's stock-in-trade and the focal point of the majority of his literary writings, but for a brief time, at the beginning of his writing career, he must have had at least a passing interest in hypnotism, for he would write, not one, but two stories dealing with the subject.

The first of his hypnotic tales was The Avenger, appearing in the March 1909 issue of *Gunter's Magazine*. In The Avenger, we meet Roger Galliphant, a man with medical training and a strong interest in psychology and psychic research. Galliphant is also a powerful hypnotist who, while performing a simple demonstration of hypnotism in front of friends, discovers that an acquaintance of his, James Chester, has used hypnotism to commit at least two murders. Roger Galliphant, knowing the difficulty of proving Chester's crimes in a court of law, plans on avenging the murder victims' deaths, and he does so by using his own hypnotic powers against those of Chester's—and thus a battle between hypnotists ensues. Roger Galliphant also appears in Sabatini's second tale dealing with hypnosis, The Dream, a novelette published in the August 1912 issue of *The Story-Teller*. Galliphant appears toward the end of the story when he is needed as an eminent authority on hypnotism, and he must decide if Francis Orpington was under the influence of hypnotic suggestion when he killed an unarmed man.

lso

What do you get when you combine "Buffalo Bill" Cody with Bernie Madoff, and for good measure throw in an actor, a cookbook author, a college founder, a faith-healer, an embezzler, and a bigamist?

Answer: Edward Oliver Tilburn

E.O. Tilburn (aka N.T. Oliver, Ned Oliver, and Nevada Ned) was a late 19th/early 20th century con-artist that has somehow flown under the radar of both biographers and historians, but in this book Donald Hartman has revealed Tilburn to the world, and his life story should be of interest to folks that are fascinated by con men, as well as to those readers that enjoy getting a glimpse into the lives of scoundrels and frauds.

Hartman included a biographical profile on Tilburn in *The Hypno-Ripper* and the *BlueInk Review* says, "However, the highlight of the book is Hartman's 40-page biography of Oliver. The editor's meticulous research enables him to engross readers with the true story of this part-time author, snake-oil salesman, minister, faith healer, medicine show barker, sharp shooter, real estate mogul, city commissioner and, likely, bigamist—proving that, indeed, truth is sometimes stranger than fiction."

Jason Half commented on the same work, "In the book's final section, Hartman provides a fascinating and well-researched biography of Tilburn, alias N.T. Oliver and "Nevada Ned", and the man's rollercoaster of a life does not disappoint. In sum, Tilburn – sometimes with an "E" at the end of his name, sometimes not, but usually with an unearned honorific like "Dr." or "Ph.D." attached – was a patent medicine huckster, an author, a preacher, a professor, a realtor, and a man of business to the American towns and people he would descend upon, swindle, and leave."